QUAKE

QUAKE

ALBERT J. ALLETZHAUSER

BLOOMSBURY

First published in Great Britain 1997

This paperback edition first published 1997

Copyright © 1997 by A.M.C. Alletzhauser

The moral right of the author has been asserted

Bloomsbury Publishing Plc, 38 Soho Square, London W1V 5DF

A CIP catalogue record is available from the British Library

ISBN 0 7475 3340 7

10 9 8 7 6 5 4 3 2 1

Printed in Great Britain by Clays Limited, St Ives plc

Albert J. Alletzhauser may be contacted at
alletzhauser<100077.64@compuserve.com

Dedicated to the memory of those who died in Kobe and to:

Thomas Dudley Cabot 1897–1995

Industrialist, philanthropist, statesman, scientist, engineer, chess player, yachtsman, horseman, hiker, canoeist, skier, hunter, rancher, author, traveller and argumentative family man. We will miss you.

AUTHOR'S NOTE

The story that follows may seem fantastic, imaginary and at times exaggerated. The interesting and perhaps disturbing part of this 'novel' is that many of the characters are based on real people, most of the events are a matter of historical record, while future events are within the realm of probability. The last chapter of *Quake* gives chapter-by-chapter detail of historical accuracy.

1

THE OMEN

The manganese mines of Wuzhou in southern China

'**F**aster, you fornicating dogs!' The mine boss was under intense pressure and swore continuously at his workers.

The peasants quickly sorted the black rocks under the hot sun. Nobody paused for rest, except for an occasional trip to the watering bucket. Fu hurriedly stuffed the rocks into red, white and blue fibreglass bags which were in turn loaded into a wheelbarrow. The other miners called him 'Quick-fingered Fu'. He was paid by the bag and on a good day earned 60 yuan – nearly $7.25.

'What's your hurry, Fu?' asked Wang, a surly, lazy worker who resented his reputation as a hard worker. 'Have you got a whore waiting for you at home, or your wife?' he asked.

'I've got two whores waiting for me at home, and one of them is *your* wife,' replied Fu, smiling to reveal his blackened teeth.

Each bag contained a hundred pounds of rock. The mine bosses were strict and usually insisted that only the heavier and better-quality pieces be sorted. The local peasants in Guangxi province called them 'heavy rocks', while geologists called them manganese. The heavier the rock, the more manganese it contained. Normally Quick-fingered Fu would be penalized or even fired for stuffing lighter rock into his bag.

But not today. Wuzhou Manganese Mine Number Three had a shipment deadline to meet.

'You work too fast,' complained Wang, jealous of Fu's success. 'You make all of us look like we're sleeping.'

As Fu loaded a rock with his right hand while searching for another with his left, he looked over at Wang. 'If you were paid for talking, you'd be the richest man in China.' And he spat on the manganese-rich boulders that lay in front of him, his saliva shimmering on the black rock before it dried quickly in the sun.

For thousands of years the Chinese had been aware of the special chemical properties of manganese. The element was to steel production what eggs were to baking – a critical bonding agent. Every steel producer in the world purchased manganese because it bonded itself to iron to make steel. The higher the percentage of manganese – and to be acceptable it had to be above 40 per cent – the better the strength of steel. South Africa had the highest quality maganese-bearing rock in the world, containing upwards of 50 per cent manganese; China had the lowest quality – less than 25 per cent. For years Japanese steel producers eager for profit had quietly bought up cheap Chinese manganese. They had long known about the massive Wuzhou deposits, and since the 1960s had sought out Chinese imports and blended it into the rails and girders that went into every railway, building and bridge in Japan. The bosses of the Japanese steel manufacturers and construction companies were proud of themselves. Nobody would ever know.

The shipment today was extra-special. It was a rush order for export to the Wakayama Steel Works in Tokyo, and there was no time even to crush or wash the manganese. The mine bosses had increased production bonuses, giving Quick-fingered Fu a chance almost to double his wages if he went really fast. He licked his lips, thinking of the juicy chicken he would bring home for dinner.

'Hurry!' yelled the head boss to the mine manager. 'Hurry!' swore the mine manager at the peasants. Quick-fingered Fu had lost all interest in what rocks he threw into his bag. His mouth watered as he thought about his wife's hot spiced chicken with green onions. He could already taste the ginger, peppercorns and dried red chilli peppers.

He emptied the bag into a wheelbarrow and a clerk put a check mark next to his name. The barrow operator took the load 50 metres to a precipice where twenty battered Ford dump trucks lay waiting below. He dumped his load, as did the nineteen other barrow operators who each worked a truck. The ancient trucks unloaded the rocks on to sturdy junks anchored in the Pearl River. The junks then sailed down the river to Hong Kong, where the manganese was loaded on to large vessels bound to Tokyo.

At six that evening, Quick-fingered Fu lined up for his daily pay. As if it were a precious gem, he pulled a half-smoked Winston stub from his shirt pocket, lit it and took a drag. He relaxed for a moment as the nicotine took effect. Then he yelled at the paymaster.

'Hurry, you son of a toothless whore!' Fu was paid on the basis of how many check marks he had next to his name and thought he could needle the paymaster.

'Twenty-four loads,' said the paymaster as he started to count Fu's money.

'There are twenty-five marks, you blind son of a goat!'

The paymaster was always trying to cheat Fu as he did all the other workers, reasoning that he too was entitled to his share of the production. 'I can only count twenty-four marks.'

Fu's face contorted. 'The market's going to close, you fatherless scum. Pay me for twenty-five loads or I'll put you into one of my bags and load you on to the truck!' He was anxious to get to the market before the choice birds were sold.

The paymaster placed 9 dirty bills into Fu's soiled-stained, blistered hand. 'Twenty-five loads . . . lets see, at 4 yuan a load that's 100 yuan,' he said.

Without looking down at his hand Fu glared at the paymaster. 'Now give me the other ten.'

'May your ancestors' graves grow untended,' cursed the paymaster as he counted out the balance.

Fu greedily snatched up the additional banknotes and ran off to the market. 'Give me a fat, juicy chicken.' He held up his day's wages to the butcher. 'The last one you gave me was so tough I lost two teeth trying to eat it.'

'You'd lose teeth eating steamed rice,' barked the butcher as he hawked on to the ground, barely missing a brace of duck and pig heads. He reached down and lifted up a plump live chicken by the neck. 'This bird's one of my best. I was going to take it home for myself, but I'll let you have it for 25 yuan.'

The chicken started to squawk and flap, so the butcher held it upside down by the legs.

'Is it tender?'

'Are you going to eat it or fuck it? Now make up your mind,' shouted the sweating man.

'I'll pay you 20 yuan.'

'Hurry up,' shouted another customer. The market stall was filling up with workers on their way home.

'Okay, give me the money.'

Fu handed over the notes and carried away the chicken.

'That stumpy-rooted dwarf,' thought the butcher. 'I should have demanded 25.' He moved on to haggle with his next customer.

That evening, when Fu chopped the head off the chicken, the headless body ran away into the bushes. Fu retrieved it, drained the blood and gave the bird to his wife for plucking. He never told his wife about the bird's headless run. It was very bad luck for a lifeless chicken to run about – many peasants considered it an evil omen, preceding a death whose victim would not receive a proper burial with his ancestors. But Fu had no cause for alarm. This omen would be fulfilled not through Fu or his family but by countless others in the distant city of Tokyo.

By the time Fu had begun picking the remains of his meal from his black teeth with a splintered wishbone, the inferior manganese was wending its way down the Pearl River. A few days later in Tokyo the 50,000-tonne shipment was unloaded and melted in Wakayama Steel's ferro-manganese plant. The usual painstaking quality controls were waived. Wakayama Steel had to hurry the order to Daishin Construction, whose ninety-storey Daishin Trade Towers in Ginza was being rushed to meet its opening date. The girders were cast from alloy containing the substandard Chinese manganese and quickly delivered to the construction site. 'Ah, the wonders of "Just in Time" delivery,' thought the site manager when they arrived. Besides erecting the Daishin Trade Towers to a tight deadline, his job was to ensure that the building inspectors from the Ministry of Construction did not examine the work too closely.

Two thousand minor tremors hit Tokyo each year and their incessant movement was slowly and undetectably wearing down the skyscrapers, bridges and railways of the city. Much of the city's infrastructure was built using the same low-quality Chinese manganese as the Daishin Trade Towers. Almost immediately, invisible stress factures appeared in the building, invisible spider's webs buried deep within each girder.

Meanwhile, the residents and commuters of Tokyo went about their daily lives with little thought of an earthquake hitting their city. The last "Big One" had hit in 1923, and as far as they were concerned this was the stuff of textbooks and ancient history. Little thought was given to the impact of a direct hit on the 34 million people living in the world's most crowded megalopolis. The results of a killer quake were too appalling to think about, so nobody did. And forget the possible death toll anyway – 64 per cent of the nation's top companies had their headquarters located in Tokyo, and a direct hit would shut down this economic superpower. For those coming out of the greatest recession since World War II, this prospect was more daunting than any massive loss of life. It was best not to think about things over which one had no control.

Thirty kilometres under Tokyo, three tectonic plates shifted restlessly.

2

THE 'A' TEAM

Winter in central Tokyo: the vacant site of the future Daishin
Trade Towers

'. . . there is no possibility of earthquake prediction.'

Charles Richter, 1958

'Scientists are on the verge of being able to predict the time,
place and even size of earthquakes.'

From a *Time* magazine cover story, 1 September 1975

The normally well-dressed woman hid under the expressway.
She had changed out of her Chanel dress into a tracksuit,
sneakers and Mets baseball cap. Hiroko Fujita was an
investigative reporter for the *Asahi Shimbun* newspaper. The sun
had just gone down and it was getting colder. Hiroko, who had been
waiting since five that afternoon, impatiently checked her watch. It
was now after six.

Suddenly she saw the headlights of a tanker truck pull into the
vacant building site. Three more tankers pulled in behind, their
diesel engines muffled by the commuting traffic on the expressway
above. Hiroko pressed the green button on her camcorder and began
videotaping the procession of vehicles.

Despite the security lights strung up in the lot, she could barely
make out the company name on the side of each truck. She pushed
the zoom lens and the name came into focus: FUJI INORGANIC
CHEMICAL. A security guard emerged from a mobile construction
site cabin and signed them in. A burly driver jumped out of the leading
truck and motioned to his fellow drivers; they all followed the guard
back to the cabin, leaving their engines idling. Hiroko kept the video
going and carefully made her way up to the trucks. She scanned
their licence plates and the external gauges which indicated that
none of them was carrying any liquid. Then she backed her way to
the bridge, the camera lens never leaving the trucks. Her hands were

freezing and, leaving one hand in her pocket, she blew constantly on her camera hand to keep it warm.

After twenty minutes the drivers emerged from the hut, jumped into their trucks and left. Hiroko switched off the video. She came quickly out from under the expressway and dashed across a corner of the vacant lot to her car. Just then the guard spotted her.

'Hey, you! Stop!'

Hiroko broke into a run.

'Stop!'

The guard was running towards her but Hiroko was already in the driving seat. She fired up her Mazda 626 and sped away, praying that the guard had not read her licence plate. She had her first piece of evidence, but she needed more.

Hiroko was a member of the *Asahi* 'A' Team, assigned to expose corruption in Japan's construction industry. The country had weathered the resignations of six prime ministers in six years, most of them the victim of pay-off or sex scandals. The *Asahi Shimbun*, one of Japan's most progressive newspapers, had formed this journalistic hit squad to ferret out corruption in government and big business. The 'A' Team sold newspapers. Unlike in Britain, where the press regularly exposed the underbelly of society, muckraking was rare in Japan where the truth was known by mainstream newspapers but never mentioned.

Hiroko had a first degree from Tokyo University and a post graduate degree from the Columbia School of Journalism. Not only was she drop-dead beautiful, she was also the brightest reporter on the newspaper. But these were not the assets which they might have been on a Western newspaper. If anything, they were just a concession to the encroachment of the West in male-dominated Japanese journalism.

The tanker trucks were supposed to be filled with sodium silicate, a chemical coagulant which hardened reclaimed land before buildings were erected. Hiroko suspected that Fuji Inorganic Chemical had been sending empty tanker trucks to the Daishin Trade Towers site, invoicing Daishin Construction for the full amount of the chemicals and paying a kickback to the Daishin chairman.

The next morning at work, Hiroko put through a call to a semi-retired seismologist and civil engineer at Tokyo University named Dr Tokai. His speciality was the effect of earthquakes upon society. Though gregarious, the spindly octogenarian was not popular among Japan's architects and builders because his gloom and doom scenario put pressure on Parliament to enact stringent building codes.

Hiroko's call went through.

'Tokyo University.'

'*Moshi, moshi.* Dr Tokai, please.'

'Just a moment, please.'

At eighty years old Tokai still came into work each day and, though a professor emeritus, picked up his own phone. '*Tokai desu.*'

'Hello. This is Hiroko Fujita, a reporter from the *Asahi Shimbun*.'

'Yes. How may I help you?'

'You were recommended as a source for a story I'm writing on the dangers of building on reclaimed land. Do you mind if I ask you a few questions?'

'Please.' Tokai was lonely, and eager for a chance to talk.

'Can you please tell me more about the hazards of such construction?'

'Young lady, you must first understand some basic facts. Most of central Tokyo lies on reclaimed land which will turn to jelly in a big earthquake. Our city was once a series of interconnecting rivers, waterways and canals which were only filled in this century. Think of Tokyo as a giant bag of rice which has settled over time. When a quake shakes the settled material, the low water table will be forced through the landfill. Most buildings will be subsumed into the liquid. We call this liquefaction.'

'Do you have any proof to back up your theories?'

'Some. But remember that the last great earthquake to hit Tokyo was in 1923, when the city had no skyscrapers. The term "liquefaction" was not really discovered until 1964 when an earthquake in Niigata sent huge fountains of water erupting through the streets. The Institute of Civil Engineers has constructed a computer model of Tokyo showing what would happen to the city during a big earthquake. Over 225 square kilometres is forecast to be in danger of liquefying.'

'What about all the reclaimed land in Tokyo Bay?'

'All that land will turn to sludge.'

'Even the Teleport?'

Tokyo Teleport was mankind's most ambitious residential and commercial development, housing tens of thousands of residents and employing hundreds of thousands of workers. It was built on reclaimed land in the centre of Tokyo Bay.

'In a big quake it will be destroyed. All the buildings will sink. Ten per cent of all the world's seismic energy is released here in Japan. Can you imagine the arrogance of building a futuristic city over the world's most active fault line? And on soft ground! And in the middle of the Ring of Fire.'

'What's that?'

'We call Tokyo Bay the Ring of Fire. We import almost all of our oil and chemicals, of which a third is stored on reclaimed land encircling the bay, just a short distance from the city centre. There are nine hundred storage tanks containing 63 million kilolitres of toxic liquid: oil, tetraethyl lead, toluene, white oil, ammonia, chlorine, cyanide acid, hydrochloric acid and sodium cyanide.'

'How's it stored?'

'Mostly in tanks built during the 1960s. The National Fire Agency didn't enact storage laws until 1976: new tanks must now sit on pilings sunk deep into firm soil. The only way to prevent liquefaction is to bury pillars deep enough in soft ground so they reach a suitable anchor. With old tanks we can only inject chemicals into the ground to firm it up. This is not very effective, and corruption occurs frequently.'

Hiroko imagined rivers of toxic waste rushing out into Tokyo Bay, fires lighting up the sky and toxic gases wafting over the city. This was worse than a Godzilla movie.

'Can I see the study done by the National Fire Agency on how to prevent and combat this disaster?'

'Mmmm. That's difficult.'

'Why?'

'They've never done one.'

'Nobody's ever studied the impact of an earthquake on the toxic waste stored around central Tokyo?'

'Correct.'

Hiroko could not believe what she was hearing. 'Doesn't the government have people studying earthquake prediction and earthquake resistance?'

'Over five hundred researchers study earthquake prediction. But it's a waste of time. Earthquake resistance is left to private companies.'

'You say it's dangerous to put a storage tank on reclaimed land. What about a tall building?'

'Where?'

'Say near Ginza.'

'Maybe you could build to forty storeys. First you'd inject the soil with a chemical coagulant to harden it. Next you would sink pilings down 30 metres, maybe more, until you hit bedrock.'

'What if the soil hadn't been prepared?'

'The building would sink or slowly topple, depending on the size of the quake.'

'And if the quake was comparable with the one in 1923?'

'Hardly any buildings would survive.'

'You're sure of this?'

'Yes. But nobody will ever know till the Big One hits.'

They were both silent for a moment, until Hiroko realized that she might have been tiring the eighty-year-old and finished the interview.

'You've been very helpful, Dr Tokai. May I invite you to lunch some time as a thank you?'

'Yes. That would be very nice.'

'What about next Tuesday?'

'That would be fine. I have a class which ends at noon.'

'Good. I'll pick you up at the university.'

'Okay. Bye now.'

'Bye.'

The following week Hiroko travelled out to the university. As she approached the ten-storey building which housed the Department of Earth and Planetary Physics, she saw a dozen students standing, hands up against the wall, as if they had been arrested. Dr Tokai, whom she recognized from photographs, was yelling at them as a coxswain would direct his oarsmen.

'Wait . . . push . . . wait . . . push . . . wait . . . push . . .'

To Hiroko's horror, the building started to sway. The students no longer needed the professor's assistance as they felt its natural rhythm.

Heads began to pop out of windows.

'Some of us are trying to work here,' shouted one of them.

'Stop that!' yelled one voice, whom a student recognized as belonging to the Dean.

'Professor, we'd better stop,' the student warned.

'Okay, okay. That's enough for today. See you all next week.'

The building came to a rest as the students picked up their belongings and went their separate ways.

Hiroko walked up to Dr Tokai. 'Excuse me. I am Hiroko Fujita of the *Asahi Shimbun*.'

'Oh, hello. I am Tokai. Nice to meet you. Just in time to see the end of my demonstration.'

'What were you doing? Was it dangerous?'

'No, there was little danger. I was showing my seismology class that every building has its own natural frequency of vibration.'

'What does that mean?'

'Every ten-storey building has a one-second frequency of vibration which means it will rock back and forth naturally every second – like a child on a swing. Did you see at the end that the building was starting to swing naturally?'

'What's that got to do with an earthquake?'

'The taller a building, the longer its cycle. Again, one second for every ten storeys. A forty-storey building will rock in four-second cycles in a longer swing. If a building is out of synch with the frequency of the shock waves of a quake – that's it. The building collapses. High-frequency waves wipe out small buildings and low-frequency waves wipe out tall buildings.'

'So your experiment could have been dangerous?'

'Only if we had rocked the building counter to its natural sway.'

The two of them were standing on the university steps, and for a moment Hiroko had forgotten that she had invited him to lunch.

'Are you hungry?' she asked.

'Sure. I know a little sushi shop around the corner.' As they started to walk off the campus Hiroko asked another question. 'So how do you predict earthquakes?'

Dr Tokai did not answer, but instead pulled open his briefcase and handed Hiroko five pieces of blank paper. 'Hold your arm out straight and drop each piece one by one from the same position.'

Passing students gave them quizzical smiles but Hiroko did as she was told and dropped the first paper. There was no wind and it landed slightly left about 5 centimetres in front of her.

'Now the second.'

This sheet landed to the right. The third landed in the middle, while the fourth hit her legs and landed on her feet. Just as Hiroko got ready to drop the last piece of paper a breeze blew across the campus, rustling the ones on the ground. She let the last sheet go and it fluttered away.

'You can't predict earthquakes any more than you can predict where a piece of paper will land. This branch of study is called non-linear physics – some people know it as chaos theory. A small change in initial conditions will greatly affect the end result. Now imagine how billions of tonnes of brittle, unstable, pressurized rock, constantly expanding and contracting, will react. A small quake hundreds of kilometres away may set off a non-contiguous chain reaction and trigger a major quake.'

They picked up the scattered papers, walked on and a few minutes later came to the sushi shop.

'Then why do you bother to try and predict them?'

The waitress handed each of them a hand towel as they both ordered the sushi set lunch without looking at the menu.

'Three reasons. The first is the grand delusion of public safety. The government pretends we are in no danger so as to instil a sense of order in the public. Secondly, the delusion of earthquake prediction saves building owners a lot of money. Most structures need to be taken down or reinforced.

Hiroko nodded, thinking of how much the owners of the Daishin Trade Towers were saving just on ground-hardening chemicals. Building codes were already lax in Japan, yet contractors still cheated.

'My profession perpetuates the myth of earthquake prediction in order to justify large construction projects. To admit error now would embarrass all previous bureaucrats, including MPs, vice-ministers and so on.'

Their lunch orders arrived. Tokai crunched away on an octopus tentacle while Hiroko let a succulent piece of tuna melt on her tongue. Then the professor reached into his briefcase again and pulled out a photocopied cover story from *Time* magazine dated 1 September 1975.

'This was the peak.'

'Of what?' asked Hiroko.

'Of the US earthquake prediction programme. It collapsed soon afterwards. In the 1960s, American researchers were envious of all the money that Japanese researchers had been allocated to predict quakes. So the Americans jumped in on a good thing and put their hand out for money in the States. And they got it. Their efforts culminated in this article.'

Hiroko delicately picked up a piece of pink ginger with her chopsticks, followed by a giant prawn which she dipped upside down in her soy sauce.

'So what happened?'

'It all fell apart. In the States, researchers must validate their research to keep their grants. Since it's impossible to predict quakes anyway, none of the scientists could keep their grants and the money dried up.'

'And in Japan?'

'The opposite occurred. Money kept pouring in. There's no academic accountability here. All the professors and researchers wanted money and as research grants skyrocketed the need to perpetuate the myth of earthquake prediction increased. To get money they had to pretend that quakes could be forecast. Now it's too late to retract their statements. Backing down would be a loss of face and the money would shrivel up.'

'So it's all a great lie.'

'I'm afraid so. They're all con artists, but I suppose my profession has taken things too far to admit it.'

The waitress cleared the table as both sipped their hot green tea. They finished and, as they rose to leave, Tokai tried to pay for the meal. Hiroko protested, but the elderly man insisted. She could see it meant a lot to him, so she bowed and waited outside while he settled up.

A moment later he reappeared.

'Please call me if you have any questions.'

'I will. Thank you again,' she said, bowing once more. Hiroko walked towards the subway while Dr Tokai went back to the university.

Over the next month she probed corruption within the construction industry with the help of Dr Tokai, who provided her with expert sources in engineering, construction and seismology. These men could not speak publicly for fear of losing their jobs, and wanted their stories aired on an unattributable basis. She obtained samples of the inferior steel girders manufactured by Wakayama Steel and samples of sub-standard Korean concrete used in the pouring of support pillars. After videotaping the empty tanker trucks, Hiroko went back to the site to record the length of the foundation pilings. Daishin Construction were now on alert and the entire site area was surrounded by blue plastic sheeting 6 metres high. Hiroko drove on to the overhead expressway and parked in the emergency lane to obtain video footage. The pile driver operators were supposed to drive the supports down 30 metres until they hit solid rock. Instead, they drove the steel pilings only 15 metres into the soft earth, then stopped. This cut the Daishin steel bill in half. Wakayama invoiced Daishin Construction for 30-metre-long steel pilings and kicked back a chunk of the savings into the Daishin slush fund.

The phoney invoices, for both the coagulants and the foundations, were in turn shown to the building inspector from the Ministry of Construction, who showed up on a construction site only twice: in mid-construction and at the end of a project, which made it impossible to determine how far the foundation pillars had been sunk. The Ministry had only three hundred inspectors nationwide and relied on the integrity of the construction industry to police itself. To Hiroko this was a joke, given the underworld's strong links with the industry.

After a month of investigation Hiroko filed her exposé. Her story never appeared.

3

THE SALARYMAN

Ninety five per-cent of all Japanese polled believe themselves to be middle-class

Nomo Watanabe sat behind his grey metal desk, his back to the window. Eight desks were lined up in two rows either side and in front of him. There was only one computer in the office.

He looked at his watch. Lunchtime. It was a scorching summer day but Watanabe put on his grey Armani suit jacket. As section manager for the Mitsukoshi department store he was expected to look like other salarymen in their short-sleeved white shirts. But Watanabe was different, and as the creative head of the men's department he dressed in tweed in the winter and lightweight designer suits in the summer. At the last minute before he walked out he took a book off his desk, a sign that he wanted to eat alone. Two rows of underlings bobbed their heads as he left. They gave Watanabe a two-minute head start, then bolted for the staff elevator.

Rank had some privileges, since Watanabe could avoid the stifling staff elevator and take the air-conditioned main elevator. He pressed the down button and a moment later the doors opened. A pretty women in white gloves and dressed in a blue and red Mitsukoshi uniform held the doors and greeted him.

'Hello, Katcho.'

Watanabe, the Section Chief, acknowledged her greeting by tipping his head.

As the elevator door closed, the girl began speaking in a sing-song voice. 'Time to descend, dear customers. We are sincerely grateful for your humble patronage.'

Watanabe scanned the customers, mostly women. His job was to attract more men to the premier department store.

'Ground floor. Thank you, dear customers.'

Everybody piled out and Watanabe walked on to the street. Elegant women with designer shopping bags slung on their arms contrasted with the sea of white-shirted men sauntering along the street, most with toothpicks dangling from their mouths and a pack of Mild Sevens stashed in their shirt pockets.

Watanabe squeezed himself into his regular noodle shop and positioned himself at a small table under the air conditioner. The waitress smiled, said nothing and brought him a Kirin orange drink. He opened his tattered book: entitled *The History of Mitsui*, it was a history of his own company written in 1937. Although under a different name, Mitsukoshi had been founded in the 1600s and was the foundation for the Mitsui empire. Mitsui, then as now, was the largest company in the world and even in those days employed over 3 million people. Many of them had been slave labourers in the military build-up to the war, and the irony of slave labour was not lost on Watanabe.

The waitress brought his spicy noodles in an oversized bowl. With the book in his left hand and chopsticks in his right, he began slurping away. Something in the company history caught Watanabe's eye and he excitedly got up from the table, paid his bill and hurried back to work.

He got out of the elevator at the top floor and, without pausing to knock, rushed into his boss's office waving his book.

'Bucho, I have a great idea . . .'

Suzuki disentangled himself from his secretary just as Watanabe entered. Flustered, the secretary hurriedly left the room head down without looking at the intruder. Suzuki was cross, but his junior was oblivious to the situation.

'What is it now, Watanabe?'

'I've got an idea on how to promote sales in the men's department.'

'Do we have to discuss this now?'

'Yes. Please listen. It came to me while reading this *History of Mitsui*. It says here that a hundred years ago our department store rose to greatness by slashing prices. Instead of accepting credit, the Mitsui family cut prices in return for cash sales. My idea is a variation of this. Why don't we have a huge discount sale on men's clothes to promote our lines?'

Suzuki, busy wiping lipstick off his face, was not interested. Watanabe continued.

'Men hate wandering up five storeys in a fashionable department store. They can't be bothered. They go from work to lunch to work to the bar. So for one week we clear out the entire ground floor and fill it with fashionable men's clothes.'

Suzuki interrupted him. 'Forget it, Watanabe. Your section is allocated the back of the fifth floor in all our stores. And a sale? You know Mitsukoshi never cuts its prices. Leave that to Daiei. Why should we? We're the best. Now leave me alone, I have work to do.'

Watanabe felt as if somebody had punched him in the stomach, and walked back to his desk without saying a word. As soon as he had left, Suzuki's secretary slipped back into her boss's office, locked the door, obediently lifted her skirt and bent over his desk. Corporate Japan was hard at work.

4

THE PARTY

The celebration for the opening of the Daishin Trade Towers in central Tokyo, June, 6.30 p.m.

> 'Graft and corruption have long been endemic in the construction industry. It is not without significance that construction companies make up the largest group of tax evaders . . .'
>
> Peter Hadfield, *Sixty Seconds That Will Change the World*

The security guard looked down at his clipboard and fumbled through the guest list as his earphone crackled. He was in charge of VIP guests and it was a problem keeping up with the stream of guests. As at most parties, everyone arrived at once.

A voice crackled into his earphone. 'Tada-san has arrived in a black Benz. Please have an escort meet him at the front entrance.'

The chauffeur opened the rear passenger door and gave his hand to a squat, overweight man in a black power suit. His shoulders were covered in dandruff and his trouser legs in cigarette ash. Black suits were usually reserved for funerals except when worn by Japan's elite such as cabinet ministers and company chairmen. As the man laboriously heaved himself out of the car, the TV crews filmed and the paparazzi began clicking away. There was a festive air, as at an Academy Award ceremony, and a crowd had gathered behind velvet ropes to gawk at arriving guests. A select number of journalists had been invited to the bash but no cameras were allowed inside. They would all be given envelopes full of fresh banknotes as 'car money' for attending. The gossip columnists, never at a loss for hyperbole, called it the party of the decade. Even of the century.

'It's Minister Tada.'

Again, the cameras clicked away furiously. Tada, Japan's Minister of Construction, waddled down the red carpet like a bulldog, head bent.

'Look, here comes Prime Minister Mori!' The entire focus of the media turned to the next guest.

Meanwhile, the security guard leafed frantically through the guest list – over a thousand names – until he finally located Tada's name, ticked it off and nodded discreetly to a group of pretty, kimono-clad females.

The hostesses were on special duty tonight for the grand opening celebration of the Daishin Trade Towers. An ancient builders' custom decreed that a maiden must be sacrificed during the celebration of a new structure, and modern society had changed only slightly. The hostesses were to escort VIPs, keep glasses filled, light cigarettes and bring plates of food to the guests. Kaelin was the prettiest of the hostesses and shuffled over in her *zori*, her formal slippers, to escort Tada to the express elevator. She was a beautiful half-Chinese, half-Japanese woman with unnaturally well-formed breasts. Taller than most Japanese men, she was a favourite hostess, and though often regarded as a 'party favourite' she rarely slept with her clients.

Kaelin bowed at ninety degrees, so that her face almost touched her knees, and kept her hands placed on top of one another just below her crotch. It was the most formal of all bows and all that Tada could see was her black coiffed hair and a lacquer hairpin. As she held the bow for a full five seconds Tada wondered what his escort was like in bed, but waited to see her face before he pursued this line of thought. Kaelin rose from the bow and Tada gasped. *The Daishin chairman has outdone himself.*

'What's your name?'

'Kaelin.'

She bowed towards the elevator and the Minister started to walk in the direction indicated. A female attendant in the sumptuous elevator, lined in Indonesian teak and Italian marble, pressed the button for the top floor. Tada cursed his luck. *Why did there have to be an elevator operator?* He had hoped to grope his escort on the way up and perhaps even convince her to feast later on his giant shitake mushroom.

'*Nanajukai de gozaimasu,*' said the elevator girl a moment later, indicating the seventieth floor.

'*Dozo yoroshiku,*' responded Kaelin.

Tada automatically left the elevator first as the attendant and Kaelin held the door for him. A man never held open a door for a woman.

He stepped out. Kaelin walked sideways, half bowing and motioning for him to enter. Tada passed the hat check counter and ignored the lacquered pot into which all the guests placed their name cards. He strode straight to the head of the receiving line where Minoru Kobayashi, the Daishin chairman, greeted him.

Kobayashi was middle-aged, short of stature and thin, with thick black glasses.

'Welcome, Daijin,' said Kobayashi, bowing obsequiously.

Kobayashi was in a state of elation this evening. His new building was the talk of Tokyo, and the man to whom he was bowing had made it all possible.

Tada nodded his head slightly.

'I have something for you,' whispered Kobayashi. 'We can go down to my office in an hour after all the guests have arrived.'

Tada nodded, moving down the reception line followed by his escort. The other ten Daishin officials dropped their heads like a row of falling dominoes as the Minister passed by. He entered the reception room, which was already packed with Japan's glitterati. Invitations to the Daishin opening were the hottest ticket in town.

The financial chieftains of Japan's 'Big Four' securities houses – Nomura, Daiwa, Nikko and Yamaichi – were huddled in conference together, attended not only by their escorts but also by their 'bag' men. These lackeys opened doors, hailed taxis, lit cigarettes, remembered names and laughed at their boss's jokes. Tonight they also warded off sycophants. The fashion, design and trendy publishing crowd was present: representatives of Issey Miyake, Yamamoto, *AERA*, *SPA!*, *Shukan Bunshan*, *Shukan Gendai*, *Bungei Shunju*, *Architectural Digest*, *Friday*, *Vogue* and *Vanity Fair* pranced about. Each media source was allowed two journalists to cover the party. Daishin assigned them a male 'escort' to influence their movements, monitor conversations and ensure that they did not snoop into Daishin affairs. Fifty or so top politicians were present, their place in Parliament assured through a time-honoured tradition of corporate fund-raisers and pay-offs.

The most powerful man in the room was neither a politician nor a corporate chairman. His name was Ken Moyama, and he was godfather of Japan's yakuza, or mafia. Minister Tada noticed him at a sushi counter surrounded by hand-picked bodyguards. Moyama was the one man whom Tada feared and respected. He tried to make his way through the crowded room to pay his respects, but failed. The room was packed, and Tada too large for movement.

Along the perimeter of the room were food stands filled with delicacies. One stand of succulent sushi featured *akagai*, or ark clams; boiled *ebi*, warm eel with a dash of black sauce; *hotategai*, juicy scallops on rice; and *shirao*, tiny translucent fish as long as a fingernail. The other stands featured *yakitori* on sticks, and cold green noodles such as *zaru soba*. On a bed of ice in the middle of the room lay giant shelled shrimps and boiled lobsters, on which guests freely gorged themselves.

From the middle of the shrimps and lobsters rose a giant 3-metre-high ice sculpture in the form of the two Daishin towers. A company photographer was taking pictures of the guests in front of the sculpture; at his side a woman jotted down the names of everyone in the pictures. Daishin would send each guest his photograph.

The ice sculpture was magnificent but could not capture the true beauty and nobility of the two towers. As the summer evening turned to darkness the guests walked spellbound around the glass reception room, staring out at the neon-filled Tokyo nightscape. Never had such a tall building been attempted in Japan.

The twin towers soared ninety storeys above the Tokyo skyscape and were futuristic in an already futuristic city. Before this, the tallest building in Japan had been the sixty-storey Sunshine Building in Ikebukuro. At great expense, Daishin had covered the towers in slabs of polished blue-white granite. All the outside windows were of smoked black glass, a relief from the drab 1960s-style glass curtain buildings that dotted the city. Daishin had built the towers on a vast undeveloped plot of land bordering Shimbashi and Ginza, near the Shuto expressway. The fishing docks were nearby to the east. For years the site had lain vacant except for the multicoloured tents of a team of archaeologists who were excavating some ancient ruins. Kobayashi, the Daishin chairman, had bribed city officials for planning permission, thrown out the archaeologists and started to build this gigantic symbol of corporate power.

'I tell you something's wrong,' said the Shinto priest to his colleague.

Both were dressed in suits and had eagerly accepted the invitation to attend the party; it was a rare event for priests to be entertained. They noisily slurped up green noodles from a small bamboo lattice tray.

'What can be wrong? They paid us enough.'

'It's not the money. This tower's standing on some sort of ancient grave. Did you see the bones they dug up when laying the foundations? There's going to be trouble, I feel it.'

'Look, both of us need the money. Just keep quiet before somebody hears you. No more thinking. Come with me. Some more sake will clear your head.'

The two priests moved over to the cask and filled their square wooden cups, drinking heavily in the hope that the evil spirits would vanish.

Contractors traditionally hired Shinto priests to appease any evil spirits living around a building site. These two priests had performed the necessary purification rituals by first building on the site a straw rope enclosure into which they had put two green bamboo trees. They had shaken smaller bamboo rods with white paper streamers and muttered a blessing. When the priests went to remove the bamboo trees, they found them blackened and trampled into the mud, a very bad omen. The priest was certain that evil spirits had moved into the site. When they told the Daishin chairman about the evil presence, both priests were paid an extra $250,000 each (nearly 25 million yen each) to say nothing of the incident. The straw enclosure was removed and building was begun.

An hour into the party Tada slipped away from the guests and made his way to the elevator. He leered at Kaelin.

'Wait here for me. We can have some fun later.'

Tada passed the gift table that had just been set up. Partygoers often received gifts from their hosts and a thousand beautifully wrapped boxes were stacked on the table and floor. The wrapping paper was specially printed for Daishin with images of the twin towers embossed on the surface. A hostess offered Tada a gift which he accepted. He took a second one. *I'll give it to one of my mistresses.*

An open elevator was waiting. 'Fiftieth floor,' he told the girl attendant.

A moment later the doors opened. Kobayashi was already there to greet him, and the two of them walked into the Chairman's office with its spectacular view of the neon-filled Tokyo night.

'May I offer you a drink?'

'Vodka ice.'

Kobayashi prepared the drinks at his private bar. He knew what was coming next, so didn't turn round. The familiar gurgling emanated from Tada's throat, then he hawked and spat into a beautiful marble ashtray.

'That's quite a beautiful flower you presented to me this evening. Does the flower blossom?' asked Tada.

'The flower will certainly open up for you.'

The Daishin chairman had put Kaelin on the company payroll to act as a hostess: her sole job was to entertain clients and VIPS such as Tada. Part of the game was to pretend to Tada that she was an amateur and under orders to massage his ego, then massage his beetroot. What Kobayashi did not know was that Kaelin was indeed an amateur.

Tada plunked his heavy body on to the leather sofa. While Kobayashi poured the drinks, the Minister inserted a ring-clad pinkie into his nostril and rotated his finger. He found what he was looking for and wiped his hand on the underbelly of the sofa cushion. At last Kobayashi turned and handed Tada his drink.

'Cheers,' said Kobayashi.

'Cheers.'

Then the Daishin chairman walked over to his desk and hauled out a large black document bag. Tada's face lit up.

'I have a little something for you, Tada-san.' Kobayashi lifted the bag with difficulty and handed it to the Minister.

Cash bribes were common in a society that relied on cash transactions. It was as if the collective mentality of Japan still recalled the dark, cold, dangerous post-war years when a cash society ruled. Deals such as Tada's pay-off were usually settled in brown paper bags stuffed with 10,000-yen notes, each note worth roughly $100. The low value of the notes was a problem in large-scale pay-offs and an annoyance to Japan's ministers, who were the main beneficiary of under-the-table payments. Every few years legislators debated redenomination of the yen in order to make bribery less conspicuous. Tada had successfully kept his inspectors at the Ministry of Construction away from the Daishin Trade Towers project, and now he peeked inside at the 10,000-yen notes.

'Thank you.'

Tada finished off his vodka in one gulp. Most Japanese rarely drank vodka and preferred Johnny Walker Black Label or Chivas Regal.

Kobayashi took Tada's glass to refill it.

'It's Daishin who wishes to thank you. We saved billions of yen thanks to you. I hope this is the beginning of a long relationship. We plan on putting up many more buildings,' said the chairman.

He handed Tada another vodka which the Minister immediately slammed back. As host, Kobayashi was required to continue filling the Minister's glass.

'Another one?'

'No, no, I must be off. I'll go straight to my car. Can you send the little flower along to me?'

'Certainly. But you might be more comfortable using my guest room on this floor,' he offered. Few companies could afford entertainment suites for midday or midnight romps, but Daishin could.

'No. The car's fine.'

Tada wanted to get to the back of the Mercedes to count his money. He rose, belched and then made his way to the elevator.

Kobayashi bowed. Tada bowed slightly and said goodnight. He did not realize how drunk he was until the elevator started moving down rapidly. He put his hand on the attendant for balance and she smiled nervously at him.

'Ground floor,' said the elevator girl.

Tada patted her on the backside and walked slowly to his car, careful not to stumble. The photographers were still there and snapped away. Nobody observed that he had entered with nothing and was now carrying a document bag. Other guests were leaving with flowers, presents, umbrellas and briefcases, so nobody noticed Tada.

Five minutes later his 'flower' – the maiden whom Kobayashi was sacrificing to propitiate the gods – arrived at the car. Kaelin's instructions were to have a 'good time' with Tada. As far as she was concerned, that didn't include sex. But Tada thought otherwise. The moment Kaelin entered the car Tada began fondling her. Kaelin began to protest, but the burly Minister ignored her.

'Home, driver.'

Tada put up the smoked interior window between the front and back seat, and as Kaelin opened her mouth to speak he slapped her so hard that he split her lower lip.

'You foreign slut, one more word and I'll really hit you,' he hissed as he ripped off her blouse and bra.

She didn't cry out as Tada tore off her skirt and pants. She didn't scream when Tada forced his way into her. This infuriated the Construction Minister, who wanted a fight. The more he hit her, the more stoical she became.

When they reached Tada's apartment Omori, the driver, got out and opened the door. Seeing Kaelin lying crumpled on the seat, his first impulse was to disembowel Tada. But Kaelin needed his help.

'Driver, take her home now. I'll see you tomorrow night.'

He turned abruptly and left them.

When Omori leaned into the car to help Kaelin, she screamed: she was in shock. Omori drove her home as fast as he could. As he parked the car, he lowered the interior window just low enough for her to hear him.

'I promise I won't harm you. I want to help you.' He had already taken off his jacket so that she could cover herself.

Kaelin refused his help out of the car, but when she took several steps and faltered, he picked her up and carried her to the door. It was only once Kaelin was safely inside her apartment that she began to cry, first softly and then in deep uncontrollable sobs. Omori held her close, rocking her in his arms until she fell asleep. Early the next morning, when Kaelin awoke, she looked up at Omori and began crying again as the memories flooded back. He took her into the bathroom, gently took off what was left of her clothes and bathed her. Kaelin didn't protest or resist.

5

THE SPACESHIP

The Tokyo Dome, 7 July

'More than two hundred thousand religions have sprung up in Japan since the 1800s.'

From a research report issued by
the Ministry of Cultural Affairs

Anti-terrorist forces were stationed throughout the stadium, on full alert against attack. The threat of nerve gas, germ canisters or high explosives being set off was taken seriously. The guards were dressed in modern-day samurai helmets with gas masks strapped to their arms, just in case.

Their concern was warranted. As the guards checked the stream of incoming visitors, two infiltrators made their way towards the entrance. Casually holding hands, the couple were dressed smartly as if they were part of the conservative gathering. As they approached the guards, the woman, Mariko, noticed a policeman coming towards them and squeezed Kato's hand. The policeman was accompanied by a golden retriever specially trained to root out explosives, chemicals and abnormal-smelling substances. Drugs were not a Japanese problem.

Sensing Mariko's fear, the dog stopped and looked up at her. Mariko looked straight ahead and smiled, holding her breath while gripping Kato's hand. Finally the retriever dropped its nose to the ground and moved on. Mariko breathed and relaxed her grip.

She tried to hide the bulge in her skirt, but the parcel pressed awkwardly against her abdomen. For a moment she felt the guilt and deception of a shoplifter – until she remembered her mission. She was on the side of righteousness. Mariko loosened up. They were almost at the stadium entrance.

The guard stared suspiciously at the pair. Thinking quickly, Mariko began chatting with Kato.

'Oh, I've never seen the Great Master before,' she giggled. She

knew an innocent schoolgirl laugh would defuse the guard's
suspicion.

Then Mariko offered her handbag for inspection, her two arms
extended over the obtrusive object hidden in her skirt. The ploy
worked. Self-assuredness was the best weapon in a society where
guile was not expected. The guard waved them through and an usher
showed them to their numbered seats.

Sixty thousand followers were busy crowding into the stadium on
this humid summer night. The Tokyo Dome in the centre of the city,
also known as the 'Big Egg', was Asia's largest indoor sports arena. A
buzz filled the air. The capacity of the Dome was fifty thousand, but
tonight the organizers had let in an extra ten thousand who stood
in the aisles or milled about the infield. Fans had paid over 30,000
yen ($300) a head for tonight's event. The dramatic tension was
the sort usually associated with the popular local baseball team,
the Tokyo Giants, during a championship home game.

This may have been the Giants' stadium, but the crowd was not
there to watch a game. Nor were they dressed for one. The men were
in fashionable Armani and Hugo Boss suits while the women wore
designer dresses. Most were urbanites in their thirties and forties.
There was no drinking.

Mariko and Kato made mental notes of the spectacular backdrop.
A three-storey stage set was cloaked mysteriously in gossamer-like
netting. Two massive high-definition TV screens were posted either
side of the stage. They could feel the excitement surging through
the audience as everyone waited for the show to begin. The buzz of
excited voices sent an involuntary chill through the couple as they
found their seats.

Suddenly the lights went out and the crowd hushed. Only an eerie
whitish blue glow from the two TV screens could be seen. Soft,
synthesized music began to fill the air. Hidden strobe lights whirled
around and turned the Dome into a three-dimensional planetarium
with revolving galaxies, comets, stars and planets. A collective shiver
ran through the crowd. The show had begun.

'*Sensei! Sensei!*' The crowd started chanting rhythmically. '*Sensei*'
was a term of honour reserved for respected members of society such
as teachers, doctors, professors and members of Parliament. Now the
crowd was on its feet and working itself up to fever pitch. They wanted
to see the 'man'. Even rock stars like Mick Jagger and Madonna had
problems getting passive Japanese audiences to their feet.

'*Sensei! Sensei! Sensei!*' The beat was quickening. The sixty
thousand fans stomped their feet, rocking the Dome. The effect

was electrifying. To these people, the evening would be worth every single cent of admission. To Mariko and Kato, it was absurd.

Yet in spite of their views the couple joined in with the crowd, waiting for the right time to make their move. Mariko shivered. She compared it to the patriotic fervour of an Olympic, Superbowl or World Cup opening ceremony . . . or, maybe more appropriately, to Hitler's Nuremburg rallies at which a million of his devoted supporters worked themselves into a frenzy.

The crowd started to scream as it spotted the orange glow of a spaceship rising from behind the stage. The chant of 'Sensei! Sensei!' reached full pitch. The audience knew their leader was making his entrance. A young girl next to Kato fainted. Friends tried to revive her. The spaceship hovered above the stage and now the crowd was going wild, screaming 'Sensei, Sensei' loud enough to be heard many kilometres away. A hidden cameraman zoomed in on the spaceship, throwing the image on to the great HDTV screens. Up stood a figure clad as an Inca emperor, bedecked in full feather headpiece. His cherubic face lit up the screen like a giant Mao poster. It was Master Wa, the founder of Japan's largest religious group, Happy Science.

Wa was the self-proclaimed reincarnation of Buddha, Siddhartha and the Greek God Hermes, all-powerful seer of the future and leader of 10 million devoted followers. He adorned himself in the garb of a mighty emperor of the ancient Inca civilization, of whom he also believed he was a reincarnation. Wa raised his hands and the crowd immediately fell silent. He allowed the silence to hang in the air.

Wa had created Happy Science in 1988, and its right-wing followers believed that their master was the modern Buddha. The number of his followers had multiplied beyond his wildest dreams. Tonight's extravaganza was a religious celebration to honour Happy Science's ten millionth member, and coincided with Wa's birthday. Every year he rented the Tokyo Dome for his birthday party and invited fifty thousand people.

His round face engendered trust and warmth, while his black, silky, closely cropped hair projected a conservative image. The most interesting and inexplicable physical characteristic of Wa's appearance was a golden 'glow' which radiated from the back of his head, reaffirming to any followers who might otherwise question his status that he was most assuredly the reincarnation of Buddha.

The netting had been unobtrusively removed from the stage. Until now the stadium had been pitch-black except for the illumination of the spaceship and Wa, but slowly the technicians faded up low-level spotlights on the stage set to reveal a throne of gold surrounded by a cutaway Inca palace. A road ran through the palace and led to Wa's version of heaven: the ninth dimension, with structures resembling golden beehives. The crowd gasped, then broke into applause.

'It's like a *Star Trek* convention,' whispered Kato to Mariko.

'No, it's like a Nazi rally with Wa as their almighty Führer.' It was time for her to act. Mariko slid the package out from under her dress and secretly put in in her lap. She aimed it at Master Wa and pushed a button. Her camcorder started whirring away as the great one began to speak.

'Two hundred and seventy million years ago El Cantare invited a billion people from Orion to enter their spaceships and fly to earth. We are descendants from this great migration.' As he spoke, the choreographed show kept time with him. Fifty dancers acted out the migration behind him on the stage. Giant spaceships filled the two screens.

The spellbound audience listened with reverence to Wa's every word. They all knew this story already, but hearing it from their master made it all the more significant.

'We are all descendants,' his voice boomed out. 'But the purity of those original voyagers has disappeared! We have fallen from grace since the great migration so many years ago. We are *evil*! We are selfish, greedy and lustful,' he said, his voice trailing off. There was an eerie silence. The audience did not know what was coming next.

Suddenly Wa exploded. 'We're on the verge of apocalypse!'

Horrific music filled the stadium and images of nuclear holocaust tore across the giant TV screens. A number of people screamed out in terror, knowing that Wa had to be right. He was omnipotent.

'We're about to be swallowed up by a vengeful mother earth.'

On the screens buildings toppled to the ground, waves pummelled the seashore and powerful winds swept across the earth. The world lay in ruins while slow, forlorn music played in the background. Some of the audience were crying now.

'We are so full of sin and uncleanliness that there's no escape. We've got to die before we can be reborn again. The Kobe quake destroyed Hanshin because of the evils of gambling, prostitution, pornography and crime. So will the same fate befall Tokyo. Death and destruction await us. There's no escape. There must be no escape, for we deserve to die. Witness our sins!'

A series of images flashed on to the screens, the first a silent clip of the killing fields of Cambodia. 'Pornography is one of our biggest sins, leading to the destruction of our youth and the decay of our society.' On the TV screens a lost child in tattered clothes wandered aimlessly, creating a visual metaphor for how lost people had become. 'Our shops openly sell pictures of naked children, pictures of violent sex and pictures defiling the act of love.'

Kato shifted uneasily in his seat, having frequently bought S & M magazines at his local news-stand.

A melange of erotic human flesh came up on the screen. The flesh began to rot and then turn black.

'Pornography is a sin which is slowly eating away at our minds and bodies. It's part of the devil's plan for winning us over to his lustful and evil ways. He thinks we are weak. He thinks he will triumph. But he *will not*!'

The crowd leaped to their feet and cheered.

'We must lead the struggle against pornography,' Wa declared when the audience had calmed down slightly. 'And we must lead the struggle against the media who distribute such filth. The executives who publish and sell these images will burn in hell, as they deserve!'

Giant balls of flame leaped up from both sides of the stage. Kato could feel the heat even from where they sat high up in the grandstands. The audience cringed.

Japan had the highest concentration of porn in the world, in both magazines and films. The movie industry alone pumped out twelve thousand porn films a year, compared to three thousand in the USA which had twice the population.

Master Wa's conflict with the Japanese government and the porn industry had been brought about by the relaxation of the ban against full frontal nudity. Magazines now published shots called 'hair nude' – slinky young girls fully exposing themselves. Before deregulation the government had been forced to employ hundreds of censors, mostly old women, whose job had been to leaf through every single pornographic magazine before it was sold and scratch out images of women's pubic hair with a small rake-like instrument. These magazines were then rewrapped in plastic and sold to millions of horny, anticipating males. They opened the magazines only to find the private parts scratched out, as if a sniffing dog had wantonly pawed away with its claws at the young girls' bodies.

To Wa, porn was like a drug. Once you smoked dope it led to snorting cocaine and mainlining heroin. Looking at naked ladies would lead to S & M, paedophilia and other perverted sexual acts.

*   *   *

'Another powerful evil stalks the earth, an evil which will chain us to servitude and take over our lives.'

Black and white clips of impoverished North Korea came on screen, depicting the destitution of a society where a corrupt and all-powerful government destroyed the soul of its people.

'Beware, Japan! One of our greatest evils is our own government. Politicians and bureaucrats survive on corruption, chained to the interest of those who feed their greedy hands. Fed by the underworld which controls porn, our legislators permit moral laxity.'

Feasting on rancid meat, thousands of maggots squirmed on the giant screens. The squeamish in the audience turned their heads in disgust.

'The evil in government grows stronger still,' stated Wa, 'compounded by fanatical religious groups intent on taking over our society.'

Tapes of the 1995 sarin gas attacks rolled up on the screen, with bodies writhing on the ground in pain. An Aum follower was shown with wires running to a metal skullcap on his head.

'The Aum Shinrikyo were the first to attempt national thought control. But there is a greater evil than Aum – the Soka Gakkai. They've already penetrated Parliament and are spreading like cancer through Shinshinto. Disguised as a reputable religion, the Soka Gakkai leaders are plotting to take over our government and destroy our society.' Soka Gakkai happened to be Happy Science's main religious competitor and had made significant inroads into Japanese politics.

More giant balls of flame leapt skywards. The show had now been going for an hour without an intermission.

'Tonight I've spoken about the rise of pornography, the proliferation of gangsterism, the corruption of our government and the blindness of our media. I feel these evils present here tonight . . .'

Everyone glanced nervously at the person next to him.

'We shall cleanse our society of them.'

Kato leaned over to Mariko. 'Nuking this stadium right now would be a pretty good start.'

'Shhhh,' hissed somebody behind them.

Kato kept talking. 'People really believe this garbage,' he said, no longer whispering. 'This is a circus routine.'

The man got up to protest, spotted Mariko's video recorder and hurried over to two guards, pointing towards the couple. Kato saw the guards start towards them.

'Uh-oh. Quick, Mariko, out to the left. Hurry!'

Mariko tucked away her camcorder and they both started moving towards the nearest exit. The fact that they were the only two people leaving went unremarked by the rest of the audience, whose attention was riveted on Master Wa up on stage.

Mariko and Kato broke into a run.

'Stop them!' yelled the guards.

The anti-terrorist squad had long since left and the remaining attendants, who worked for the owners of the Tokyo Dome, did not want to get involved in conflict. Kato and Mariko were too quick for the guards and had a 100-metre start. They jumped a metal crowd control fence and ran into the main street, where a dozen taxis waited expectantly for the event to end. Mariko and Kato jumped into the leading taxi just as the guards ran up to the taxi rank.

'Kodansha headquarters, please.'

The taxi sped away, leaving the guards flustered. They were paid to protect the stadium, not to chase interlopers. They shrugged their shoulders and returned to the show.

'This is going to make a great lead story for next week's magazine,' said Kato jubilantly to Mariko.

The couple were reporters for *Friday* magazine, Kodansha's best-selling weekly publication. Intent on destroying Wa, Kodansha had sent in Kato and Mariko to witness the celebration and then write a hatchet job on Master Wa, whom they considered a huckster. Wa's persistent attacks on pornography and Kodansha's magazines had hurt the circulation figures.

Back in the Tokyo Dome, images of Nostradamus flashed across the screen. 'Listen, my people, we must prepare ourselves for a great tragedy.' The visuals of the sixteenth-century astrologer were cleverly used. In 1994 Master Wa had produced a best-selling movie on his prophecies which had had Japanese audiences repenting in the aisles.

'Our earth is a living being with a conscience. The evil actions of the Japanese people have disrupted the harmony of the earth, which will purge itself of materialism and hedonism, just as a man must scratch his face when he has an annoying itch,' he declared.

'Tokyo is doomed! We all are doomed!' This was moving fire-and-brimstone oratory straight out of the Old Testament. 'Those of you who are evil will die!' He paused for maximum effect. '. . . Those who follow the path of enlightenment will survive the coming horror.' Wa closed his eyes, as would a fortune teller.

Having torn them down, he would now built them up. The ethereal sound of harp, violin and piano filled the Tokyo Dome. Pastoral views of the ninth dimension, Wa's view of heaven, filled the screens. Wa took his place on the Inca throne. He looked neither imperious nor arrogant. Palace attendants walked slowly around the stage set.

A young woman in her twenties, obviously frightened, approached the throne, led by two of Wa's dancers. She was dressed in a grey Chanel skirt and white silk blouse.

'Welcome.' He led the girl down to the front of the stage, where the entire audience could see her. Wa paused again for effect. He could milk an audience better than the best. 'I wish to introduce the ten millionth member of Happy Science. Miss Yuki Noguchi.'

He stepped back, allowing Yuki to stand alone in front of the multitude. The fans went wild, throwing flowers on stage and taking photographs. Thousands of flashbulbs blinked as the crowd started chanting 'Yuki, Yuki.' The applause was thundering. Behind Yuki, Wa beamed, then moved forward again.

Yuki bowed before the master. Wa then placed over her head a gold necklace emblazoned with a giant 'W'. Yuki was so overwhelmed, not only by the honour but also by the rush of adrenalin, that she felt like fainting.

Wa waited for the applause to die down enough to be heard above it. 'You are my ten millionth follower. Be proud of it. Wear it . . .' He picked up the necklace, '. . . as an honour.'

He turned to the audience. 'Tonight we welcome number ten million. But soon we will have another ten million followers, and then another ten and another.'

The crowd was on its feet, cheering. It took several minutes for them to calm down. During that time Yuki was escorted off the stage, to more flowers and camera flashes.

'Our numbers will swell very soon. A new order of the ages is upon us – a Japan where spiritualism, entrepreneurialism, a free economy and a free government will flourish. But first the old order must be destroyed. Purged. Expunged.'

Music was building underneath him, and suddenly Wa's voice boomed out louder than during the entire evening. 'This summer Tokyo shall experience an earthquake unprecedented in the annals of Japanese history. It is the end of the world as we know it. And the beginning of a New Order as I've predicted. Prepare yourselves!'

A giant flash blinded the audience. A rumbling, thunderous crash was heard, replicating an earthquake. All the seats in the stadium began to vibrate – an effect which frightened even the most hardened earthquake veterans. The stage was enveloped in smoke and the entire stadium went black. When the stage lights came on, Wa was gone. The Inca palace lay in ruins. In the distance the audience could see Wa walking down the yellow road to the ninth dimension, his arms outstretched. Another quake was felt, and the remaining blocks of the palace fell to the ground. The lights of the ninth dimension were dimmed and then blackened. For a second time Wa disappeared, this time for good.

'*Sensei! Sensei!*' chanted the sixty thousand, hoping for an encore. They screamed for another two minutes before the infield lights at the Giants' Stadium came on.

The show was over.

6

THE CATFISH

Sunday at the Watanabe home in Chiba, a north-eastern suburb of Tokyo

'The doctrines of the Hindi avatar, the Hebrew Messiah, Christian millennium and the Hesunanian of the Indian Ghost Dance are essentially all the same.'

Nineteenth-century anthropologist James Mooney describing how the Indian tribes hoped to incorporate the American New Madrid earthquake of 1811 into their mythology in order to overthrow their white oppressors

With his trousers pulled down around his ankles, young Matsuo Watanabe, aged three, was standing over the yellow plastic bucket that his father had brought home. 'Now aim carefully.' Matsuo's eight-year-old sister Naomi was potty training him and held the bucket under the yellow stream of urine.

'What are you two doing?' shouted their father, interrupting Matsuo's concentration.

The young boy looked around at his father as the stream trickled down.

'Not my new earthquake kit,' he moaned. Watanabe was not given to harsh reprimands. 'Matsuo, we only pee in the potty or the toilet.'

His son looked confused. 'But Daddy, the bucket looks just like my potty . . .'

Nomo Watanabe pulled his son's wet trousers off, took the bucket to the outside tap and washed it out. The previous contents of the bucket were strewn all over the lawn. 'Come, help me pick these things up,' he gently commanded his family.

He stooped down to pick up a flashlight, radio and book of matches. The EQ Utility Bucket was a Californian import which the Mitsukoshi department store sold throughout Japan. The trendy yellow bucket was a best-selling conversation piece – few thought to buy it on the grounds that it might be useful in the event of an earthquake. The container included a first-aid kit, goggles, gloves, Swiss Army knife, ten cartons of AQUA, Kleenex, twelve orange and green Snaplights, a BRW space blanket, a chemical miniheater, toilet bags and a deck of cards. Japanese consumers snatched up the EQ Utility Buckets at 20,000 yen a piece.

Watanabe snapped the lid on, walked inside and was putting the bucket on a high shelf when he was interrupted. Fujimoto, who had just wandered into the house, was a widower who had been married to the second cousin of Watanabe's wife. She had died, leaving him to manage the family shop nearby. Fujimoto had borrowed some money from Watanabe to settle some gambling debts, pretending he needed the money to increase the inventory in his corner shop.

'What are you doing?' enquired the visitor.

'Getting ready for an earthquake.'

'What earthquake is this?' scoffed Fujimoto.

'Haven't you been following the news? Every week this year there has been a quake in the Pacific: Taiwan, Manila, China, Japan, the Sakhalin Islands. And read this,' said Watanabe, throwing him a copy of *Friday* magazine. He stabbed with his forefinger at the article written by Mariko and Kato.

'BUDDHA FORECASTS QUAKE: Sixty Thousand Fans Prepare for Doom!' read the sarcastic headline. 'Master Wa, dressed as an Inca Emperor, rallied Tokyo Dome last week to virtual hysteria. The highlight of the annual birthday celebration of the self-proclaimed Buddha was his prediction of an imminent earthquake to hit Tokyo. The frenzied fans were reminiscent of Nazi brownshirt rallies with Wa as their Führer . . .'

The article went on to trash Wa. The publishers, Kodansha, claimed the golden sheen on the back of Wa's head was chemically induced. 'Fraud!' they cried. His radiance was sleight of hand, much like the crying madonnas and bleeding Jesus figures that popped up around the world. The article also poked fun at his claims that humans were formed from Venusians, a race of beautiful intellects with sparkling bodies and IQs over 300. According to Wa, some of these Venusians had travelled to earth in spaceships from the ninth dimension.

'You believe in this guy?' asked Fujimoto incredulously.

'No, no, not the religious part. But the earthquake makes sense.'

'Bah, you're a fool to waste your money on such nonsense.'

Fujimoto was jealous of how easily money flowed in this household, and was not sorry he had played upon family obligation in weaseling the loan out of his relative. He reckoned Watanabe must be making good money as a section chief at Mitsukoshi. His own corner shop was not doing so well, for which he blamed the large department stores. But the housewives knew he overpriced the goods.

'We have no worries. Our houses are all sturdy. They've lasted fifty years and they'll last another fifty,' insisted Fujimoto. 'And what are those?' he asked, pointing to a pile of plastic tiles.

'The builders are going to put them on the roof next weekend.'

Plastic tiles were lightweight and much safer than top-heavy ceramic tiles. A wooden home, as most were in Japan, with ceramic tiles was like a book balanced on pencils – in an earthquake it would easily splinter and crush the occupants.

'Well, do as you like,' said Fujimoto in a disparaging tone before remembering why he had called. 'I should soon have the money you loaned me.' His tone softened slightly.

Fujimoto had borrowed the million yen – nearly $10,000 – over a year earlier but had no idea how he was going to repay the money. He had read in a book that it was best not to avoid people to whom you owed money, so each week he dutifully promised payment.

Watanabe ignored his comment. 'You must prepare yourself. The Big One is overdue.'

But Fujimoto was more concerned about money, and seeing expensive roof tiles lying on the ground convinced him that Watanabe was in no hurry to get his money back.

'Yeah, yeah. If you're so sure about the Big One hitting, let's make a small bet. If the quake comes by September, I pay you an extra hundred thousand in interest. If not, then I can extend my loan an extra year,' bargained Fujimoto, forgetting momentarily that he had promised to repay Watanabe soon anyway.

Watanabe shook his head sadly. 'No bets. You're family. I just want you to be safe.'

'See you next week,' said Fujimoto. The shopkeeper was relieved that Watanabe was not going to demand his money back.

That evening the two Watanabe children cuddled up to their mother and father for their Sunday evening story time.

The Watanabe family was typical of most Japanese households. Life revolved around their single-storey wooden house in Chiba, across the bay from Tokyo. Their home was perhaps a bit bigger than most: it had a cheery Western-style living room with wall-to-wall carpeting, sofa and TV with the latest Sega game system. The family slept in two tatami-matted rooms with futons. Most homes were not so large or so well decorated. A tatami mat was roughly the size of a human body – 1 metre wide and 2 metres long. But Watanabe had a twelve-tatami house and was proud of this achievement. Most homes were six, eight or ten tatami in size.

Nomo Watanabe was not your prototypical salary man and seldom went out drinking with colleagues or friends, preferring to spend time with his family. He did not smoke, play golf or have a mistress, and he loved his wife and her company. Not that Watanabe was a wimp: he was ambitious and had strong views at work of how to improve Mitsukoshi. At home, though, he relaxed and felt no need to be domineering or engage in false male bravado. He enjoyed cooking dinner at the weekend and even washed the dishes on occasion.

Every Sunday evening was story night in the Watanabe home. Instead of watching TV or playing Sega CD games, young Matsuo and Naomi listed wide-eyed as their father told stories: some were from Japanese mythology, others pure fantasy. Now he sat in his armchair, a birthday gift from his wife. The armrests were dark from use.

'What story shall I tell you tonight?'

'Please tell us the story of the giant *namazu*,' urged Matsuo. A *namazu* was a catfish.

'Again?'

'Oh please, please, please,' pleaded Naomi.

'That's what you get for telling them an earthquake's on the way,' teased Mrs Watanabe.

Young Matsuo jumped up from the armchair screaming. 'The fish story, the fish story!' He ran in small circles around the room.

'But I told you that story last week,' Watanabe began to argue, knowing he would lose.

'Fish story, fish story,' Naomi and Matsuo began chanting together.

Watanabe finally gave in, as he always did – but he loved to watched them plead with him and sometimes was able to cajole a big hug. 'Okay, okay, I'll tell you the story of the mischievous catfish.'

Immediately his two children jumped on to his lap and snuggled themselves into position, Matsuo on one leg, Naomi on the other. This was all part of their Sunday evening routine. He looked over at his wife, who smiled back at him and nodded.

'Once upon a time, deep in the mud below the earth, lived Wato, a giant catfish. His whiskers were as thick as tree trunks and as long as the longest train.'

Naomi interrupted him.

'You mean even longer than the Shinkansen, Daddy?'

'Yes, darling, even longer than the bullet train,' replied Watanabe, who seldom got through an entire story before Naomi had exhausted him with questions and Matsuo had fallen asleep.

'Now Wato was a troublemaker,' started Watanabe.

'Daddy, you mean like Matsuo, don't you? Remember when he poked his finger through the *shoji*?' (The *shoji* was a paper screen.)

'Yes, I remember,' Watanabe said. 'Now let me tell the story. The giant catfish was very mischievous and so reckless that the gods decided that Kashima, protector of the earth, had to keep him still. Kashima took a giant rock and placed it on top of Wato. Wato tried to shake the rock off but it was no use. He couldn't move. But Kashima liked to enjoy himself. Sometimes he liked to go out drinking with the other gods and relaxed his guard on Wato. Whenever Wato sensed this, he thrashed wildly around in the mud.'

Matsuo was already asleep and Naomi was fading fast.

'Wato's frantic movements are why we have earthquakes,' said Watanabe. Then seeing that Naomi was down, he smiled at his wife. Rarely did the children go to sleep so easily. It was going to be a quiet evening.

They took the two children into their sleeping area, laid them side by side on the futon and put a light cover over them. Then they went back to the living room where Watanabe sat down in his armchair again and picked up his favourite book.

'I've got to go into the Ginza store to take inventory on Tuesday.'

His job was to calculate what brands would sell. Last season, Watanabe had taken a big gamble. He had bet that foreign designer names like Ralph Lauren, Brooks Brothers, Paul Stewart, Timberland and Armani would be a big hit for men. Watanabe reasoned that Japanese consumers were fanatical fashion snobs – the more Western and elite the brand, the more appealing. Watanabe also bought most of his foreign labels in dollars. The dollar had plunged and Mitsukoshi had made a fortune. By taking inventory, he could see how successful his gamble had been. But Mrs Watanabe sensed that he was less enthusiastic than usual about this task.'

'Is everything all right at work?'

'Mmm. I had another fight with Suzuki over increasing sales. They don't listen to me and will only promote according to my age, not my ability. I guess it gets tiring reporting to men with a salaryman mentality.'

'But, dear,' said Mrs Watanabe in a soothing voice, 'you are a salaryman, and almost every man works this way.' She was worried about her husband. Though good-natured, he had been complaining more and more about work.

Watanabe went back to his reading, then put the book down again. 'Where are the new thinkers and entrepreneurs of Japan? Where are the Henry Fords, the Richard Bransons, the Sam Waltons and Bill Gates of Japan? Our Matsushitas and Sonys have grown too large. The little guy is snuffed out by the big companies.'

Mrs Watanabe tried to soothe her husband. 'Tomorrow is tomorrow. Come to bed now. I'll give you a massage.'

Watanabe looked up at his wife and smiled. 'Sorry, I guess I carried on.' He paused. 'I am the luckiest man in Japan.'

He took her hand and led her into the bedroom. Neither of them could possibly know this would be the last massage Watanabe would ever receive from his wife, and that tomorrow night would be their last together.

7

THE SCAM

A summer Saturday

'No earthquake has ever been predicted in the history of mankind.'

Dr Robert Geller at the Department of Earth and Planetary Physics, Tokyo University, 1995

A lex sat down at the kitchen table and his mother stood by the stove. The room began to shake gently and Hiroko stopped to check on her son. Her research into earthquakes for the *Asahi Shimbun* made her feel uneasy about the slightest trembling.

'Hey, Mom, feel that?' laughed Alex. 'That's a wimpy quake, maybe a three.' So many earthquakes hit central Tokyo that he knew the difference between a mild tremor and the 'Big One'.

Suddenly the room shook violently from side to side. Hiroko was standing but could not move forward.

'Mom!' shouted Alex in fear, unable get out of his chair.

'Don't worry, Alex.'

The room was vibrating erratically and threw her off balance. Her arms were pinned to the wall. The quake reached six on the Richter scale. Alex's chair had fallen backwards and he was on his back, kicking his legs like a turtle.

'Help! Mom! Make it stop.' Alex tried to curl up. He put his hands over his head, fearing the worst.

As the room was moving sideways a savage vertical shock wave hit. The room was thrown up and down. The quake reached seven and was rising. All movement was impossible. Mother and son looked like a pair of crash test dummies thrown from a flying vehicle.

'Please! Stop!' yelled Hiroko, as she was hurled from side to side.

A moment later all movement and rumbling stopped. The kitchen door was thrown open and a pair of attendants in white overalls rushed in.

'Are you okay?' The attendants unstrapped Alex from his chair and Hiroko from the wall. The ride was over.

Hiroko felt ill, as did her son. Assisted by the Tokyo Disneyland workers, she and Alex staggered down the steps.

Quakemaster was a hydraulic brainchild conceived for children who were ever more demanding in the rush for adrenalin-filled thrills. Tokyo might have thousands of minor earthquakes a year but that did not prevent children forcing their parents to fork out 1000 yen each to experience the 'Big One'.

'Pregnant women and those with heart problems are not allowed on this ride,' read a notice as she and Alex queasily passed a long line of eager children holding reluctant parents by the hand.

'They don't look so good,' whispered one father to his child, 'maybe we should go on the Dumbo ride.'

'Dumbo's for babies, Dad.'

His father did not pursue the matter, not wanting to embarrass himself or look cowardly in front of fifty other parents. The fathers had already paid 1000 yen each in advance, a wise move by Tokyo Disneyland management since parents would have been unable or unwilling to pay for Quakemaster after the jarring ride.

Hiroko stumbled behind a bush and vomited. As if vomiting was contagious, Alex felt his mouth filling with water and watched as his breakfast hit the ground. An unpleasant tang filled his mouth and he looked over at his mother.

'Let's go again,' he said mischievously and with a straight face.

Hiroko didn't hesitate to call his bluff. 'Okay.'

'Forget it Mom, the queue's too long,' he added, suddenly feeling ill again.

Hiroko walked slowly over to the soft drinks stand. 'Let's get something to wash this taste out of our mouth.'

She bought two Cokes and gave one to Alex. Hiroko usually forbade Alex to have soft drinks, but she had read somewhere that Coke settled the stomach. She handed one of the cans to her son.

'Spit the first sip out, then you can drink the rest.'

Feeling slightly better, Hiroko and Alex walked around Disneyland for a while, but avoided any further rides. Half an hour later they called it quits and went home to Mitaka, a western suburb of Tokyo, to spend the rest of Saturday recovering.

Hiroko's own mother, Michiko, had already left for work when they got home, but her tell-tale, foul-smelling cigarette smoke lingered in the air. This did not please Hiroko, who allowed her mother to live with them on the understanding that there was no smoking in the apartment. Michiko had emphysema and was slowly drowning from liquid in her lungs. Her hacking and gurgling was not so much an annoyance as an anxiety to Hiroko, who realized her mother would not live long. Michiko had spent her entire adult life as a bar hostess and now owned a snug bar in Ginza called the Gaslight. The bar resembled its owner: small, thin, purple-tongued and raucous. Michiko worked six nights a week at the Gaslight. She left at five each evening and returned home at four in the morning with her clothes and body reeking of smoke and alcohol. Despite her fatigue, Michiko awoke to see her grandson off to school before collapsing again on her futon.

Michiko had worked this punishing routine for thirty years. Her first years as a bar hostess had been lucrative as bureaucrats, businessmen and yakuza kingpins convened at the Gaslight. Michiko was known for her ability to keep secrets, and kept a special back room where she served her more clandestine clients. With her pretty face she lived the high life as the mistress of various wealthy patrons, one of whom was Hiroko's father. Hiroko herself had grown up with dozens of 'uncles' and promised herself that one day her own home life would be warm and stable. The decline of Michiko's fortunes as a hostess was stemmed when Hiroko's mystery father made Michiko an outright gift of the Gaslight. Though the bar supported her family, all she had to show for thirty years of work was the Gaslight, her daughter, her daughter's education and jewellery given to her by once-adoring clients.

But Hiroko was determined to earn enough money to help her mother retire. That was not yet possible on a reporter's salary and, since Michiko's savings had put Hiroko through college, she repaid this obligation by allowing her mother to live in their Mitaka home. The strain was compounded by the lack of privacy. Bringing home boyfriends was slightly embarrassing: single mothers were not common, especially when they came with baggage like Michiko. Hiroko kept her tough-talking, bar-owning mother a secret and projected a well-educated, well-dressed, cosmopolitan image to those at work. Hiroko seemed the consummate female professional of the modern era, but like many women was defined by her complex relationship with her mother.

Her son grew up with fewer complexities and was adored by mother and grandmother. Alex had been born in New York while Hiroko had been a student at Columbia University's School of Journalism. Alex's father was Alexander Fitzgerald, a professor of poetry with whom Hiroko had fallen in love. When Alexander died in a car accident,

Hiroko was shattered and out of sheer paralysis had remained in New York for a year. Then mother and son had returned to Tokyo where Hiroko landed a job at the *Asahi* newspaper. Only a small group of people knew that Hiroko had a son and nobody knew about her mother. Professionally Hiroko was determined to rise above her past.

Mother and son had an evening ritual and that evening, while Hiroko heated the milk, Alex put three white marshmallows into each of the two New York Mets coffee mugs they had bought at Shea Stadium. It had to be three marshmallows – not two, not four. Then mother and son would curl up on the sofa and Hiroko would read to her eight-year-old until he fell asleep on her lap. Her husband had not left much money but had left Hiroko with a special gift – a delight in the English language, which she was now passing on to Alex. Each night Hiroko read to young Alex – first nursery rhymes, then fairy tales and now the Hardy Boys.

Hiroko lifted Alex up and carried him to bed, covering him with a blanket and thinking how lucky she was to have him as a son. Then she laughed, remembering how he had conned her on to the Quakemaster ride earlier in the day.

Hiroko brushed her teeth and washed her face. She changed the cover on her mother's futon and sheets and threw out the crumpled tissues in the wicker basket. It was then that she noticed a flash of colour in the tissues. She picked up one of them, to find it covered in dried blood that her mother had coughed up.

Hiroko made a note to visit her mother's doctor the next day. Then she broke down and cried herself to sleep.

Fifth floor of the *Asahi Shimbun* headquarters in Tsukiji, Monday morning

The fifth floor was the nerve centre of the *Asahi* newspaper. Filled with chain-smoking, casually dressed reporters, many with long hair, it seemed an unlikely source for much of the nation's news. The reporters lived one step above bag people – a utilitarian existence geared toward producing stories. Nobody noticed the ugly redbrick building or open-plan office lit by fluorescent lights. The *Asahi* bosses had tried hard to create a brightly lit workspace for their reporters: a blue industrial carpet dotted with cigarette burns contrasted with the white metal shutters on the windows.

The newspaper was in the business of exposing secrets. Every journalist had a satellite phone which in the field could be plugged to grey Toshiba laptop computers with built in modems and colour screens. Reporters simply wrote their copy on assignment and transmitted the copy from the laptop via telephone to the *Asahi*'s main computer in the Tsukiji headquarters. Articles were docked to the reporter's private e-mail box, and from here the editors cut and pasted the copy before each evening's deadline.

'The meeting's tonight.'

'Where?'

Hiroko Fujita was talking on the telephone to Kaelin, who had now been forced to become Tada's mistress.

'Tada's apartment.'

'Can you tape the meeting?'

'I'll try.'

'You have to.'

There was a long pause on the other end of the line. 'Okay, but if he finds out he'll kill me.'

Before Hiroko could reply, the line went dead. Hiroko hated putting her 'source' into such danger, but she had to get her story and needed proof of Kaelin's allegations. This could be the opportunity she needed. Her editor had quashed the exposé on the Daishin corruption scandal and refused to print it until she had more evidence.

Hiroko was excited and turned to Jiroo, a close friend and colleague. He lived near her in Mitaka, and together they rode the Sobu line to work each day. More than once he had intervened on her behalf when some randy businessman had tried to chat her up during the forty-minute ride. He was also about the only man in the office who hadn't tried to get into her pants. Not that he didn't want to. Jiroo fantasized often about Hiroko, especially on the train where her presence drove him wild.

Jiroo's professional expertise was in financial matters.

'This will bring down the Japanese government,' Hiroko whispered to him.

'Tell me what you've got.'

She explained the Daishin Construction stock scam.

'Three months ago Daishin's stock price on the Tokyo Stock Exchange was 750 yen. Today it's almost quadruple that. My source says that Daishin had a meeting three months ago with their banker, their stockbroker, the Prime Minister and the Transport Minister. The bank agreed to lend a billion yen to the Prime Minister and another billion to the group to buy up Daishin shares. The meeting to unwind the scam is being held tonight at Tada's apartment.'

'You're so naive, Hiroko-chan,' interjected Jiroo. 'That's how Japanese politicians have always raised money. It's just that nobody's allowed to write about it. Including you.'

'This is different,' Hiroko explained defensively. 'First, I think I can get direct evidence of the ministerial involvement. Secondly, this scam is not just a passive crime of stock manipulation. Daishin's actions are life-threatening since none of their buildings are being constructed to withstand earthquakes.'

Jiroo knew Hiroko was intent on breaking the story. 'I'll help you present the story, but it's your job to get it printed.' That meant getting it by Sam Tanaka, their editor.

'Oh, thank you, Jiroo!'

Jiroo took out a piece of paper and drew a chart. 'First Daishin decides to raise money for expansion by issuing new shares to the public. It's more profitable to raise money at 3000 yen than at 750 yen a share. Right?'

Hiroko nodded, following his logic.

'Once Daishin makes the decision to issue new shares it's a sure bet that its share price will skyrocket before it's formally announced the decision. The banks then lend a billion yen to the Prime Minister, who's the first to buy shares at 750 yen through a nominee front. The second billion's lent to the front organizations of secondary ministers such as Fujimura and Tada. Underworld kingpins then force themselves into these buying syndicates. The entire scam is orchestrated by the stockbroker.'

He drew in the names of the insiders at the top of the chart. The first round of insider buying had pushed Daishin over 1000 yen a share.

'If the insiders all bought stock at low levels, then who's left to push it to 3000 yen?' asked Hiroko.

'That's no problem. Daishin's stockbroker draws up a list of preferred clients to whom favours are owed. These include senior politicians, stockbroking executives and clients who have previously lost a lot of money in a bad recommendation. By the time all these preferred clients and insiders have bought, the stock rises to, let's say, 1250 yen a share. The brokerage firm then instructs its construction analyst to write an optimistic report on Daishin. The broker faxes this handwritten "buy" recommendation to top Japanese insurance and fund management firms.'

That had pushed Daishin's price to 2000 yen a share.

'The analyst then mails a more formal, printed "buy" recommendation to the broker's institutional client base: corporate
accounts, smaller fund management firms and a handful of wealthy
individuals.'

That had pushed Daishin to over 2500 yen a share.

'Almost last on the financial food chain are the foreign investors.
An English language report is faxed and mailed.'

That had pushed Daishin's price above 2700 yen a share.

'But when does everyone get out? And who gets out first?' asked
Hiroko.

'The sucker in this whole scam is the little guy. The Japanese
broker, in this case Marayama Securities, has thousands of brokers
whose sole task is to stuff individual clients full of worthless shares.
The "sell" signal in this scam will be when retail brokers begin
jamming Daishin Construction down the throats of housewives
and shopkeepers. Private clients are known as the "little fish with
the big mouth" for their ability to snap at a baited hook. Each of
the Big Four brokers has millions of retail clients serviced by their
branch network. During their morning meeting hundreds of branch
managers order thousands of retail brokers to push Daishin shares.
They hit the phones, whispering to their clients that Daishin is a
political stock. By then it's too late. The share will rise another 200
or 300 yen during which time the insiders will all be selling.'

Jiroo finished his chart.

DAISHIN SHARE SCAM

750 yen	High-ranking insiders begin buying: Prime Minister, cabinet members and yakuza chiefs. Banks finance the politicians.
1000	Senior politicians, high-ranking executives in Daishin's main stockbroker, and those who are owed favours, begin buying.
1500	Top fund management firms, insurance companies and banks are sent handwritten 'buy' report with verbal confirmation over the phone that Daishin is a 'political' stock.
2000	Entire institutional client base of Daishin's underwriter are told to buy Daishin shares.
2500	Foreign institutions are sent a glossy 'buy' recommendation.
3000	Retail clients are phoned by thousands of aggressive brokers; insiders bail out. Daishin announces in the

newspapers that it will issue new shares to the public
at 3000 yen a share.

This type of stock scam had been the backbone of Japan's
economic miracle, keeping the stockmarket inflated while filling
corporate war-chests and political coffers.

Hiroko's allegations were startling. Though the nation's power
elite had been embroiled in scandal before, few were ever directly
linked to pay-offs. Usually an underling admitted vague blame in
order to deflect criticism from his boss. When the media and police
investigators started circling for the kill, a politician, bureaucrat or
company president usually resigned. Few facts ever became public.
Hiroko had the evidence by which the *Asahi Shimbun* could topple
the Prime Minister.

Each time Hiroko presented evidence at the weekly 'A Team'
meetings, however, her leads either dried up or Sam Tanaka asked
her for yet more evidence.

'Who's the mole?' Hiroko wondered aloud.

Jiroo shrugged and leaned towards her, breathing in her intoxi-
cating perfume.

'It could be anybody,' he whispered. 'We've interviewed so many
people. Any of them could be crooked.'

Hiroko shook her head in frustration. Jiroo glanced around to
see if they were being observed.

'Wish me luck.' Hiroko walked over to discuss the latest develop-
ments with Sam Tanaka, determined to get her exposé into print.

As Hiroko walked over to the editor's desk it was as if all the
men within a 5-metre radius had been zapped by an electric shock.
Some sneaked glances, others watched openly as she moved across
the room. Most of them only came up to her chest. They did not
complain about this. Almost every newsman, single and married, had
tried to sleep with Hiroko Fujita – unsuccessfully. Today she wore a
lightweight grey wool dress by Chanel. Like most Japanese women,
Hiroko spent most of her disposable income on clothes and jewellery.
The Japanese had the best-dressed females on earth: Gucci, Armani,
Versace and Chanel were standard gear for all women above 'OL' or
office lady level. Unlike her mother, whose expensive dresses never
quite fitted properly, Hiroko wore her clothes well. This particular
number hugged her slender hips and superb breasts.

'Tanaka-san?' said Hiroko softly.

She sat across the desk from her editor. His desk stood against the
wall and faced the entire office, so Hiroko had her back to the work

floor. She sat back and crossed her legs provocatively. Growing up
the daughter of a bar hostess had taught her the practical side of
being a woman.

'Tanaka-san, I've worked very hard on my corruption story. Tada,
Mori and Fujimura are all guilty. It's time to publish it, don't you
think?' She wore a pouting smile.

'No, no,' he stammered, 'there is not yet enough evidence to link
them to the bribes.' He listened to Hiroko, as he always did, because
she was beautiful.

In a mischievous mood, Hiroko leaned over and lowered her
breasts on to the editor's desk, squashing them slightly.

'Tanaka-san, if I can get you a tape recording of a meeting between
Mori and Tada discussing the bribes, will you print it?' She was careful
not to mention when the tape was being made.

Tanaka's face was now fire engine red and he involuntarily blurted
out a response. 'Yes, I'll print it.'

'Put your hand on your heart like this and swear,' demanded
Hiroko as she placed her left hand between her breasts.

Tanaka started hyperventilating but did as he was told. 'I
swear.'

Mission accomplished, thought Hiroko. She sauntered off to her
desk, thinking of the humiliation she had to endure to get published.
Hiroko often wondered at how her mother seemed to enjoy flaunting
her womanhood in return for favours, even bragging how, as a young
woman, she had won a five-carat diamond in a 'dare' by stripping in
a bar full of customers. Hiroko felt guilty enough just manipulating
Tanaka.

Tanaka figured, wrongly, that he could sleep with Hiroko if he
printed the story. Going to bed with her was almost worth his life.
Almost – and five minutes later, when he lost his erection, he thought
better of it.

Hiroko looked at her watch. Almost eleven o'clock. She had to
meet her mother's doctor at noon, then conduct an interview at
two-thirty. All eyes followed her out of the door.

8

THE GAIJIN

Monday on the Salomon Brothers trading desk in central
Tokyo

'There are over 120 billionaires in America and most of
them made their money by owning companies listed on the
stockmarket. No wonder the words 'stocks and shares' hold
such magic to college graduates.'
A US financial magazine describing Wall Street's allure

The traders cursed and shouted as the stockmarket fell.
Blinking red lights flashed the latest Tokyo stock prices
on the 6-metre-long blackboard. Each flash represented a
price change, and the continual flashing spelled danger.

Dougie Douglas shouted down the intercom to his trader in
Singapore: 'Sell two thousand contracts!' He quickly switched on
the intercom to his Osaka office: 'Buy two thousand contracts!'

Douglas left both lines to Singapore and Osaka open, awaiting
confirmation that his trades had been completed. His desk looked
like a spaceship with hi-tech trading machines surrounding him:
Reuter's for foreign exchange, Bloomberg for bonds, Quick 10
for stocks.

Douglas sweated. All he could do was wait, which was not
something traders did gracefully. Salomon Brothers was Japan's
largest foreign brokerage house. The present was not a place to
linger for Dougie or Salomon.

Born in Brooklyn into a lower middle-class family, he had been a
child chess prodigy, travelling the eastern United States to compete
in weekend tournaments. At the age of twelve he achieved a Master's
ranking in chess, winning tournament after tournament. When not
on the road he earned up to $500 a week playing chess on Brooklyn's
sidewalks, fleecing older men who arrogantly believed it impossible
for one so young to be so calculating.

Douglas spent his entire life planning ahead. At fourteen he knew he would attend Columbia University, the ultimate dream of his father, a motor mechanic who had saved for Dougie's college education. But the boy didn't need his father's savings – Columbia gave him a full work-study scholarship after he scored a perfect 800 on his mathematics achievement test.

He was popular in college, working as a bartender. He boasted that he could make any drink – or woman – in the bar. His party trick was being blindfolded and guessing the name of whatever drink or cocktail was placed in front of him. Good-humoured, he only lost his temper once in four years at Columbia – when someone spiked his tomato juice cocktail with urine.

Dougie graduated *summa cum laude* with a degree in advanced mathematics. He had saved enough money to travel through Europe for a year after college with his room-mate Wayne Herman. Wayne's family had lived all over the world and his father was reportedly the number three man in the CIA. The two young men received a very warm welcome in Europe, confirming Dougie's suspicions of the Herman family connections. More importantly, Dougie ended up one short of screwing a girl in every country he visited. His nemesis was Luxembourg. Stupid little country. The place was so small there were no good-looking women.

Back in New York he landed a job with Salomon Brothers, who were always on the prowl for 'rocket scientists' whom they could convert into traders. Starting in their training programme, he worked his way up through the trading desk. Wayne Herman landed a job at Kroll Associates, the premier American detective agency, most of whose employees had intelligence contacts around the world. Both men promised that the first one to make his fortune would help the other up the ladder. Both stormed up the ranks quickly. Dougie had four qualities that made him shine at Salomon: a sense of humour, a lightning-quick brain, determination and a capacity to drink late into the night. One day he was told to fly to Tokyo to fill in for a trader on holiday and never came home. The absolute decadence of the expatriate Tokyo lifestyle was perfect for him. For the first time in his life, Dougie was not planning his moves in advance.

The stockmarket continued to fall.

'Come on dickbag. Confirm, confirm,' muttered Douglas to himself.

Sugimoto, the Japanese trader and Douglas's best friend, listened in on his conversation in order to improve his English. The two had been close friends ever since Douglas had visited Sugimoto's brother in hospital where he had been admitted for a bone marrow transplant. Douglas had taught the fifteen-year-old how to play chess, and had played the teenager each day after work. Chess was their only form of communication, and the companionship helped his recovery. Sugimoto's resultant devotion to the American had made the pair inseparable. Together they hoped one day to earn enough money at Salomon Brothers to start their own company.

'Douglas-san, what is meaning of "dickbag"?'

Douglas laughed. 'It's like the other words I taught you. It has no meaning.'

'*Ah so desu ka*,' Sugimoto nodded. 'I understand. You mean like pin-dick, button-head and fuckwad.'

Sugimoto carefully wrote down 'dickbag' in his notebook next to 'douchebag', 'hosebag' and 'scumbag'. *Americans have so many bags, thought Sugimoto. In Japan we only have shopping bags.*

Sugimoto taught Douglas Japanese in exchange for English lessons. The American's idea of the Japanese language was a universe of thirty words. When he first moved to Tokyo, Sugimoto took Douglas out on the town. They had jumped into a taxi with Sugimoto shouting, '*Eto, Teikoku Hoteru onegaishimasu.*' Even Douglas knew that '*onegaishimasu*' meant 'please', and the word '*hoteru*' was easy. '*Eto*' was a new word.

'What does "*eto*" mean?' Douglas had asked.

'Nothing,' replied Sugimoto. 'It's sort of like the English "um"'.

When they had arrived at the hotel, Sugimoto ordered drinks: '*Ano, biru nihon onegaishimasu.*'

'What does "*ano*" mean?'

'Nothing really,' Sugimoto had responded.

Douglas just shook his head, thinking that the Japanese had more ways of saying nothing than any other race.

Later they went out for sushi, and once again Sugimoto ordered. '*Ja, sushi seto onegaishimasu*,' Sugimoto asked the waiter.

Douglas listened carefully. He knew what 'sushi' was. 'Seto' was obviously the word for 'set' while '*onegaishimasu*' meant 'please'. That left '*ja*'.

'What does "*ja*" mean?' pestered Douglas.

'Just another filler word.'

This was great news to Douglas, who had been struggling with Japanese. He calculated that 70 per cent of the language consisted of negative space and filler words like *ja*, *ma*, *ano*, *eto* and *ne*, foreign words like *takushi*, *biru* and *hoteru*, and basic words he was forced to learn like those for 'thank you', 'please' and 'straight', 'right' and 'left' so that he could direct taxi cab drivers home after his late-night drinking binges.

Sugimoto wrote down all the filler words for Douglas, who learned them overnight. With a bit of arm twisting, Sugimoto also threw in a few good phrases like 'You have beautiful skin' and 'Would you like to go to a love hotel with me?' Douglas used that last one with consistent success. Sensitive Westerners such as English teachers and Buddhist wannabes could spend the rest of their lives learning fluent Japanese. Douglas had better things to do with his life. He certainly was not going to learn how to write complicated Japanese characters, or 'barbed wire' as he called them.

Meanwhile the stockmarket kept falling.

'Come on, douchebag, confirm.'

Douglas flicked his intercom to Singapore to talk. 'Yo! What's the hold-up?'

'Done. We've filled your order,' replied the Singapore office.

Douglas spent his time playing the Simex and Osaka futures exchanges off against each other. Theoretically both futures markets consisted of many of the same Japanese shares, so when one futures market got too expensive while another was underpriced, Douglas swooped in and simultaneously bought one and sold the other in equal amounts. Douglas figured they were like financial elastic bands that, when stretched, had one day to return to their normal position. When they came back into parity he unwound the positions for a hefty profit.

Douglas flipped the intercom to Osaka. 'I need to cover, guys. What's the story?'

'Just a minute, it's illiquid today.'

Actually the Osaka trader had forgotten to process Douglas's order. The Osaka office, mostly Japanese, were not about to admit that to Douglas, who was a *gaijin* or foreigner.

'Filled. You buy two at seventeen five,' Osaka confirmed thirty seconds later.

Douglas was overjoyed. He had needed to purchase 2000 contracts simultaneously with a sale of 2000 at 18,000 with Singapore. Osaka's delay meant he had bought back each of his contracts much cheaper. Their mistake had just earned Salomon $2 million. What made this mistake even sweeter was that Salomon Brothers paid Douglas 10 per cent of all net profits on his trading. Luckily, he did not share in any losses. He had just made a quick $200,000 bonus.

Douglas thought for a moment. If he were always slow to cover one side of his trades, he could earn a fortune. Then he remembered

Nick Leeson, the Baring's trader who in 1995 had lost over a billion dollars of Baring's money on a gamble that Japanese stocks would rise. The bet had ruined one of the great names in finance. What Leeson had not anticipated was the great Kobe earthquake, which in January 1995 had brought about an unprecedented and unexpected six-month collapse in Japanese share prices.

Bad luck, thought Douglas, who empathized with Leeson. *Who could have predicted an earthquake? I'll never have to worry about that problem.*

Salomon Brothers' management had come down hard on internal controls after the Baring's collapse. 'In case of an earthquake, we need back-up systems outside Tokyo,' they cried, forcing the Osaka office to replicate the Tokyo records. Salomon was full of cowboys who bet billions of the firm's capital each day. The Salomon chief executive hired internal policemen whom Douglas and his buddies called the 'SS', short for 'Salomon's stooges'. They had virtual firing power if they felt traders were exceeding their limits.

Still, controls in the Asian brokerage industry were lax.

'Fucking A, we're gonna get shit-faced tonight, Sugimoto,' whooped Douglas as he slapped his friend on the back.

Sugimoto whipped out his notebook and scribbled 'Fucking A' and 'shit-faced' into his diary. Sugimoto then turned to ask Douglas what 'A' meant, but the American was already dancing around the office slapping high fives.

After work nine traders headed towards the elevator and out of the doors of the Urbannet Building, also known as the 'Tower of Bubble', referring to the extravagance of the go-go eighties. The building was famous for its negative space – the eighteen-floor atrium was surrounded by prominent financial institutions such as Union Bank of Switzerland, Barclay's, Salomon and Nomura. The scarcity of land in Tokyo prevented atria; the Urbannet Building welcomed the feature – it was a statement that its tenants could afford to rent vacant air. Both Nomura and Salomon had insisted on taking the top floor as a sign of superiority over those below. While this was to be Salomon's Asian headquarters, the floors rented by Nomura were simply overflow from its Nihonbashi headquarters. Salomon outbid Nomura to get the upper floors.

Everyone piled out of the elevator and on to the street. Dougie flagged down two taxis but there was only one problem. Each vehicle held only four passengers – three in the back and one in the front.

Nine traders, eight seats. Mathematically, the logical choice was to split the group into three. But the laws of mathematics did not apply to a group of nine fully charged human beings anxious for a good time.

'You four take the front taxi,' Douglas instructed four of his companions. 'We'll pile in here. Yuki can sit on my lap.' Yuki was his trading assistant and the woman whom Master Wa had pronounced as the ten millionth follower of the Happy Science group.

Yuki blushed. She had a crush on Douglas, but was too shy ever to have asked him out. Every day Yuki waited expectantly for Douglas to invite her out, but their only time spent together was in after-work drinking sessions. Instead she had to listen to Douglas call his girlfriends from the trading desk to arrange liaisons. Worse still, he dated three or four women a week. What really hurt her was when Douglas's potential dates did not speak English. All he wanted to do was sleep with them. The language barrier did not thwart Douglas, and when a potential conquest did not speak English he simply handed the phone to Yuki who told the women when and where to meet him. Occasionally Yuki thought some of his potential Japanese conquests were a bit loose and to 'protect' him said the woman did not want to see him. Yuki reckoned she 'screened' out one of every four dates, but wished she could screen all of them.

Douglas was good-looking – he was five foot eleven with stocky shoulders, brown hair and athletic body. Yuki saw a lot more in Douglas than his macho trading guise. Her first glimpse into his inner personality was at a party given at his $120,000-a-year apartment in Hiroo Garden Hills. Salomon Brothers paid the rent, the utility bills and Douglas's $3000 a month phone bill. The Japanese women at the party had gawked at the sheer luxury of his apartment with its three bedrooms, kitchen, living room and maid's quarters. Most were lucky to live in an apartment the size of Douglas's Filipina maid's quarters. While most of the men and women flirted, Yuki used the time quietly to find out more about Douglas.

Lined along one wall of his apartment were a series of forty or so framed black and white photos, obviously taken by a professional. Each had a caption describing the situation, making the collection a rare fusion of photography and literature. Many photographers let their pictures stand as detached observations of humanity. These particular scenes were poignant because the artist delved and engaged his subject matter – a crippled street urchin begging in Calcutta, a bag lady who lived in the lobby of the World Trade Center in New York, a dispossessed Bosnian refugee looking for work in London, and homeless victims of the 1995 Kobe earthquake.

Few people at the party more than glanced at the pictures. When Yuki pressed Douglas to tell her where he had bought them he blushed and, swearing her to secrecy, admitted he had taken them himself. 'I don't want the guys to know,' he had told her. Yuki later discovered that he had taken time off from Salomon Brothers and quietly gone to Kobe the day after the quake to work on relief efforts and take photos. After that evening Yuki was hooked. She knew that he was the man she would some day marry – even though Dougie hadn't yet shown the slightest romantic interest in her.

Luring Douglas was not entrapment, she reasoned. Yuki was doing what every other woman in the world did when she fell in love. Women called it falling in love, while men called it stalking their quarry. Tonight was a big chance for Yuki. She had prepared for just such an opportunity, having changed in the ladies' room into a black miniskirt, fishnet stockings, camisole and white silk blouse. She liberally sprayed herself with Chanel Number Five and put on a light pink lipstick. *I'm twenty-five*, she thought. *If I don't hook Douglas, I will have to marry a Japanese salaryman and be a housewife for the rest of my life.*

Douglas climbed into the taxi. 'C'mon, Yuki, climb in.' Her miniskirt rode up her thighs as she placed her right leg over Dougie and sat back against him.

'Shinjuku, please,' Dougie told the driver in Japanese.

A thrill ran through her as she sat pressed against Douglas, but he did not seem to notice. She was wrong: Dougie was intoxicated by Yuki's perfume and the feeling of her body turned him on. For the first time he looked at her closely. *This woman's beautiful*, he thought without letting Yuki know he was examining her.

Without it seeming like an embrace, Douglas moved his arms around Yuki's slim waist. 'I'll be your seat belt,' he joked.

Yuki sensed an easy victory and adjusted her body as if to get more comfortable, her left breast touching his chest. Dougie was hooked.

All the entertainment districts in Tokyo were different. The famous Ginza was the high-priced dinner-cum-hostess haunt of senior executives. Dinner for four here could run to 100,000 yen, more than $1000. Roppongi was the nerve centre of Tokyo's drinking and dancing scene, while Shibuya catered for teeny-boppers. Shinjuku, where Douglas was taking his trading team, was a world of its own.

To Douglas, the place was like a *Bladerunner* fantasy – as if he were living in an animated fairyland. Like Ginza, Shinjuku was filled with neon lights that seemed to swirl around his head. It was always the most crowded of Japan's night-time haunts, full of street musicians, flower women, beggars, fortune tellers, hawkers, labourers and pedlars.

Since Shinjuku was situated in the western part of Tokyo, in an area of solid bedrock and slightly less prone to direct hits from earthquakes, this was where corporations built their skyscrapers. It was also known as the centre for Tokyo's infamous gangsters, the yakuza. Pachinko and tattoo parlours, hostess bars and nightclubs were crammed into seedy back alleys. Shinjuku rail station was one of the largest in the world, a transit point for all commuters heading to the western suburbs. Since most shopping in Japan was centred around major commuter points, the rising affluence of Shinjuku-based commuters meant a rise in nightlife. Out of its dingy origins sprang trendy clubs. The 1990s saw the outing of gay bars in Tokyo, particularly in Shinjuku. They popped up everywhere with names like the Mars Bar, Zip, Madonna and GB, while jazz clubs, reggae and hard rock establishments also dotted the landscape.

When they got to Shinjuku, Douglas signalled for both taxis to stop. Yuki climbed out, making a point to slide across his lap. This move was not lost on Dougie, who quickly slipped his hand into his pocket to conceal his erection. He paid for both fares, then led the way under a pink sign which said 'AV BAR', short for 'Adult Video bar'.

The AV Bar was located on the ground floor, the first signal to the traders of its exclusivity, since few bars could afford ground floor space which was normally reserved for expensive shops. The inside was fitted with black polished granite and marble lit by low-voltage lighting and judicious use of blue and pink neon. Douglas immediately thought of a *Miami Vice* stageset. Sade-esque music eased the group out of business mode and into party mood. One of their first sights was a giant 2-metre television screen, which for the moment was playing a music video.

The mama-san guided them to their seats. What embarrassed Yuki was the waitresses, who were topless and wore only short black leather skirts. This was the kind of decadence against which Master Wa had preached. But Yuki hid her embarrassment and knew she had to endure the next few hours to win over Dougie.

Once they were seated at the table, a beautiful topless waitress sauntered over to them. Yuki had to admit the woman had a magnificent body, shown off to best possible advantage in her leather microskirt. When the waitress leaned forward to take their drink orders, Yuki wondered whether she was wearing any pants.

Yuki blushed. The waitress turned, saw Yuki staring at her naked backside and winked.

'What's the matter, Yuki? Haven't you ever seen an ass before?' asked one of the group, Wada, whom Salomon office girls had nicknamed 'The Pig'.

'I've seen plenty, Wada-san – just never 10 centimetres from my face.' She tried to hide her discomfort.

'Come over here, my small sake cup, you can sit on my face any time,' said Wada to the waitress. A small sake cup was schoolboy slang for 'virgin'.

The entire table broke into laughter. As the group ordered drinks, Yuki turned her attention to the side of the table where a TV screen was encased in black marble. An erotic porn movie was playing. Yuki did a double take, looking from the video to the waitress and back again. The waitress was starring in the movie! Yuki looked around the AV Bar and noted that all the waitresses starred in the movies playing at their tables.

'Does that turn you on, Yuki?' Wada leered.

'Lay off, buttplug,' said Douglas, protecting Yuki and staking his claim. 'Yuki's with me.'

The tension was broken a second later when the traders looked more closely at the videos.

'Hey, that's our waitress in the video!' somebody yelled.

The Japanese traders went wild. This was a new twist to porn, even for porn-ridden Japan.

'Can I have your autograph?' shouted Wada. 'You can sign my aching Swahili.' He began to unzip his fly.

The waitress casually walked over to Wada and sensuously zipped his fly back up.

'Maybe later,' she cooed. 'If you're a good boy and order lots of drinks.'

'Tequila slammers for everyone,' shouted Wada. 'Two rounds, no . . . make it three.'

'Anything else?'

'Yeah,' replied Wada. 'Do you like music?'

'Of course. Why?'

'I'd like you to play my skin flute and swallow the music,' roared Wada.

Again the table erupted into laughter. The waitress gave a slight, high-pitched whistle like a flute, smiled and replied instantly. 'I am sure your *gobo* plays a wonderful song.'

A *gobo* was a long thin beetroot. The Japanese language was very colourful when it came to describing penises as vegetables. A *kyuri* was a cucumber about 12 centimetres in length, which was the size of the average Japanese penis when erect. An *imo* was a short fat sweet potato – a large unshapely mass – while a *matsutake* was a long, thin mushroom with a large head. A *hine daikon* was a shrivelled radish.

'Maybe you will give me a big tip later,' she joked.

By the fourth round of slammers most of the group were hopping around the dance floor. Yuki noticed that dance partners had miraculously appeared for the men, whose ties were undone and shirt-tails hanging out. The enormous TV screens turned from music videos to erotic films.

Dougie divorced himself from the antics of the traders and spent most of evening talking with Yuki, a tiring exercise. Usually, Japanese used non-verbal signals to communicate, and during meals they concentrated on their food in silence. Americans hated silence.

The mama-san approached their table. She asked Douglas a question and he leaned over for a translation.

'What does she want?'

'Would the gentleman like to take his waitress to the special room in back?' the mama-san had asked.

Yuki smiled and turned immediately to Douglas. 'She asked if you would like sea snail as an appetizer with your next round.'

Douglas looked up at the mama-san with a disgusted look and said 'No' in Japanese.

Yuki then excused herself from the table, found a pay phone and dialled Douglas's home phone number.

'*Moshi, moshi*,' answered a sensuous female voice, obviously Douglas's date for later that evening.

'Do you speak English?'

'No.'

This is my lucky night, thought Yuki.

'I am Mr Douglas's assistant. He won't be home this evening but will call you later next week.'

Yuki hung up and returned to the table.

'Oh, Dougie, I forgot to mention that a woman called this afternoon saying she could not meet you tonight. She said you would know what she meant.'

Douglas shrugged his shoulders. *Who cares?* He was having more fun with Yuki. He grabbed her hand and led her out on the dance floor. To Douglas's surprise, Yuki was a great dancer. The way she smiled at him made him wonder why he hadn't paid more attention to her.

He noticed her staring at him. 'What's so amusing?'

'You've stopped dancing.'

'C'mon, let's go,' said Dougie, taking her hand.

It was two in the morning. Dougie flagged down a taxi and told the driver to take them to his apartment as Yuki had hoped.

As the taxi came to a stop Yuki leaned forward and whispered something to the driver, who smiled and nodded. Douglas climbed out and paid the driver, then helped Yuki whose shapely legs he eyed with lust. He would have to have been a eunuch not to be aroused by her body and couldn't wait to make love to her.

Walking to the door, Yuki held Dougie's hand. Her entire body tingled. As Dougie fumbled for his keys, Yuki turned him around and kissed him, savouring the moment. Dougie dropped his keys to the ground and wrapped his arms around her warm body. Yuki found his tongue and sensuously lolled around his mouth. She could hear his breathing increase and felt his heartbeat against her own throbbing breasts. Then slowly she drew herself away.

'Yuki, what's the matter?'

He tried to draw her close to him, but Yuki gently resisted. 'You don't have to play games with me,' he said. 'I know you've been planning this all evening.'

It was Yuki's turn to be surprised. 'How?'

'I understand more Japanese than you think. The mama-san would be very upset if she knew you compared her hostesses to sea snails,' grinned Dougie.

'Why eat sea snail when you can have lobster?' said Yuki, recovering from her shock.

Dougie took the opportunity to embrace her once more, but Yuki again pulled away. 'I've had a wonderful evening, Dougie.'

'Uh . . . right.'

She pecked him on the cheek and walked back to the taxi, knowing that he was watching her.

'Thanks for waiting,' she said to the driver as he sped away.

The flame was lit.

9

THE PROVIDER

Monday in a wealthy Tokyo hilltop suburb: the 8000 square metre compound of Ken Moyama, head of Japan's underworld.

The underworld has helped finance almost every Japanese Prime Minister since 1955.

Factoid

Ken Moyama was dressed in slippers and a *yukata*, a lightweight cloth kimono. He stepped outside to his koi pond and put his hand in the pellet bowl. The fish gathered expectantly and then thrashed madly as Moyama threw them their food. This thrilled him. Some of the brightly coloured orange and white koi had cost him over 10 million yen each, nearly $100,000.

Most Japanese collected koi for their beauty, grace and elegance. Not Moyama. He was a provider. As the koi fought for their meal, Moyama remembered 1945. Food had been scarce and Japanese men, women and children had fought among themselves as American servicemen unloaded rations. Ten per cent of Japan's population at that time lived in air raid shelters and warehouses. Those who controlled the food reigned almighty – gold, silver and sexual favours were given to the food rationers. The trains out to the countryside were crowded with men prepared to fight for rotten potatoes, black lettuce and a handful of rice for their family.

Moyama had been sixteen at the end of the war. He had fended for himself. His mother had been killed in the Tokyo firebombing and, though friends said his father was a powerful wheeler-dealer, Moyama had never heard from him.

Moyama had vowed never to become an animal himself, as he watched people fight like koi over scraps of food. He wanted more than food, he wanted power. He wanted to be the man whose food was being unloaded from the back of a lorry, not one of the hungry mob. Late one night Moyama and his friends raided sardines, milk, oranges and chocolate from an American depot and sold them on for a vast sum.

Looking down at his koi, he thought how like people they were. As he continued to feed them, he recalled his supreme moment of pleasure standing on the back of the food lorry, looking down on the hungry faces of those who eagerly handed him gold and silver. Moyama had felt like a powerful god. Food was officially rationed; Japanese families were handed out coupons but never enough, and families were force to buy on the black market. Well-heeled families even had to bring their own food for restaurants to cook. Moyama had charged for food as the whim took him: a man who had punched an old woman when forcing his way to the front was charged three times the already inflated rate for a small bag of rice; Moyama gave a woman with a child strapped to her back a free bag. She hid the rice under the baby for fear of being arrested. Though food rationing ended in 1950 the legacy of coupons lived on, and they were still used in restaurants until 1968 when they were abolished.

The Americans shut down Moyama's black market operations in 1946 and threw him into Sugamo prison alongside the Class A war criminals. Fortunately, Moyama had squirrelled away a fortune in gold before he had been caught. His years in prison were surprisingly easy and his fellow inmates called it the 'crossbar hotel'. Guards and prisoners treated him with respect. The American guards taught him English, and gifts of food and clothing were delivered by guards to his cell.

Convinced that his treatment was a reflection of his stature, Moyama was humbled to discover that there was a more powerful man in Sugamo prison. That man was Moyama's own father, Yoshio Moyama, who by 1945 had amassed a $175 million fortune through control of industrial wealth in Japanese-occupied China. Yoshio Moyama had been a middleman for the Japanese military during the war. As an ultranationalist he was given preferential and lucrative government contracts, bartering Chinese minerals for heroin. Operating out of Shanghai, he supplied Japan with everything from iron ore to industrial diamonds, cobalt to platinum. He had even tried to procure uranium for Emperor Hirohito's nuclear bomb experimentation, a secret which had remained closely hidden for fifty years after the war. Much later the imperial family would reward the Moyamas for being able to keep a secret.

Late in 1946 Ken Moyama was introduced to his father in Sugamo. 'Son, you will work for me now,' said the elder Moyama at their first meeting. No tears, no hugs, no greetings, and until his father's death in 1984 the father-and-son team were inseparable.

The Americans released both Moyamas in December 1948 on the condition that they dispose of the Communist 'problem' that had arisen in Japan. The elder Moyama hired yakuza bands to thump socialists into submission, and by 1950 he had become recognized as the 'godfather' of the Japanese underworld. Every yakuza gang paid him homage and money, adding to his already sizeable booty.

With his fortune, the elder Moyama bankrolled the formation of the Liberal Democratic Party in 1955 and was a behind-the-scenes force in the party that ruled post-war Japan until his death in 1984. The son then inherited his father's entire empire.

A rare albino koi jumped part way out of the water and broke Ken Moyama's concentration. He walked back to his office and picked up a heavy black telephone handset. Japan led the world in advanced telecom production, yet many older men like Moyama still used a rotary dial telephone. His only luxury was a second handset for incoming calls. A fax machine lay in the corner of his office, unused and still in its box.

Moyama called his stockbroker. One of his jobs was to orchestrate the sharp rise of Daishin's share price. Brokers called this a 'ramp', and most ramps were organized by speculative groups backed by yakuza money looking for a tax haven. Daishin Construction shares had been the darling of the stockmarket, rising from under 750 to 2650 yen a share in three months. Most attributed the rise to the corporation's success in constructing the Daishin Trade Towers. But the only reason Daishin was on the move was because Ken Moyama wished it to be so. He alone pushed the stock, and he alone doled out the profits to the Prime Minister, Construction and Transport Ministers.

His broker answered the phone. 'Buy me 500,000 Daishin Construction up to 2700,' ordered Moyama.

I'll just tweak the shares. Moyama was a master stock manipulator. The order was worth just under $13.5 million and was the last of five similar purchases he had made over the last few months. His average price on $50 million worth of Daishin stock was just under 1500 yen a share.

'Book the shares to my charity account,' he instructed.

This signalled to the broker that Moyama was purchasing the shares on behalf of a syndicate. The broker placed Moyama's order, but only after picking up a few shares of Daishin for his own family at 2650. The Moyama order pushed the stock straight to 2700.

Moyama picked up the handset again and called another broker. 'Sell 10 million Daishin Construction,' he ordered and hung up. Moyama trusted nobody. The key to a successful manipulation was selling while a stock was hot. He had no intention of hanging on to Daishin any longer. Moyama had been selling more of the share than he had purchased for three straight days.

As Daishin's stock price rose, interest in the share was aroused at street level. 'Improved earnings,' waxed the brokers to their clients. 'Political stock,' they whispered, pretending to be insiders and buying heavily from the reservoir of shares that Moyama had dumped on the market.

His deal complete, Moyama turned his attention to the meeting later that evening at Tada's apartment.

10

THE PROPHET

Central Tokyo, the headquarters of the Happy Science
religious sect

'It was God's revenge because the country used its economy to
serve the devil.'

Libyan leader Muammar Gaddafi
on the 1995 Kobe earthquake

'Have the public relations team come up to my office,' Master
Wa instructed his secretary in a soft voice.

The wealthiest and most powerful religious leader in
Japan was unhappy – his Tokyo Dome prophecies had been ignored
by the media. The press treated him as a charlatan and a 'prophet for
profit', a creeping form of cancer that was silently but begrudgingly
acknowledged. Few articles ever appeared about Happy Science,
despite their growing numbers and power. Some sections of the
non-believing public still treated them as a cult group, associating
them with radical cult kidnappings and gas attacks.

Three well-dressed men appeared within seconds. 'Yes, *sensei*.'

They bowed at a deep seventy-degree angle, soaking up the light
of their master. Wa was nattily dressed in an expensive suit and
shirt with gold cufflinks. Many pictures of him were hung around
the office and, superimposed on the shining gold image of a Buddha
figure, were used in the Happy Science publicity material. Buddha
and the Master were almost indistinguishable.

The three men were breathing heavily and the gold medallions on
their chests bobbed up and down. Each wore a golden moon pendant
around his neck with the initial 'W' emblazoned across it. It was a great
honour to work for Wa, and, though the most prestigious public relations job was widely considered to be that of an aide to the Prime Minister, nothing could coerce these men to swap jobs. The Prime Minister
was a mere mortal. Here they worked for Buddha himself.

'I wish to make a press statement.'

'Yes, *sensei*.' One of them set a micro-cassette recorder going.

'A great earthquake is about to destroy Tokyo. The Japanese people have less than one week to change their evil ways,' he stated with precision and confidence. Most futurists worked on a greater margin of error.

The public relations men gasped. They were devotees who believed every word uttered by their masters, and immediately their thoughts turned to their homes and families. But the three managed to overcome the urge to rush to a telephone and call home.

'Less than one week,' he confirmed.

One out of every twelve people in Japan was now a devotee of Wa, and his rise had been remarkable. With an astounding IQ of 170 he had graduated as Japan's top high school student before sailing through Tokyo University. Then he had joined Toyo Menka, a large trading house, but after a few years began to see and hear a series of revelations which made him abandon his business career. He then wrote his first book, *The Laws of the Sun*, which became a massive best-seller and formed the basis for Happy Science.

The growth rate of his fledgling group was staggering: four hundred followers in 1987, two thousand people in 1988, ten thousand in 1990. In 1991, more than fifty thousand people filled the Tokyo Dome to hear Wa reveal himself as the re-incarnation of Buddha. More importantly, Wa by 1992 had over 5 million paying members of Happy Science, a figure which ballooned to more than 9 million three years later. His books regularly sold over a million copies each, and his 1994 hit movie *Nostradamus* had had people repenting in the aisles. His Happy Science publishing empire sold cassettes, videos and books through magazines and bookshops, but what made his publishing empire so impressive was that many of the books were written by Wa himself.

Wa's public relations team waited patiently for their master to continue with his press release.

'I have had a vision of death and destruction. The Japanese people must prepare themselves for the coming disaster.'

Wa bowed his head slightly and went into a meditative state. The three men took their cue and left.

Once outside the door, they scrambled to their phones to call their wives. 'Stock up on food and drink,' they ordered. The press release was then faxed to fifty news organizations and sent via Nifty e-mail to members. The Happy Science press machine in top gear was an impressive sight.

But though the press release was sensational ('PREPARE FOR
DISASTER: Quake to Hit Tokyo in the Next Week'), few outside
the Happy Science group took any notice of Wa's prophecy. Japan's
media were tired of religious fanatics.

11

THE NET

Monday afternoon at the Japan Meteorological Association
in central Tokyo

The Massachusetts Institute of Technology announced an
annual spoof award based on the Nobel Prize. They called it
the Ignoble Prize and one year awarded it to two organizations:
an Alabama church which claimed it had devised a mathematical
formula for determining the number of souls burning in hell, and
the Japan Meteorological Agency for spending $100 million of
taxpayers' money on analysing the twitching of catfish as a
means of predicting earthquakes.

H ow ugly. Hiroko emerged from the subway station and
stared up at the Japan Meteorological Agency, the nation's
command centre for earthquake information, which inex-
plicably came under the control of the Ministry of Transport. The
JMA monitored all seismic activity in Japan and issued alerts and
information concerning earthquakes and the tidal waves known as
tsunamis. The structure was an ageing grey concrete box with a
bunch of hi-tech antennae and dishes on its roof. Constructed in
1963, it was, like many of Tokyo's office buildings, nothing but a
ferro-concrete box hung with glass. What a contrast to the beautiful
East Garden of the Imperial Palace across the street, with its pine
trees, manicured lawns and finely raked gravel.

There were no security guards, so Hiroko walked straight into the
building. She thought it strange that there was no security, especially
after Tokyo's terrorist threats and subway gas attacks. Hiroko's
apprehension increased as she made her way into the building.
Her imagination was always active and she imagined a terrorist
organization taking over the building, issuing a false earthquake
alarm and exploiting the chaos. Hadn't Shoko Asahara, leader of
the Aum Shinrikyo, the Supreme Truth cult, almost created an
Armageddon?

Hiroko took the elevator straight up to the seventh floor and found Hamada crammed into an office with a dozen other seismologists. He was a thin, bespectacled academic.

'Hamada-san?'

'I am Hamada. Nice to meet you.'

'I am Hiroko Fujita. Nice to meet *you*.'

They exchanged business cards and examined them. Her card only said 'reporter' for the *Asahi Shimbun*, and made no mention of her being on the corruption desk.

'Please come in.'

Hamada was a civil engineer who was an expert on earthquake-proof buildings. Most seismologists specialized in areas with names such as geomagnetic phenomena, seismic array, acoustic emission, strain accumulation, and strainmeter, extensionmeter and tiltmeter technology.

Hamada's work area looked as if an earthquake had just struck. Twelve metal desks were squeezed together, each piled nearly a metre high with papers. Glass-fronted cabinets, filled with more books and papers, lined the walls. Computers and printers were stacked or perched precariously on the desks. Seismographs spewed out paper near the doorway and on to the floor. Overworked plugs with multi-adaptors lay on the floor like miniature octopi. On top of one cabinet a TV had the sumo wrestling tournament tuned in with the volume off.

'Thank you for seeing me at such short notice. I'm writing an article concerning earthquake-proof buldings.'

'*Ah so desu ka*.' Hamada nodded in approval.

'They say you're the world expert. I'm particularly interested in what the law requires a contractor to include in each building.'

'Yes. But before we discuss earthquake proofing I must explain about earthquakes, so with your permission I'll give you a short, painless lesson.'

Hiroko nodded.

'The first thing is that Japan has two types of earthquakes: interplate and intraplate. Interplate means movement between two or more tectonic plates beneath the earth's crust. We sit on the edge of three plates: the Eurasian, Philippine and Pacific. The Philippine plate to the south-east is slowly moving towards us and colliding against the Eurasian plate 100 kilometres south-east of here. When the plates crash together, one of them must give way. The Philippine plate moves or 'subducts' underneath the Eurasian plate, creating an earthquake.

'The best example of an interplate quake is the great Kanto earthquake in 1923. Such interplate quakes are the strongest and most deadly. 'An intraplate quake is like the Kobe quake in January 1995, which was the result of fault patterns within the Eurasian plate shift. Most Japanese earthquakes are of this type. They're not usually over seven on the Richter scale.'

'But look at the devastation of Kobe,' protested Hiroko.

'Exactly. Now you can imagine how bad an interplate quake will be for Toyko.'

Hamada went on to explain that the JMA had seismographs all over Japan to detect earthquakes. He handed Hiroko a booklet which showed the locations of 73 seismographs designed to show long-term ground motion, 87 stations to detect short-term ground motion, 76 stations to detect very slight motion, two ocean bottom seismographs and 31 micro-volume borehole strainmeters.

It was too much to take in all at once, so Hamada explained.

'We call this the Tokai net, where the JMA has nearly three hundred stations. After Kobe we managed to get funding to bring this up to a thousand. Tokyo University has sixty stations and the fire department is planning ten while the utility companies have their own network. We 'surf the net', jumping from shockwave to shockwave in hope of finding interesting data.'

Hamada liked this expression and felt it gave his profession a macho tag. He and his colleagues liked to think of themselves as the geological equivalent of trekkies, but instead of travelling through time and space they travelled through time and earth. Hamada continued.

'Just concentrate on the boreholes. We dig a hole 15 centimetres wide, deep into the earth, which sometimes costs taxpayers upwards of a billion yen. In these holes the slightest movement is picked up. We hope erratic borehole activity will warn us of the Big One.'

'Hope? What do you mean, "hope"? Haven't you ever predicted an earthquake?'

Hamada paused and sucked his teeth. 'Well . . . mmmm, that's a very difficult question.'

'Has *anyone* in the world ever predicted an earthquake?' she asked, giving Hamada a way out.

'Only once.'

'Where?'

'Manchuria in 1975. A town called Haicheng. There hadn't been an earthquake in that province for over a hundred years. Then suddenly there were five hundred tremors in three days.'

'What happened?'

'The Chinese government claims it ordered 3 million peasants out of their homes at two in the afternoon on the final day of the tremors. It was February and freezing cold, but they all obeyed. Five and a half hours later a massive quake wiped out the province. Only three hundred people died instead of tens of thousands.'

'Do the Chinese have more advanced warning systems?'

'No, it was luck. We actually found out later that the Chinese government may have been lying and never ordered the city to evacuate. Panic had set in, and people left their homes in droves. The government just took the credit. Eighteen months later a quake wiped out Tangshan, which is only 160 kilometres east of Beijing. Over three-quarters of a million people died. As usual, officials doctored the figures and journalists were kept out. Thirteen million Chinese have died in earthquakes over three millennia.'

'Any other predictions?'

'No, I'm afraid that was the only one and that's dubious.'

'And what about tsunamis?'

'Let me explain. As you know, a tsunami is a giant tidal wave created by an underwater earthquake. The speed of the wave increases as it spreads from its source and as the ocean depth gets greater.'

'So what happens when it hits land?'

'Something spectacular. The wave slows down and sucks up coastal waters in a vicious undertow. The height of the wave rises dramatically, sometimes as high as 30 metres, carrying away homes and people.'

'Have you ever seen one?'

'Not exactly, but I've seen the results of one. Five years ago we monitored an 8.2 underwater quake off the island of Hokkaido. We tried to warn the residents of a remote fishing village called Aoki, but nobody could get through on the phone. We alerted the army, then flew up to Sapporo and drove up the coast to Aoki. Everything appeared normal. We were sure the tsunami had hit but could find no evidence.'

'So what happened?'

'Just before we got into Aoki, I looked up and saw seaweed hanging from the trees. When we got there, there was nothing left. All the houses had been swept out to sea. The only things we found were a few scraps of wood and a Toyota Land Cruiser sitting on top of a tree on a distant hill.'

'So you predicted the tsunami?'

'Mmmm, well . . . not exactly. We were six minutes too late to warn residents.'

'So prediction of earthquakes and tsunamis is impossible?'

'Our monitoring systems aren't foolproof, but I'm sure that, should we detect an earthquake, there will be sufficient time to warn the public.' That was what the government told the Japanese public.

'Assuming you predict an earthquake, what happens then?'

'We call out the Six Wise Men.'

'Who?'

'Six of the most eminent seismologists in Japan. Their technical name is the Earthquake Assessment Committee. Each man is required to carry a beeper around the clock. They are signalled, called in and picked up by a nearby police car. Lights flashing and sirens wailing, they are brought here to convene an emergency meeting at the command centre.'

Hiroko found it hard to believe that anybody could predict an earthquake, but tried to keep quiet. Hamada was the expert and presumably knew what he was talking about. Her journalistic instincts took over, however.

'Wait a second. You mean to say that you can predict an earthquake and then have time to race six old men here to hold a meeting?'

'Yes, that's right.'

'What will they accomplish?'

'Their job is to examine the warning signs, arrive at a consensus and alert the Director General of the JMA,' replied Hamada.

'Who then does what?'

'The director general calls the Prime Minister.'

'Aaaaaaand?'

'He will convene a cabinet meeting,' said Hamada, unaware of how ridiculous this chain of events seemed.

Hiroko just managed to stop herself rolling her eyes in disbelief. 'What happens then?'

'The cabinet arrives at a consensus as to whether the Prime Minister should alert the public and begin an evacuation. If they are in agreement, the Prime Minister issues a warning statement. Here, take a look at this.' Hamada handed her a glossy purple brochure on the JMA and opened it at the sample warning on page seventeen which would be sent to the media. Hiroko read the paragraph.

Abnormal data was simultaneously obtained at approximately 5 a.m. on 1 September by the strainmeters at Omaezaki, Fujieda, Shizuoka and Fuji, tiltmeters in Okabe and Fujigawa, and water level meters in Hamaoka and Shimizu. Based on this data, and since many earthquakes have occurred in the south of Suruga

Bay, the EAC was held at the JMA at 8.30 a.m., and a discussion ensued to determine whether this data was a large earthquake precursor. As a result, the JMA Director General reported to the Prime Minister that a large earthquake would occur in Suruga Bay and its southern area within the next two or three days, followed by the Prime Minister issuing a Warning Statement. If an earthquake occurs, the seismic activity is estimated to be greater than six in the Shizuoka Prefecture and the Intensified Area, and approximately five in its adjacent areas. A large tsunami is also expected on the Izu Peninsula and Suruga Bay Coasts, with people in these areas being required to prepare for an earthquake/tsunami.

Hiroko looked up. 'By the time everyone finishes reading this an earthquake will have come and gone,' she said.

'If we need to act quickly, the Prime Minister will address residents through our public address system.'

Hiroko had always wondered why Tokyo was dotted with greyish loudspeakers hanging off utility poles and subway ceilings.

'Will anybody pay attention?'

Hamada sighed. 'Probably not. Most Japanese won't believe in the Big One until after it occurs. But that doesn't mean we don't have the responsibility to warn them.'

Very Japanese, thought Hiroko. *And doomed to failure*. The Japanese government liked to think it could control nature. She wondered if the government really believed this, or whether it was just propaganda to stave off panic. Life in Tokyo was already stressful enough.

'We can even issue broadcasts and link into the national media from the EAC command centre,' said Hamada proudly.

'Can I see the conference room?'

'Yes, this way.'

They took the elevator down to the second floor. The dimly lit passageway to the conference room was partially blocked by boxes and spare cabinets, and Hiroko saw that half the bulbs were blown out. She did not hold out much hope for six old men making it through this mess in a quake.

They entered an ante-room with grey metal lockers against one wall. There were also some chairs and sofas.

'Each of the Six Wise Men has a change of clothes here,' said Hamada. 'A three months' supply of food and water is stored in those cupboards.'

Next came the command centre. A large conference table surrounded by twenty chairs stood in the middle. Six seats were equipped with NEC computer screens, and a huge NEC multi-screen faced the room. Hamada saw Hiroko's curiosity.

'The wise men are elderly and can't see well,' he explained, laughing.

'I hope they can see well enough to read their beepers,' said Hiroko.

'We can transmit seismographic data easily for them to evaluate and see. If they have good eyesight, their desk is equipped with a smaller screen. But most of the older men don't like any of this new technology. Our screens are linked to the NEC mainframe and Sun work stations further down the passage. This fax machine has a dedicated line to the Prime Minister's office.'

Hiroko wondered what would happen if the telephone lines went down. Utility poles were the first things to crash in a quake. She could not see any back-up Satlink phones.

'We're also directly linked to you.' Hamada meant Asahi Radio and TV, and pointed to a button. 'We can simultaneously broadcast to all the major TV and radio networks via satellite from this room.'

'Shouldn't your entire facility be underground in case of a quake?'

'No. Why?'

'It's safer to be underground in a quake, isn't it?'

'Yes, it's safer underground – and we often hear of those in tunnels or in subways who don't feel the slightest tremor during a big quake. But we're safe here.'

'What a relief! May I ask you about earthquake-proof buildings *now*?'

'You mean like the Daishin Trade Towers?'

Hiroko was taken aback.

'Like you, I have my sources,' he said, smiling. 'I'm well aware of what you're doing. But don't worry, I applaud your motives and hope you can reveal the corruption in our society so Tokyo can be a safer place.'

Hamada continued. 'When I left university I became an adviser in Kajima Construction's earthquake-proof division. My job was to develop and test new technology. We developed a new shock absorber.'

'I've heard of it,' she said. 'But how does it work?'

'We build an 1100-kilo sandwich of rubber and malleable steel a metre and a half thick and place it under the structure to be built or an existing structure. The rubber and steel absorb the shock and reduce it by half . . . Warn me if I get too technical.'

'No, no. The more detail you give me about construction, the easier I can pinpoint corruption.'

'We scientists measure the acceleration of earthquakes in terms of ground acceleration levels, which we call Gals. A Gal is one centimetre per second per second. When the ground starts moving horizontally, that's when trouble starts. A Richter scale 7 earthquake will normally have a peak acceleration of 600–700 Gals at the points closest to the fault. Not many buildings will withstand horizontal forces of 800 Gals. The Kobe quake had a maximum acceleration of a thousand.'

'And you say the Big One will be many times worse?'

'The maximum acceleration may not be much worse, but the duration may be a minute or two rather than ten seconds. Combined with lower frequency seismic waves, which cause damage to high-rise buildings and storage tanks, the result will be catastrophic. But our device at Kajima reduced the horizontal Gal forces by almost half.'

'That's incredible – a rubber shock absorber can really save a building?'

'Yes. But unfortunately only a dozen buildings in Osaka and a few hundred in the Tokyo area have the shock absorbers. Tokyo itself has over 9 million buildings.' Hamada sounded dejected. 'That's why I left private industry. Clients have short memories of the Great Quake of 1923. The cost is only 5 per cent of the total building, yet hardly anybody is willing to invest in this technology. They're more interested in lining their pockets than saving lives. And besides, nobody believes the Big One will really hit Tokyo.'

'Will it?'

'I'd bet my life on it.'

'When?'

'Only our equipment will tell us,' he smiled.

Hiroko continued her interview. 'What are contractors required to do by law to make buildings safe?'

'Concrete's the biggest worry. As of 1981 all vertically bunched steel bars must be wrapped by hoops spaced every 15 centimetres. Think of a hoop as the piece of seaweed that holds the sushi together. The steel bands hold the steel bars together within the concrete. All buildings put up between 1971 and 1981 have hoops 30 centimetres apart. Buildings erected before 1971 are unsafe.'

'All buildings?'

'Yes. In a 400–500 Gal quake all pre-1971 buildings will collapse,' stated Hamada.

'Even this one?'

'Sort of, except that we reinforced it in the mid-1980s.'

'Do all construction companies comply with building codes?'

'Well, that's difficult to answer,' replied Hamada.

'You mean no?'

'Yes. I mean no. Most construction firms have historical links to the yakuza. This is traditionally where their pool of labour derived. It's a very rough business. This traditional link to organized crime makes the construction industry rife with corruption.' Hamada paused. 'Corruption in the Japanese building industry is a vicious circle, with no beginning and no end. You will find it impossible to expose it.'

'How do I save or skim on the cost of a new building?' Hiroko went on. 'Hypothetically of course.' Her rapport with Hamada was such that she could now ask him direct questions.

'You begin by ordering Korean concrete, you purchase inferior steel made with Chinese manganese, you fail to insert steel hoops every 15 centimetres, you invoice the client for work not carried out but passed by the building inspector, you space the sprinklers wider apart and bill the client for a more advanced fire detection unit than the one he has paid for. That should add 15 to 20 per cent to the net profit of the job.'

'You should start your own construction company,' teased Hiroko.

'I would die of poverty,' he said. 'Most contractors cut corners which will forever remain undiscovered. Until an earthquake.'

'Is skimming the norm?'

Hamada read Hiroko's mind. 'Just take a look at the Daishin Towers. That building will be the first to fall during an earthquake. It's built on reclaimed land, and so many corners have been cut that the building should be round.'

Hiroko laughed.

'But a story like the one you're contemplating will never be printed. Prime Minister Mori, Construction Minister Tada, Transport Minister Fujimura and the yakuza are too strong. I'm sure they already know of your exposé and, though I pray your voice will be heard, I believe it won't be. I left Kajima because it was difficult for honest firms to earn a profit when most contractors were bid-rigging. And then there was the frustration of so few company chairmen believing an earthquake would hit Tokyo. My dream is to use the JMA as a mouthpiece to convince the owners of new buildings to use the shock absorber.'

He fell silent. Hiroko realized the interview was over and rose to leave.

'On our way out let's look into our main control room,' Hamada added. 'Let's see if there have been any quakes over the last day.'

They walked down the dim passage to a brightly lit room full of new computers. She looked through the glass window. Everyone was wearing slippers and blue smocks.

'Here.' He handed Hiroko a pair of guest slippers. 'It's a clean room.'

The dust-free EPOS centre was where live time seismological data was fed into computers for processing. It was a seismologist's dream play room, full of seismometers, strainmeters, extensionmeters, tiltmeters and tide gauges. Twenty workers were hunched over computers, receiving and analysing data. Hiroko and Hamada walked up to the seismograph.

'Now this is very interesting.' He ripped a piece of white paper off the seismograph.

Hiroko just saw a bunch of squiggly lines.

'An earthquake waveform is constantly erratic over a forty-second period. This indicates that there has been seismic activity offshore. Nothing to worry about, though.'

Actually, Hamada was disturbed by the wave form, but hid his anxiety. He showed Hiroko back to the ante-room and she slipped on her shoes again.

'Oh, before you go I have something for you,' said Hamada as he handed her a box. 'Don't open it now. Wait till you get home.'

Hiroko bowed. 'Thank you, but I should be the one making you a gift.'

'No. No. I enjoyed our meeting.'

'So did I. Goodbye.'

'Bye.'

Hiroko could tell that Hamada wanted to get back to his graphs. 'I can find my own way out,' she said, squeezing through boxes piled in the hallway and walking down a flight of stairs.

She was glad to be outside again. The JMA building was the last place in Japan she would like to be in an earthquake . . . except perhaps the Daishin Trade Towers.

THE ANIMAL

Monday evening

'The yakuza are employed widely in Japanese politics – as fundraisers, bodyguards, and campaign workers . . .'

From David Kaplan's
The Yakuza

The phone rang once but there was no answer.
'Where's that whore?' *If she doesn't pick it up by the fourth ring I'll beat her senseless.*
Kaelin answered on the third ring.
'Where've you been? Never mind. Hook up the recording equipment and stay in the upstairs room. I'll be home shortly.'

Japan's Construction Minister was in the back of the Mercedes on his way home. His car was fitted with a TV, bar and fax machine. It was only a ten-minute ride home, but Minister Tada wanted everything ready for his big evening. This included super-sensitive snooping devices.

Tada was fascinated by gizmos and had purchased an electronic bug made by Microtronics of Osaka which was hidden in his pen. Japanese business executives used Microtronic's pens when wrapping up deals with Western businessmen. They'd place the pen on a table and leave the room in the middle of a negotiation. But Tada had a different plan this evening and wanted a recording of the meeting. The bug transmitted to a receiving/recording unit upstairs in his bedroom. An AV camcorder was also positioned in his wall cabinet to record the proceedings on video.

A select group of Japan's power elite were due at Tada's home at 7 p.m. to discuss the Daishin stock ramp. Besides Moyama, the group included Minister of Transport Fujimura and Prime Minister Mori. Unknown to Tada, Kaelin had promised a copy of the videotape to Hiroko for her story at the *Asahi Shimbun*.

Once Tada had hung up on Kaelin he lit another cigarette, but immediately started wheezing badly and stubbed it out. Ash fell all over the black leather seats. Omori, the driver, cringed, knowing what came next.

Tada gargled on his own phlegm and then spat a stream of green mucus into the brass spittoon in the back seat. Omori wanted to retch as he listened, knowing that he would have to wash out the spittoon later. He hated Tada. No, 'hate' was not strong enough. He would have cut out Tada's heart with a blunt instrument. Daishin Construction had given Tada use of the Mercedes with Omori thrown in. Although Tada had the use of a Nissan Century and driver from the Ministry, he had sent them down to Kobe to ferry his wife around. 'That'll keep that nagging wench quiet,' Tada had figured. The Mercedes supplemented his 25 million yen government salary, as did the additional income from bribes, share manipulations and gifts.

To Omori, Tada was subhuman. The man picked his nose and ears and belched and farted whenever he wanted. Most people at least waited for privacy. Luckily the Mercedes had smoked windows and a glass partition between the front and back seats.

Nobody had warned Omori about Tada's revolting behaviour, so on his first day of work, when he opened the back door to help his boss out of the car, he had reeled from the stench. It gave Tada great pleasure to see a grown man throw up, so he had gone to great lengths to leave a mess behind for Omori to clean up. Omori now wore a white surgical mask for protection against – and in defiance of – Tada.

The jet-black car glided to a halt in front of Tada's Kojimachi apartment. As Omori opened the door for Tada and pulled him up from the seat, he observed the deep, now permanent indentation in the upholstery from his boss's overweight bulk.

Tada lurched out of the back. 'Driver, pick me up tomorrow morning at the usual time,' he grunted. Omori had driven Tada around for two years but 'driver' was the only name he had ever used to address him.

Omori bowed and closed Tada's door without looking into the spittoon. He had learned to hold his breath discreetly until he could close the door.

As Tada waddled laboriously to his apartment the normally reserved Omori spat on the ground where the Construction Minister had just stood. Then he jumped quickly back into the driver's seat and called Kaelin. His spirits lifted as he waited for her voice.

'Hello, Kay-chan.'

'Hello, my darling,' she cooed.

'The animal's on his way up,' he warned her.

'Is he in a bad mood?'

Omori shook his head in anger. 'He's always in a bad mood, but I don't think he'll hit you tonight.'

'I love you,' said Kaelin.

'I love you too, Kay-chan. Don't worry, some day we'll be together. We'd better hang up now.'

Tada's elevator was ready to open at his floor.

'No, wait,' urged Kaelin. 'I just want to feel you're with me for a moment longer,' she pleaded.

Tada had stepped off the elevator and was moving towards his apartment door.

'No, it's too dangerous. I love you,' said Omori, hanging up to protect Kaelin.

Kaelin hung up the upstairs phone just before Tada came through the door.

Tada was merciless in his perverted lust for Kaelin. Any self-respecting Japanese would have made her his wife number two, but not Tada. His courtship was the threat of having Kaelin fired from Daishin Construction unless she became his mistress. Kaelin needed her job in order to survive. There had never been any question of going to the police about Tada's rape. The embarrassment would have been suicidal, and as the woman all the stigma would have fallen on her, not him. Later, Tada had forced her to pose naked for photographs or be beaten up yet again. Afterwards he had threatened to sell the pictures to Japan's porn underground if she refused to perform the acts he required of her. The greatest hold that he had on Kaelin was her own personality. As the daughter of an alcoholic, Kaelin was attracted to and easily manipulated by abusive males. When Tada got drunk he beat her and blamed Kaelin for not serving properly and not attending to his wishes. Soon Kaelin believed that she was at fault and 'deserved' to be hit. Deep down she knew Tada would kill her if she tried to leave.

Tada took off his shoes and yelled for Kaelin, who was upstairs setting up the tape equipment.

'Oi, woman, is everything all set?'

Kaelin appeared, limping slowly, her leg still bruised from his last beating. 'Yes, the audio tape and video recorders are prepared,' she said, head bent.

'Okay, go into the bedroom. Don't make a noise. When you hear the doorbell, start both tapes. Before you go, make me a drink.'

He walked away towards the bathroom.

Tada's apartment exhibited the vulgarity common among those who had purchased class. The brown velvet chairs and sofas were adorned with gold tassels. A glass-topped table stood on a wall-to-wall beige shag carpet. Fake third-rate Picasso and Monet sketches hung on one wall.

Five minutes later the doorbell rang. Kaelin started the tape and video recorders while Tada's maid opened the door.

'Please come in,' Tada's voice boomed from inside.

All his guests had arrived on time and together, and were now jammed in the entryway. A black and white scroll hung in the *tocunoma*, or alcove of honour, but there were no flowers as one would have expected in a Japanese home. Everyone began taking off their shoes as Tada came out to greet his guests: Ken Moyama, godfather of Japan and head of the yakuza; Kobayashi, the chairman of Daishin Construction; Fujimura, the Minister of Transport; and Prime Minister Mori. The mood was festive.

Tada smiled as he bowed. His remaining teeth were black from lack of brushing. Tada adhered to the Eastern custom of washing his mouth out with tea each evening. Chewing on the leaves, he believed, would prevent his teeth from decaying. His acquaintances sat as far away from him as possible and behind his back called him 'Dragon Breath.'

The men took off their shoes and slipped into the black cushioned Pierre Cardin slippers which faced them. Nobody made a move until Tada invited them inside to indicate who was to have the seat of honour.

'Did you see Daishin's share price today?' chirped Kobayashi proudly as he put on his slippers. 'Twenty seven hundred, a new record.'

A company's absolute share price on the Tokyo Stock Exchange was considered a status symbol. If Daishin Construction were trading at 2700 a share while premier construction firms like Shimizu or Kumagai languished below 1500, then Daishin was considered a superior company.

Moyama observed Kobayashi's mood. *Funny*, the yakuza leader thought, *this man actually believes there's a connection between share price and reality. What a fool*.

'Yes, congratulations, Kobayashi *kaicho*. Daishin will now have a very successful fund-raising,' said Tada to the chairman. '*Dozo*.' This way.

Tada waved his guests inside, motioning for Prime Minister Mori to sit with back to the wall, facing the front door. This was the seat of honour. The other men sat down randomly. Tada lit a cigarette and the ministers did likewise. Green jade ashtrays were by their side.

The maid brought a tray containing a bottle of 1928 Macallan Glenlivet and three glasses.

Prime Minister Mori let out a gasp. 'My favourite.'

Tada knew that the Prime Minister was a connoisseur of fine malt whisky, and at the last Christie's auction in Glasgow he had paid £2000 each for two bottles of the world's finest malt. One bottle was for this evening and another as a gift for the Prime Minister. Tada later intended to use the empty first bottle for 'second-rate guests', refilling it over and over with cheaper whisky.

Tada personally poured the whisky into the three glasses, savouring the moment. He handed the first one to the Prime Minister, who sniffed his glass lovingly.

The maid knew what Moyama wanted and discreetly brought him a cup of hot green tea. She then placed a double vodka on the rocks next to Tada.

The men raised their glasses. '*Kampai!*'

Tonight was the final meeting to discuss the Daishin Construction fund-raising through Marayama Securities.

'Thank you for coming, gentlemen,' said Construction Minister Tada as the group prepared to get down to business. 'Shall we ask Moyama-san to brief us?'

Moyama was the most powerful man in the room – and indeed the whole country. The pretence that Tada was leading the discussion was only for the sake of propriety.

'Our operation is almost complete,' said Moyama. 'My records show a substantial profit in the charity account.'

'How much?' asked Fujimura, trying to hide his greed. The Transport Minister had some personal debts to settle, and the Daishin scam would bail him out.

'Nearly 5 billion yen,' Moyama told a gleeful audience. That was $50 million. They all toasted again.

'I'll start taking profits tomorrow when the Marayama Securities brokers begin pushing Daishin to their individual clients. Mori-san, you, myself and Tada have a billion profit each. Fujimura-san, we have allocated half a billion for you, and half for you, Kobayashi-san. The extra billion will be used for special payments.'

Fujimura and Kobayashi were considered lesser mortals in the hierarchy of politics and pay-offs.

Tada poured another round of Glenlivet. The maid brought

Moyama more tea and Tada another double vodka. Meanwhile Kaelin remained upstairs, listening and keeping watch over the tapes.

Though Moyama had already been secretly selling shares already, he wondered who had been buying the syndicates shares so aggressively. Even Marayama's client base was not strong enough to push Daishin's stock so strongly. *I bet it's that dog Tada*, Moyama thought. *I don't trust that man. He's a pig.* Moyama's distrust ran so deep that he was carrying a Hitachi counter-surveillance device. Although Moyama was old-fashioned, he had asked Hitachi engineers to design this scrambler after discovering that somebody had wire-tapped his home, presumably to make money off his insider tips. When Moyama spoke, the device scrambled the frequency of his voice. Any listening device only picked up a garbled noise.

'Mori-*sensei*, please tell us your plans,' asked the yakuza leader.

The Prime Minister spent five minutes discussing the Liberal Democratic Party members who had been bribed to ensure he remained in office. The Prime Minister would get to keep his entire billion yen profit. After it was channelled into an aide's fictitious account, the money would be distributed widely throughout the party.

Next it was Tada's turn and, knowing that the recorders were running, he was noticeably brief.

'My side's all taken care of.'

His reticence set off warning signals in the mind of the yakuza boss, who knew that Tada liked to hear himself speak, belch, fart and spit. Moyama was glad he had brought his scrambler, and intended to make Tada squirm.

'Have all the building inspectors been paid, Tada-san?'

'That is Kobayashi-*kaicho*'s responsibility.'

He deflected the question, knowing that a percentage of the bribes to his building inspectors had already found their way to his own pocket. The Daishin chairman was in an effusive mood and began speaking.

'Yes, work went well on the Towers. We have paid all the inspectors, as you know, and finished the building in time for the party.'

Kobayashi was a nuts-and-bolts man, and launched into details of his operational savings generated by kickbacks. In the construction industry, kickback savings were part of every normal budget.

'Our profit on the chemical coagulants was huge since we never hardened the reclaimed land. The Fuji tanker trucks arrived empty and they invoiced us for the chemicals, of which 70 per cent will be reimbursed to our syndicate. I'm slightly worried, though, because an intruder was seen taking pictures of our empty tankers.'

'What about profits on the construction materials?'

'We made good money. Skipping the steel bands saved us a hundred million; we used Korean concrete to save another 1.2 billion; Chinese manganese saved us 3.6 billion on girders. As agreed with the Tokyo municipal government, they will subsidize the cost of the earthquake-proofing in return for our constructing the Towers in their district. We have billed them for the rubber shock absorbers. Naturally they don't exist.'

'Thank you, Tada-san, for arranging everything so well,' said Kobayashi.

Tada stiffened.

Moyama was feeling mischievous and stood up. 'Yes, I'd like to drink a toast to Tada-san, who helped arrange this entire Daishin operation.'

Everybody rose, shouting, '*Kampai! Kampai!*'

Tada now wished he had not asked Kaelin to tape the meeting. But then he could always erase part of the tape. 'You're welcome.' Tada bowed.

But Tada had more important problems to worry about. He had secretly borrowed 2 billion yen from Sumitomo Bank to purchase 800,000 Daishin shares outside the group's scam. He knew it was late in the secret operation, but even a small 10 per cent profit amounted to a lot of money. Moyama had promised to keep him informed of all market operations. Tada's average price was 2500 yen a share before costs, and he figured that Moyama would not begin unloading for another week. He wanted to start selling tomorrow before the yakuza leader dumped the syndicate shares. *Too bad I can't get him drunk so he wakes up late*, thought Tada. The market opened at nine. *Who cares?* He was beginning to feel the alcohol. *Once the Marayama brokers start buying, we can all get out.*

The meeting broke up. Everyone left in high spirits, knowing they were going to make a fortune tomorrow. As his guests were putting on their shoes at the door, Tada presented everyone with wrapped gifts: lacquer ware for everyone except the Prime Minister, who received the second bottle of 1928 Macallan Glenlivet.

Once they had gone, Tada staggered upstairs. Drunk and in a frisky mood, he felt like smacking Kaelin around for fun. He needed to feel powerful again after spending an evening with

Moyama. Kaelin was already cowering in the corner, knowing what was to come. Tada leered at her and slammed the bedroom door.

Nobody heard her screams.

13

THE TWINS

The basement of the Palace Hotel, the morning of the quake

'We are confident we can predict an earthquake in time to warn the public.'

The Japan Meteorological Agency

'Disposable Fuji cameras?'
    'Five more.'
    'Cigarette lighters?'
'Let's order another box.'
'Condoms?'
'We need three more boxes of the Rough Rider and one of the Silk Road.'

Miss Noichi moved to the glass-fronted refrigerator. 'Pocari Sweat and Orange Hi-C?'

'We're out of both.'

It was the middle of summer and the tourists had made a run on the Noichi twins' cold drinks. Fifty-year-old spinsters, they ran a brisk business in the basement of the Palace Hotel selling items such as cigarettes, drinks and newspapers. Being unmarried meant that the sisters were considered strange and slightly unnatural by their neighbours. 'Maybe they're gay,' they whispered, and avoided the pair. The twins had few friends and relied on one another for companionship. Both had had fiancés when they were in their early twenties, but the prospective husbands had abandoned the girls. The rumour was that investigations conducted by the grooms' parents revealed that a Noichi uncle had once been treated for mental illness, and the weddings were called off.

During the day they ran the shop and at night they played Go. Their only other comfort in life was Mushka, their Siamese cat. Mushka came into work each day and curled up under the counter to sleep, coming out only to rub herself against the legs of the twins as they worked. The sisters kept Mushka's pink plastic water and food dishes under the counter.

Their shop was five times the size of a coffin. The Palace Hotel was situated on the inner moat of the Imperial Palace and teemed with well-heeled holidaymakers. Though foreign tourism was non-existent due to the high cost of the yen, local tourism was booming. Children were off for summer vacation, while fathers had taken their annual two weeks' holiday.

The sisters were able to charge an extra 50 yen on the Fuji disposable cameras and 10 yen on soft drinks, since there were no other shopping facilities within a ten-minute walk. But families staying in the Palace Hotel could afford the premium – less affluent tourists stayed in outlying second-rate hotels and were bussed in to wander reverently around the Imperial Gardens. Palace Hotel clients could walk.

'BIC disposable razors?'

'We haven't sold one.'

'Sanyo electric razors?'

'Order two.'

The twins did not question the logic of their consumers. When a man left his electric razor at home he simply bought a new one rather than a cheap plastic disposable. 'One for home and one for work,' reasoned the buyer.

'Toothpaste?'

There was no response from her sister.

'Kiko, what's wrong?'

Her sister stood frozen to the spot.

'Kiko, please speak to me. It's your rheumatism again, isn't it?'

Tokyo's hot, humid summers inflamed her sister's knees. She nodded and sat down on a small wooden stool next to the refrigerator to relieve her joints. She rubbed her right knee and continued downward, massaging her calf and ankles. Kiko took off her household slipper and worked her right foot. But something else was bothering Kiko, and Keiko knew it. Twins did not spend fifty years together without knowing each others' innermost thoughts.

'No, not an earthquake – please tell me it's not an earthquake,' said Keiko. She had never seen her sister in so much pain.

Kiko winced, holding her right knee and then her left. Ever since the age of ten she had been able to predict earthquakes. Both her knees burned in excruciating pain just before a tremor was going to hit. A few racy magazines had run stories on Kiko's premonitions and scientists had even run tests on her inflamed joints. They had kept Kiko under observation, hoping for an earthquake during her stay, but nothing happened. Though not mocking, the scientific community was sceptical.

Kiko looked up at her sister as if to say goodbye, and finally spoke. 'Under the counter, Keiko. I'll join you in a moment.'

Keiko jumped under the small check-out counter and cuddled up to Mushka just as the rumbling started, but Kiko, her knees throbbing, was unable to stand up. Then their entire world turned black.

14

THE TRAIN

Tuesday morning in Hiroko Fujita's home in Mitaka, a
western suburb of Tokyo

'If you are driving when an earthquake strikes, pull your car
into a parking space or on to the side of the road. Turn off
your car, leave the keys in the ignition and proceed on foot.'
Tokyo Metropolitan Police pamphlet

'Due to severe congestion of city streets there is little or no
street parking available in Tokyo's five main wards. In many
streets there is barely room for a single car to pass – we therefore
request all commuters to take trains and subways.'
Japanese government handout

All night $10 billion worth of seismographical equipment
whirred and hummed silently at JMA headquarters. All was
quiet on the Tokai fault.
It was 7.15 on Tuesday morning.

'Alex, honey, time to wake up.' Hiroko kissed her eight-year-old son
on the cheek, but he didn't stir. 'Let's go, Alex. Time for school!'
This time her voice was louder as she tried to sound stern.
Alex stirred slightly.
'Come on, get dressed,' she urged, tossing him his blue school
uniform.
'Mom, I hate wearing these clothes. They don't wear uniforms in
the States,' he moaned, his head still partly under the pillow.
'This is Tokyo, not New York. Here we follow rules. No
individualism, obey orders and be a sheep,' she said half jokingly.
Alex reluctantly slipped out of his sweat pants and into his
blue school uniform. 'I feel like a zipperhead in this stupid
uniform.'
'Uniforms cannot be stupid – only humans can be stupid. The

uniform teaches you to respect yourself and others – it is also a sign of authority.'

Alex was cheering up. 'I'll make your coffee, Mom.'

He tipped the ground Brazilian mocha into the Braun coffee-maker. Out came the Mets coffee mugs. Hiroko poured Alex some hot chocolate. The morning *Yomiuri* newspaper was lying on the breakfast table. A front page picture of fish swimming near the surface of the ocean accompanied the headline: 'Record Hauls off the Coast: Fisherman Report Biggest Catch in Twenty Years'. One fisherman reported fish jumping high into his boat and said there were so many that it looked as if the sea were boiling.

'Mom, when am I going to get another father?' Alex's question caught Hiroko off guard.

'That's what I keep asking her,' replied another voice in the room.

It was Michiko, Hiroko's mother, who had come home from work at about 4.15 that morning and had woken to see her grandson off to school. She smiled, showing a set of brown, stained teeth, and then began coughing uncontrollably. This coughing was now continuous and so severe that earlier that year Michiko had broken two ribs. Privately the doctor had told Hiroko that he did not expect her mother to live more than two years if she kept on smoking.

'*Ohayo*,' Michiko managed to splutter in greeting to her family.

'*Ohayo*.'

'*Ohayo*, Grandma.'

'So. When am I getting a new father, Mom?'

'Yes, Hiroko, when are you planning to remarry?' asked Michiko mischievously in between coughing fits.

'When I find a man I like, and good men are hard to find in Japan.'

Hiroko was in no hurry to marry again, and found Japanese men chauvinistic. Most adopted the Confucian adage that a woman should obey her father in youth, her husband in matrimony and her son in old age. Hiroko was now thirty and people found it strange that she was not married. Some day, however, she needed to find Alex a father . . .

Hiroko looked at her watch. 'Time to get ready for school.' She lifted Alex up and gave him a big hug.

'I hate school,' he said, rolling his lower lip inside out.

'Alex!' yelled his grandmother. 'Your face is going to freeze if you do that. It took me eighteen years to get your mother to stop that annoying habit.'

Hiroko and Alex both rolled their lower lips inside out and began laughing.

'Bet you can't do that, Grandma.'

'Okay, watch this,' she said, touching her tongue with her nose. Both Hiroko and Alex tried and failed.

'Let's go, Alex,' said Hiroko, smiling broadly.

She threw her handbag, Satlink phone and wallet into an oversized carrying bag. Thinking she might go to the gym after deadline, she tossed in a water bottle and sneakers. As she dug through her bag, Hiroko found the gift that Hamada had given her the day before. Curious, she opened the box and took out a white plastic machine the size of her satellite phone.

'Shaking Boy,' read the label.

'Hey, what's that, Mom?' asked Alex, taking it from her hand. He shook it.

'QUICK, DIVE UNDER THE TABLE,' shouted a voice. Alex hit the floor as his mother explained.

'It's an earthquake alarm. We'll leave it here just in case. Now let's get ready.'

'I want to go to work with you.'

She ignored his comment.

'Then can I go to work with Grandma?'

Both women laughed.

'Do you know where Grandma works?' asked Hiroko, whose turn it was to be mischievous.

'Sure. She has a coffee shop in Ginza.'

Both women laughed again.

'Soon you'll be old enough to visit me at work. Now listen to your mother and get ready for school. Don't you have an exam next week?' said his grandmother.

'Don't remind me.'

'Next weekend I'm taking you to the Shrine of Wisdom to make sure you pass,' said Michiko.

'Mother!' protested Hiroko. 'This is the late twentieth century. A bunch of priests banging on drums, ringing bells and singing chants won't help him if he hasn't studied.'

'I know the priest,' said her mother, 'and he'll do the school examination ceremony for only 4000 yen. Alex can pat the holy rock and drink the holy water. Now that's a bargain. What have we got to lose?'

'I don't want my son believing in all this nonsense.'

'Nonsense? Don't be so irreverent. Besides, it's a good insurance policy.'

'Enough of all this. Off to school, Alex. Now come and give me a big hug,' Hiroko said, kissing her son. 'See you tonight.'

'Bye, Mom. Bye, Gran.'

After Alex had left, Michiko pressed her daughter about remarrying. 'So just when are you going to find another husband?'

'Mom, let's not discuss this now. I want to talk about *you*. I saw your doctor yesterday.'

'What? Behind my back?' This revelation brought on a new coughing fit.

'About your health. We're both concerned.'

Michiko was coughing so hard she could not respond.

'Mom, this is serious. He said you'd die if you didn't stop smoking. Please listen to me. You remember our agreement.'

Just at that moment Hiroko smelled stale smoke on her mother's nightgown, though she could not detect any smoke in the house.

'Where have you been smoking, Mom?'

'Our agreement is that I don't smoke in the house. You shouted at me on Saturday and I swear that I haven't smoked inside since then.'

'I'm sorry, Mom. I just don't want to see you die. If I've been a bit anxious it's because I'm also under pressure at work. My editor's still sitting on my Daishin story and claims I need more evidence. I thought this was my big break.'

'Maybe I could be of help . . .'

'Thanks anyway, Mom. Now please think about what I've said. I've got to catch the train.'

Hiroko stepped out of her apartment, and as she closed the metal door looked down at the concrete floor. Five Mild Seven butts were stamped out in the concrete. A pang of guilt swept over Hiroko for forbidding Michiko to smoke in the house. Her own mother was reduced to sneaking a smoke in the dark, early morning hours. *She's really trying to make an effort*, thought Hiroko.

She quickly opened the door again, stuck her head inside and looked at her mother standing in the kitchen. Michiko quickly hid her cigarette under her palm, though a wisp of smoke wafted towards the ceiling which Hiroko ignored.

'I love you, Mother.'

'Ehhh?'

'I said I love you. I'll see you tomorrow.' Hiroko closed the door again and began to walk to the station.

With her daughter gone, Michiko silently looked at her cigarette and put it out. She had to stop smoking somehow, but it was just too difficult. Ten minutes later she wandered out on to the concrete staircase and lit up another Mild Seven.

Hiroko usually managed to find a seat in the front car, which stopped nearest the exit at her first destination, Akihabara station. That meant fewer crowds to contend with and, more importantly, fewer groping salarymen. Her 'A Team' associate and good friend Jiroo Matsuoka was usually on hand to fend them off anyway. In Akihabara she switched to the Hibya line, which took her to Tsukiji station near the *Asahi* headquarters. The whole journey took about forty minutes.

The train stopped at Shinjuku station. White lines on the platform marked precisely where the train stopped and the doors would open. Long lines of patient commuters had formed between the white lines. Recently the *Asahi* had run a story on how Tokyo trains were filled to 200 per cent capacity.

Through the subway door Hiroko could see Jiroo's smiling face. Hiroko appreciated his efforts to be the first in line every morning just to sit next to her.

'*Ohayo gozaimasu.*' He sat down in the seat next to her.

'*Ohayo.*'

The train quickly filled up. Standing commuters gripped the beige plastic handstraps or the shiny metal bars above. As the train lurched forward, those standing pressed against the seated pair.

Hiroko and Jiroo seldom talked during their daily ride. The press of people made private conversation impossible. For Jiroo, just to be next to Hiroko was exciting. The ride to work was a time of fantasy for him.

Yet more commuters boarded. The train left the station and had been running about a minute when Hiroko saw they were travelling high above the traffic, approaching a green metal bridge. The train slowed to a crawl, then stopped. The train had just been shut down from railway headquarters.

Japan Railways took a pragmatic view of earthquakes and figured that prediction was impossible. They relied instead on the first set of small shock waves to trigger a trip switch, which shut down JR trains before the violent tremors hit thirty seconds later.

Initially the passengers felt nothing. But looking out over Tokyo, Hiroko noticed that the buildings were swaying dangerously. It was as if a giant unknown force had pulled a rug out from under the city. The train keeled to its side as the bridge buckled. Many of the passengers screamed. One woman fell to the floor; another was flung violently through a window to her death 15 metres below. One elderly man died of a heart attack. But the worst was yet to come.

Pandemonium reigned. People began clawing at each other to try and open the doors, forcing the train to lurch precariously. The conductor, shaken, had the microphone in his hand.

'Please don't panic,' he shouted. 'Everyone stay where you are. Don't move. We will receive instructions.'

Nobody moved. He repeated his instruction several times before normality returned. Some people had died, while others were injured. Fear gripped them all, yet strangely nobody moved – simply because of the conductor's orders.

The train was tipped at a precarious angle on its right side, where most of the passengers had fallen. Asphyxiation was the most immediate problem, several people having been crushed by the weight of fellow passengers. One pretty teenager had her head wedged between the window and the man behind her. She was making involuntary faces on the window in an effort to breathe. She could not even scream, and soon suffocated to death.

Hiroko and Jiroo, along with a few other passengers, had held on to the metal bars to prevent sliding downwards.

The train lurched again to the right from the weight of the passengers. Another mass scream erupted.

'Please don't panic,' the conductor shouted again. 'Help is on its way.'

This momentarily calmed the train. But the conductor was a fool – no help was coming and it was clear that the train was about to topple off the tracks at any moment. He seemed more concerned with order than survival.

'Quick, let's open the left-hand doors,' Hiroko shouted to Jiroo. Her companion hesitated. Even he was waiting like a schoolboy for official instructions.

'Now!'

Jiroo responded automatically to her order and jammed his hand into the conductor's booth, trying to switch open the doors. He stretched as far as he could, but couldn't reach the lever.

'I can't.'

'Try harder,' Hiroko urged him.

Jiroo's face was pressed against the shiny metal, his hand so close to the lever but still not touching.

'It's too far,' he breathed.

Suddenly the train lurched once more.

'Again!' shouted Hiroko.

This time Jiroo stretched, nearly pulling his arm out of its socket, and managed to flip the switch.

There was a hiss. The doors opened but only 20 centimetres or so. Hiroko pushed her body into the opening and wedged herself between the rubber doors, then pushed with all her strength.

'Help me open this. Quickly – we must get out.'

Jiroo prised the doors apart. Another man came to his aid and the two of them continued to push. The remaining passengers were either crying or in shock. They looked like scared rabbits.

'Do not leave the train!' ordered the conductor. 'It's against regulations.'

'To hell with the regulations – do you want to die?' yelled Hiroko, surprised by her own aggressiveness. Her stint in New York had given her an edge unknown to most Japanese.

The three of them managed to push the doors open enough to squeeze through. Hiroko threw her bag to the ground 15 metres below, then crawled out on to a short metal ladder at the bottom of the train. After that she jumped on to the bridge. The two men followed.

'Come on. *Jump!*' she shrieked to the passengers. 'You're going to die just sitting there.'

'No!' shouted the conductor. 'Help is coming.'

Nobody moved.

The three began to make their way down the side of the bridge, and as they jumped to the ground a massive aftershock hit. They could hear the passengers scream again, and then watched helplessly as the train plunged on to the road. The leading carriage was tossed far from the bridge, its 30-tonne frame hurtled effortlessly into the sky. Nobody could have survived the appalling impact. This scene was being replayed throughout Tokyo. Those who followed instructions died; those who thought for themselves lived. Disasters were intended as lessons in the survival of the fittest. The first rule of survival in Tokyo after the quake was that there were no rules.

Hiroko looked around her in shock at the smoke, fire, dust, noise and confusion. An arm was sticking out from underneath the wreckage and she rushed over.

'Hold on, I'll help you.'

Hiroko grabbed the twitching hand and pulled, only to find the arm no longer connected to its body. She fell to her knees.

Fires were raging everywhere. She heard a person call out from inside the train. Someone must have survived after all, and she called Jiroo for help. They scrabbled their way into the mangled carriage, but could only see a mass of twisted bodies among the tortured metal and shattered glass.

'Where are you?'

'In here,' responded the muffled voice.

The sound came from deep within the pile of dead passengers. Jiroo and Hiroko tried to untangle the bodies but found it was like trying to untangle dozens of sewing knots – the difference being that humans were very heavy when dead.

'There's no way in,' said Jiroo, giving up in despair.

It was true. Hiroko looked around for help, but there was none. They were on their own.

'Please hurry . . . I have very little air left . . . I'm having trouble breathing,' faltered the voice.

'We'll have you out soon.'

For the next few minutes Hiroko sat on a mound of bodies, talking to the victim in a reassuring tone. But gradually the voice grew weaker and weaker until there was no reply at all. Hiroko's sense of failure overwhelmed her and she began to sob.

Then she remembered Alex and her mother. *Oh my God.* Hiroko spotted her bag, ran over to it and grabbed her Satphone. She dialled her home number. No signal. She then dialled Alex's school. No ring. Panic began to grip her. Michiko was a street fighter and survivor, and if anybody lived through an earthquake it would be her mother. But her son . . .

She tried her work number. Again, no ring. Then she rang through to the editorial desk at the *Asahi* office in Osaka.

Someone answered.

'Help, help!' Hiroko pleaded into the phone. 'I have to find my son!'

'Who's this?' demanded the man.

'Fujita. Hiroko Fujita. You have to find Alex. I can't get through.'

'Hiroko, calm down. This is John. John Nakamura.' He was the Osaka metropolitan editor.

'Nakamura-san, you must find Alex.'

'Why, what's wrong?' Osaka had only felt a mild tremor.

'What's happened? A quake. Tokyo's been destroyed.'

'What?' shouted Nakamura. He was stunned. So the Big One had finally hit Tokyo. 'Tell me what happened, Hiroko. Tell me everything.'

Nakamura snapped his fingers and a secretary ran over. He put his hand over the mouthpiece.

'Get Asahi Broadcasting and Asahi Radio on to me now, then call CNN International in Atlanta. Head of syndication. Now!'

'Nakamura-san, please help me find Alex,' Hiroko said again in desperation. 'Here's his school number,' she said, reading out the numbers. She began sobbing uncontrollably again.

'Hiroko, stay calm. I'll have one of our team find Alex. Don't worry about him any more.'

Nakamura knew that the Tokyo quake was the story of a lifetime, and Hiroko was his lifeline to an exclusive story where opportunity was measured in minutes, even seconds. He motioned for his assistant to dial Asahi's Tokyo office, but there was no answer. Almost all of the capital's 12 million phone lines had been severed. There was no way he was letting Hiroko off the line.

'Don't hang up. This way I can keep you updated on our search for Alex,' he lied.

'Oh, thank you, Nakamura-san.'

'We'll find him, but in the meantime you must talk me through the quake. Tell us what happened. No one here knows.' Nakamura picked up a dictaphone and started recording.

'Anything as long as you find Alex.'

'Get me a TV and radio crew over here now,' the Asahi editor shouted to his staff. A minute later they were assembled. The production manager of TV Ten yielded to Nakamura's seniority and found himself taking orders from the newsman.

'Begin broadcasting live,' Nakamura ordered. 'Tokyo's been destroyed and we're the first with an eye-witness account.'

Five minutes later a deal was struck. CNN purchased the exclusive English language rights to Asahi's broadcasts by Hiroko – their attempts to contact their Tokyo bureau had proved fruitless since the headquarters had collapsed. Asahi was to be paid one million dollars in cash for the rights, five times the going rate. Asahi guaranteed CNN an English-language broadcast for as long as Hiroko's Satlink batteries lasted. CNN figured that they could have a crew in Tokyo by then. In the meantime all other world TV and radio stations had to deal with CNN to buy Hiroko's rights. A day later Nakamura also negotiated for Hiroko's commentary to be printed daily in *USA Today*, a deal which would later have a big impact on Hiroko's life.

'Hiroko, please speak in English. How long will your battery last?'

'Sixteen hours.'

A dazed Hiroko obeyed his request to speak English. 'You keep phoning Alex's school. I'm heading west to Shinjuku to find my son.'

And so Hiroko's harrowing tale began. Mesmerized, the world listened.

15

THE ARMY

First Army Command Headquarters

'Because no one asked me to.'
> The Defence Minister on why he didn't deploy the
> military as soon as he heard about the Kobe earthquake

General Mishima was the ageing, crew-cut, barrel-chested leader of Japan's 150,000-man army. The nation's leaders didn't call it an 'army', of course; they called it the Ground Self-Defence Force, on the pretence that Japan would never again resort to the militarism of World War II. General Mishima's daily responsibility was command of Japan's Eastern Army based in Nerima, a grey suburb outside Tokyo. His other task was that of commander-in-chief of Tokyo's rescue operations should a crisis arise. But few ever did – an occasional plane crash, evacuation of civilians from the banks of a steaming volcano or the defusion of a World War II bomb found in some school yard. He didn't even get to deal with terrorists. The riot police got all the fun.

The general took out his handkerchief, dusted the three gold stars on both shoulders and looked out of the window. His troops were doing their callisthenic exercises in the courtyard. There wasn't much else for him to do. After forty years of service he was about to retire from a long and undistinguished career. No wars and no invasions. It wasn't exactly the kind of career he had intended. Though he was also head of Japan's five regional armies, he had never even fired a shot. His ancestors would be laughing over that one. Descended from samurai, Mishima counted among his most famous relatives his great-uncle Tojo whose illustrious wartime career ended swinging from an American gallows. Mishima planned a healthier ending to his own career.

Mishima sighed and began to daydream about his retirement. Soon he nodded off to sleep.

A moment later he was jolted awake. Bouncing in his chair, through the window the general caught a glimpse of the chaos outside. His men were flying through the air. One army truck jumped up and down like a plaything thrown by some wanton child

General Mishima knew that this was the Big One. It was funny the things that ran through a man's mind at a time of danger. The only thing he could think about was making sure no blame stuck to him when the rescue operations went wrong. He had successfully passed all blame for the failed Kobe rescue operations on to the local army boys. He might not be so lucky this time.

The shaking subsided. Mishima was now lying on the floor with his back covered in window glass. Through the doorway and further down the passage he could see that a ceiling had caved in. The furniture in his own office had toppled over. The building seemed to be at an odd angle, so he popped his head up and looked out into the courtyard. Men in green army uniforms were rushing around in all directions, while some lay on the ground motionless. The nearest barracks was destroyed. His men were already digging in the rubble with their standard-issue shovels.

Shit, thought Mishima. The army didn't even have its own construction equipment. *We'll have to borrow from the Ministry of Construction and private construction companies.* What a mess.

His aide came running into the room, blood running down the side of his face. A splintering window pane had gashed his cheek.

'General, are you okay?'

'Yes, I'm fine, I'm fine,' he barked in an irritated voice. His honourable retirement was now at risk. 'Get me a damage report on our own troops. Put the First Army on alert. I want shovels, helmets, rescue supplies, tents, hospitals and water tanks prepared. Then report back. Send up a UH-1 observation chopper now. Most of our choppers are in Hokkaido. Get them flown down here immediately.'

'Yes, sir.' The aide was scribbling madly on a pad as blood ran down from his face on to the white paper.

'Get me the Defence Minister, then the Tokyo governor, then the head of the navy and air force on the line.'

'Lines are down, sir.'

'I don't give a shit. Use our special satellite link or the two-way radios. We just paid over 500 million yen for the radio system. Just patch me through.'

'Yes, sir.' The aide knew there was little hope of finding the two-way radios, which were stored in boxes somewhere.

'What time does the Disaster Prevention Bureau open at the

National Land Agency?' demanded Mishima. 'This is their problem.'

'Not till 9 a.m., sir.'

'Those lazy bastards. I don't suppose we'll have any chance of reaching them?'

'No, sir.'

'Then who the fuck's going to call an emergency meeting of the government? Never mind, just get a move on.'

'Yes, sir.'

'Oh, shit.'

'What's wrong, sir?'

'We need to evacuate the Emperor to his villa in Kyoto. His call sign is "Overlord". See if you can reach the Imperial Household Agency. If not, get a chopper over there straight away.'

'Yes, sir.'

Though General Mishima had just put 22,300 troops on full alert and could call on another 14,600 within two days, his men had almost no disaster equipment. The government spent more than $50 billion a year on the military budget, yet the only disaster equipment they purchased consisted of a thousand radio transceivers.

There was another major problem, too. General Mishima could not commit his army to rescue operations until the Tokyo governor had approved the mission. On paper, he had the power to commit the SDF in case of life-and-death, but that would mean acting on his own initiative, something Japanese bureaucracy did not allow for. Mishima would wait for the governor's approval. The only problem was he remembered reading in the morning paper that the governor was holidaying somewhere in the South Pacific.

16

GINZA

Tuesday morning at Ginza crossing

The safest place to be in an earthquake is in a new skyscraper. The bigger the quake, the taller the building, the safer you are.

Conventional Japanese wisdom

Nomo Watanabe got off the subway at Ginza crossing, Tokyo's elite shopping district. He climbed the stairs to the exit and emerged next to the Wako department store. As he waited for the light to turn green to cross over to his own store, Mitsukoshi, he looked up at the two Daishin Trade Towers and gasped at their beauty.

Like a giant mole travelling at high speed, the first primary wave moved through the earth just as the light turned green. Watanabe heard the quake before he felt it. A deafening roar filled the air and, as he stood looking up at the gigantic building, granite slabs came hurtling down on to passers by below. A quarter-second after hitting the Daishin Towers the P or primary wave hit Watanabe and threw him 10 metres into the middle of the intersection. It was as if somebody had punched him in the chest. He did not try to stand up and attempted instead to roll over on to his stomach to protect his face from flying missiles, but movement was impossible. The pavement buckled all around him and Watanabe was certain he was about to be swallowed up by the earth.

Explosions filled the air. The liquid petroleum gas tank of a taxi near him burst, sending a fireball into the air. Glass from the Mitsukoshi department store and nearby shops blew out into the street and filled the air with lethal fragments. The P wave knocked the Mitsukoshi department store a metre sideways as the secondary wave lifted the building a metre off the ground. The girders supporting each floor snapped, and all the floors collapsed to the ground.

The twin Daishin Towers never had a chance. The steel supports built with Chinese manganese were already cracked, and needed little impact from the tremor to make them sever completely.

The P wave roared like an express train, squeezing and expanding the rock as it moved, shook the two towers violently and threw the western one sideways. Four seconds later a secondary wave, known as an S wave, hit and sent the tower into a vertical shake. The ground acceleration level of the shock waves registered 1200 centimetres per second per second, three times what it would have taken to wipe out every building erected before 1971. Average quakes registered 200–300 Gal in horizontal acceleration. By the time the third set of waves, called surface waves, hit the Daishin Trade Towers the damage had been done.

The simultaneous horizontal and vertical force of the quake sheared the ground-level supports of the western tower. Momentarily it sagged to its knees, before teetering slowly to lean on its companion 20 metres away.

Two hundred and fifty-five square kilometres of Tokyo instantly liquefied, turning to a grey, gelatinous slurry. The water pressure under Ginza reached nearly 15,000 kilos per square centimetre, enough to blast a hole through the side of a steel ship. The pressurized water followed the path of least resistance and forced its way through three hundred years of loose sediment to the surface of the earth. Geysers of grey mud spurted high into the air, while the water directly under the Daishin Towers followed the newly sunk pilings upwards. Water sprayed 30 metres up the side of the building like oil from a wildcat strike.

With only 15 metres of support at its liquid base, the east tower gave way as it was hit by the west tower. Both collapsed, taking with them ten thousand occupants. The death toll included the head of Daishin Construction, who had built his own inferior-quality coffin.

The quake had lasted barely a minute, and had released forty times more energy than the 1989 San Francisco earthquake.

The dazed Watanabe thought that North Korea must have launched a nuclear strike against Tokyo and prepared himself for death. But when death never came he slowly hauled himself to his knees. Blood was running down his face and he felt a strange feeling in his mouth. A 10-centimetre-long shard of glass had embedded itself in his cheek, penetrating his mouth. He gently pulled it out and put his tongue against the small hole in the side of his face. Tearing off a piece of cloth from his shirt, he put it on the outside of his cheek. The blood held it in place.

Watanabe staggered with difficulty to his feet. The Ginza looked as if somebody had crossed the stage set for *Godzilla* with that for *Last Exit to Brooklyn*. Most of the buildings had collapsed and the thick, choking dust made it difficult to see. Glass and broken neon signs littered the streets, covering the bodies of the dead and injured. Fires were just starting to break out and thick black smoke poured from some of the buildings. Most of the LPG-driven taxis were on fire. Watanabe found it difficult to stand – the street surface had ruptured everywhere and some parts were 2 metres higher than others. To make matters worse, brown liquid was shooting out of the earth – some of it from broken sewage pipes, some from broken water mains and some from liquefaction. So many buildings had toppled on to the street that the main road was hard to identify, and the few survivors were those who had been crossing the main street.

Watanabe's first instinct was to find his family. He looked for a payphone, then realized the futility of it. He sat down in the middle of Ginza crossing to clear his mind. Worrying about his family wouldn't help him – he knew that. They were either dead or alive, and no amount of premature grief would change that.

He looked around him. Screams filled the air. Fires were now blazing out of control and would continue to do so until they burned themselves out. The sprinkler systems in Tokyo's buildings were connected to water mains which had fractured.

After a full three minutes of meditation Watanabe rose calmly, with a look of determination. During those three minutes he had reasoned through the quake. It was clear that all emergency and telephone services would be useless in Tokyo's present state. It was also clear that it would take him four or five days to walk home. With luck his family's home in Chiba would not have been hit by the disaster. Meanwhile his time was best spent helping those in Tokyo. It was the right thing to do, and he hoped that in Chiba there were others like him, if necessary helping his family.

Watanabe remembered the storage depot in Nihonbashi where Mitsukoshi kept all its food supplies. If he could make it to the depot and set up a system of rationing, he might save some lives. Normally the walk would take him no more than forty minutes, but not today.

There could be no firm planning in this crisis – every plan had to be flexible. Today was a day of instinct and resourcefulness, and part of his meditation told him to take things as they came.

Watanabe's thoughts were interrupted by an arm waving for help from under a manhole cover in the centre of Ginza crossing.

'Help us.'

He crawled over to the manhole cover as quickly as he could, trying not to step on the bodies of the dead and dying.

'Please help!'

The cover had been dislodged and the hand was waving frantically. 'Help us,' the voice repeated.

As soon as Watanabe heaved the manhole cover open a little further, a man crawled out of the hole gasping for air.

'We were . . . trapped in the subway. The subway filled up . . . with water. The lights were out. We crawled along the dots.'

The man was referring to the yellow Braille-like squares that covered Japan's subways and walkways and guided the nation's blind around street corners and train stations. The man stopped talking for a second and looked at the carnage above ground. More people began climbing up the metal ladder through the hole; miraculously the entire group was uninjured. The last person up was an old man.

'Here, take my arm,' offered Watanabe.

'Thank you,' he panted, out of breath.

Watanabe sat him down and looked round to see if anyone else needed his assistance. Several of the survivors had begun to wander off when a high-powered hissing sound was heard. A young woman was standing frozen in the middle of the street, shaking uncontrollably, with smoke coming out of her mouth, ears and eyes. Another woman in the group ran to help her.

'*No!*' cried Watanabe.

But it was too late. The woman grasped the young girl's hand, and the other survivors looked on in horror as her body pulsated to the ground as if she were slam dancing.

Several of the women began to cry, and others started to run away.

'Nobody move!' shouted Watanabe. 'There may be an aftershock. You could all be electrocuted.'

Most of the group did as they were told and huddled together, both through fear and their natural instinct to obey authority. Watanabe suddenly found himself in charge.

'I have to find my family,' cried out one woman.

'I have a little boy at home,' said another.

Watanabe spoke again.

'We all have families, but there's nothing you can do for them except survive. Tomorrow, when the aftershocks have passed and the electricity is turned off, it will be safer. Buildings are still falling. Be patient.'

One businessman ignored Watanabe and began walking home, picking his way through the rubble. A wide variety of plastic signs had previously dotted the Ginza streetscape, while advertisements in the form of real cars and giant plastic crabs had hung from buildings. According to the Building Standards Law these ads had to be securely bolted, but this law was never enforced. The ads had now become lethal projectiles, and after the businessman had gone a short way a two-storey neon sign fell and crushed him.

This did not, however, deter the old man in Watanabe's group, who also got up and started walking. But after taking a few steps he stumbled in one of the many cracks in the pavement, falling over the legs of a body. Watanabe hurried over and helped him up.

'Old man, where are you going?'

'I must see if my building is still standing.'

'Are you crazy? You can't do that.'

But the man stubbornly kept walking.

'Wait, old man. Where's this building of yours?'

'Just around the block.'

'You'll never make it that far.' Fires were burning all around them, and visibility was limited to 15 metres. 'You'll be killed,' insisted Watanabe.

'I'm eighty-five years old, and if I could survive the war I can survive this. If I die walking to my building, then it's my time.'

Sometimes Watanabe hated the fatalism of Japanese society. 'It's still too dangerous. Look at those two women who were electrocuted.'

'They were stupid.' He kept walking.

Watanabe turned to the small group of survivors. 'I'll be back in half an hour. If you wish to help me on relief efforts, and get home to your families, then remain here.' Then he turned and took the old man's hand. 'Okay, old man, lead the way. And tell me what's so important about this building of yours.'

17

THE HAND

Tuesday morning on the Salomon trading desk on the top floor of the Urbannet Otemachi Building

'The bone.'

A surgeon's response to the toughest
part of performing an amputation

'Did you sleep well?' asked Dougie.

Yuki nodded.

He studied her.

'What's wrong?' she asked.

'I just wondered why I never noticed you before last night . . . I mean in *that* way.'

'What way?'

Dougie took her hand and smiled. 'How long have you been planning this?' he asked her.

Yuki blushed. 'It's impolite to ask such a question,' she said and turned away, bending over the desk to pick up her trading sheets.

Dougie moved behind her and whispered something in her ear; Yuki giggled. Then Dougie sat back in his trading seat and got down to business. He was nervous. Yuki knew something was wrong by the way he clicked his pen – Dougie furiously clicked the top of his ballpoint whenever he was pensive. It was the type of observation that only a poker player would make. Or a woman in love.

'Doug, can I get you a drink?'

'Sure, thanks,' he said absent-mindedly.

Yuki did not bother asking what he wanted. She knew he only drank fruit juice and health drinks. His latest kick was Pocari Sweat, a clear, isotonic sports drink popular in Japan. Dougie liked the idea of drinking something that sounded as if it had been extracted from human armpits. He had even sent a case of Pocari Sweat home for his family.

'If I want to drink bodily fluids, I'll wait till I'm adrift at sea for a few weeks,' said his father as he poured the Pocari Sweat into the sink. A motor auto mechanic, he only drank Coke and Budweiser.

'Dougie says it's really popular over there in Japan,' defended his younger sister.

'I'm not surprised – those Japs will eat and drink anything. They even eat fish without cooking it. Fucking barbarians.'

That was the end of the Douglas family cultural experimentation.

Dougie looked at his watch: twenty past eight. The stock market opened in forty minutes. He had bet $100 million of Salomon's money that the stockmarket was going to fall and kept clicking the pen. *Did Yuki remember to hold back the confirmation slip to the Salomon settlement department?* he wondered.

Every time Dougie finished a trade in the stock or futures market, he was required to submit a trading slip to Salomon's settlement department. Today Douglas was unwinding an arbitrage position. The previous week he had simultaneously bought 5000 futures contracts on the Nikkei 225, where they traded on the Singapore International Monetary Exchange, and sold 5000 contracts of the Osaka 50 on the Osaka futures exchange. Both these indices moved in tandem. When they were out of kilter, he bought one and sold the other until they came into balance. In liquidating an arbitrage position, his bosses required Dougie to unwind them simultaneously to avoid undue risk. He had purposely ignored this requirement.

As his assistant, Yuki was required to ensure that each of the buy and sell slips reached the Salomon back office. By instructing her to hold the sell slip, the back office would not know that Dougie had not yet 'bought' in the other half of the trade. When selling the Simex position yesterday he had told the trader to 'book' it over and not report it for a day. This bought Dougie time. Technically it was illegal, but all securities houses breached financial regulations during the course of business. Douglas was worried that Yuki had inadvertently reported the trade.

'Where's Yuki?'

'Getting you a brewski,' replied Sugimoto.

'Thanks, bud,' said Dougie, running off to the kitchen.

'You're welcome.'

Sugimoto flipped open his English notebook to find the word 'bud'. His entry read: 'Bud. All-American beer only to be drunk cold and out of the bottle. Usage in a sentence: "Yo, bartender gimme a Bud wudja." ' Sugimoto scratched his head. Maybe Dougie had said 'Pud'. He flipped the page to 'Pud: also known as Big Dick,

Johnson, Willy, Fred, le grand Zozo, the Sequoia or the aching Swahili. As in pulling my pud or yanking my chain.' *The English language is difficult*, thought Sugimoto, giving it one last try under the world 'spud'. 'Abbreviation for couch potato and spudinski. As in "Cummon you spud let's go rock the town tonight." ' Sugimoto gave up.

Dougie found Yuki in the kitchen. She had just poured his Pocari Sweat into a glass and was looking for a knife to cut the toast she had made him. Dougie liked his toast cut in sharp triangles.

'Yuki, did you report that sale on the 5000 futures?'

She didn't turn round, but instead stiffened and looked intently at the clear liquid she had just poured.

'Yuki, what's wrong?'

The liquid in the glass was vibrating as if dinosaurs from *Jurassic Park* were invading Tokyo. As Dougie reached for her hand, the glass started shaking violently while the kitchen rocked back and forth. Then the whole building began to collapse.

Douglas awoke in agony. He tried to move, but his right hand was pinned under a concrete slab. He felt as if he were outdoors but everything seemed grey. The noises around him were not familiar: strange hissing and crackling sounds, the splintering of glass, far-off explosions. Douglas had a hard time breathing – dust filled the air and was mingled with a strong smell of gas. *Shit, I've got to get out of here*, he thought. Forgetting that his hand was pinned, he tried to stand. A searing pain shot up his right arm and he almost passed out.

A minute later a violent aftershock shook the wreckage. Dougie screamed out as the giant concrete slab mashed his hand into a thousand splinters without letting him go. The pain was unbearable and he lapsed into unconsciousness . . .

Douglas awoke for a second time. His right arm was throbbing but there was no feeling in his hand. As his eyes gradually grew accustomed to the grey light, he spotted Yuki at his feet. She was moaning and, though it was hard to tell in the dimness, it looked as if she were bleeding from the head.

'Yuki, wake up. Please wake up.'

Dougie gently prodded her with his foot.

Yuki stirred. 'Doug,' she cried fearfully. 'Are we dead?'

'No, we're alive. Are you okay? Can you move?'

'Yes, I think so.'

Both were under a giant piece of concrete which had fallen like a lean-to over them.

'Yuki, listen carefully. We have to get out of here. I smell gas all around us. Just one spark will blow this place up. See if you can crawl over me and get my hand loose,' he instructed.

Yuki crawled over him. Her eyes had adjusted to the gloom and she could just make out his right hand.

'Can you move it?' he asked desperately.

Yuki looked at his hand.

'Try to get it out,' he pleaded again.

Yuki reached down, grasped Dougie's forearm and pulled. He let out a blood-curdling scream and passed out. Yuki leaped back in terror, then began to cry.

Douglas awoke for a third time with Yuki bent over him. She had found a can of Coke, torn off a piece of her dress and soaked it with the beverage. She was applying the compress to his head.

'You've got to get out of here.'

'No, *we* have to,' she said.

Douglas knew he would die unless he acted quickly. He thought back to his trip to Kobe, and recalled three cases where those trapped under eaves and concrete had had to cut off a limb to save themselves. Two had had to amputate just ahead of an advancing fire and the third before a gas main blew. Only one was lucky enough to be saved by a rescue team with morphine and a surgical saw.

'Yuki, you must save yourself. Climb out towards the air. Find help.'

She started to cry again.

Douglas knew he could not allow her to watch the amputation, and he did not want her there if he failed. Shock was setting in, and he supposed he would simply use a piece of sharp concrete or pipe to cut his hand off. If he didn't keep passing out from pain, or bleed to death, he felt he could survive.

'I'm not leaving you,' said Yuki, bringing her sobs under control.

'If you stay then you must help me cut my hand off,' he said, thinking that that would give her an excuse to find help.

'I can't do it!'

Douglas could not wait any longer. He picked up a nearby piece of broken pipe and raised it high above his body. As he brought it down quickly on his wrist, Yuki turned away. Dougie passed out again. Blood was now spurting from his wrist.

Yuki gained control of herself and realized that Dougie would die without her help. She quickly tore another strip from her dress and tied a tourniquet just above the wrist. The wound was still bleeding profusely. Yuki then took off his necktie and tied it tightly around the cloth. The bleeding stopped at last. For several minutes she looked around their crawl space before finding the knife she had used to cut Dougie's toast. The smell of gas was getting stronger.

Yuki put the serrated edge of the knife on his wrist and began sawing, repulsing her gag instinct. Finally she hit bone and the knife would go no further. Desperately, she picked up a piece of concrete and slammed it down on the knife. She heard a cracking sound and continued sawing until Dougie's wrist came away from his hand. She wrapped up the stump and pulled Dougie on to her lap. As she stroked his hair, she began to sob uncontrollably, praying that he would live.

'Wake up, Doug-chan, wake up,' she repeated over and over.

Five minutes later Douglas awoke. Disorientated and in deep shock, he looked at his arm. There was no pain.

Yuki took over. 'Follow me,' she commanded as they began their crawl to freedom.

As the eighteen storeys of the Urbannet Otemachi Building had fallen to earth, only those on the top floor had stood any chance of survival. The arrogance of Salomon Brothers, insistent on taking the top floor, had ultimately saved the couple. All those lower down had been killed.

18

THE SIX WISE MEN

'Closing down Tokyo by means of an earthquake warning will cost the nation 720 billion yen [$7.2 billion] a day. It'll never happen.'

A government official on the economic reasons
why the Japanese government would never issue an
earthquake warning

The metal hedgehog stirred slightly. The Swiss-made seismometer was one of two hundred recording devices located deep beneath Japan. The device stirred again, its advanced electronic innards rapidly memorizing the seismic frequencies of the big quake, registering every movement in analog encryption and converting the data to a digital format. An open telephone line trailed out of the back of the hedgehog like a tail. The data sped over the NTT phone line, and a minute after the quake the seismographs at JMA headquarters began spewing out graphs. Moments later they fell silent as the telephone lines into Tokyo were severed.

Four minutes after the earthquake the pagers of the Six Wise Men started beeping: 'URGENT. PLEASE COME TO JMA HEADQUARTERS IMMEDIATELY. BIG EARTHQUAKE IMMINENT. CONTACT LOCAL POLICE FOR TRANSPORT.'

The pagers were marvels of Japanese workmanship. Four of them beeped for twelve hours next to warm corpses – two-thirds of the seismological dream team. Three were men over the age of seventy who had died peacefully in their sleep. The fourth had his skull crushed when rubble from a building hit him on the way to work.

Meanwhile another of the six wise men, a Tokyo University professor, was at his home in Choshi, a large town on the Pacific 130 kilometres north-east of Tokyo. Choshi had been largely unaffected by the tremors. He frantically called his local police station, which sent a squad car to his home. Lights flashing, they drove at breakneck pace across the Chiba peninsula to the main highway leading into Tokyo. At this speed, the professor estimated it would take just over two hours to reach Japan Meteorological Agency headquarters. Not today. Half an hour into the journey, traffic came to a standstill.

'Use your radio,' the professor ordered the driver. 'Find out what's wrong.'

'This is squad car two, calling central headquarters. Over. Can you please tell me what the hold-up is on the highway? Over.'

The radio box squelched, but there was no reply.

If the professor had been in a helicopter he would have seen traffic backed up for 80 kilometres into Tokyo. Actually 'backed up' would have been the wrong word once inside the city limits. The mangled Shuto expressway did not exist – it had collapsed on its side, taking with it all the commuters on top and all the buildings beside it.

After waiting three hours in the squad car without moving, the professor decided to use his own initiative. 'I'll walk,' he said stoically, slinging his suit jacket over one shoulder. Nobody ever saw him again.

The sixth Wise Man had the best chance of making it to JMA headquarters. He was Dr Tokai, the spindly, octogenarian professor who had helped Hiroko in her research into earthquake-proof construction. Tokai was due to deliver a 9 a.m. lecture to Tokyo University students. He had been in his office, a small one-storey add-on structure with a light roof, when the quake hit. Dr Tokai took pride in immediately identifying it as higher than eight on the Richter scale. He was sure that the seismometers had not even squeaked before this one.

Tokai already knew that he would have to walk to the Meteorological Agency. He did not bother trying his phone or his car – the phone lines would be dead and the streets blocked. *I should have had one of those new-fangled satellite phones*, he reprimanded himself.

Dr Tokai was excited. Instinctively he knew that this was one of the greatest geological disasters ever. He filled a bottle from the water remaining in the pipes, put on a hard hat, threw the papers out of his briefcase and replaced them with medical supplies. At the last minute he threw in a disposable Fuji camera. Tokyo University was in the eastern part of the city, only a few kilometres from the JMA building. At the age of eighty Dr Tokai set out on the field trip of his life. He glanced briefly at his watch, which now read 8.45 – another fact which worried him. It meant that the staff of the National Land Agency, which was responsible for coordinating disaster relief, would be trapped en route to work. The Disaster Bureau of the Land Agency did not open until 9 a.m.

19

THE FIRE

Tuesday morning in the area of the Watanabe family home in Chiba

Tokyo has 9 million buildings; 7 million are made out of wood.

Fujimoto stirred; the greedy shopkeeper lay buried in his own home. He tried to open his eyes, but at first it was impossible. Then he slowly wiped away the caked-on dried blood and managed to open them.

What he saw appalled him. A large wooden beam hovered just above his head. Memories came back. He had been in an earthquake. Pain began to register all over his body; he was certain something was broken. *Get out of the house*, Fujimoto told himself. The one thing he remembered from an earthquake pamphlet was that aftershocks could be expected. He eyed the wooden beam apprehensively as he made for a tunnel of light.

After thirty minutes of crawling and scrambling through the wreckage, an exhausted Fujimoto found himself outside. Oddly, he was still holding his morning newspaper. Though it was 9 a.m., the sky was black with smoke. Fujimoto could only see a few hundred metres ahead, but what he did see was shocking. There was almost nothing left of his street. He looked back at his own house. The roof had caved in to one side. Luckily he had been in his study near the front door. Fujimoto thanked the gods for his good luck. Then he panicked, thinking about his shop. All his money was tied up in it – he had to rescue the store or he was doomed.

Fortunately Fujimoto had not broken anything as he had assumed; he was just bruised and sore. He hurried towards his store past the remains of the Watanabe home. As Fujimoto ran past, he heard screams from inside. Like most other wooden houses in central Tokyo, the building had collapsed under its heavy roof tiles. This was the primary killer in residential areas, where millions of homes were made of wood.

'Help me,' pleaded a weak voice within the rubble.

Fujimoto approached the house. The smell of gas was everywhere.

'Help.'

Watanabe, thought Fujimoto. He had survived. He briefly thought about rescuing Watanabe and his wife, then remembered the million yen he owed them. His first impulse to help his relative was lost in a moment of greed.

Fujimoto looked around, rolled up his newspaper and lit a match. Then he neatly made a small pile of wood under a corner of Watanabe's home and put the torch under the wood. Soon a nice crackling fire was going. Screams could be heard coming from inside the house, which was now a blazing inferno. Fujimoto backed away.

Why can't I ever make a nice fire like that at home? he wondered as he walked to his shop. He had gone barely 20 metres when he heard the explosion, and turned to see Watanabe's home go up in a fireball. The leaking gas had ignited. After that there were no more screams.

Fujimoto smiled and continued walking towards his shop, a free man.

A young girl stood in the street watching the horror, too frightened to scream as the fireball came towards her and knocked her unconscious.

20

THE TONGUE

Tuesday morning at Ken Moyama's home

'Snakes awoke from hibernation; rats appeared in groups so agitated that they did not fear human beings; small pigs chewed off their tails and ate them. Wells began to bubble.'
From Andrew Robinson's *Earthshock*, a description of strange behaviour before the 1975 Haicheng earthquake

It was quarter past eight and Ken Moyama had been working since 5 a.m. He adroitly racked up the wooden beads on his abacus, figuring out June's income, and jotted the totals down on a piece of scrap paper:

Gifts from yakuza gangs	10 million yen	($100,000)
Prostitution, gambling and protection	120 million	($1.2 million)
Property income	200 million	($2 million)
US cash, stocks and bonds	100 million	($1 million)
Japanese cash, stocks and bonds	25 million	($250,000)

He had over $275 million invested in America, which he was beginning to let his student son manage from UCLA – the yakuza leader was pleased to see that his monthly income from the States was nearly a million dollars, or 100 million yen. Moyama was not pleased to see that his $450 million Japanese portfolio only brought him in $250,000 a month. *That couldn't be right.*

Moyama checked all his bank accounts again to see if he had forgotten some. They were all registered in the names of his cats, dogs and koi. He ran down the list. 'Sasha, Ling Ling, Pookey . . .' They were all there.

All bank accounts with less than 3 million yen were untaxed by the government, which meant that the rich often evaded tax by opening twenty or thirty accounts. Moyama had more than fifty.

Since banks did not require proof of identity to open an account, the public took full advantage of this by registering in the names of their family pets. The authorities turned a blind eye to this massive tax evasion since the nation's huge savings had been the driving force behind the Japanese economy. The banks paid a derisory amount of interest on savings accounts, which was why Moyama felt cheated.

Suddenly he was disturbed by the thrashing of his koi. *How strange. I fed them at six.* His fish only jumped when it was feeding time.

Instinctively he rushed outside and shouted to his family, domestic staff and retainers. 'Get out of the house now! Everyone in the courtyard!' he yelled, not masking the panic in his voice. Moyama ran over to the koi pond and turned on the water tap full blast. Within minutes his wife, kitchen staff, gardeners, bodyguards and assistant were all milling around the yakuza boss.

'What's wrong, Ken-chan?' asked his wife, worried that he was going to fire one of the staff.

'Just wait. Nobody move.'

The entire group was terrified. They had never seen Moyama act in such an odd manner.

Somewhere Moyama had read the results of an eight-year study in which scientists had determined that koi could predict earthquakes. He had dismissed the finding until he saw them thrashing about his pond. As Moyama and his household looked out over the city, they saw blue-orange flashes which they mistook for power short-circuits. The grinding of the earth's crust had generated an aurora from the electricity it threw off. These brilliant flashes were seen 2–3 metres off the ground.

Suddenly the earth roared and everyone was thrown off their feet. Each time Moyama tried to stand, he was thrown down. Movement was impossible. The group lay entangled for sixty terrifying seconds. Then it was over.

The Moyama household were fortunate. Their compound was on top of the highest point in Shirokane. These hills were of solid bedrock and were one of the safest places to be in an earthquake. Everyone picked themselves up and brushed themselves down. Except for the roofing tiles, which had cracked and fallen, there was little damage. The only injury was to Tessie, their Filipina maid, who bit her tongue off in a fright. Much later Moyama laughed over this irony and hoped it would cut down on her phone calls to Manila, which cost him a fortune.

Moyama's two bodyguards tried to act bravely. From 5 a.m. until 5 p.m. each day they protected Moyama until they were relieved by the second shift. The two bulky men weighed over 100 kilos each – more than twice the size of the average Japanese.

'That wasn't so bad,' lied Mata, the largest bodyguard, whose hands were shaking. Mata had styled himself after Luco Brazi in *The Godfather*, which he had seen dubbed into Japanese. *The Godfather* had been a big hit with the yakuza. Mata's large head appeared to be joined directly to his shoulders with no neck in between. He walked like a penguin, his arms at an angle to his body. His other distinguishing feature was that the top joint of the little finger on his left hand was missing.

Moyama ignored Mata's stupid remark and pointed towards the city. 'Look.'

The group looked in horror at the skyline – which no longer existed in its familiar form. Shinjuku, Tokyo Tower and the Daishin Trade Towers had gone. The Daishin Trade Towers were supposed to be quake-proof, but Moyama was not surprised that the building was no longer standing: so many people had dipped their hand into the money bucket. Much of the city had been vaunted by the government as quake-proof: bridges, towers, buildings, expressways – now they had gone in less than thirty seconds. Moyama shook his head as smoke billowed from the city below.

Then the second tremor hit. Once again everyone was thrown to the ground. After it had subsided, Moyama gathered everyone together. The Filipina was crying in agony. Moyama picked her tongue off the grass, washed it in the koi pond and handed it to his wife. 'Hold this for a minute,' he instructed. His wife didn't want to touch the disgusting thing, but did as she was told.

'Nobody's allowed in the house. More quakes are on the way. There's plenty of water in the koi pond for drinking.' The flood from the tap was now reduced to a mere trickle. Moyama knew that Tokyo would have no water. He motioned to Mata. 'Give me the Satlink phone.' Then he ordered the bodyguard to go into the maid's quarters to find a needle and thread.

Moyama walked to a corner of the garden and thought for a moment. *This is just like World War II. The city is destroyed. Chaos and confusion will reign. Few in Japan remember the war, and fewer still will be prepared to act. This is my time.* Moyama dialled his Osaka headquarters and his chief there answered the phone.

'Yes, boss?'

'Listen closely. Tokyo has been destroyed by an earthquake. I want you to take my helicopter and fill it with medical supplies, blankets, water and food. You will fly it to my home in Shirokane immediately.'

'Yes, sir, but what about airspace regulations? Where will I land? What – ' Moyama cut him off. 'There are no rules any more. Do as I say!' he barked.

'Yes, sir,' said the apologetic lackey.

Moyama continued. 'I also want a thousand armed men shipped into Tokyo by freighter. They must have one leader who will report to me, and a leader under him for every hundred men. I will leave it to you to figure out how they get here. After you have given these orders I want you to locate ten more helicopters and a transport aircraft. Fill them up as with the first. They will all land on my hill. I will call about how to handle the aircraft later.'

'Yes, sir.'

'Oh, and one last thing. Please bring twenty Satphones and a hundred batteries.'

'Yes, sir,' answered the chief, wondering where the hell he was going to find a hundred phone batteries.

Mata returned with a needle and thread.

'Tessie, come here.'

Despite her pain the Filipina maid walked over when Moyama called. He motioned to his wife to bring the tongue and thread the needle. 'Mrs Moyama is going to sew your tongue back on, Tessie.'

The maid fainted.

'Good, that makes your job easier.'

He wiped the blood away as his wife reattached the tongue to Tessie's palate. In fifteen minutes the operation was complete and Moyama began to give orders to his bodyguards. 'You.' He was pointing to Mata. 'You're on guard duty to protect my family. Begin patrols around the house. Anyone seen looting or being part of a gang except ours is to be killed on sight.' Moyama still remembered the gangs that roamed post-war Tokyo, looting and raping. 'Any civilians in distress, needing food or water are to be sent to the helicopter landing site.'

Mata scurried off to do his boss's bidding.

'You,' said Moyama, motioning to the other bodyguard. 'Find a landing spot for the helicopter. Make sure you are armed.'

'Yes, boss.'

Then Moyama called Osaka on the Satlink again. 'Bring a welding torch and an acetylene tank. Then call the underground headquarters of Aum Shinrikyo. They're in hiding in the hills above Kyoto. Pick up some Semtex.'

The household stood around gazing at Moyama, wondering what he would do next. He had forgotten how much he had enjoyed wartime Japan. The yakuza boss was now happier than he had been in years. Once again he was Moyama the Provider, and from that he took strength.

For his next call Moyama needed complete privacy, but signalled to his son Ken to join him. Ken Moyama, proudly named after him, was studying computer science and economics at UCLA but was home from California for the summer. Moyama was old enough to be his son's grandfather, having sired him when he was over fifty. Such testimony to his virility gave Moyama great pride.

He walked over to a secluded part of the garden and dialled Las Vegas. The phone rang twenty times. *This would never happen in Japan*, thought Moyama. His own people were under strict instructions to apologize if the phone rang more than twice before they picked it up.

A brusque voice answered. 'Yeh.'

'This is Moyama.' He spoke very slowly. Moyama had learned basic English in Sugamo prison from the American guards, but was very embarrassed about speaking it. It was about the only thing in life he was not confident about.

'I please speak Mr Berman,' he said carefully.

Moyama heard the man put his hand over the receiver. 'Yo, Tony, some gook is on the line.'

Moyama winced.

'Sounds like a Chink to me.'

'Hello, Tony Berman here.' Berman, of Italian Jewish origins, had been guardedly admitted to the mafia's ranks after marrying the daughter of a ruling boss. As a lawyer, he protected the mob's legal interests and tried to keep his family and their soldiers out of jail. But he wasn't too good a lawyer, and a number of his family were fuming away at him in prison, waiting to get even.

'Mr Berman, this is Moyama.'

Berman got excited. 'Moyama-san, how good to hear from you. How can I help you?'

Tony Berman was also old man Di Angeles' son-in-law and the mob's guardian for family gambling, drug and prostitution interests in Las Vegas. The Di Angeles branch of the mob had long considered breaking into the Tokyo underworld. Every year at the family general meeting, Berman pushed for overseas expansion. Many of the older conservative family members did not like this. Berman discussed the idea of earning in yen in addition to dollars, but the old-timers just shook their heads. Berman pursued the idea anyway, figuring that the older Sicilian members would be edged out in the coming years. Moyama and Berman had met twice, both times in Tokyo. Though the Di Angeles family had vetoed any mafia ties to Japan, both sides remained friendly.

The old man had allowed Berman to take over the family's Las Vegas interests, but he was not happy about his decision. Not only did Berman drink and gamble but he was abusive. Reports had come back that Berman had continually beaten his wife – Di Angeles could forgive any other sin, including Berman's penchant for little boys, but he could not forgive anybody hurting his daughter. The old man was biding his time, waiting for a chance to nail his good-for-nothing son-in-law.

Moyama had started off the conversation but was now happy to hand the phone over to his son. 'Just moment please. My son.' He turned to his son. 'Speak English to this guy. This is what I want . . .'

'Mr Berman, this is Ken Moyama junior. Tokyo has just had earthquake. If you fill plane with medical supply and blankets, he will allow you to join us. The plane must be here tomorrow and we will fax you a list of supplies and a flight plan in fifteen minutes. The plane must be loaded with morphine and heroin.'

'This is very sudden.' Berman was absorbing the importance of what Moyama was offering. The mention of morphine and heroin was exciting. The most effective means of starting addiction was through legal medication, because patients found the treatment hard to break. If Moyama allowed Berman to continue supplying morphine into Japan after the crisis, the American would make a fortune.

'Mr Berman, this opportunity my father extends but once. You choose. In or out.'

'We're in,' said Berman hurriedly, not even thinking of consulting his father-in-law back east. Making a move into a new market was normally unheard of without family permission.

'Good. My father says he looks forward to seeing you Wednesday Tokyo time. Goodbye.'

The two men went over to Moyama's topsy-turvy office and picked a pen off the floor. Moyama dictated a fax. After they had finished, Moyama handed him the cellular phone.

'Now hook the fax up to my phone and send it to this number. I don't understand these new things.'

His son did not bother telling him that the fax machine was outdated and had been replaced by interactive e-mail and Satlink computers. The young Moyama looked at the fax machine. It was still in the box and had never been used.

Moyama the Provider knew that chaos was a time to make money, so he began to hatch a scheme. But he would have to act quickly.

THE CAMPAIGN

Tuesday morning at the Ginza branch
of Marayama Securities

'One of our salesman – a grown man – had his chair taken away
from him for two months and was forced to stand throughout
the day like a schoolboy.'
A quote from *The House of Nomura* by ex-stockbroker
A. J. Alletzhauser, describing one punishment
for not meeting daily sales quotas

The Marayama stock salesmen all stood in line at attention, having just finished their morning callisthenics. The Ginza branch manager was giving them a pep talk at their 8 a.m. meeting. The chairman of Marayama had had a phone call from Ken Moyama late the night before, hoping that all would go well on the stock campaign today. The chairman in turn had called the Ginza branch manager. Everyone was under strain to ramp the Daishin share price.

'I want our branch to place buy orders for half a million shares of Daishin Construction. We need to show we're the best branch in the country. We're number one,' yelled the branch manager.

Usually the pep talks were run by the sales manager, but this stock campaign was too important. Ginza was the most aggressive and profitable of Marayama's 150 branches.

'Head office has awarded triple bonus commission to anyone selling Daishin Construction shares to clients.'

Unlike most Japanese firms, Marayama worked on an incentive basis. The manager handed out a crib sheet full of analyst's notes on Daishin which the top brokers ignored, relying instead on instinct to jam shares down a client's throat. Each retail salesman's commission income would be posted at 12.15 and 5.15, as it was each day, and pressure was enormous.

'*Banzai*!' shouted the manager.

'*Banzai*!' yelled the frenzied stockbrokers.

The entire sales team raised their fists as if they were going into battle. With a nod from the branch manager they scattered, running for their phones. 'Buy Daishin!' they continued shouting.

Thousands of Marayama Securities stock salesmen throughout the nation's branches were engaged in the same morning ritual, preparing to stuff their clients into Daishin shares.

'Prime Minister Mori is behind Daishin,' whispered one Marayama broker.

'Daishin is an upward-related stock.'

'You can't lose money on this one.'

'It's the beginning of an upside technical breakout.'

'I promise the stock will rise to 3500 in two weeks,' swore another broker in an effort to clinch a sale.

'Ah, a political stock,' nodded customers who did not care about fundamental performance. Once they heard that Daishin was 'political and upward-related', the buy orders poured in. Only the rookie brokers read the analyst's quickly typed note:

> Daishin is a visionary company. Most construction firms earn money by erecting a building for a profit. Daishin goes one step further and keeps a stake in every building it puts up. Why leave money on the table for real estate and insurance companies, reasons Daishin's chairman Kobayashi. Daishin has purchased large stocks of land in the Tokyo/Yokohama area for development. Our analysis shows that over 60 per cent of Daishin's worth is tied up in buildings and development projects. Look for earnings to rise over 40 per cent this year with Daishin Trade Towers' rental income coming on stream. Strong buy recommendation.
>
> T. Kawasaki, construction analyst

The Tokyo Stock Exchange computer had buy orders for 1.2 million Daishin shares by 8.20 a.m. Only half a million shares were recorded on the sell side. Clearly Daishin was in for a spectacular rise.

Tada had been at work since 7.45. It was now 8.15.

Omori, his driver, was worried about Kaelin because she normally rang him on the car phone at eight, just after Omori had dropped his boss off at the Ministry. The two lovers usually chatted each day for fifteen minutes. Early morning was a good time – Tada was at work organizing his day while Omori was supposed to be washing and waxing the Mercedes. But Kaelin hadn't rung this morning. Omori concentrated on the car, rubbing the wax in hard circles. He pretended he was erasing Tada's face. Omori rubbed harder.

Tada meanwhile sat in his office thinking. The Tokyo Stock Exchange opened at 9 a.m. and he desperately needed to sell his 800,000 Daishin Construction shares before Moyama began selling the syndicate shares. Tada owed Sumitomo Bank 2 billion yen for the loan to buy the shares. He prayed that Marayama's private clients would be given the buy signal by the firm's domestic branches. *I'll stuff them with my shares before Moyama can sell*, thought Tada.

He rang DaiNippon Securities, a small Tokyo Stock Exchange broker whom he used when conducting secret deals, and waited impatiently for his call to be answered.

'*Moshi, moshi*,' said the trader's voice.

'Tada here.' He didn't bother saying 'Hello.' He never did, and this morning he was more abrupt than usual. Orders had to be in early to be tapped into the Tokyo Stock Exchange's dealing computer. 'Sell 800,000 shares in Daishin Construction.' Tada spat as he spoke. Though he had a spittoon near his waste basket, the floor around was dark and moist from where he had missed. 'I want them sold today.' Tada belched and then continued: 'Marayama Securities should be a big buyer. How does the market look set to open this morning?'

The broker knew that Tada expected a positive answer, so he invented a reason for the market to be strong. The broker also knew that if Daishin Construction were not strong today, Tada would blame him and he would lose his job. The ideal of lifetime employment was a myth – Tada could have him fired at any time.

'Investors are confident of the new government spending package and look set to bid up shares today,' lied the broker. In fact share prices had been very weak overnight.

'Today,' grunted Tada.

The broker heard a static-like noise on the phone and knew that Tada was coughing up phlegm again.

'All sold today, or you find a new job.' Tada then hung up.

When the quake hit a few minutes later, Daishin ceased to exist as a viable company. Trillions of dollars' worth of prime Tokyo and Yokohama real estate and buildings vanished, including Daishin's flagship twin towers. Tada had 800,000 shares of worthless Daishin paper and a 2 billion yen loan to pay back, but, as Kaelin had rightfully predicted, Tada survived the quake. Many people would live to regret it.

Kaelin regained consciousness at about 9 a.m. Fortunately the

Kojimachi area was situated on bedrock and, though all the glass had blown out of the windows, the apartment building had survived. The bedroom lay in ruins, a giant crack in the ceiling. The glass doors leading to the terrace were shattered.

Gingerly she stepped out of bed but a pain shot through her head. At first she thought she had been injured in the tremor, then remembered the previous evening. Tada had slapped her around. Drunk, and feeling the need to reassert his power after a meeting with Japan's kingpins, he had hit her in the jaw when she refused to have sex. She had blacked out around midnight. Kaelin felt the swelling on the side of her face. *Thank God Tada's not around.* He had left for the office at 7.30 that morning. She put on her slippers and limped slowly to the bathroom. The mirrors were shattered and the cabinets ripped apart. Kaelin turned on the tap, but only air hissed out and the pipes shrieked. A dribble of brown water appeared. Kaelin turned the tap off again.

She went back to the bedroom and tried the phone. Dead. The power was off. Light and air streamed in where the terrace doors had been. Kaelin picked up some clothes strewn on the floor, putting on jeans and tennis shoes. She had to locate Omori. She picked up the Satphone near the bed and dialled Tada's car phone. The phone rang but there was no answer. Kaelin rummaged through the bedside drawers and found a flashlight.

She left the bedroom and made her way past Tada's study. The flashlight picked up a gleaming object behind Tada's desk. Kaelin carefully made her way through a foot of fallen bric-à-brac that had toppled off Tada's cabinets. She waved the light behind his desk. The wall was cracked, revealing a hidden walk-in closet. Nervously she entered. Finding it difficult to walk, Kaelin waved the light at her feet. A hundred or so hard core porn videos lay in a jumbled mess on the floor. *That pig*, thought Kaelin, *I'm leaving.* She recognized one of the videos as the tape of the previous night's share scam operation, and took it with her.

Kaelin heard crying from across the room and made her way over. There on the ground was Carlotta, Tada's Filipina maid. A bookshelf had fallen over on her leg.

'Carlotta, are you okay?'

'Yes, I theenk so.'

Kaelin tried to move the bookcase, but Carlotta winced.

'My leg. I theenk eeets broken.'

Kaelin put down the flashlight.

'I need to lift this off you,' said Kaelin. At that moment an aftershock hit, the tenth since the big quake. Kaelin lost her balance and fell backwards just as a ceiling beam came crashing down.

Fifteen seconds later the tremor subsided. 'Let's get out of here, Carlotta.'

Then Kaelin saw the growing pool of blood running from under the beam, which was now embedded in Carlotta's skull. There was no point in checking whether she was still alive.

Determined to find Omori, Kaelin made her way via the emergency staircase to the open air. She silently prayed that Omori was still alive. And that Tada was dead.

22

TOP GUN

Almost all those who die in an earthquake die in the first eight minutes, most from suffocation.

The American Seventh Fleet was patrolling the South China Sea when it received the distress signal.

'Come in USS *Ranger*, this is Washington.'

The communications officer of the *Ranger* immediately picked up the emergency message. 'We read you, Washington.'

'A massive quake has just hit Tokyo. *Ranger*, we request you proceed at full speed to Tokyo Bay to assist in rescue operations.'

'Roger.'

'*Ranger*, this mission is authorized by the Big Bird himself. Further rescue supplies en route from Pearl Harbor.'

'Roger. Any other instructions?'

'Negative. Oh, keep CNN tuned in for updates.'

'Roger. Over and out.'

'Washington out.'

The radio operator smiled bleakly to himself. *What a hoot! The Japs wipe us out in Pearl Harbor, and here we are airlifting supplies to them over half a century later.*

But the American rescue operation had a precedent unknown to most modern sailors. Immediately after the tragic 1923 earthquake which claimed 140,000 lives, President Calvin Coolidge had deployed the US Pacific Fleet to Yokohama. The first vessel arrived in the harbour on 3 September, two days after the quake, and helped ferry rescue supplies from Asian ports.

Now, moments after the order came down from Washington, Captain Dennis McFlynn of the *Ranger* gave the command: 'Full speed ahead.'

Earthquake surveillance is considered a security matter by the United States government. Silent cheers go up when an enemy is hit by a quake, though for humanitarian reasons this is never acknowledged. The centre of America's surveillance is the small

town of Golden, Colorado, the headquarters of the US Geographical
Survey whose National Earthquake Information Service is linked to
hundreds of seismographs around the world. The moment a quake
hits anywhere on the planet, the USGS knows its origin, epicentre,
hypocentre and magnitude. Seismologists in Colorado had a direct
phone link to the National Security Agency, and within an hour the
President had ordered the Secretary of Defence to move. He in turn
called the Head of the Navy, who in turn ordered the USS *Ranger*
to steam into Tokyo Bay.

The *Ranger* was the grand-daddy of the US armada, an aircraft
carrier known as the 'Top Gun' of the Pacific Fleet. With a steel
deck over 300 metres long, the 81,000-tonne *Ranger* patrolled the
seas of Asia with five thousand combat-ready Navy and Marine
troops. Their average age was twenty. The attack planes which
once bedecked the *Ranger* had been scaled down in recent years:
the F/A-18 Hornets, E-2C Hawkeyes, EA-63 Prowlers and KA-60
Intruders were in some cases now replaced by reconnaissance planes
and civilian rescue choppers. There was no doubt, however, that the
Ranger was still a force whenever American interests in Asia needed
protection.

The *Ranger* was a floating city with its own restaurants,
mess halls, theatres, shops, video arcade, bowling alley, barbers'
shops and hospital. Though the ship had been commissioned
in 1957 and destined for retirement in 1993, the navy had
persuaded the US government to keep her on active duty. She
had once commanded operations in the Pacific, a task now
entrusted to a giant Nimitz-class supercarrier of the Seventh
Fleet.

Captain McFlynn had been in a similar emergency situation
after the 1995 Kobe earthquake. Then the US government had
authorized the *Ranger* to anchor offshore to despatch emergency
medical supplies, tents, doctors, troops, food and water. The fax offer
from the US Navy lay unnoticed on Prime Minister Murayama's desk
for three days before the offer was curtly turned down. 'We don't need
American forces infringing on our sovereignty,' the Japanese cabinet
decided.

This time things would be different. The captain of the *Ranger*
hoped to be anchored in the harbour by 5 a.m. on Thursday. With
direct authority from the President of the United States to offer any
assistance necessary in helping Tokyo's victims he did not intend
to be thwarted by Japan's bureaucracy, and did not radio ahead to
Japan's Maritime Self-defence Force.

Captain McFlynn had forty-eight hours to figure out a way to land in Tokyo Bay without creating an international incident. He opened his safe, pulled out America's 1960 defence treaty with Japan and began reading.

23

THE GREAT LIE

Tuesday, shortly after the earthquake

I love you.
The cheque's in the mail.
Earthquakes can be predicted.

The three great lies of mankind

Hiroko's phone rang and she picked it up excitedly, hoping for news of Alex. '*Moshi, moshi.*'

It was John Nakamura from the *Asahi Shimbun*'s Osaka office. 'Hiroko, we'll be broadcasting your voice live in two minutes.'

'Have you heard anything about my son?'

'Please speak only in English and describe exactly what's happened in Tokyo.'

'I told you I'm searching for Alex. That's all I'm interested in. If you want me to broadcast on my walk toward Shinjuku, fine – but I'll do so only if your team try to locate my son.'

'Hiroko, we're searching for him,' lied Nakamura. He had long given up his family life to pursue his journalistic career, and now lived alone. All he cared about was his story. Without her he had no live broadcast, no exclusive and no CNN. He had to appease her.

'Hiroko, I swear by all the gods that we're trying to find Alex. Now compose yourself, we're going live.'

Hiroko kicked off her black Ferragamo shoes, dug deep into her bag, pulled out her sneakers and put them on. A photo of Alex fluttered out of her wallet. Hiroko picked it up, kissed her son's face and put the photo in her shoe. Then she began walking west with her companion, Jiroo, towards Shinjuku, a journey which would normally take six hours on foot and might now take her more than a day.

It felt like dusk. No sunlight filtered through the smoke and dust and it was difficult to see. Screams and explosions filled the air.

'Hiroko, can you help me?' Jiroo's arm was still bleeding badly, having been caught on a jagged piece of the subway car. Hiroko bent down and tore off a piece of cloth from a woman's dress, wrapping it around Jiroo's arm.

'Hiroko, stand by to go live.'

She ignored Nakamura and finished tying off the bandage.

'Thanks. That's the second time today,' said Jiroo.

'Don't worry. You will be saving me before the day is over,' she replied. Then 'Okay . . . I'm ready,' she said to the voice in Osaka.

'Stand by,' said the *Asahi* editor down the line. 'Are you ready?'

'Yes.'

'You're sure?'

'Yes, I'm sure.'

'Okay, you're on.'

'Hello. My name is Hiroko Fujita and I am speaking from Tokyo, a city which 12 million people once called home. Most no longer have a home. The streets around me are filled with glass, concrete, cables, cars, poles and dead bodies. Buildings that have not collapsed look as if they are about to do so. Fifteen minutes ago I was on a train with over two hundred people. Now only a handful of us are alive. An earthquake has destroyed the city. I don't know how many people have died nor how bad the damage is elsewhere. Nor do we know how far the quake has spread. The greater Tokyo/Yokohama area is the largest concentration of humanity in the world, with over 34 million people. Judging from the rising smoke around the city, my guess is that death and damage are widespread.'

The earth began to shake again and Hiroko lost her balance. A powerful noise like a low-pitched electrical hum could be loudly heard. A live wire lay across the top of the metal subway car and was melting the contents of the carriage. The smell of human flesh rose.

Jiroo was the first to act and pushed Hiroko further away from the appalling sight and stench.

'It's ghastly,' she wept. 'Their faces are frozen in terror. Some have no faces or limbs.'

Hiroko was openly weeping. Millions of listeners around the world felt her anguish.

John Nakamura came on the line and tried to compose her.

'Hiroko, can you tell us – was the earthquake restricted to your area or was all of Tokyo hit?'

'Help me! Help!' came a voice from under three bodies lying in the street. A pool of blood was congealing next to them.

Hiroko tucked her phone into her belt and put her hand on the woman's head. The phone line was still open.

'Where are you hurt?'

'I don't know,' she moaned. 'I just feel sleepy.'

Hiroko propped the woman on to her chest. It was then that she and Jiroo spotted the pool of blood. The woman's legs had been sheared off, and two bloody stumps stuck out from under her dress. Hiroko breathed deeply, trying not to show fear, then looked into the woman's face.

There was a look of gentle sadness in her eyes. 'Please tell my son that I love him. I'm just going to have a little rest now.' Then her body went limp.

For the second time Hiroko wept. By now 30 million Japanese viewers elsewhere in the nation were tuned to Asahi's Channel 10, while CNN figured that the number of viewers had shot up to 100 million. Hiroko's live report was quickly tuned in to by heads of state around the globe. Offers of relief were made through Osaka, since there was no means of contacting anybody in Tokyo.

'Jiroo, please find out who she is so we can tell her son.'

He slipped the woman's handbag from her arm, took out her driver's licence and put it in his pocket.

The first thing that struck Hiroko as odd was that the roads – cracked, filled with toppled buildings, burning cars and live power lines – were filled with panic-stricken drivers attempting to get out of Tokyo. *What can these people be thinking?* Hiroko asked herself.

'This city's burning, the roads are impassable and I'm witnessing an attempted mass exodus, driven by fear. Drivers are waiting patiently in their cars for somebody to clear the road or direct traffic. They wait for help, yet they only wait for death. I'm proud to be Japanese . . . But sometimes I wonder at our nation's collective ability to process information . . . Yet it is the most absurdly polite panic – there isn't even the honking of a horn. If this were not sad, it would be comic. Don't get into your cars. There is nowhere to go. The risk of explosion and electrocution is high. I appeal to the authorities to turn off the electrical supply to Tokyo.'

But Hiroko was not the only live radio voice being broadcast in Tokyo. Although her telecast was the focus of the world, dozens of other stations had Satlink communications with survivors. This was more destructive and created more unease and confusion than anyone might have imagined. Each eye-witness was an island of misinformation.

'And now I see group of Koreans stripping a body for money,' reported one survivor over the radio. The Koreans had actually ripped off a man's jacket and torn open his shirt in an attempt to resuscitate him.

'The road near us in Shinjuku looks safe and traffic is now starting to move.' By some quirk of fate the solid bedrock of western Tokyo meant that some buildings and major roads were not damaged. This report sparked a wave of fleeing motorists, blocking some of the few fire and ambulance crews that had been able to get out and might have been able to save lives. The same radio station predicted that no more than two hundred people would have been killed in Tokyo and said that, from its vantage point in Shinjuku, damage appeared to be limited.

A third station reported that Tokyo Electric Power had cut off its main power grid and it was now safe to re-enter homes. Tokyo Electric Power had done no such thing, yet listening residents believed the report and put themselves at great risk as they tried to retrieve valuables.

An eye-witness on Tokyo Bay was confused by the damage. 'It looks as if a tsunami has hit the waterfront, with all the buildings demolished, boats overturned and water everywhere.' The man was standing near a boat repair yard where the boats in dry dock had been overturned. The presence of water was caused by the liquefaction of the waterfront, not by a tsunami. Those near the water panicked and, at great peril, fled inland.

Meanwhile, Hiroko and Jiroo were trying to survive their own dangers. They had finally figured out how to dodge live power cables, scouting ahead a distance of 5 metres. If they saw loose wires, flying sparks and a blackened roadside, they veered around the area.

The pair made for a hill in the distance and knew that the Imperial Palace lay ahead. They bypassed a taxi whose rear end lay in flames. The black, charred remains of the driver and a female passenger gave off a sweet, nauseating smell. Hiroko gagged. Then something caught her eye.

Crawling on the road was an infant. The baby's hands and knees were bleeding from cut glass and she was crying. Hiroko ran over and picked up the baby. It was a girl, no more than a year old. Still clasped in her hand was a pink rattle. Hiroko looked over at the taxi. Obviously, the mother's last act before being burned to death had been to open the door and set her daughter free. The mother had one leg outside the taxi. Hiroko tried to get closer to the flames to discover the mother's identity. She began vomiting after what she saw next. The mother had been trying to save two children. The first had escaped. The second was a newborn baby burned beyond recognition, still held deep in its mother's embrace.

CNN's viewership had now swollen to a quarter of a billion people – fed only by Hiroko's voice and visual back-up. But for a moment after this shocking experience there was no sound from Hiroko.

'Are you still with us, Hiroko?' asked Nakamura.

'Yes,' she said softly, not wishing to describe the scene. Instead she looked into her bag and found her water bottle. It was half full. Hiroko sparingly dabbed water on to the girl's hands to wash off the blood.

'We've found a little girl whose mother has died,' she continued. She paused and looked down at the baby. 'I'm calling this little girl Hope.'

The phone lines at CNN headquarters in Atlanta were instantly jammed. Later CNN calculated that over five thousand viewers wanted to adopt Hope. Their central switching system was designed to take over five hundred calls simultaneously, but the thousands of callers swamped the system, shutting it down for three hours.

Hiroko had no bandages, so ripped her Issey Miyake scarf into shreds. She wrapped the silk pieces gently around Hope's tiny hands and then they continued on their way to the Imperial Palace.

A wind had blown up, clearing the thick black smoke that enveloped Tokyo. Small fires, now flamed by the wind, spread, setting alight gas pipes and wooden houses. More explosions were heard. They climbed a hill and looked out over the city.

'Oh, my God!'

'Hiroko, Hiroko, what's wrong?' asked her Osaka editor.

It took a moment before she could speak. 'Tokyo is completely destroyed.' She let the words sink in and composed herself. 'Our view from just east of the Emperor's Palace is one of complete devastation. I'm reminded of my grandfather's recollection of the US fire-bombing of Tokyo in 1945, the worst single slaughter of people in the history of mankind. We have no way of determining how many have died today, but we are witnessing one of history's great tragedies.'

Hiroko was now playing the role of correspondent. Watching the city, however, she found it difficult to choke back her fears for Alex. She and Jiroo were still a kilometre from the Imperial Palace's east garden.

Those gardens were anything but calm. The forecourt garden of the Imperial Palace was one of 134 Special Evacuation Areas, or SEAs, open to refugees.

Residents of the city's financial district and other areas without parkland had no escape from the fire. Even in the evacuation areas little food and water had been stored away and, though these places acted as havens, one became a deathtrap.

The people of Sumida in eastern Tokyo knew that their only refuge from fire lay in a local park that served as a firebreak. There was little panic. Residents took time to carry out furniture and family treasures at an unhurried pace. Those who had first taken refuge in the park, jealous of those who had retrieved belongings, went back home to recover what they could. At one o'clock the fires that had been raging in the downtown area of Nihonbashi merged with those of Sumida and leapt across the 200-metre-wide Sumida River. There was still little panic in nearby Sumida Park.

As the flames approached the park, more and more residents jammed into the Special Evacuation Area. The crowds swelled to thousands and then to tens of thousands. By two o'clock the whole area was a jostling mass of sixty thousand refugees laden with furniture and baggage. Meanwhile, the flames from Asakusa, to the north-west, leaped the Sumida River and merged with the fires from Nihonbashi. The Special Evacuation Area was now under attack from three sides.

Fire has the characteristic of being drawn towards other fires. A super-heated vacuum was formed in the air between and above the fires, creating a dry wind that sucked the flames together, torching everything in their path. The thousands trapped in the supposedly 'safe' area realized the horror of their plight. A hot, burning whirlwind emerged from the wall of flame and swept across the ground, raining down burning cinders on the screaming thousands. The furniture and baggage caught alight. Giant, blazing thermals sucked up individual refugees high into the air and spat them out as charcoal corpses hundreds of metres away. All but a few of the tens of thousands who had sought refuge in the government Special Evacuation Area perished.

Hiroko could see nothing of this horror a few kilometres to the east as she looked down on the Palace Gardens. Streams of injured and frightened shoppers from Ginza, businessmen from Marunouchi and bureaucrats from Kasumigaseki had fled to the outer gardens. From the hilltop above, Hiroko noticed an absence of billowing smoke in the Palace. Every other part of Tokyo was now enveloped in fire.

By 11.30, three hours after the quake, Hiroko's group arrived outside the East Garden. The headquarters of the *Mainichi* newspaper, which bordered the gardens, had collapsed.

'We're now at the Imperial Palace,' she reported, 'which seems from here to be the only place of safety in Tokyo.'

Although the broadcast was live, Hiroko asked about Alex in front of half a billion listeners. 'Nakamura-san, any word about my son yet?'

The Osaka editor was flustered.

'Not yet. Our Asahi crew is still trying to find news of his school.'

'Please, John, I need to find my son. You promised.'

'We'll find him, Hiroko, don't worry. We've had two people searching for him,' said Nakamura, glib as ever. He aimed for the mute button on his phone and then called over one of his assistants. 'Look, I forgot to have somebody check on Hiroko's son. This woman is giving me a headache. Get her off my back and have somebody make their way over to the Mitaka primary school. His name is Alex Fujita. I don't have a picture of him, but see what you can do.' The problem was that Nakamura had hit the memory button of his handset instead of the mute button. Hiroko and half a billion listeners heard the conversation.

'You son of a bitch!' she yelled down the phone. Hiroko always used American expressions when she was angry.

'Fujita-san, I . . .'

'Be quiet! I kept my end of the bargain and I'm broadcasting for you. Now you keep yours.' Millions of listeners were cheering Hiroko, who now decided to take matters into her own hands.

Only a block from the JMA headquarters, she led Jiroo and Hope along the perimeter of the Imperial Palace, past the subway station to the Japan Meteorological Building. Thousands of refugees were fighting their way into the gardens, and they were going against the flow. The east-facing side of the JMA building was ripped apart. Hiroko ignored her editor and began broadcasting again.

'I'm reminded of the Oklahoma City Federal Building blown up by a terrorist bomb in 1995. It's as if some unseen force, wielding a dull knife, had dissected the building. Workers are visible, dead in their chairs and lying over their desks. Steel-reinforced rods and concrete hang down. Papers are everywhere. There's no fire.'

World viewers, although still without visual hook-up, were captivated by Hiroko's vivid description.

'The JMA headquarters is the centre for seismological research and its nerve centre is the earthquake command centre on the second floor. The satellite media links and TV cameras enable the director general, and, if necessary, the Prime Minister, to address the nation.

We're making our way into the building now. If we're successful we may be able to give listeners a visual hook-up.'

Actually Hiroko had little concern about the visual convenience of world viewing audiences. She had other plans . . .

The west entrance was relatively unblocked. They fought their way past refugees and into the lobby, which was, surprisingly, dimly lit. Then Hiroko remembered the back-up generator system in the basement. The JMA used a series of emergency generators called a Unitary Power System, which in keeping with the Japanese love of acronyms they referred to as the 'UPS'. The group made their way up the western staircase to the second floor. Light from the generators guided them through the hallway. Boxes and toppled cabinets littered the floor. They went past the Earthquake Phenomena Observation System, known as the EPOS room. Now the room was devastated and nothing seemed to be functioning. Three men lay slumped in their chairs.

Hiroko heard a rustling of paper and peered into the EPOS room. There on the floor sat Dr Tokai, the only survivor of the Six Wise Men, oblivious to the destruction around him. He was poring over sheets of seismological data which had earlier spewed continuously from the machine. The sheets covered the floor like old-fashioned ticker tape gone wild.

'Dr Tokai?'

He paused in his analysis. 'Huh? Oh, oh, hello there.' Tokai popped to his feet like the Scarecrow in *The Wizard of Oz* and bowed to Hiroko. 'What are you doing here?' he asked.

'We're looking for the audio-visual hook-up. And you?'

'Looking over data. I guess I'm the only one of the Six Wise Men to have made it.'

'We're heading toward the command centre. Can you help us?'

Tokai was like a child who could not put down his toys. He pulled the paper from the seismometer and began rolling up the sheets. 'Okay, just give me a minute,' he said. After he had finished, he ripped a few pieces of paper from an overturned machine.

'Let's go. But first let's see about Dr Hamada.' Hamada had given Hiroko the interview at the JMA earlier.

They climbed over debris and several bodies strewn in the EPOS room, making their way to Hamada's corner office. Jiroo had to clear away some boxes before they could proceed.

Hamada was seated at his desk, staring blankly at the wall.

'Dr Hamada,' started Hiroko before recoiling in horror.

The man had been severed at the torso by the thick sheet of glass that had covered his desk. She turned away and left the room. Tokai was staring at Hamada. *What folly. Hamada should have known better.* The post-quake analysis of the Kobe disaster clearly indicated the dangers of glass desk-tops. Shockwaves sent objects, including human bodies, travelling horizontally at over 300 kilometres an hour.

They proceeded down the corridor to the command centre, with Jiroo carrying Hope. The ante-room was topsy-turvy – all the lockers and cabinets installed for the Six Wise Men had fallen over. Hiroko made her way into the committee room, where the emergency lights were on. The room was dishevelled but not seriously damaged. The giant NEC multi-screen had fallen, but the TV equipment stored in a cabinet underneath was undamaged. She started giving orders.

'We're going to set up a TV studio. See if those TV backlights are hooked up.'

She pulled the cameras out of their metal luggage containers. Jiroo handed Hope to the old man and helped Hiroko.

'What's a backlight?' he asked.

Hiroko showed him.

'Now hook them up to the UPS system.'

'What's a UPS system?'

'The power supply.'

'Dr Tokai, can you tell us how to hook the cameras up for broadcast?' asked Hiroko.

Tokai pointed to a plug which was labelled: 'Simultaneous broadcast: national media'.

The backlights suddenly lit up and startled Hope, who began to cry. Hiroko dug into her bag, pulled out the water bottle and gave it to Tokai. The old man put a drop of water on Hope's tongue, but the baby wouldn't stop crying. Tokai took her into the ante-room where, as he had expected, he found some rice crackers among the supplies in the overturned lockers. Soon the pair returned, Hope's cries subsiding as she happily gnawed away at a cracker.

Hiroko, meanwhile, had handed the portable video camera to Jiroo. 'Hold this portable camera at eye level,' she instructed, standing in front of the TV lights. 'I'll tell you when to start recording.'

Jiroo lifted up the camera and focused on Hiroko, who took a deep breath and then nodded. Jiroo pressed the red record button.

Hiroko was now on Japanese national television via satellite hook-up. Though nobody in Tokyo could watch since there was no electricity, Hiroko estimated there were another hundred million viewers elsewhere in Japan who could.

Hiroko reached into her bag and pulled out a picture of Alex.

Her hands caked with blood, she held the Satlink phone close to her mouth. First she spoke Japanese, then translated it into English. 'My name is Hiroko Fujita. Many of you have been listening to my broadcasts on the Tokyo quake.'

Japanese viewers were shocked at Hiroko's appearance. They were used to middle-aged male presenters, always well groomed. Now they were staring at a young woman with tangled hair and torn clothes. Black soot covered her face, while blood from the woman whom she had tried to save smeared her silk blouse. Viewers could even pick out Hope's tiny bloody handprints on Hiroko's shoulder. A woman's customary role on Japanese TV was to smile sweetly and sell detergent, chocolate, deodorant and vacuum cleaners.

Jiroo was a novice cameraman and had been instructed to focus on Hiroko's head and shoulders. But he inadvertently kept moving the camera. Her skirt was gashed and torn in front, exposing her upper thigh. Some male viewers who had just tuned in found this erotic and, still not aware of the seriousness of the earthquake, looked upon Hiroko's telecast as some sort of sensuous, beach-wrecked publicity stunt. The seriousness of the quake, however, was about to be revealed.

The strain of the past three hours had at last become too much for Hiroko, who began to crack on camera. 'Please, I must find my son Alexander Fujita. He's eight years old and goes to Mitaka primary school.' Weeping now, she took out the little boy's picture. 'This is my son. Please help me find him. The *Asahi Shimbun* Osaka office can contact me. Thank you for listening to my plea.'

Back in the Asahi offices in Osaka, John Nakamura was fuming. Calls had already been coming in asking why Nakamura had not been more diligent in looking for Alex. Now Hiroko had usurped the Japanese airwaves to find her son. Nakamura was directly responsible for Hiroko's quake broadcasts and was getting worried about keeping his job.

His fears ended sixty seconds later. CNN were on the line: they wanted a visual hook-up to Hiroko's broadcasts. Another million-dollar fee was agreed. CNN had Hiroko on air within thirty seconds. There was a five-second delay between her telecast and CNN's broadcast to the world, but CNN called it live anyway. Atlanta computer graphics specialists quickly choreographed a series of background visuals entitled 'THE TOKYO QUAKE' with the words written in a vibrating manner, the 'E' of 'QUAKE' falling off the earth. A haunting sound bite from Wagner's *Götterdämmerung* accompanied the visual lead-in.

By the time Hiroko had finished her plea for Alex, CNN were 'live'. She continued: 'Some of you have heard of the little girl we found.' She motioned for Tokai to bring her over. 'This is Hope. Her mother and little brother are dead. If you know her family, please contact the Asahi Osaka office.'

Hope squinted as she looked into the bright camera lights, then broke out in a smile and shook her rattle. Viewers could see the makeshift bandages over her bloodstained hands. Hiroko gave her a kiss and handed her back to Tokai. Then she began speaking rapidly in Japanese.

'If anybody in Tokyo is listening over the radio, my advice is this: think for yourselves. Don't wait for help.'

Nakamura tried to interrupt, to force Hiroko to speak English, but she ignored him. She had to get her message across to Tokyo listeners.

'Those of you who act on instinct will survive – those who wait for instructions from government or rescue organizations will wait in vain. The fire department isn't coming. The police aren't coming. Your city doesn't exist any more . . . Don't get into your cars. Most importantly, don't go inside your home or any building. The gas pipes and electricity supply may not have been switched off, and if you're using a candle or lantern the risk of explosions is high. If you're in need of water in central Tokyo, go to the Imperial Moat. Its water isn't fresh, but the ruptured sewage pipes don't seem to have polluted it.'

Nakamura finally managed to break in to tell her of their global TV audience. Hiroko seized the opportunity.

'I'm begging all international governments who want to send aid not to wait for the Japanese government to respond to your offers. We are unsure whether the government actually exists, and too many people are dead or dying for you to wait for authorization.'

She caught her breath.

'This quake is one of the worst tragedies ever to befall Japan. As a journalist, I recognize that preliminary estimates of damage and death are always low. Nobody is ever sure how serious a situation is. We need your help. On behalf of Japan I formally request your assistance.'

In Osaka, John Nakamura was going wild. Asahi was certainly going to fire him. One of his journalists was live on world television soliciting international aid on behalf of the government. TV ratings continued to soar, however, and Hiroko was doing just fine. Dr Tokai, meanwhile, had been examining his roll of seismological data. Hiroko called him over.

'This is Dr Tokai, a world-famous seismologist, professor emeritus at Tokyo University, and a member of the six-man Earthquake Assessment Committee. In Japan we call them the Six Wise Men,' stated Hiroko. 'How bad was the quake, Dr Tokai?'

'Hmm. This data shows that the first shock wave at 8.26 a.m. measured 8.6 on the Richter scale.'

'What does this mean in terms of damage?'

'Very few buildings will be left standing in Tokyo.'

Tokai shuffled loudly through his papers. 'The acceleration of the shock waves measured 1200 centimetres per second per second.'

'What does that mean exactly?'

'Most buildings would have been wiped out with half or a third of this acceleration.'

'And do you have any advice for listeners in the Tokyo area, or do you need to contact any members of the EAC or Prime Minister's office?'

Tokai surprised Hiroko by launching into an anti-government tirade. 'No. Earthquake prediction is a joke. Impossible. Earthquakes are a part of non-linear physics, which means controlled analysis of their impact is beyond human comprehension. For years our government has convinced the Japanese people that it could forewarn residents of a big quake. Billions have been spend in this effort,' said Tokai.

He was now on a roll, and Hiroko let him talk on.

'We Six Wise Men secretly called this the Great Lie. It kept the fabric of Japanese society intact. The earth and sea around Tokyo are wired with sensing equipment. Tokyo itself is wired with loudspeakers to warn of impending disasters. All this supports the Great Lie. Nobody can predict an earthquake far enough ahead to warn people. Our entire nation has been lulled into complacency. We worked and played, unaware of the dangers which lurked under Tokyo. If our government had come out and stated that a great quake was a certainty, our lives would have been different. The Great Lie meant we could build elevated highways through our city instead of building them on ground level with broad avenues. Our buildings could have been built lower and further apart. All buildings could have been constructed on top of a rubber shock absorber. Power cables could have all run through underground tubing. Nobody would have worked or lived on reclaimed land. A replacement for glass would have been found. Aren't we Japanese supposed to be the most innovative people on earth? Why must we only invent electronic gadgets for money? We churn out futuristic transistors, Walkmans, cars, cameras and compact discs, yet we can't even protect our own people.'

Dr Tokai had run out of breath. He realized he had overstepped the bounds of protocol and waited to be reprimanded. Instead Hiroko and her viewing audience had been captivated by the truth of his words. Nobody had ever dared voice such an opinion before.

Hiroko broke the silence. 'Dr Tokai, do you have any advice for us?'

'No. It's too late for advice. The dead cannot be brought back to life. There is only one thing to do now: find food and water. Do not under any circumstances enter a building. There will be as many as a thousand aftershocks in the next week. In fact we'd better get out of this building now,' said Tokai, gathering up his papers.

Hiroko took over. 'I'll continue to report as I make my way to find my son. Given the mass destruction of the quake and the large numbers of refugees migrating to the Palace grounds, we'll try and travel through the main Palace. We'll then see if the Parliament building and ministries are still standing to determine whether Japan's government is operable.' She found a remote transmitter and hooked up a medium-range receiver to the broadcasting console. 'We will film as we walk,' said Hiroko.

Once outside the building, Jiroo panned the JMA's emergency camera on the thousands of Japanese fleeing towards the Palace. The team were swept away by the crowd.

24

LITTLE BUDDHA

Tuesday morning at the home of Master Wa

'Believers who donated over $2000 received the best prize of all: two gallons of Shoko Asahara's dirty bathwater.'
From David Kaplan's *The Cult at the End of the World*, describing how easy it was for cults such as Aum Supreme Truth to blossom in Japan

Master Wa was furiously tapping away at his Mac keyboard when he heard the first rumblings of the seismic 'P'wave. Fingers glued to the keyboard, Wa hit 'S' for 'save', 'Q' for 'quit' and 'E' for 'eject' in rapid succession. A whirring noise ejected his disk. He stuffed it in his shirt pocket just before the secondary wave ripped through his home three seconds later. The last thing Wa remembered was grabbing his Satphone.

Wa's study resembled an air traffic control monitor, with projectiles flying through space at various altitudes and speeds. Ordinary household objects had become missiles: the Apple Mac flew 2 metres before exploding on to the floor, a glass-framed picture of Wa shattered and then hurtled across the room like a Ninja death star. A bookcase bolted to the wall and laden with hundreds of books on philosophy, religion, economics and history jumped into the air and then hopped forward before toppling. A decorative vase hit Wa on the head and knocked him out cold.

The day of the quake was an important milestone in Wa's career, not just because he had prophesied it but because he had just completed his most important book. Unable to sleep, he had been beavering away on *The New World Order* since 5 a.m. He often flicked on his Mac at four or five in the morning and, trance-like, could write for six hours without a break. *The New World Order* described how the evils of pornography, government, false religion and materialism would be eradicated by a great earthquake. A spiritually bankrupt public would flock to Happy Science and the frenzy would spread to other nations, creating the world's fifth major religion.

Wa had worked at a feverish pace to ensure that *The New World Order* would be on the shelves by July, a remarkable feat. Japan had one of the world's fastest turnaround times in publishing. While it took anywhere from one to three years to get a concept into print in the West, in Japan it took a matter of weeks.

Wa wrote on the most powerful graphic/text computer in the world, a Power Mac 71/80 with 80 megahertz clock speed. A lightning-quick response time in commenting on world events had brought Happy Science waves of new followers. Gas attacks, earthquakes, tsunamis, bombings, local wars – any disaster served as fodder to boost membership. The word was spread through Happy Science's weekly magazine and through quick-release books. The stunning rise in the number of Wa's followers – from 10,000 in 1989 to 10 million at the time of the quake – was due to the development of desk top publishing.

A book could now be typeset, printed, bound and distributed in eight days rather than eight months. The Kobe earthquake was a perfect example. Two months after the quake, Happy Science had a paperback on the shelves which outlined what had happened and described preventative measures for similar future occurrences. The public scooped up the book.

When Master Wa came to ten minutes later he did not even bother checking the damage to his home. His family were safe in Osaka where they were visiting relatives. The quake was a signal, and Wa had to act. Passing what looked like the morning after a wild party, he picked his way carefully to the front door. It had been ripped off its hinges, so Wa stepped into the street. An aftershock rocked the ground, knocking Wa to his knees. *The earth is still angry. I must act.*

He dialled his Osaka office.

'*Moshi, moshi*,' answered a pleasant female voice.

'This is Wa. Put me through to Haruma, please.'

Down in Osaka the receptionist bowed into the phone, convinced that Wa had supernatural powers and could witness her every move. 'Yes, *sensei*.'

The phone rang internally and his Osaka chief picked up.

'*Haruma desu.*'

'This is Wa. My prophecy of a major quake has been fulfilled.'

'Congratulations, *sensei*.'

Wa looked around at the damage to his street. 'Tokyo is heavily damaged. Please listen carefully. I want our public relations team to meet at our Osaka headquarters. Our printing company is to be on standby to print my book. Remember our Kobe exercise? Volunteers are to be called throughout Japan in the name of Happy Science to assist in rescue operations. I need transport to Osaka immediately.'

'Yes, *sensei*. But how can we – ?' Wa interrupted.

'We have two helicopters. One in Tokyo which is likely to be damaged, and one with you. Have the pilot meet me at the Yasukuni shrine in three hours.'

Wa hung up.

The Yasukuni shrine and park lay only four blocks away. Wa did not bother searching for food or water. All he needed was the manuscript for *The New World Order*, which was stored on the disk in his shirt pocket. Wa walked there in a trance, feeling his way through the rubble and oblivious to the screams around him. *They have paid for their sins*.

The chopper picked up Wa at noon.

'Sorry I'm late, *sensei*,' apologized the pilot over the roar of the blades.

After handing the religious leader a set of headphones so that they could talk over the intercom, the pilot explained. 'The yakuza leaders in Osaka are searching Kansai for helicopters, paying over 10 million yen to borrow them for two days. We had to fight off Yamaguchi-gumi members just to take off at the airport.'

They will pay, thought Wa. A battle had been looming for years between the conservative religious leader and Japan's underworld. In Wa's opinion, the yakuza were the primary reason for the Kobe quake purging the earth of evil: for over a century the Osaka/Kobe area had been a centre for gambling, prostitution and pornography. The gang leaders of Hanshin had easily manipulated the Japanese and foreign press as yakuza gang members had been photographed off-loading rescue supplies to Kobe victims. Their pillaging of abandoned homes had gone unrecorded except by Master Wa, and now the yakuza were out to get him.

Wa pointed skyward. The pilot took off.

'Where's the phone jack?'

The pilot switched the headphones from 'intercom' to 'phone'. Wa dialled the Osaka office again.

'Can we land on the Happy Science building to avoid the yakuza at the airport?'

'Sssssss. I'll try, *sensei*.'

Wa hung up. The Happy Science Osaka headquarters had a beer garden on the roof. Haruma realized that his master's question was not a request and had his staff tear down the fake Bavarian trelliswork, the colourful plastic banners and tubs of flowers.

Two hours later Wa landed and walked straight to the permanent office he kept.

'Are the printers ready?'

'Yes. Toppan Printing have their modem line cleared for your transmission.'

Wa flicked on his Mac, waited ten seconds and then inserted his disk. He opened *The New World Order* file, turned on his Comstation modem and pressed 'E-World'.

E-World requested the e-mail address to which he was sending the manuscript. Wa tapped in Toppan Printing's identification number.

Two circles came up on the screen. Wa smiled. He had requested this high-security service from E-World. There were two options: security access code required for retrieval, and open retrieval. Wa now chose the security option. Almost all the Internet mail services posed security risks. Hackers took less than five minutes to enter the main mail box of CompuServe, Prodigy and American On-line, but Wa's data would be safe.

Wa hit SEND. Thirty seconds later the four-hundred-page document was being downloaded to Toppan Printing's pre-press unit. One of Toppan's graphic design experts laid out the text, while another began quickly drawing sketches to appear in the book, for which Wa had left blank pages. An artist designed the jacket.

The Happy Science public relations team went into high gear. Copywriters churned out leaflets explaining temporary survival techniques, outlining emergency services in Tokyo and asking residents to consider forward planning after the shock wore off. These leaflets were airdropped over the Imperial Palace and other evacuation centres. Wa took charge of the entire operation.

'First, I want translators to take the text of my book and translate it into English, Spanish, Mandarin, Hindi, German and French. They have a week. This quake is going to take us global.'

Toppan's pre-press unit now sent Master Wa's book internally on disk to a Komori high-speed web printing machine, which read a digital imprint and downloaded it on to another Apple. A machine operator on the Komori press pushed a few buttons: the data was fed digitally to an electronic make-up system and imposed directly on to a laser imaging device. These plates were strapped to the printing press cylinders in the form of a new technology called Laser Optical Recognition, or LORE, which shot a laser directly on to the paper. The book was printed in sections of thirty-two and sixty-four pages and spat out at the end of the printing machine in stapled sections. From these they were sent to the bindery, to be bound with hot glue and have eight-colour, glossy covers attached. Within eight days, Toppan Printing would send a 200,000 print run to Japanese bookshops. Japan published books like it built cars and electronics – quickly and efficiently.

Wa's new book, like his previous ones, would then get rammed down the throats of consumers through thousands of bookshops and newsagents. *The New World Order* would be on sale everywhere except in Tokyo, where Happy Science volunteers would hand out free copies.

Playing on the public's superstition was easy for Master Wa. After all, many of Japan's inhabitants still believed that deities existed behind every rock and tree, so convincing them to appease the gods by converting to his religious sect was easy. This was a public that believed the 1923 earthquake had been caused by Japan's enemies, who had supposedly invented a giant earthquake machine.

But Master Wa had bigger plans than just taking over the nation's lost souls. He wanted to become a global icon. This earthquake was his chance, and he began plotting his next move.

25

THE WAVE

Monday evening, Salomon Brothers' world headquarters

'*That* is fuckin' awesome. I mean *fuckin*' awesome. I *fuckin*' mean fucking awesome. You are one Big Swinging Dick, and don't ever let anyone tell you different.'

The head of Salomon's bond trading department to Michael Lewis, author of *Liar's Poker*, after Lewis stuffed a French client with $86 million of unwanted bonds

The black limousines were parked outside Salomon Brothers' Broad Street headquarters in lower Manhattan. The drivers chatted, smoked and stubbed their butts out in the gutter as they waited to chauffeur top management to their homes in Greenwich, Far Hills and the upper East Side. It was 7 p.m.

Once a week the eight members of the Salomon management committee met in the firm's oak-panelled board room to decide on policy, strategy and problem-solving. The meeting had just broken up when a trader named Ralph Gazinsky burst into the meeting uninvited.

'Turn on CNN! Quick!' he yelled in panic.

Gazinsky traded Japanese government bonds, so his working day began at six in the evening and ended fourteen hours later to fit in with Japanese time. After this brief outburst he rushed out of the room again.

Derek Hunt, the Salomon chief executive, flicked a remote control and CNN came on. It was 9 a.m. in Tokyo and Hiroko Fujita had just begun her live, voice-only broadcasts. A 'still' frame of a Japanese city engulfed in flames and smoke appeared on the screen. The caption said 'Tokyo', but the photo was from the CNN archives of the Kobe disaster.

Hiroko's voice filled the room. '. . . I'm naming this little girl Hope.'

'Gee, that's sad,' mocked one of the executives, feigning tears.

'And I call my prick Herman. Let's get the fuck out of here and head home.'

He was heading for the door when Alanda Voltaria of CNN came on the screen. Voltaria was a blonde, and he had a weakness for them.

'Awwooo, Awwooo,' he howled like a wolf. 'Boy, I'd like to get her lips around Herman.' Such conduct was acceptable at Salomon Brothers and, indeed, almost mandatory.

'This is Alanda Voltaria reporting from CNN in Atlanta. The eyes of the world are on Tokyo where a massive earthquake has just hit Japan's capital. Initial reports indicate the tremor registered 8.6 on the Richter scale.'

Video footage came up with the subtitle 'file'.

'What the fuck?'

'Shut up,' said Hunt. 'Listen to what she's saying.'

'We have no indications of the death toll yet and damage is unknown. A CNN team headed by our roving anchorman Craig Huntley is on its way to Tokyo. Until then Hiroko Fujita, our Tokyo correspondent, will keep us updated with exclusive live coverage.'

Everyone began talking at once.

'Holy shit.'

'8.6 is enormous!'

'How big was San Francisco?'

'What the fuck is this? Jeopardy?'

'I'll take Earthquakes and Natural Disasters for 100.'

'Everyone *shut up*!' yelled their chief executive. The room fell quiet.

'We have Dr John Bailey on the line, a seismologist from the University of California at Berkeley. Dr Bailey, can you speculate about the impact of this quake on Tokyo?'

'At 8.6 on the Richter scale this is by far the largest earthquake ever to hit mainland Japan. It would be comparable to dropping a small nuclear bomb in an urban area,' said Dr Bailey.

'Can you explain the Richter scale for our viewers?'

'Charles Richter invented the scale in 1933 after journalists kept pestering him to compare various earthquakes. It measures the magnitude of an earthquake by analysing seismic energy released by disruption of rocks deep within the earth. A quake registering 7 generates seismic waves having ten times the amplitude and 30 times the energy of a quake registering 6. To put this in perspective, this quake released 500 times more energy than the 1989 San Francisco quake. The Japanese have a different scale called the Shindo scale, which rates earthquakes non-scientifically on the basis of intensity 1 to 7. This was 7 out of 7.'

'Can you give us an idea what damage can be expected?' pressed Voltaria.

'Few buildings will have withstood the impact. The death toll will be very high.'

'Can you hazard a guess?'

'Hundreds . . . no, thousands, maybe even tens of thousands will have been killed.'

'Get on the fucking blower to Tokyo!' yelled Derek Hunt. Hunt had made his reputation by running the Tokyo office some years ago. It had a very low staff turnover and Hunt knew many of the employees on a first-name basis.

Someone tapped on the speaker phone and hit the direct dial code for Tokyo.

The phone droned dead in the background.

'Redial,' ordered Hunt.

'Dr Bailey, what was the world's worst earthquake?' asked the CNN interviewer, knowing that viewers enjoyed disaster details.

'Tangshan, China, in 1976. Over 750,000 Chinese died, though the government doctored the figures and only reported a quarter of a million deaths.'

'We're talking about huge numbers of lives. Is there a precedent for a quake of this magnitude in Japan?' pressed Voltaria.

'Yes,' replied Bailey, shuffling papers. 'The 1923 Great Kanto earthquake registered 7.9 and killed nearly 150,000 people. All the other quakes over 8 took place offshore and generated tsunamis close to 30 metres high. This quake could be as bad as the one in 1923.'

'By tsunami you mean a tidal wave? You're saying Japan can expect tidal waves from this earthquake?'

'No, not necessarily. If the epicentre was under Tokyo Bay, then the damage might occur in California or South America.'

'What! I've got a fucking property in Malibu,' yelled one of the executives.

'You're saying a tidal wave might endanger the California coastline?'

Voltaria had a hint of scepticism in her voice. Although CNN was telecast globally, the commentators tried to find an American angle to every story. Parochialism reigned, even at CNN. A quake had just wiped out Tokyo and CNN was analysing its impact on America.

'A giant wave *is* possible. When the coast of Chile was struck by an 8.5 earthquake in 1960, 6-metre waves hit the Japanese coast

10,000 kilometres away twenty-two hours later. We might expect the same here in California,' said Bailey.

Within seconds, phone calls from desperate California home-owners were swamping the CNN switchboard, wanting to know when the wave would hit. The switchboard was already overloaded from listeners wishing to adopt Hope. Within thirty minutes, traffic jams blocked coastal routes inland from San Francisco, Los Angeles and San Diego. It was an exodus that only paranoid Californians could stage. Unfortunately TV and radio editors were unwilling to refute the tsunami warning outright, since the possibility did exist. The media were worried that, if they refuted the warning and a wave did hit, they would attract massive liability claims.

Voltaria continued, unaware of the mass panic the well-meaning doctor had initiated. 'Well, thank you, Dr Bailey, a seismologist from Berkeley who warns California, 'Watch out, the surf's up.' As soon as we have an update on the severity of the Tokyo quake, we will report. Meanwhile back to Hiroko Fujita, a quake survivor reporting exclusively for CNN.'

'Try the Osaka office,' commanded Hunt of the man who was failing to get Tokyo. It was busy.

'Try again and keep trying till you get through.'

The executive hit the automatic redial button and went to pour himself four fingers of Chivas in a Lalique tumbler.

'Bring over the whole bottle,' someone yelled.

Japan was the main source of Salomon profits and therefore of executive bonuses. The committee were worried.

Finally, on the fourteenth attempt, the phone rang. 'Yeah, got 'em,' shouted the executive as if he had just scored the winning touchdown in the Super Bowl. It was now 9.15 a.m. in Japan.

'*Moshi, moshi. Salomon Brothers de gozaimasu,*' answered the receptionist.

'Speak fucking English,' shouted one executive.

The receptionist was flustered.

'Hey, cut the shit,' ordered Hunt, who, having lived in Japan, didn't appreciate his colleagues' cultural barbarism. He took over.

'*Moshi, moshi. Derek Hunt desu. Tanaka san onegaishimasu.*' Hunt had identified himself and asked for the branch manager, Mr Tanaka.

'Just a moment, please,' she said, putting him through.

The Salomon chief spoke in English. 'Tanaka-san, this is Derek Hunt from New York. What's going on? We hear there's been an earthquake in Tokyo.'

'Ah so. Quake very big. Very bad. Maybe 8 on Richter scale.'

'Eight point six,' shouted a chorus of executives. It did not sound as if Tanaka was going to be a fount of timely information. Salomon Brothers' executives were information junkies.

'So what's the damage?' asked Hunt.

'Mmmm. Maybe not so good.'

Hunt knew that to a Japanese this meant very bad.

'How bad?'

'Very bad.'

'How very bad?'

'Hmmm. Maybe Salomon Tokyo building not standing.'

'What the fuck do you mean – our building might not be standing?'

Hunt was frustrated that no facts were available. He hated not being in control of a situation.

'Well then, can you tell me our exposure?'

The Osaka office kept back-up records of all trading done for the Tokyo office.

'So. Hmm. Morning report say we own 220 billion yen of Japanese government bonds and 17 billion yen in Japanese shares. We also short 20,000 Osaka futures contracts,' read Tanaka from a computer printout.

'What's that in real money?' shouted a New York-based board member.

'Over 2 billion dollars in bonds and 170 million in stocks,' replied Tanaka. Salomon Brothers was in the business of running massive stock and bond positions for its own trading account, but even this amount was staggering and set the board room into chaos.

'Shit.'

'Fuck me.'

'There goes our bonus.'

'Jesus fucking Christ, I just bought a third house in Palm Beach. I thought the bonus was in the bag.'

The Salomon chief took control again. 'Fax me the printout. When will the markets reopen?'

'Ssssss. The Tokyo Stock Exchange might not reopen.'

'Tanaka-san, I want you to call me back with details of how long the Tokyo Stock Exchange was closed after the Great Kanto earthquake in 1923. There's got to be a precedent.'

'Hai.'

'Keep us posted,' he finished, tapping off the speaker phone. Then 'Get me that trader. Now!' yelled Hunt.

The man came running in a moment later.

'What's your name?' asked the chief executive.

'Gazinsky. Ralph Gazinsky.'

'Okay, Ralph. The other traders have gone home, so you listen closely. You're in charge of liquidating our Japanese exposure. We've got 220 billion yen in Japanese government bonds. Find out which ones and bang 'em the fuck out. Call up your buddies at Merrill and try to stuff them. Next, I want you to sell all our fuckin' Japanese stocks. Take any discount you need to sell this shit,' ordered the Salomon boss.

'Gotcha,' said Ralph, already halfway through the door.

'Hang on, Gazinsky. What do we do about our 20,000 short contracts in Osaka?'

Ralph smiled. 'It's Salomon's lucky day. The stock market's gonna get hammered when it opens – if it opens,' he said, starting to leave the room again.

'Hey, Gazinsky.'

'Yeah,' said Ralph, turning again.

'Don't fuck up.'

There was a moment of silence, then he nodded and ran off.

Salomon's eight almighty leaders waited in the board room like schoolchildren. The last thing they needed was a quarter billion-dollar write-off. They opened a second bottle of Chivas.

'Shouldn't we tell our drivers we'll be late?'

'Fuck them, that's what they get paid for. The longer they wait, the more they make.'

Ralph ran to his desk and flicked his direct line to Merrill Lynch. His hands were trembling.

'Hello,' answered the Merrill trader.

Salomon's central tape recorder began rolling.

Ralph knew that the Merrill Lynch trader had heard of the earthquake and played it cool. 'Need a bid for 99s in size. Any action?' he asked.

Ralph and Jimmy had been out drinking the previous evening. Ralph knew that Merrill Lynch thought Japanese interest rates were going to increase. Merrill had a massive short position in the Japanese government bond market and had to buy the bonds back some time.

'Well,' Jimmy started to say.

Sensing that he was vacillating, Ralph went for the throat. 'Jimbo, I'll give you sunshine on your position. Low bid me for 2200 bars of 99,' asked Ralph, who was now sweating. He downed a mouthful of Evian and wished he had a bottle of the Chivas they were swilling in the board room. He had asked the Merrill Lynch trader to buy 2.2 billion dollars' worth of Japanese government bonds due in 1999.

'Well . . .'

'Listen, Jimbo, I'm over my limits for the third time. I gotta knock this shit out or compliance'll have my ass,' lied Ralph.

Wall Street's traders were all given trading limits, and in fits of inspired exuberance over-extended themselves. This had driven the toothless compliance departments crazy in the 1980s, and by the 1990s they were able to fire traders for irregularities.

This sales pitch struck a chord in Jimmy, who was weighing up other factors in deciding whether to buy the bonds from Salomon Brothers. The two traders rented a beach-house together in Easthampton on Long Island. Ralph had introduced Jimmy to 'wicked' Wanda, a Salomon groupie who worked for a third-tier Wall Street broker. Unknown to Jimmy, Wanda was known as the Salomon house slut, whose motto was 'so many men and only one pussy'. The Merrill trader was thankful to Ralph for getting him laid the previous weekend, so Jimmy decided to buy the bonds as a favour.

Having decided to commit $2.2 billion of Merrill Lynch's money based on friendship, alcohol and sex, Jimmy wanted to see how much money he could make. How far could he press Ralph? 'I'll bid 75 for 2200 big ones of the 99,' he said.

The Salomon trader jumped at the bid, spilling Evian all over his desk and lap, but quickly controlled himself.

'Done. We sell you 2200 big ones of 99 at seven five. You saved my backside, buddy, I owe you one. I'll ask Wanda to come out again this weekend. See ya then. I gotta put on my skates. Thanks, bud.' Ralph hung up.

'Yeeeee-haaaa!'

He had unloaded Salomon's bonds, and now it was time to unload the stock position. Bond traders hated trading in shares and despised equity traders. The small dollar size of the trades was demeaning, and bond traders revelled in their lack of expertise in the stock market with a mentality which declared: 'I don't know shit about shares, but who cares?' Clear trading lines were drawn between stocks and bonds, and it was rare for Ralph to be handling such a trade.

He examined the printout of Japanese shares. *Hmm . . . about $170 million of stock. Not much*, he thought and hit the Morgan Stanley direct line to a trader whom he knew slightly.

'Yeah.'

'Hi, Kevin, Ralph here at Solli.'

Kevin was surprised to hear him. 'Hey Ralphie, wotcha doin' tradin' stocks?'

'Client just came in with a $170 million portfolio trade. Everyone else has gone home. Can you see if you can bid me net for the block?' offered Ralph.

'Sure, Ralphie, tell me what you've got,' said the Morgan Stanley trader, hoping to worm out details of the Salomon portfolio.

Traders never revealed their individual stock positions in block portfolio trades, but only the class of stock: 'A' for blue chip, 'B' for second line stocks and 'C' for illiquid third-liners. If the seller had a portfolio worth $170 million, then the buyer would evaluate the number of A, B and C stocks and put in a blind bid, say at $161.5 million. Ralph knew this practice but figured he could trick the Morgan Stanley trader into buying the portfolio by acting like a sucker himself.

'Let's see,' said Ralph, slowly leafing through the portfolio as he played the dunce. 'All blue chips. Sony, Pioneer, Toyota, Sumitomo Bank, Japan Airlines.'

Ralph was aware that Morgan Stanley would know about the earthquake. 'Oh, here are a number of construction stocks,' said Ralph, purposely mispronouncing their names: 'Kumagai, Obayashi, Kajima, Taisei and Daishin Construction.'

Jimmy got excited. After the Kobe quake, construction firms had reaped two years of rewards redeveloping the city. Though news of the Tokyo quake was beginning to filter through, nobody had yet gauged the enormity of the disaster. New York's traders figured that Tokyo had had a slight jolt and the market would be up and running again tomorrow. No big deal. But Salomon Brothers had figured, as its executive committee so aptly put it, 'that Tokyo was fucked and it was time to bail out'.

The Morgan Stanley trader ran some numbers through his calculator. 'Okay. Look, I'll do you a favour and bid you $160 million for the block.' He thought the Tokyo Stock Market would open down a bit the next day, but the $10 million discount would give him a profit.

It was Ralph's turn to get excited now. 'Done. I sell you $170 million "A" stocks for $160 million.' He then read off the name and number of shares in each stock he had just sold, and hung up.

Then he rushed back to the board room, but had to wait to report on his success since the Osaka branch manager was on the speaker phone again. 'The Great Kanto earthquake destroyed Tokyo on 1

September 1923 and the Tokyo Stock Exchange was closed down until 27 October.'

'And the Osaka exchange?' asked Hunt.

'It reopened one week later.'

'Thanks, Tanaka-san.' Hunt hit the speaker button and turned to Ralph, who was clearly pleased with himself.

'We stuffed Merrill Lynch on the bonds and Morgan with our stocks. Took a 5 per cent hit on each,' he said.

'Yeeee-haaa! Morgan takes it up the backside again,' squealed one executive.

They had reason to be exuberant. Morgan Stanley was Salomon's mortal enemy.

'Gazinsky, this calls for a celebration,' shouted Hunt.

'Champagne!'

An ice-cold magnum of Dom Perignon was popped open. Hunt poured Ralph's glass first.

'I'm proud of you, young man,' said the Salomon chief. He poured the other glasses and proposed a toast.

'To Ralph Gazinsky.'

'To Ralph Gazinsky,' shouted the executive committee, who were now drinking champagne on top of whisky. Ralph knew he was on the road to big success and big bucks. After several more toasts, including one to the demise of Morgan Stanley, the party ended. With a giddy buzz, all the executives piled down to the lobby to their waiting limos.

Ralph, with a headache coming on, headed back to the trading desk. He popped two extra-strength Tylenol and put his feet up on the desk. Another lonely night at the office. He turned on CNN and saw Hiroko Fujita on the air. Suddenly he felt horny and wished wicked Wanda were there, sitting on his magic wand.

Haunting images were now hitting world viewers. Ralph looked at ravaged Tokyo.

Fuck Tokyo, thought Ralph. *Thank God I sold out.*

26

THE CREDIT

Atlanta, Tuesday, shortly after the quake

Shake 'n' Bake
The mischievously named movie double feature of the late 1970s, when *Earthquake* and *Towering Inferno* were released

'Carol, do we have enough Crunchy Nut Corn Flakes to last me three weeks?'

'Craig, I bought you twelve boxes.'

His assistant smiled, one step ahead of her boss. Huntley opened a new box of cereal every other day. 'I like my cereal fresh,' he always told the news team.

Craig Huntley was CNN's global anchorman, a sort of roving firefighter who was airdropped into world disaster areas. Tall, swarthy, eloquent and single, he was well liked. Huntley was not a prima donna like many anchormen, and the CNN staff liked him for being down to earth. The women liked him because he was single. So when Huntley asked for his usual food and drink to be loaded on the Cathay Pacific flight to Hong Kong, Carol laughed.

'Every time a disaster hits, the price of Kellogg's stock skyrockets,' Carol joked as she prepared his other requests, including special bottled water and long life milk but no Coca-Cola. Most Atlanta residents were fervent Coke drinkers and proud of their city's principal product, but not Huntley. He wasn't a health addict, but didn't like the thought of dissolving his insides. 'My Dad used Coke to take the rust off our old cars,' Huntley told people. Any of the other staff who had special requirements had to fend for themselves: CNN provided some essential emergency supplies, but otherwise everyone was on their own. No danger pay and no food was part of the business.

With the precision of a military campaign, CNN mobilized its news force to go to Japan. The initial wave of reporters left the Hong Kong bureau aboard the first available commercial flight to

Osaka. Stringers from Beijing and Bangkok also descended on the city, all with a mandate to make their own way to Tokyo. The two crews had only small hand-held cameras and recording equipment; the heavy-duty equipment was on its way. Within an hour of the quake Atlanta had chartered a jumbo jet to fly its remaining reporters, engineers, technicians and cameramen to Hong Kong. From there CNN chartered a Hercules C-140 transport plane to ferry their team to Osaka. Although CNN had begun as a cable news network, all its live transmissions came via satellite. In the field CNN used satellite transmitters slightly smaller than the massive receiving dishes used by farmers in Kansas and embassies around the world to pick up distant TV signals. Each dish weighed 700 kilos and fitted into ten large boxes. The engineers packed two generators, which were also stripped down and packed in boxes a metre square. Five Satlink M-phones were loaded, along with five Sony editpacks. The price of a Satlink phone call was $10 a minute and it enabled the CNN reporters to place a call anywhere in the world, be it in the African desert, the jungles of Indonesia or the rubble of Tokyo.

An editpack contained all the equipment necessary to tape, edit and send out a broadcast. Each weighed 90 kilos. CNN field correspondents could shoot forty minutes of film from which they could edit down to a two- or three-minute broadcast, which was sent directly via satellite to Atlanta and then sent out untouched by headquarters. Five Apple Mac laptops with built-in modems and CD capacity were also loaded. On this trip the CNN charter also carried a doctor along with food, water and medical supplies.

Huntley was nearly airborne for Hong Kong by the time Hiroko began her televised broadcasts. Carol had prepared reading material on previous earthquakes: Kobe in 1995, Los Angeles in 1994, Cairo in 1992, San Francisco in 1989 and Armenia in 1988. Carol had also thrown in a few books on Japanese culture. Having arrived at Hong Kong's Kai Tak airport, Huntley cleared immigration and boarded the waiting Hercules. The transfer of equipment to the transport plane took time, so Huntley watched the footage of Hiroko's telecasts. 'She's beautiful,' he thought, making a mental note of her torn grey skirt and cream blouse. Huntley was intrigued and slightly aroused.

A staff reporter filled Huntley in on the latest unconfirmed reports that the Prime Minister had been killed, but his main concern was getting from Osaka to Tokyo. Every television news agency had descended on the city to find a way through to Tokyo: CNN, BBC, Sky News, CBS, NBC, ABC, the German networks ARD and

ZDF, and TF1 from France. The world's big three news agencies, considered poorer relations of the networks, were there: Reuters, Associated Press and WTN. Fifty major newspapers had also sent teams to Osaka. But Ken Moyama's gang leaders in Osaka and Kobe had already commandeered most of the area's spare helicopters.

Huntley possessed not only on-screen talent but the flair of a hard-hitting reporter. He knew how to cajole, bluster, force, charm and wheedle himself into – or out of – any situation. On landing in Osaka he used his 'charm' technique, combined with a bit of bluster, and called Isao Nakauchi, chairman of the Daiei department store. Daiei was a mammoth retail chain with headquarters in Osaka, and Nakauchi was its dynamic, worldly and wealthy founder.

Huntley's Japanese assistant put him through.

'*Moshi, moshi, Nakauchi desu.*'

'Hello, Mr Nakauchi, this is Craig Huntley of CNN.'

'Ahhhh, Mr Huntley, I'm honoured to speak with you. I'm a big fan of yours. How may I help you?' CNN had a devoted international audience in Japan, which had grown considerably after the Gulf War.

'I spoke with my boss, Mr Turner, and he very much wants to invite you to Atlanta as his guest to watch the Braves play.'

Nakauchi was a baseball fanatic and owned the Daiei Hawks, a major league team. 'Now this is indeed a very great honour. I should be delighted to accept his invitation.' There was a pause. 'How may I help *you*?'

Huntley had brilliantly created an obligation on Nakauchi's part of which the elderly Japanese tycoon was well aware. He waited with amusement to see what CNN really wanted. It was as if CNN had magically created a credit in a fictitious bank account and now had to spend the money.

'Thank you for accepting, and I shall relay the good news to Mr Turner himself. In fact, he suggested I speak with you on another matter. We have our entire news crew here in Osaka but are without transport. We were wondering if we might borrow your personal helicopter to cover the Tokyo quake.'

Nakauchi could not believe his luck. Allowing CNN the use of his helicopter would be a fabulous piece of international publicity. He tried to contain his excitement.

'Hmmm. Well, you know Daiei is committed to the relief effort and we would be reduced to only one helicopter. But since CNN's effort will create international awareness of our disaster, I think for the sake of Japan, and because of my

friendship with Mr Turner, we can give you use of the helicopter.'

'Thank you, Mr Nakauchi. Mr Turner and I really appreciate the
favour. Our team is at the Osaka airport. How shall we arrange to
meet the Daiei helicopter?'

'I'll have it sent over to you with a pilot.'

'Thank you very much,' said Huntley. 'And I look forward to
seeing you in Atlanta.'

'And I look forward to seeing you on TV.' *In my helicopter.*

Nakauchi was about to bask in the credibility he had long awaited.
Daiei had almost been wiped out during the Kobe earthquake in
1995 and had suffered losses of over $2.5 billion. Tokyo-based
rival department stores such as Mitsukoshi, Seibu, Tokyu and
Takashimaya had croaked with secret pleasure at his misfortune.
Tokyo stores had always considered themselves a cut above those
in Osaka/Kobe, since Tokyo's elite clientele were considered more
cosmopolitan than the country bumpkins of Hanshin. Now Nakauchi
could change all that, turning the Tokyo quake to Daiei's advantage
and expanding in Tokyo while his rivals licked their financial
wounds.

He placed an urgent call to his helipad. 'Hello, this is Nakauchi,'
he told the manager. 'I want our corporate helicopter to fly to Osaka
airport. Our chopper and pilot are at the disposal of CNN.'

'Yes, sir.'

Then he gave the man another set of instructions.

'Yes, sir, we'll do that immediately.'

Two hours later Craig Huntley and his crew were boarding the
chopper. Armed with a notepad, Huntley was about to step up
into the passenger seat when he dropped his pen on the tarmac.
He stooped to pick it up and put one hand on the metal frame for
balance. His hand stuck slightly, and when he pulled it up he saw a
glob of red paint stuck to his palm. Huntley chuckled, retrieved his
pen and climbed into the chopper. *Nakauchi's a smart old codger*,
he thought. The word 'Daiei' had just been painted in large letters
on the belly of the chopper.

27

OVERLORD

Outside the Imperial Palace hours after the quake

'The courtesans and geisha poured in from the north like a disordered field of flowers.'
> Nobel prize-winning novelist Kawabata Yasunari,
> describing the refugees fleeing the fires of
> the 1923 great Kanto earthquake

Hiroko was swept away by the mob, and as its numbers swelled she was driven involuntarily towards the Imperial Palace. With Hope in her arms she needed help – she called to Jiroo, but the noise of the panic-stricken refugees drowned her voice. All her concentration was centred on keeping her footing. Jiroo was almost close enough to touch her, but she had to shout his name five times before he heard her.

'Over there,' she said, pointing with her head.

After ten minutes of exhausting jostling, Hiroko manoeuvred out of the torrent of bodies on to a small highway which divided the Palace from Kitanomaru Park to the north. Empty cars, some still burning, littered the road. The refugees, unable to enter the locked Palace grounds, were making for the park. Famous for housing the Budokan where foreign rock groups played to adoring Japanese fans, it had now become a sanctuary. The park was desperately overcrowded, as were all the other Special Evacuation Areas throughout the city.

The sea of jostling, frightened refugees made further passage impossible. 'What do we do now?' asked Jiroo, who was claustrophobic and close to fainting. Tokai had now managed to join them.

'Follow me,' Hiroko yelled.

They began climbing the hill which led to the Imperial Palace. Except where the highway abutted the palace, the Imperial grounds were surrounded by a moat 50 metres across, the remnant of the Sumida River which had once flowed past the Palace. As additional protection for the Emperor's forces in ancient times a steep hill had been constructed around the Palace, giving guards a view of anyone trying to struggle to the top. A 6-metre-high stone wall encircled the hilltop. Only the most tenacious samurai would have been able to swim the moat, climb the hill and scale the wall while under attack.

The little group were now under the stone parapet.

'What now?'

'Over the wall.'

Hiroko handed Hope to Jiroo, scrabbled her way up a nearby pine tree and jumped on to the stone fortress. Jiroo tore some strips of cloth from his shirt to make a sling for Hope, and then climbed the tree with the baby on his back. He handed her to Hiroko and then went down again to bring the equipment.

Tokai was unsure whether he could scale the pine tree and wall. 'I don't think I can make it,' said the eighty-year-old seismologist.

Jiroo jumped back down again to help him.

Once they were all at the top they looked down into the Imperial Palace. Though occasionally a person could be seen running, there was little movement. Far in the distance was the home of Emperor Akihito.

'Turn on the camera.'

Jiroo panned the quiet, spacious gardens, then swung the camera down on the refugees packed into Kitanomaru Park.

'This is Hiroko Fujita. We are now looking inside the Emperor's Palace.'

Most viewers, Japanese or Western, had never had a glimpse of it. The camera scanned the wide gravelled roads, greenery and manicured lawns; because of its location it was the most expensive piece of property on earth, said to be worth over a trillion dollars – more than the value of Canada. The majestic villas and outbuildings had had their tiles ripped off but were otherwise sound. Smoke billowed from the rest of Tokyo, but the Imperial gardens remained relatively peaceful.

These grounds had been built to withstand disaster. Three hundred years earlier the Palace had been the five-storey stronghold of the ruling shogun. By imperial decree, no buildings were allowed to surpass it in height. Back then the Palace area was crowded with buildings and bustling with activity. The entire city grew up around it and a spiralling system of moats, and gradually the Palace became a lonely shrine to times past.

When General MacArthur officially stripped Emperor Hirohito of his divinity in 1945, the Palace became even lonelier. Despite this, it remained Tokyo's physical hub – rail and subway lines swung in large loops around it, imitating the concentric circles of the moats.

The Japanese now had mixed feeling about their Emperor's status. Fewer than 1 per cent still believed him to be divine, and most of those were over seventy. Roughly a quarter of the population revered Emperor Akihito, a quarter respected him, while just under half were indifferent; 2 per cent actually disliked him.

While Hiroko was broadcasting, her phone rang.

'Hiroko, this is Nakamura again. I've switched off our live hook-up for a moment so we can speak privately. There's been a radio report that the Prime Minister is dead. An amateur reporter for a small radio station claims he saw Mori's body in the rubble of his official residence. We think it's unlikely since he's supposed to be on holiday in the mountains with his family. Can you make your way across the Palace grounds to his home?'

'Only if you swear that a team will be despatched to find my son.'

'I swear on my ancestors' grave. I'm putting you back live.'

Emperor Akihito and Princess Michiko had not been injured in the quake. The roof had fallen in places and many of their possessions, historical relics housed in glass cases, had been damaged. Members of the household rushed over to check on the Emperor. He had switched on his emergency generator and was watching CNN as Jiroo's camera scanned over the refugees.

'Countless hundreds of thousands, maybe millions, of survivors are rushing for the safety of the Imperial Palace, yet the gates remain closed. We are making an urgent appeal to the Emperor to open the palace to Tokyo residents,' said Hiroko.

As she was broadcasting, the prop wash from a giant transport helicopter drowned out her voice. The rescue chopper was no more than 30 metres overhead and coming in to land near the Emperor's home. The noise was deafening and Hiroko was forced to stop.

Under General Mishima's orders, the First Army command had sent a twin-rotor IHI-built V 107 transport chopper to ferry the Imperial family to safety. Their mission was to get them to the Imperial villa in Kyoto, but there was a problem. Sato, head of the Imperial Household Agency, was first to meet the evacuation team and explained the situation.

'I'm sorry. The Emperor and his wife refuse to leave,' he told them. 'But the rest of the family is assembled. Do you have enough room for everyone?'

'Yes,' shouted the evacuation captain above the noise of the chopper blades, 'But I need to radio First Army Headquarters to take advice on the Emperor.'

After worried chatter between General Mishima's office and the evacuation team it was agreed that Sato would 'encourage' the Emperor to leave after he had 'overseen' the initial rescue operations at the Imperial Palace. A compromise was reached whereby the Emperor's wife joined the evacuation party to 'oversee' the family in Kyoto.

With that agreed, the chopper took off for nearby Akasaka Palace to pick up the remaining members of the family. The Emperor began giving Sato his orders.

'I want you to open the gates and allow the refugees access to our gardens. Also please find the young woman roaming the grounds. I wish to speak to her.'

Sato's job was to protect the Emperor, not the residents of Tokyo. 'Your majesty, opening the Palace gates isn't such a good idea. The refugees will ransack your home. The East Gardens will be sufficient,' said Sato.

The East Gardens had been opened to the public since 1968. Already they were brimming with refugees.

'Sato, I appreciate your concern, but the people of Tokyo need space. Open the gates. Now.' The Emperor was firm. 'And please find that woman. I have an idea.'

'Yes, your majesty,' said Sato, his displeasure evident. Sato walked briskly back to the Imperial Household Agency a few hundred metres away and began barking orders. 'Find the woman reporter near the north gate. She's with two men and a small child.'

He then sat down at his desk, picked up his Satlink phone and dialled Ken Moyama. The Imperial Household Agency seldom had contact with the yakuza leader, but this was an emergency. He was at home in Shirokane where the first wave of supplies was due to arrive on his hilltop by helicopter.

'Moyama-san, this is Sato of the Imperial Household Agency.'

Normally the yakuza leader would have been surprised to hear from the Imperial family, but he had learned to accept strange circumstances at times of crisis. 'Sato-san, are the Emperor and Empress uninjured?'

'They're fine, thank you. I'm calling because the Emperor has decided to open the Palace to quake victims.'

'Good idea. How can I help?'

At heart, Moyama was an imperialist bent on restoring the Emperor to his rightful place as head of the nation, with the full powers of a reigning monarch. Opening the Palace, in his view, was a good public relations gesture. Historically the yakuza had controlled right-wing hit squads who silenced the Emperor's critics and, though the squads had had their heyday in the 1930s, they still existed.

'We're in need of medical supplies, blankets, food and water and phones.'

'Hmm . . . I'll need a helicopter landing site. Could you please clear a space in the west quadrant of the Palace. Our supplies will take a few hours to arrive.'

'The Imperial Household thanks you, Moyama-san.'

'You know my strong beliefs, Sato-san. It is my duty and pleasure to assist the Imperial family.'

Moyama hung up and smiled. The whole purpose of ordering supplies from Osaka was to give Japan's gangsters a new image. The Kobe earthquake had been a remarkable public relations success, with his gangs handing out food, water and blankets to survivors. Hardly any of the media reported on his vulture-like scavenging of abandoned homes. Tokyo would be an even more spectacular victory in changing the attitudes of the Japanese people. The yakuza were no longer ruffians to be shunned, but a caring, honour-bound group who deserved acceptance in society. It was Moyama's ultimate scam. Once society let down its guard against the yakuza, the underworld could penetrate legitimate business. All Moyama had to do was divert his choppers from Shirokane to the Imperial Palace.

Sato spent fifteen minutes detailing how the Imperial gardens were to be used as an evacuation area. He then sent the plan by messenger over to the Emperor. Sato then gathered together his staff, of whom only two had been injured.

'The Imperial Palace is to be opened to refugees,' he informed them.

A look of horror came over the staff. They were used to dealing with royalty, not commoners.

'We'll all be killed.'

'They'll over-run us.'

'They'll steal our food and drink all our water.'

Sato was stern. 'That's the wish of the Emperor, and his orders will be obeyed. Anyone not obeying will be dismissed immediately.'

That meant having to survive in a Tokyo which no longer existed, and the group fell silent.

'Thank you. We'll begin by dividing the Palace into a grid system. Refugees will be assigned in Hiragana syllabary order according to their surname and the fifty-one characters.'

The hiragana syllabary was Japan's phonetic alphabet, which began with 'A' and ended with 'yo'. The division of fifty-one sectors corresponded roughly to the twenty-six letters of the Western alphabet. Sato handed out photocopies of a plan of the Palace divided into fifty-one sectors. One of the four-year-olds in the Imperial Household had Hiragana flash cards, which Sato now put to good use.

'Glue these cards to wooden boards or cardboard and attach them to a stake. When that's complete, inform me and we'll open the gates.'

'How many people shall we let in?' somebody asked.

'All of them.'

'But there are millions of them!' blurted a gardener in fear.

'Silence!' Sato glared at the man. 'You'll join the guards at the gate.'

Sato turned to leave and hurried back to the Emperor's residence where he spotted his assistant escorting Hiroko and her team through the side door.

'Fujita-san?' Sato was out of breath. 'Fujita-san. The Emperor wishes to assist you. I'm not sure what he has in mind, but please follow me.'

'Me?' she asked in surprise.

'Yes. Please. This way.' Sato led Hiroko, Tokai, Jiroo and Hope into the Emperor's home.

The Emperor had just finished reading the handwritten sheet that Sato had sent him. As Hiroko was brought before him she bowed, then motioned for Jiroo to begin rolling the camera. He was frightened of violating Imperial privacy, and refused. Hiroko insisted, but Jiroo remained frozen.

'Fujita-san,' began the Emperor. 'You may film the announcement I'm about to make.'

Jiroo immediately turned on the cameras.

'I wish to announce that the Imperial Palace is open to all victims of the quake.'

Hiroko moved her hand-held phone nearer to him so that he could be heard.

'All refugees will be treated as guests of the Imperial Household and placed according to surname in fifty-one designated areas. We expect emergency supplies by nightfall. Phones will be available at each of the fifty-one sectors, thanks to NTT and KDD of Osaka. I ask everyone in Tokyo listening by radio not to panic. For those rescue agencies both in and outside Japan, I request that food, water and medical supplies be sent urgently. We've arranged for two helipads to be established: one in the Marunouchi Gardens and another in the western section of the Imperial Palace.' The Emperor spoke with an air of authority.

Hiroko, ever the reporter, spoke out. '*Heika*, your generosity is overwhelming. Thank you. But has the government approved of your request for foreign assistance?'

'If the Prime Minister or any of the cabinet members are still alive, I welcome their suggestions. We're in a crisis. I can't wait for bureaucratic consensus when lives are at stake. Neither can the millions of our citizens.'

He was right. Japan was in turmoil and needed a leader. The Emperor was fulfilling a role that no one had thought possible. Most Japanese considered him only a titular head of state, not unlike the Queen of England.

The Emperor motioned for Jiroo to bring the baby to him. Hope was eating a cracker which, in its sodden, chewed state, dribbled all over the Emperor. He laughed.

'Fujita-san, we'll look after Hope. Your duty now is to your nation and to your son.'

'How did you know about Alex?'

'We watch CNN too.'

Hiroko chuckled. Hope was now climbing over the Emperor.

'Two of my Imperial guards will join your group and show you across the garden to the Parliament building. Then they will help you get to Mitaka to find your son. You must take food and water. The Japanese people thank you.'

Jiroo kissed Hope, who was still in the Emperor's arms. Tokai too was to remain at the Palace, having decided that at the age of eighty he was best not walking any further. Hiroko was the last to say goodbye to the infant and held her close for a long time.

'You'll see her again,' said the Emperor. 'And you'll find your son too.'

Hiroko followed Sato out. He motioned for Jiroo to turn the camera off and for Hiroko to put her phone on mute. Sato then whispered in Hiroko's ear.

'What I'm about to show you is a state secret, so please find a reason to be off the air for fifteen minutes.'

Hiroko discreetly turned her phone off, and for the next fifteen minutes the world wondered what had happened to her.

'Follow me.'

A moment later the group stepped into a gardener's shed. A staircase descended into the darkness. Sato flipped a switch and an emergency generator roared to life.

'This is our secret passage. It was constructed in the 1930s, and leads under the Imperial Moat straight under the Parliament building. Even MacArthur's troops never knew of its existence. This is where many of our national treasures were hidden during and after the war. The passage is well lit. You will emerge in the ante-room of Parliament . . . if it is still standing. An alternative exit leads to a similar gardener's shed in the back of the Parliament gardens.'

Each of them was handed a backpack with water, food, flashlights and first aid kit.

'Good luck,' urged Sato.

The team, four-strong, descended into the passage.

Meanwhile, under the ruins of the Palace Hotel across the street, Keiko Noichi was still trapped. She opened her eyes but everything was black. Keiko lifted her head a little and it 'hit' concrete. Tons of rubble lay above her head.

'Kiko?'

There was no answer from her twin sister.

She tried to move, but her legs were pinned and it was no use. She began groping around in the dark with her hands, collecting small items. Two of them felt like tubes of toothpaste and she put them safely under her arm. What would she do if her sister were dead? The twins had spent their life together and Keiko would not know how to live without her companionship. Her sister was the only friend she had. Then Keiko felt something warm snuggle up to her and realized that Mushka, her cat, had survived. Keiko closed her eyes and went to sleep to the sound of Mushka's gentle purring.

28

THE TUNNEL

Tuesday, late afternoon, below the Imperial Palace

'We only make computers, we don't use them.'
A quote from the Prime Minister's office, which
was criticized for not having a state-of-the-art
'situation room' for national emergencies

The tunnel was cool and moist, the earthen floor soft underfoot. Hiroko led the way. While the outside air was dry and parched from the thousands of fires raging in Tokyo, here it was like drinking cold, fresh water. Hiroko wished she could stay in the safe cocoon of the tunnel, free from death and destruction, until she was safely home with Alex.

Despite the auxiliary generators, the light was dim. Many of the bulbs were old and blown out. Hiroko fished out a flashlight that Sato had given her and flicked it on.

The walls, of whitish stone, were wet to the touch. The secret tunnel had not been used in years and cobwebs criss-crossed the passage. Like the air, they were damp, and they caught in Hiroko's hair and mouth.

'Jiroo, hand me the camera tripod, please,' she called back.

He took the lightweight aluminium stand out of his equipment bag and handed it to her. For carrying, the stand collapsed into a 30-centimetre baton. Hiroko opened it to a length of 120 centimetres and expanded it into a tripod.

'There.' She held the tripod base in front of her to catch the cobwebs as the group moved on.

The journey was quiet for the first five minutes. Then the far-off squeaking of a rat could be heard and Hiroko froze.

'What was that?' she whispered, knowing exactly what it was.

'It's just a – '

'Don't say it.' Hiroko shuddered involuntarily. 'I hate rats. Why do there have to be rats?'

Jiroo looked at her and then laughed.

'It's not funny,' she admonished him. 'This is like *Raiders of the Lost Ark*. You walk in front, and if you see a rat kill it before I die of a heart attack.'

It was another kilometre underground to the Parliament building. They heard the rats but saw nothing. After twenty minutes the tunnel began to rise and the air became drier.

When the group came to the fork, Hiroko took the left tunnel as Sato had suggested. This led directly into the Prime Minister's ante-room. They reached a stone staircase. At the top of the stairs was a large wooden door with an iron ring bolted in the centre. Hiroko pulled. Nothing happened. The Imperial guards squeezed to the front.

'On three,' they said.

'One, two, three.'

The door loosened slightly. The next time they pulled, it flew open. A blast of dry air hit them.

Hiroko was now leading again. The Parliament ante-chamber was heavily damaged. 'The main house is to the left and the upper house to the right,' she said. All Japanese reporters were familiar with the layout of the Parliament building. 'Jiroo, please turn on the camera.' Hiroko then dialled the Asahi Osaka office and her editor answered.

'Fujita-san, what happened? We were all worried about you.'

'My phone battery went dead and we had to find another one.'

Nakamura was actually more worried about his audience. CNN had scrambled to fill up thirty minutes of air time with seismologists and 'rock hounds'. But world viewership had remained steady at half a billion. Most wanted to know why Hiroko had blacked out with no explanation. Others were waiting for news of a disaster, enjoying CNN's live coverage in the way that some viewers watched race car racing for the crashes. Many remembered the American attack on Baghdad and thirsted for action – 'technical difficulty' in a crisis indicated chaos, which was more fun to watch than polished anchormen.

The camera was recording. 'This is Hiroko Fujita. Having walked from the Imperial Palace we're now across the street in the Parliament building. Our Parliament and Prime Minister are the heart of government, where the executive branch rules the nation. Our 512 representatives are elected directly by the people but are more of an elite club than the voice of the people.'

The group picked their way among splintered glass, overturned cupboards and shattered desks. A secretary lay under a heavy filing cabinet. Hiroko asked the Imperial guards to lift the cabinet off her and listened for breathing, but it was no use. The woman had died of suffocation. Hiroko gently closed the victim's eyes and folded her hands over her chest.

'Please take a picture of this woman's face,' she requested of Jiroo. He moved in for a close-up while Hiroko continued off camera. 'We'll be filming dead bodies as we continue, so that families or friends may identify and, in time, burn their loved ones. Though non-Japanese viewers may find this peculiar, we Japanese consider it very important to recover bodies in order to hold a proper funeral.'

The group moved on.

Nakamura, the Asahi editor, came on the line and briefly cut the transmission to CNN in order to speak to Hiroko. 'CNN cut away before you closed that woman's eyes and we don't have playback facilities here. They'd like you to do it again when I cue you.'

'What? Tell them to go to hell.'

The group had now reached the assembly room of the main House of Parliament, and stood staring into the room. The stained glass ceiling had crashed down on the assembly room, but fortunately no meeting had been in session. Shards of glass lay embedded in chairs, desks and four cleaning women. Back in 1986 the lower house had debated the topic of what to do in the event that a quake brought down the stained glass. Hard hats as worn by building workers had been put forward as the obvious answer, and the motion was debated.

'Helmets are ugly and unfashionable,' was the consensus. Instead the house voted to have trendy polyethylene hoods made. The hoods, felt the macho house members, made them look like samurai. The members of the upper house wished to show their independence from the lower house and decreed that they would protect themselves from flying glass by putting their suit jackets over their heads.

The cleaning women had had no time to put on the special hoods. The glass had cut straight through their flesh even faster than it had torn through the wooden tables.

Jiroo filmed the carnage.

CNN warned viewers that parental discretion was advised in watching the coverage, but this only increased the number of viewers. Nobody turned off their sets. The world had been waiting for blood and here it was.

Hiroko and the guards looked for survivors.

'Aaaaaaa . . .' A moan, barely audible, could be heard from under the speaker's podium. A cleaning woman, old and withered, lay partway under it. Her legs had not been able to fit under the box and were nearly severed. She lay in a pool of blood and Hiroko knew she did not have long to live. Jiroo rushed over and videotaped Hiroko as she crawled down and offered her water, asking if there were anything she needed. She sipped from Hiroko's water bottle.

'I'd like to see your smile,' she whispered.

Hiroko looked down at the dying woman, confused.

'The villagers where I come from in Kyushu . . .' Her breathing was getting more difficult. '. . . believe that if we die . . .' Her body was starting to go limp. '. . . among those who are smiling . . . we will be happy in our next life . . .'

Hiroko looked down on the stranger and forced a smile.

The woman smiled back and then died.

Hiroko backed out from under the podium and decided to head for the nearby Prime Minister's residence where the nation's leader had been reported dead. Her phone line was live and the camera whirring.

'The earthquake has impaired Japan's central government. Unlike in the West, the division of power among executive, legislative and judicial has never been balanced. Most power has traditionally rested in the executive branch, which in turn has been funded by big business and organized crime. Amazingly, despite this power the Prime Minister is forbidden to act in a crisis without the consent of his cabinet.'

Experts tracked Hiroko's journey, explaining to viewers the significance of the footage being transmitted. The CNN news team in Atlanta provided anchor woman Alanda Voltaria with a large map of Tokyo for viewers.

One constitutional expert explained that inability to find the Prime Minister to convene Parliament brought the government to a halt. Voltaria interviewed Hiroko by phone, adopting CNN's usual chatty style.

'Hiroko, what's going on with rescue operations? We understand that the city's come to a standstill,' she said.

'Rescue operations can't begin without authorization from the governor and consensus among the thirty-three government organizations represented in Tokyo.'

'Who can set the rescue in motion?'

'There are only four men who matter now. The governor of Tokyo, who is somewhere in the South Pacific, the Prime Minister, who is presumed dead, the Cabinet Secretary, deputy prime minister and Chairman of the National Land Agency, none of whom can be found, and General Mishima of Japan's Eastern Army who has the military on full alert.'

'So why not send in the army?'

'That would be viewed as unconstitutional without permission from the city authorities.'

'If the Prime Minister were alive, presumably he could act.'

'Not really. This is Japan. He could invoke an obscure law called Article 125 of Basic Law of Disaster Response, in which he takes control of the military, the police, firefighters and other government agencies. But no Prime Minister has had the courage to invoke this law because of fears that the people would brand him a dictator . . .'

'We're now heading for the Prime Minister's house just across the street,' Hiroko added, giving CNN a cue to cut to other interviewees.

The reaction to the disaster within Japan's government district had been orderly. Ministerial aides, secretaries, office staff, gardeners and helmeted riot police (assigned to guard the government office blocks) had been the first to filter through to the northern section of the Palace. They were followed by daytime dwellers further 'inland' – refugees from the entertainment districts of Roppongi and Akasaka. There was a reason for less panic to have been shown in the government district of Kasumigaseki: the buildings were squat and less dense than in the rest of Tokyo, and the streets broad. Though many of the ferroconcrete glass structures had been razed, most were built on large plots, surrounded by grass and set back from the road. Many were protected by large walls and heavily guarded entrances fortified by anti-tank barriers to thwart militant students and radical demonstrators. Fires were isolated within individual buildings and had little chance of jumping the wide streets. Traffic was minimal, since only government vehicles used the streets and most bureaucrats did not start work until 9 or 9.30 a.m.

Prime Minister Mori had actually been in his official residence in Tokyo when the quake hit. In order to catch up on some work he had just returned early from his family holiday in the mountains, leaving his wife and children behind. The staff had the day off and were not expecting him back.

Hiroko approached what remained of Mori's home. The stone building, erected in 1928, had been cut in half. As she approached the main entrance she saw the Prime Minister's body lying under fallen rock. Jiroo filmed the body.

'We've found the Prime Minister, and it looks as if the radio report of his death is accurate.'

It was the Mori nose that made the Prime Minister distinguishable from other men, and Hiroko noticed it straight away. The short, pointy, upturned nose protruded through a tangled mass of grey hair, blood and glasses. Hiroko checked for a pulse.

A moment later a call came through from the Asahi offices. 'Hiroko, that's not the Prime Minister.'

'What are you talking about? It most certainly is.'

'No. Just listen. It's his brother. Mori's wife just called to say that the pair of them drove back together the previous evening. She's seen the pictures and she says it's not her husband. The Prime Minister must still be inside.'

Hiroko wasn't sure of herself and hesitated.

'Mrs Mori says look at his right hand.' There's a mole on it, she says.'

'Yes,' said Hiroko a few seconds later. 'I've found it.'

'The Prime Minister has no mole. Now please see if you can find him.'

Hiroko hated taking orders from Nakamura, but did as she was told. The team entered the Prime Minister's home and explored the uncollapsed section of stone still standing.

Gingerly Hiroko climbed up the main staircase, afraid it would fall at any time. Jiroo was a few paces behind her, filming as he went. At the top of the stairs she peered into the Prime Minister's bedroom, then quickly motioned for Jiroo to stop filming.

Her phone started ringing immediately. Nakamura was on the line. 'Keep the camera rolling. What's going on?'

Hiroko ignored the Asahi editor while she, Jiroo and the Imperial guards rushed into the bedroom to help the Prime Minister, whose legs lay pinned under a cabinet. He was unconscious but breathing.

'Quick, let's get him outside before this building falls,' yelled Hiroko. 'He needs a doctor.'

On the four-poster bed a partially clad young girl lay on her stomach. The stone ceiling had collapsed and fallen on her. Hiroko checked the girl's pulse, but her body was cold and rigid. While the guards attended to Mori, Hiroko awkwardly dressed the young girl and with Jiroo's help took her down the stairs and outside, where they covered her face with a sheet.

Her phone rang constantly as Nakamura tried to reprimand her for going off the air, but Hiroko continued to ignore him and began broadcasting again.

'We've located the Prime Minister, who is injured and unconscious but still alive. The mistaken reports of his death were confused with that of his brother, who is now confirmed dead. We urgently request a doctor at the Prime Minister's home.'

Nakamura interrupted. 'Where are you taking him?'

'To the medical facilities at the Imperial Palace.'

'Don't you think it would be best to leave him at his residence and office so he can coordinate the rescue efforts?'

Hiroko was getting annoyed at Nakamura's interference. 'Coordinate with what? There aren't any communication facilities in the Prime Minister's home or adjoining office. This isn't the White House. There can't be more than one computer in this building, for Christ's sake. And frankly, at the moment he's in no state to coordinate anything.'

Nakamura changed the subject. 'Whose body is covered with the sheet?' he asked in front of half a billion viewers.

'Oh, a passing worker whom we tried to save. Her face is too disfigured for recognition,' lied Hiroko, who wanted to preserve some dignity for the dead girl and her family. Japan needed Prime Minister Mori to lead it out of this crisis, and Hiroko decided that a scandal would only hamper an already flawed rescue process.

The rescue chopper was on its way to pick up Mori, and when it arrived Hiroko and her team headed for the National Land Agency. Viewers stayed riveted to their television screens as Jiroo filmed the devastation.

29

THE SCATTERLINGS

Tuesday, late afternoon and evening at the Imperial Palace

'**The government has no crisis management system.**'
                          Former Prime Minister Hosokawa
'**Japan needs a Disaster Czar.**'
          Dr Robert Geller, outspoken critic of Japan's lack
                                    of earthquake preparedness

'I can throw further than you can,' challenged Sachiko in the universal children's tone of 'na, na, na na, na'.

'Can't.'

Sachiko was six years old and had found a playmate, a boy named Taro who was the same age.

'Can too.'

She picked up a small stone and threw it down into the moat. Taro did the same thing. Brightly coloured orange koi came to the surface in the hope of food. Throwing bread to the koi was a favourite pastime for Japanese tourists and thrilled the young children.

Absorbed in their own little world, the young pair were oblivious to the chaos around them. They followed the koi as they swam along the water's edge, throwing small stones to keep the fish bubbling along the surface.

'Sachiko? Sachiko, where are you?' called out her mother. Mrs Ota looked behind her and to the side, then frantically twisted in a circle. Fear now gripped her. 'Sachiko!' she screamed.

But her voice was lost in the din of 3 million refugees who now encircled the Imperial Palace. Throngs of dazed survivors jostled past the panic-stricken mother, concerned with their own problems. Her voice was one of thousands mingled with the screams of those in need of medical attention, dehydrated survivors yelling for water, wailing relatives grieving for lost ones and occasional cries of startled joy by reunited office workers.

Mrs Ota tried to remain calm but found it impossible. Her stomach, heart and throat were frozen in chilling panic, as if she had swallowed a block of ice. Any parent who has momentarily lost a child in a busy supermarket or on a crowded beach knows the fear than ran through Mrs Ota. She thrashed through the crowd, pushing people aside in her search for her daughter.

Meanwhile Sachiko and Taro had walked a hundred metres down the moat edge. Mrs Ota looked down the bank of the moat, her eyes desperately canvassing the area. Thirst-craved survivors knelt at the water's edge and drank the green, algae-ridden water. But there was no sign of Sachiko. Her eyes rapidly glanced over her daughter but without recognizing her, for the swarm of people created a multi-coloured blanket of humanity.

Mrs Ota turned her attention elsewhere. It was getting dark and the chances of finding her daughter were fading. Worse, she was no longer in control of her movements as she was swept towards the Palace gates.

'Let us in!' cried desperate voices as they pounded on the gates. Tens of thousands pushed their way to the front of the main north gate, crushing those in front. Mrs Ota was pushed forward against her will. The crowd was so dense that she was unable to lower her upraised arms to ease the pressure on her chest. Breathing became difficult.

Mrs Ota was a small woman in her mid-thirties and slightly frail. She wanted to cry out for air but could not breathe. She brought her elbows down on the shoulders of the man in front of her and pushed for her life. A small space opened between the two and she sucked in air, then immediately brought both arms down in front of her chest as passengers are taught in emergency plane crashes. This gave her space to breathe. Others, whose arms were by their sides, had them pinned as if held down by unseen manacles.

Sato, the head of the Imperial Household Agency, was on the parapet and knew he had to act quickly to save lives.

'Open the gates,' he commanded into his walkie-talkie.

The eight massive wooden gates to the Imperial Palace slowly creaked open. Fortunately they opened inwards. Two dozen bodies lay at the foot of the north gate. Like soldier ants who use the corpses of their colleagues to form bridges and ramps, so those in the front clambered up the growing pile of dead in an effort to scale the gate.

'Quick, clear those bodies,' commanded Sato.

But it was useless. The guards had no chance of penetrating the solid wall of oncoming people.

Sato used his bullhorn. 'Those at the back please move. Do not push.'

Nobody listened. Three million people made for eight gates which would only take ten people at a time.

In her struggle to survive, Mrs Ota momentarily forgot about her daughter. A short woman next to her was sandwiched in the mêlée and propelled forward, her feet off the ground. Nobody noticed that the woman had died from suffocation and was how a corpse being carried along with the tide. Mrs Ota stumbled on a body but kept her balance thanks to the pressure from behind. To stumble in this crowd meant certain death.

Hundreds were crushed as the torrent of humanity surged ahead, while others were propelled safely into the Imperial Palace grounds where fear was replaced by a craving for food and water. But for many thousands the fear continued as they wandered about trying to find friends and family. Some were successful, but most workers lived far outside Tokyo and had no family there to comfort them.

On top of the stone parapets, the head of the Imperial Household Agency canvassed the crowds. 'We need volunteers to guide everyone to their sectors and to distribute food, water and medicine. Volunteers will work in twelve-hour shifts with a five-hour allotment for sleep. Please line up outside the gates.' To discourage those who might just be interested in seeking water and food, Sato emphasized that volunteers would be given last priority. He also seconded hundreds of policemen who had been found wandering where the west gates, they had drifted from their guard posts at the various ministries in neighbouring Kasumigaseki. Ten policemen were assigned to each gate.

Once inside, the mob mentality was quelled. The police presence acted as a mass tranquillizer, reassuring the crowd that they still lived in a sane world of rules and authority. It was an uneasy calm. Giant boards greeted the refugees, telling them which sector to camp in.

'Please go straight to your sector,' the gatekeepers yelled through their bullhorns. 'There will be water available in each sector.'

Five Imperial policemen were assigned to each of the fifty-one sectors, their main task to prevent fights over water and camping space. Campfires began to dot the landscape. And from high points within the Palace grounds, the burning of Tokyo could be clearly seen. The skyline remained orange throughout the night.

'Mommy!' yelled Sachiko just as it turned dark. Her terror was contagious and soon her young friend was crying too, yelling in panic for his mother. But Sachiko would never see her mother again. Mrs Ota had died in the rush to the gate.

By nightfall the smell of freshly grilled fish wafted through the grounds. This surprised Sato, who was inspecting the rescue operation. Huge fish were roasting on open campfires. *Where did they get the fish?* Sato picked up the discarded outer skin of one – it resembled a small, clear plastic shopping bag, maybe even an oversized condom. Then Sato realized to his horror that it was orange. *The ungrateful commoners*, thought Sato. *They have been fishing in the Imperial moat.* Hundreds of refugees were feasting on the Emperor's koi.

'You, where did you get this?' he shouted, grabbing one young man who was picking choice bits of fish off the fire.

The man stared mutely at Sato.

'You water-guzzling peasant – you've been fishing in the Emperor's moat, haven't you?' Sato accused him. He was guarded by two Imperial policemen, so the man would be unlikely to fight.

'No, I swear I wasn't fishing. I bought the fish at the main gate,' he said, pointing.

Sato hit the 'talk' button on the walkie-talkie. He was seething. 'This is Overlord Two. Poachers are taking koi out of the Imperial Moat. I want ten armed men to meet me at the main gate in five minutes.'

Sato and the guards ran over to the gate, which was lit by auxiliary generators. An enterprising fellow was standing over a blanket-covered pile, doing brisk business with an eager group gathered round. Sato saw him pocket some money, reach under the blanket and pull out a 50-centimetre koi by the tail.

'Arrest that man,' Sato screamed at the guards.

The crowd ran off and Sato pulled the cover off the mound of fish. He had never known that the Imperial koi grew so large. Bright orange, white and mottled fish lay in a neat pile.

'Where did you get these?'

'From the moat fisherman,' he said, pointing outside the gate.

Sato began questioning the fishmonger. It turned out that the man worked in the Tsukiji fish market, auctioning fish. Much of Japan's sushi originated in the Tsukiji docks where massive slabs of tuna, yellowtail, swordfish, bream, snapper and shark were auctioned. Tourists got up at five in the morning to visit the fish market, gawk at the tons of raw fish and eat sushi for breakfast. By 6 a.m. the market was closing down. The fishmonger and his mates had finished work and were drinking in a local bar when the quake hit.

It was a crude straw-built affair, so nobody had been injured. When they heard that the Palace was opening for refugees, the drunken group somehow stumbled there through the carnage.

'We just thought we could make some quick cash. I guess we were kind of drunk.'

'You.' Sato pointed to one the Imperial policemen. 'Climb up there and turn the spotlights on the moat.'

Using cracks in the rocks to lever himself, Sato climbed the stone wall and looked where the floodlights shone down. A group of six men had taken the moat's orange underwater garbage net and, three to a side, were trawling the moat for koi. He also noticed a large group of children standing by the side of the moat. Their presence went forgotten for the moment as Sato flew into a rage, hitting his walkie-talkie button again.

'I want those fishermen imprisoned. How dare they sell the Imperial koi for food!'

A crackling sound came over the radio. 'Overlord Two, this is Overlord One, do you read?'

'I read you, Overlord.'

'The fish now belong to the people. Anyone may fish in the moat. This is my wish. Out.'

'But your majesty . . .'

'That is my wish. Over and out.'

'Yes, majesty. Overlord Two out.'

Defeated, Sato turned to his men. 'Release the fishmonger and turn the spotlight off the moat.'

Sato hated it when the Emperor played on the walkie-talkie set. He was like a little kid who had seen too many movies.

'Wait a minute. Put the spotlights back on.'

The moat lit up.

A group of twenty children were playing by the water's edge. When Sato looked closer he noticed that they weren't playing but looking for food. He shouted down from the stone wall: 'You children, what are you doing out so late? Where are your parents? Wait there, I'm coming down.'

'Hide, quick,' said the twelve-year-old ringleader. They all ran off before Sato could get down to them. Six-year-old Sachiko and Taro trailed behind.

'Who were those children?' Sato asked a guard.

'Vagrants, sir. I think they've lost their parents.'

Alone and without food and water, the orphans of Tokyo banded together to save themselves. Scrounging through rubbish, fishing in the moat and begging for food, they roamed the city streets. They became known as the Scatterlings.

Less than a thousand metres away, the twins had been trapped for twelve hours under the rubble of the Palace Hotel. Mushka nuzzled up against Keiko and licked her face. The cat purred thankfully as Keiko opened her eyes. She was now worried for her sister.

'Kiko?' she called out. She estimated that only an half an hour had passed since the quake.

Keiko heard a moan.

'Kiko, you're alive!'

'*Hai*,' came a whisper.

'Are you all right?'

'*Hai*,' came another weak reply.

Mushka walked over to Kiko and mewed at her.

Kiko had had no protection from the falling ceiling, which had broken her back. Breathing was difficult and talking almost impossible. She was paralysed and only able to move her left foot, but was determined not to worry her sister.

'I'm collecting things for us to live on,' said Keiko. 'Try to drink something. The refrigerator must be near you somewhere. Can you touch the drinks?'

Kiko was immobile. '*Hai*.'

'Good. Good. Don't talk any more for now.'

Keiko, who was protected by the counter top, began foraging with her hands. She collected some cardboard and placed it under her head before she went to sleep again.

Mushka curled up to the injured sister as if to protect her, and went to sleep.

30

THE LOOTING

Ginza, Tuesday morning, shortly after the quake

Things to do after an earthquake:
1. Under no circumstances re-enter a house or office building. Flicking on a switch or lighting a candle may ignite gas. Aftershocks are likely.
2. Keep phone lines free for emergencies.
3. Avoid panic. Hoarding food, supplies and cash will only lead to panic buying and bank runs.

What would you do immediately after a great earthquake in Tokyo? Most common answers from a 1983 poll of Tokyo residents conducted by the Disaster Prevention Council:
1. Run back into the house to save valuables.
2. Quickly call friends and family.
3. Run to the store to stock up on goods.
4. Run to the bank to take out cash.

'Eight, eight, eighty-eight.' The elderly Kozo Taishowa read out the combination to his safe.

Nomo Watanabe, the department store manager, and Kozo Taishowa stood on the Ginza plot where Taishowa's wooden house had been. His house had been thrust out into the road. The movement of the heavy tiled roof had overpowered the fragile wooden supports and it fell like a book supported by pencils. The entire structure had fallen forward in one piece, leaving the interior of Taishowa's home intact, though dishevelled.

Watanabe knelt at the safe. It was an old safe, waist-high, with the name of the manufacturer embossed in faded gold lettering on the front. Watanabe turned the combination slowly but had trouble concentrating. Power lines crackled around him. Dust and smoke filled the air as the screams of unseen voices pleaded for help.

Kozo Taishowa was unperturbed by the mayhem around him. As

a teenager he had lived through the American fire bombings of 1945. Nothing would ever equal the horror inflicted by Americans upon men, women and children. Taishowa had found it outrageous that historians seldom mentioned that atrocity. 'Atrocity' was a term invented by the winners of wars to describe the actions of the vanquished. Nobody even considered the American bombing an atrocity, since the action was justified in winning the war. One hundred and forty-five thousand people were burned or suffocated to death in the raid – more than in any other single act of destruction in the history of mankind, including Hiroshima and Nagasaki. Taishowa thought of the 6 million Jews who had died at the hands of the Nazis. Most of them had been gassed before being burned in the ovens of the death camps. The Americans were worse than the Nazis in Taishowa's opinion. Americans had burned innocent Japanese civilians alive. He remembered how he had watched a young girl, no more than twelve years old, get hit by a piece of inflammable gel. The girl had literally melted in front of him.

Although Taishowa was a kindly old man, certain events triggered a steely detachment in him. News of hi-jackings, regional wars, bombings, genocides and other crises evoked no emotion in him, for he had already seen man's ultimate capacity to inflict death. His mind blanked out, as it did on this day. Taishowa remained calm in the death storm that raged around him.

'Steady,' he told Watanabe, who was still fumbling with the combination.

Watanabe started again. Eight, eight, eighty-eight. The number eight signified health and prosperity in Asian culture. Taishowa was superstitious and used it for all his secret codes, as did thousands of Chinese and other Japanese.

Watanabe turned the combination slowly. He wanted to hurry, but forced himself to take his time. *What can be in the safe that's so valuable to the old man?*

The lock clicked at last. Watanabe turned the large steel handle downwards and the heavy metal door opened. Watanabe gasped, then looked up at Taishowa – who said nothing. Watanabe turned his attention back to the safe. Shiny bars of platinum, worth over half a million dollars, were stacked wall to wall. *No wonder he wanted to return*, thought Watanabe as he took a bar out of the safe.

'Leave it. Take out the brown envelopes and lock the safe up again.' Taishowa was clearly used to giving orders.

Watanabe was surprised, but did as he was told. He climbed out of the wreckage and handed the envelopes to Taishowa.

'You're going to leave the platinum?'

'Young man, listen to me. The platinum is of no use. It will weigh us down. The next few weeks are about survival. During the war we took only what we could carry. All that matters now is food and water.'

'Then why did we come back?'

'One must plan ahead,' said Taishowa, stuffing the envelopes into his shirt pocket. He turned to go, then looked back at Watanabe with a whimsical smile, patting his shirt where the envelopes lay safe. 'I'll tell you when the time is right.'

The two began their tortuous journey back to Ginza crossing, where they had left the group of subway survivors. Watanabe had no idea that the envelopes were much more valuable than the gleaming bars of platinum that he had left behind.

What the envelopes contained were the title deeds to Taishowa's properties scattered throughout Japan. Much of his land was in Ginza, making him a dollar billionaire on paper. Taishowa had hurried back to his safe because he remembered the confusion of 1945. Land records were destroyed during the fire bombings. Most Japanese had lived in small wooden houses and kept their records squirrelled away under the floorboards or in locked wooden cabinets. Few had strongboxes or safes. After the city was gutted by fire, land ownership fights broke out. Yakuza gangs, insurance firms and real estate companies grabbed all the prime land at that time, throwing out all small landowners without title deeds. Taishowa knew that the post-quake confusion would result in land expropriation, but his own property was now safe.

As they neared the group, Taishowa surprised Watanabe by stepping over the body of a woman lying crumpled in the street. She wore an expensive dress, with lovely pearls and gold earrings. Watanabe stooped down to see if she was still alive. She was dead. He couldn't believe that the old man could be so callous, since it would have taken only two steps to walk respectfully around the body.

'Why did you step over her?'

Taishowa stopped. 'Look around you. There are bodies everywhere.'

It was true. Over a hundred corpses lay strewn about. Watanabe's thoughts turned to his own wife and children.

Taishowa touched his shoulder. 'Don't dwell on this, my young friend. Nor think ill of me. I didn't step over this poor woman's body out of callousness or indifference. It is fate.' Like most of his fellow countrymen, Taishowa was a Buddhist and fatalistic about certain aspects of life and death. 'She's dead. I can't bring her back. If we mourn every soul lost today, then our lives will be worthless. To save your subway victims, to save those who survived the quake, you must make your way to the food hall in Nihonbashi. Before today the walk would take you half an hour. Today, who knows how many hours or days it will take. Forget the dead. It's your job to save the living. Concentrate. You're now their leader.' Now it was Taishowa who looked down the street – not at the bodies but at all the rubble, glass, electric cables and fires. 'The task won't be easy.'

When the two men arrived back with the survivors they were still sitting in the middle of Ginza crossing. It was an absurd sight. Half an hour earlier these people had been well-dressed, purposeful contributors to Japan's economic miracle. Now they sat huddled, confused and without direction. The absurdity of the situation seemed a metaphor for Japan. The Ginza, a materialistic magnet that drew Japan's shoppers in droves, lay in ruins: Mitsukoshi, Wako, Matsuya, Takashimaya . . . Three-storey neon signs were shattered or fallen. The pavement was buckled. Geysers of brown mud had subsided into mere fountains, the brown water draining itself down into the subway caverns that burrowed throughout Tokyo. The air was dry. Although the taxi-cab LPG explosions had abated, they had been replaced by fires.

Watanabe addressed the small crowd had gathered.

'My name is Watanabe and I'm from Mitsukoshi. We're going to walk to Nihonbashi.'

A man interrupted him. 'Why? What's in Nihonbashi?'

'Food. And water. We have a warehouse full of it.'

Another man spoke up. Watanabe recognized him as a section manager in the accounts department, a year younger than himself.

'The Mitsukoshi warehouse? We need permission. We can't just force it open.'

'Yes,' murmured some dissenting Mitsukoshi clerks who agreed with the accountant.

They were all over-ruled by Watanabe. 'I'll take responsibility as the eldest class member of Mitsukoshi. Our job will be to distribute food and drink to those in need. First I need a doctor. Is there one here?'

A man raised his hand. A nurse spoke up too.

'Okay, you'll be our medics. As we walk down Chuo-dori you can attend to any emergencies. Next, does anybody have a Satlink phone?'

'I do.' A smartly dressed woman raised her hand.

'Do you mind?' he said, gently taking the phone from her hand and switching it off. 'How long will your battery last?' he asked her.

'About sixteen hours.'

'This is now our emergency phone. Each of us has a family. When we reach our food depot, we'll take turns to call outside the Tokyo area.'

'Why can't we phone now?' asked someone.

'First, all the terrestrial phone lines are down in Tokyo. You can't help your relatives if they're dead. First we take care of ourselves and then we'll think of our loved ones.'

Watanabe was speaking to himself as much as to the group. The jabs in his chest went burning through him as he thought of his family.

He looked up Chuo-dori, Japan's most photographed street. Here had once stood the glittering Ginza shops, bars and restaurants. Now the street was utterly devastated and full of sharp objects. Walking was going to be hazardous.

The women had no shoes, having discarded their high heels to climb the metal staircase leading from the subway to the manhole cover. They had to find some shoes to protect their feet. But Watanabe knew that the women would never scavenge shoes from bodies in the street. His countrymen never wore used clothes, especially shoes. Japan was a nation of compulsive foot washers, and the thought of putting one's clean foot into an odour-filled container of dry sweat was repulsive. Cleanliness pervaded society to such an extent that the country even had a national shoe-burning day. Fortunately the Esperante shoe boutique lay in ruins 50 metres from Mitsukoshi.

'Wait here,' he ordered the women, then pointed to two men. 'You – and you. Please come with me.'

The three men walked down the littered street and into the lobby of the boutique, a small two-storey building. Watanabe picked up a steel pipe and broke the remaining shards of glass sticking up from the showroom window. 'Get us something to put these shoes into,' he said to one of the men. Five minutes later they were carrying twenty pairs of shoes to the women.

As they left the building, as an afterthought Watanabe ran back in. He opened his wallet and left his business card on the cash register, writing on the back: 'I owe you for twenty pairs of shoes. N. Watanabe.'

All the women in the group now had footwear, mostly mismatched sandals, loafers and boots. But fashion was no longer a concern and they were grateful. The group moved off and followed Watanabe and Taishowa down the street.

With the danger of electrocution gone now that the power supply had been turned off, many Ginza survivors found themselves surrounded by various treasures. A pearl necklace lay in the street. *Surely it would be impossible to identify*, reasoned one scavenger. *Who would miss it amidst all this confusion?* The small baubles in the street led to greater treasures within ruined shops. Curious treasure hunters outside the Watanabe group, immune to the death around them, pretended to be searching for victims in the rubble. Jewellery shops were first prize and those not completely destroyed were filled with 'rescue' workers wandering through the wreckage, heads bent. Most carried large leather bags, also 'liberated' from nearby shops, to hold their booty.

The scavengers ranged through business executives, shopkeepers, elegant middle-class women, restaurant cooks and passers by of every description. At first they were discreet about what they were doing, but this shyness was soon overcome as looting fever spread among the survivors of Ginza. Soon brazen fortune-seekers, many of them well dressed, were openly stripping corpses of rings, necklaces and watches. Looters learned to distinguish between the rich booty which adorned wealthy shoppers and company executives: gold necklaces and diamond rings on ladies, fancy Seiko, Rolex and Gucci watches on men. Special bonuses were discovered on senior executives. Most salarymen wore company pins on the left lapel of their suit jacket. Senior executives had specially designed ones, usually some sort of diamond or platinum affair celebrating long service to their company. Looters quickly learned to bypass low-level office staff and young salarymen whose gold-plated trinkets were worthless. By the end of the day Ginza's shops and corpses had been picked over as if by hyenas.

Another rumour flew through the Ginza that the Sakura Bank near Tokyo station had survived the quake. Groups of scavengers fought their way through the rubble, mud, fire and bodies in their rush to the bank. Like vultures, the first group circled outside before their leader made his way forward as if to peck at a corpse. His entry gave courage to the growing mob, who followed him into the lobby. A single bank clerk remained, a young man no more than twenty-five. His colleagues had fled, died or lay dying.

The mob leader jumped the teller's cage.

'You can't do that. Please leave,' said the junior clerk.

The leader laughed. The group close on his heels smelled money.

'Nobody is allowed back there,' the clerk said loudly, his voice annoying the leader.

'We heard there's 50 million yen in the drawers.'

'It's now my responsibility to guard this money,' said the clerk, standing behind the counter with a metal rod in his hand. 'I apologize, but if anyone touches the money drawers I shall strike them.'

Suddenly the leader jumped forward and the clerk lashed out, hitting him in the shoulder.

'I'm sorry, but I must protect the bank. Anyone else who – ' But his voice was drowned out as the money-hungry crowd, driven by avarice, rushed the teller's desk. A frenzied war cry broke out as a pack of 10,000 yen notes was discovered. The clerk was trampled in the mêlée. But there was hardly any money in the drawers. The Sakura Bank did not open for business until 9 a.m., and only two tellers had begun filling their money drawers at the moment the quake struck. This angered the mob, who moved on to the Sumitomo Bank across the street.

A man lay dying in front of the building, but the mob ignored him.

'Please help me,' he gasped as he lay on his stomach.

By now the mob was now used to dispassionately stripping corpses. 'He's going to die anyway,' reasoned one of them. 'Why not take his things now before somebody else does?' He bent down to pick up the dying man's wallet.

'No. Please. Help me,' he pleaded.

They opened the wallet and found 30,000 yen which they split among them, throwing the wallet on to a pile of rubble. One then pulled off the man's gold wedding band, while his companion pocketed the watch.

'Please. I have a wife and children.'

Ignoring him, the bandits ran off, leaving the clerk to die. Three weeks later when a pick-up truck came round to gather corpses for burning, the body of their victim was found. He had no identification. The body collectors marked him down under 'unknown'. His wallet and identification lay 2 metres away under a light covering of rubbish. He was just another of Tokyo's unidentified bodies.

Watanabe's group, too, was not immune to the looting fever that swept Ginza. Though they had travelled light, Watanabe had insisted that his group pick up survival equipment such as matches and flashlights along the way. Tiffany's had a diamond exhibition in its show window. The display window, on the ground floor of the Takashimaya department store, was dressed up with nineteenth-century mining equipment from the Kimberley diamond mines in South Africa. When Tiffany's windows were blown out, the equipment scattered on to the street. Watanabe retrieved a pickaxe and shovel. He noticed some of the women in his party picking through the broken glass after he had asked them to look for a rock hammer. *Good*, he thought to himself, *they are finally helping*. For the tenth time on that journey Watanabe left his business card in a shop window. 'I borrowed your pickaxe and shovel. Thank you. N. Watanabe.'

A middle-aged woman whispered encouragingly to a young office girl near her, 'I've got a sapphire surrounded by diamonds. Forget trying to find single diamonds – they're too hard to pick out from the glass. Go for rubies or emeralds.'

Dejected, the typist poked around in the glass one last time. Suddenly she gave a gasp. On the ground was a diamond necklace with sixty-six two-carat diamonds encircling a magnificent forty-carat pendant. A tiny gold tag simply said 'Made by Harry Winston of Fifth Avenue'. Harry Winston was the world's premier jeweller. The girl quickly stuffed the necklace into her bag, but she was not quick enough and the eagle-eyed older woman was instantly by her side.

'I'll trade you everything I found for that necklace. I must have it.' Her mouth was twisted with greed. In desperation, she took off the black-faced Bulgari watch that her husband had given her for her fiftieth birthday and shoved it into the girl's hand. 'Take this to replace your Swatch.'

The typist relented. What would she do with a diamond necklace anyway? The older woman dumped her treasure into the office girl's bag and grabbed the necklace before the girl could change her mind.

The middle-aged woman smiled all the way to the food depot. In her handbag she had the most glamorous piece of jewellery in Tokyo, a real Harry Winston creation, probably worth over 300 million yen – nearly $3 million. What she did not know was that the necklace was a Tiffany prototype used by the store to procure orders. The most valuable part of the necklace was its platinum setting: the rest was just $700 worth of zirconium.

31

THE RING

Tuesday, late afternoon, near the Mitsukoshi warehouse in
Tokyo's financial district

'We are responsible for the prevention and fighting of fires. The
problem of leaking chemicals and toxic waste is a matter for the
Ministry of Health and Welfare.'
The National Fire Agency, responding to a question on how
it would combat toxic fumes and waste should any of the
nine hundred storage tanks in Tokyo Bay explode or leak

Watanabe doubled over, convinced he was having a heart
attack.
Each time he thought of his family a similar burning
sensation seared through his chest. He had not experienced such pain
since the Mitsukoshi department store sent him on a training course
twenty years ago. He had been a newly-wed. For three months he
lived in Mitsukoshi dormitories around Japan, so forlorn that he
was unable to go out for a meal or a drink with his colleagues. The
thought of being away from his new wife sent spasms through his
heart. Convinced he was having a seizure, Watanabe took medical
advice in Osaka. 'Doctor, I think I'm having a heart attack,' he had
told the man.
The doctor asked two dozen questions about Watanabe's eating
habits, lifestyle, medical history and personal life. Then he put down
his stethoscope and chuckled. 'Young man, you're in love. My advice
is to get back to your girl as quickly as possible.'
Watanabe went to his boss at Mitsukoshi, pretending that his
grandmother had died and that he needed to return to Tokyo for
the funeral. It was the only time Watanabe remembered telling an
outright lie. His entire savings went into buying a round-trip bullet
train ticket. That weekend was one of the happiest in his life. When
it was time to leave his young bride again, Watanabe cried. The
pains in his chest continued until his return a month later. From

that day until the earthquake, Watanabe had never spent a night away from his wife. And now the burning chest pains had returned after twenty years.

The group reached the remains of Mitsukoshi's flagship store in Nihonbashi, a walk of 4 kilometres in nine hours. Watanabe prayed that the nearby underground storage area had not been flooded by liquefaction and instructed the survivors to begin digging through the sludge and rubble to locate the entrance. But first he had to quell a revolt incited by the Mitsukoshi accountant.

'Stop! We must wait for instructions,' the man insisted. 'This isn't our property. Head office must approve our opening this warehouse.'

'There's no head office,' said Watanabe. 'Look over there. The Mitsukoshi headquarters has been destroyed. People will soon be dying of hunger and thirst. No, we're going to open this warehouse.'

'Then I insist you call the branch manager at Osaka. He's a main board director.'

'Okay. And I suppose you have that number with you?'

'Yes. Here it is.' The accountant pulled out an electronic Casio directory and gave Watanabe the number. Reluctantly he dialled Osaka, got through to the manager of the main branch and explained how he wanted permission to open the warehouse to feed survivors.

'It's not my area of responsibility,' replied the manager. 'I'm only in charge of Osaka. You must contact an executive director with duties in Tokyo.'

'Impossible. You're the only senior executive who can be contacted. You must decide.'

'No. It doesn't fall under my jurisdiction. I have no authorization to say yes.'

'That means you also have no authority to deny permission.'

'No.'

'No meaning I am correct? Or no meaning you deny me permission?'

'No, I have no authority to speak on the issue.'

'Thank you,' said Watanabe in disgust, hanging up.

'Osaka refuses to make a decision. As the ranking Mitsukoshi executive I have decided we will proceed.'

'That's illegal, I'm warning you,' threatened the accountant.

'Look, I've had enough of your threats. Your objection is noted. We're entering this warehouse without your assistance. My job now is to save lives. Clearly no rescue is imminent. Everybody with me, please begin digging.'

All but the accountant and two junior Mitsukoshi clerks started clearing rubble. They uncovered an entry and forced open the door. Watanabe flipped on the auxiliary lighting, and back-up generators whirred into life. He looked around to find the vast warehouse dry. Fortunately the developers of the railway lines who had built the warehouse for Mitsukoshi had built thick walls to protect against high water tables. The waterproofing had been effective.

'Okay, everybody in.'

Watanabe helped old Taishowa down the stairway, then grabbed a clipboard at the entrance and took down everybody's name. The group now numbered about forty, additional men and women having joined them along the hazardous walk. The accountant and clerks stubbornly remained outside.

Amazingly, the warehouse had barely been affected by the quake. Ground acceleration forces had almost no impact below the surface. The shelving was still bolted in place, although most of the goods had been jostled around or thrown to the ground. Battery-operated forklifts were parked unscathed in one corner.

The survivors gasped in fascination – they had never seen such a big place. It was more than three football fields long and two wide, with goods stacked some 12 metres high. Few members of the group were used to such space and quantity. Food in shops was usually presented in tiny, elegantly wrapped packages, and mass production behind the scenes was seldom revealed.

Watanabe watched the enchantment on their faces. Everyone forgot their problems as they wandered around, some ripping open drinks while others simply gaped.

'Taishowa-san, look at them. They're like little children. All their worries are forgotten.'

'But I see yours aren't.'

'Am I that obvious?'

'Yes. It's clear you miss your family.'

'I must get home.' Heartache swept over him again. 'Taishowa-san, I must find them. Tonight I'll organize relief efforts here, but tomorrow I must leave you. I promise to be back after I have ensured the safety of my wife and children. You will be in charge in my absence. The group needs wisdom.'

'I'll wait for you.'

Watanabe climbed the staircase to the concrete mezzanine, preparing to address the group.

'Thank you all for working so hard in clearing the entryway,' said Watanabe, his voice echoing in the vast cavern. 'First we'll divide into four groups: water and food relief, excavation and medical treatment. Volunteers from each group will be taken for excavation. Rows 1–3 are filled with AQUA, Coke, Perrier, HI-C, Brazilia, Nutrament and other soft drinks. Please help yourselves. We'll then restack the shaken goods, take an inventory and ration the drinks. We'll do the same with food. Our goal is to help as many people as possible. Tonight we need rest, and at daybreak we'll begin our relief efforts.

'Anyone wishing to call home outside Tokyo may form a line at the head of the stairs. We must be above ground for the Satlink signal to work. There are forty of us, and I suggest a one-minute maximum until we can find another battery. For those in need of a toilet, I'm sorry but you'll have to go outside. We can build some latrines tomorrow. Since this is a food warehouse. Mitsukoshi does not have blankets here for our bedding. I apologize. We must make do.

'Tomorrow I'll be leaving for a short while, but I'll return shortly. Kozo Taishowa has kindly volunteered to organize the relief in my absence. Thank you.'

Watanabe took the phone above ground. It was now dark and the accountant and clerks had cleared a place to sit in the rubble, still defiantly boycotting the warehouse.

'Please join us,' offered Watanabe.

One of the clerks moved to get up, but the accountant held him back.

'We won't be a party to such banditry.'

'If you change your mind, just enter.'

'We won't.'

Watanabe hit a button on the Satphone and the numbers lit up. He dialled 119 for emergency services, and to his surprise somebody picked up. All 119 calls usually came into the Tokyo Fire Department in Otemachi, but they now had been diverted to an outlying district.

'Emergency services. May I help you?' asked a young woman.

'Yes, my name is Watanabe and I work for Mitsukoshi. A group of us have uncovered the Mitsukoshi food storage warehouse in Nihonbashi. Can you please send out a radio message to survivors in the area that we will be distributing food and water tomorrow morning? We're one block north of where the Mitsukoshi department store once stood.'

This really got the accountant worked up and he began shouting. 'You can't do that. That's theft. Don't listen to him.'

Watanabe ignored him and concentrated on the woman's response.

'Yes,' she said. 'We've had a number of calls from the Nihonbashi area and will pass your offer on. I'm not sure about the radio, but I'll try.'

The accountant wasn't about to let Watanabe pillage Mitsukoshi goods. He rushed over and lunged out at him. 'Thief!'

Watanabe thanked the woman and hung up just as the accountant tried to grab the phone. He missed and fell to the ground.

Watanabe handed the phone to the next in line and the survivors formed a protective circle around the caller. They were anxious to reach their relatives and did not appreciate the accountant's behaviour. He returned to his concrete stool, to find only one clerk left. The other had ducked into the warehouse during the commotion.

'Traitor!' he yelled.

Watanabe descended into the cool warehouse, found Kozo Taishowa and pulled a small black truncheon from his knapsack. It was a stun gun. 'I picked this up by an overturned police car, just in case looting or mob rule breaks out. This button will turn the rod on and send 90,000 volts of electricity through a person. It's meant to stun them, not kill them.'

Kozo Taishowa took the device and buried it deep in his shirt. 'Everything will be fine. Just find your family,' he said.

Watanabe announced lights out at 10 p.m. and left flashlights for those needing to urinate outside. He curled up near the old man on the concrete floor, and used his arms as a pillow.

The next morning he awoke to the sound of machinery. While he had slept, the excavation team had opened up the main cargo loading area. A concrete ramp led to the ground level and allowed light to pour into the depot. The team was already shifting goods by forklift to the ground level and Watanabe could hear a crowd outside the loading dock. Emergency services had broadcast Watanabe's message and those with portable radios in Nihonbashi and outlying areas had flocked to the warehouse. Others came through word of mouth.

Kozo Taishowa's stentorian voice could be hear above the noise of the crowd. Watanabe smiled, then packed his knapsack with water and biscuits and joined Taishowa above ground. A few thousand people were gathered. Although Taishowa had demanded that the crowd form an orderly queue the refugees remained bunched towards the front, afraid that supplies would run out before they had a chance to drink and eat. Taishowa used the warehouse bullhorn to quieten the crowd.

'We have enough food and water for many weeks. Again I ask you to form a single line.'

This seemed to pacify them.

'We'll register your names here and allocate a daily ration per person. I repeat, there's enough for everyone. Those needing medical attention, please report to the side entrance for help.'

Kozo signed off when he saw Watanabe approaching.

'I'm off, my friend.' He bowed to the old man.

'I hope you find your family well and safe. Don't worry about these people. I can handle things.' Ten people were waiting to speak to him. 'I feel young again. Off you go,' he said, and turned to deal with those needing help.

Watanabe set off. He had given little thought on how to reach his home in Chiba, north-east of Tokyo, which was normally a three hour journey by car during the rush hour and an hour and a half each way by train. Walking would take days through the mangled wreckage of Tokyo. The main highway in that direction, the Shuto Expressway, had toppled on its side much like the Hanshin Expressway had during the Kobe earthquake. Watanabe just followed a wide boulevard eastwards towards giant billows of thick black smoke and knew he was heading in the right direction.

On the reclaimed shores of Tokyo Bay lay the storage depots which fuelled Japan's mighty economic machine. Nearly all the nation's oil was imported through Tokyo Bay, and along it the country's nine oil refiners had massive plants which together produced over 80 million kilolitres of oil a year. Nine hundred storage tanks held a year's supply of refined oil. The massive petrochemical plants alongside the bay were called *kombinato*, after the Russian word for 'complex'.

The convenience of Tokyo Bay to major industry made it an ideal storage area. Little thought was given to the fact that this Armageddon-in-waiting lay next to the world's largest megalopolis. So convenient was the landing point that the chemical companies used tanks which ringed the bay to store their toxic fuels: hydrochloric acid, ammonia, methylene chloride, sodium cyanide, cyanic acid, toluene and ethylene.

When the first jolt struck, Mitsui Storage Tank No. 13 slumped to its side, its foundations finding little support in the reclaimed land. The ground had turned to slush and the steel buttresses riveted to the tank buckled. Though most storage tanks were required to have support pilings buried more than 18 metres deep through the soft, reclaimed land, Mitsui's were exempt from this requirement. Their tanks pre-dated 1984 and were only required to put up buttresses to prevent the tanks falling over in a quake. Though tilted on its right side, Tank No. 13 held. The refined oil in the half-full tank began rocking like water in a bathtub. It picked up speed, assisted by the long amplitude of the shock waves. The rocking motion of the oil became more powerful, and the liquid crushed its floating ceiling and spilled over the side of the tank.

The authorities who regulated this toxic time bomb had taken a few other precautions. Mitsui Storage Tank No. 13 had been required to be built with a concrete holding tank around the main storage tank to deal with any leakage. The capacity of the encircling tank was 110 per cent of that of the main tank. Unfortunately the outer tank cracked, and the oil spilt out on to the ground and into the bay. The main oil pipe running from Tank No. 13 to the off-loading bay, like the thousands of kilometres of other piping, was instantly ruptured. The edges of jagged steel where the pipe had ripped apart grated against one another and, although the first spark did not catch, the second did, setting the fuel alight. The flame followed the oil pipe like a fuse to a keg of dynamite.

But the National Fire Agency felt it had taken adequate precautions against just such an emergency.

Each oil and chemical company had its own fire-fighting team, equipped with a fire engine, fireboat and chemical agents to douse the flames, who reported to the NFA. None of the fire-fighting teams could be relied upon during the confusion of this particular holocaust. Not only were they frightened by the blast of Tank No. 13, but most of them ran for their lives and were dead within an hour. The reclaimed land on Tokyo Bay had turned to jelly and fire-fighters were unable to escape themselves, let alone fight a fire. Eighty million kilolitres of fuel were about to go up.

The inferno of Tank No. 13 was the first of a series of explosions that rocked the entire *kombinato*. Residents of Seoul in South Korea, across the Sea of Japan, claimed to have heard a series of explosions. The ammonia tank adjoining the Mitsui complex was next to go up, sending a plume of poisonous white smoke high into the air. Fortunately for Tokyo's refugee population the prevailing wind was north. The residents of Urawa, north of Tokyo, were not so lucky as the white cloud moved on its path of death and hovered over their town. First came a slight stinging sensation to the eyes, then a burning in the lungs, quickly followed by the vomiting of blood. The lucky ones died immediately. Wheezing survivors blinded and crippled by the white cloud wished for death.

Within ten minutes the entire *kombinato* was ablaze. Some of the black billows rose 600 metres into the sky. Scientists later recovered satellite photographs of the black clouds and remarked that it looked as if dozens of atomic bombs had been detonated over the city. The American satellite photos were developed immediately, and so alarmed the government that additional rescue ships were ordered to Tokyo Bay. As Watanabe followed the black clouds, the sun was blotted out and a dusk-like darkness descended upon him.

He walked to the banks of the Sumida River which flowed into Tokyo Bay, but to his frustration the bridge lay in ruins. He scrambled down to the riverside to find a way across and found that a number of boats, freed from their moorings, had drifted downstream with the outgoing tide. Many of them had been caught on the concrete and iron remains of the bridge. A small powerboat lay pinned against the wreckage, the tidal rush pushing it against the bridge. Watanabe grabbed the bowline and pulled the boat forward out of the wreckage.

As he was pulling the boat, he lost his footing and slipped into the fast-running water, his hand still gripping the line. He struggled to keep his head above water as the current pulled him out to sea. The boat rocketed downstream and the bow glanced off the side of his head. Watanabe saw stars, and knew that if he blacked out now he would never see his wife and children. Man and boat rushed towards Tokyo Bay with the outgoing tide. It was not until they hit a little eddy that he was able to work his way back and climb aboard by the stairs in the stern. Head throbbing, he manually fired up the two Yamaha outboard engines.

Chiba was 30 kilometres across the bay from Tokyo. He eased off the throttle as he passed under the remains of the various bridges. Then, finding himself in the middle of Tokyo Bay and away from the fire storm onshore, he opened up the engines. The engines churned through the thick oil and toxic chemicals.

As he raced across Tokyo Bay his heart soared to think that in an hour he would be reunited with his family. After thirty minutes Watanabe made out the Chiba waterfront. He headed for Water World, a family outdoor centre only a ten-minute walk from his house. He eased off the throttle again and pulled up to the bulkheads. The giant concrete breakers had been strewn about. Watanabe carefully navigated among the sunken hazards and tied the powerboat up alongside a broken pier.

Excitedly he began jogging towards home. Chiba looked less damaged than Tokyo and this gave him hope, so he began to run faster. As he came around the bend he saw Fujimoto's shop-front.

Home was only a hundred metres away now. Watanabe slowed down and began walking. Something was wrong. Most of the homes on his street no longer existed. Smoke rose from smouldering embers. Where his own house had been, only his mailbox was left standing.

Frantically Watanabe leaped into the ashes and began digging with his hands.

'No, no, Kimi-chan,' he cried.

After an hour he found his wife's body where the kitchen had been. Her corpse was charred but Watanabe knew Kimiko's tiny shape instantly. The gold ring he had given her on their engagement was still on her blackened finger. Crying, Watanabe picked up her hand and held it in his. The ring was still hot and burned Watanabe's palm, leaving an imprint. When his flesh had absorbed the heat of the ring, he lifted his wife's corpse and gently laid it in front of the house.

Head bent, he slowly walked back to Fujimoto's shop, entered and sifted through the items strewn over the shop floor. Fujimoto was in a total state of fright and did not move. *I thought I had killed him.*

Watanabe took a blanket, some oranges, chopsticks, rice and a bottle of water. 'It's Kimiko. She's dead. I'll pay you later,' mumbled Watanabe. He walked slowly home in shock.

Worried that Watanabe's ghost had come back to earth to pester him, Fujimoto fretted the rest of the day and could not sleep all night. He thought he had successfully done away with his distant relative and neighbour.

Watanabe returned home, wrapped Kimiko in the blanket and covered her face. He kissed her burnt head and laid oranges by her body. Then he made an open fire and boiled some rice in a pot which he uncovered in the kitchen. He left the rice near her body, the pair of chopsticks standing straight up in the rice, and then left to find his children.

The primary school was only two blocks away. In agony, Watanabe plodded towards the school. He passed neighbours along the way and asked about his children, but nobody had seen them.

Ahead a rescue team was busy at work. The brick school building had collapsed. The scene was bleak and grey, the only colour coming from the children's bright orange safety hats which lay strewn on the ground like dead flowers. Most of the children had died in the school and their bodies were carefully laid out in the playground for parents to identify. Wailing mothers cried over their dead children.

Most fathers had not returned, either dead or unable to get back from Tokyo.

Watanabe instantly recognized young Matsuo's body. His limp figure seemed untouched. Most of the children had died from suffocation and in death seemed only in a state of sleep. One of Matsuo's sneakers kept emitting a red light. Matsuo was proud of the sneakers his father had bought for his birthday: with each step, the pressure lit up a red strip along the heel. Matsuo had changed from his school uniform into his sneakers for playtime outside. Neither he nor any of the other children in his class made it to the playground. Watanabe took off Matsuo's tiny sneakers and held them in his hand. Tears poured down his cheeks.

'Daddy, daddy,' shouted a familiar voice across the playground.

His daughter Naomi came running up and hugged him. She did not know about Matsuo or her mother.

'Daddy, I was so scared. We were in the playground when the quake hit. Just like the story you told us the other night. Oh Daddy, I was so scared. I looked everywhere for Matsuo but I couldn't find him.'

Then Naomi spotted the little body. She tore herself away and knelt beside her brother.

'Matsuo, wake up, wake up,' she said, shaking him.

Her father knelt down beside her. 'Naomi-chan. Matsuo's dead.'

The little girl looked up at her father questioningly. 'Dead? You mean he can't play with me any more?'

Naomi did not seem to understand. Watanabe picked up his tiny son and walked home with his daughter at his side.

Watanabe performed his own funeral service for his wife and son instead of the usual three-day ritual. He and Naomi slept in the open air that night with the bodies. The next morning Watanabe went off to Fujimoto's store to buy two white and blue ceramic urns for their ashes.

'I'm sorry to hear about Kimiko and Matsuo,' said Fujimoto. His devious mind had been at work all night. 'You were too distressed yesterday to talk, but now I can tell you what happened.' Guilty of killing Mrs Watanabe, Fujimoto did not want to be a suspect. 'I tried to save your wife,' he lied.

This caught Watanabe's attention and Fujimoto went on, holding up his right forearm which had been badly burned. He had been doing a bit of night-time looting through neighbours' homes, searching for valuables, and had brushed his arm against some red-hot copper plumbing. Striated tube marks were clearly imprinted against his forearm.

'I went into the flames to save her but was burned myself.'

Watanabe bowed. 'I am in your debt. Thank you very much, Fujimoto-san, for risking your life.'

Fujimoto was playing with Watanabe's emotions and sensing that he would cancel the million-yen debt. Purposely he did not bring the matter up. Instead Fujimoto feigned a solemn expression, forced a tear to his eye, bowed and handed Watanabe the urns. They cost 2500 yen each. Watanabe also purchased various other items, including some kerosene fire starter.

'Here, take these urns. This is a time of grief and mourning for you. Please don't repay me,' said Fujimoto.

'I'll be back to thank you.'

When Watanabe had left, Fujimoto rubbed his hands. He knew he had his victim hooked.

Watanabe laid his wife and son in the centre of the ashes of the house, doused their bodies with fire starter and lit them. Mrs Watanabe was already well incinerated and the carbon on her remains lit easily. Naomi cried as the two bodies burned, but Watanabe had no tears left. Two hours later he scraped their ashes into two separate urns. Normally the bodies would have been entirely destroyed in a fiery crematorium, but here charred remains of their skeletons remained. Watanabe buried their bones and put up a wooden plaque near their heads.

'Here lie Kimiko and Matsuo who shall remain untouched in this spot until one day their entire family is united in death. Nothing shall grow and nothing shall be raised in this spot. We miss you. Love, Nomo and Naomi.'

Both Watanabe and his daughter signed their names. Then the two of them headed back in the speedboat across Tokyo Bay to start a new life.

32

THE PIPE

Kaelin escaped from Tada's apartment and made her way to the Ministry of Construction in search of her lover.

She reasoned that Omori had been washing Tada's Mercedes when the quake struck. Kaelin walked outside where she spotted the car, its front end crushed by a concrete support. Terrified of looking inside, Kaelin made her way to the front and peered in, half expecting to find Omori lying dead. But he was nowhere to be seen. She cautiously moved up the passenger door and took a sudden intake of air when she realized he wasn't there. The car was empty! Maybe he was still alive.

If anything has happened to Omori, I will kill Tada, she vowed. Tada . . . Tada would know where Omori was. Kaelin looked up at the Ministry building. She could see that the seventh floor, where Tada's office was located, had not been destroyed. Maybe Omori was up there with him. She took a deep breath and looked for a way up. The bottom four floors of the Ministry had fallen to the ground, leaving an empty shell with the top three floors intact.

The emergency staircase nearest her was undamaged and stood like a concrete sentinel, attached to the main building's upper floors. Kaelin stumbled blindly over the rubble to the stairs and began climbing. They ended on the sixth floor and she stared across into the Ministry of Construction. The side of the building was gone and Kaelin could see all the desks, chairs, papers and cabinets thrown about. There was a metre-wide chasm separating the staircase from the main building. Not looking at the 15-metre drop, she jumped, landing in a passage. Tada had a corner office on the seventh floor above her.

'Anyone up there?' she cried out.

'Up here. Help!'

Kaelin waded through the debris in a nearby office and looked up at a hole in the ceiling but couldn't see anything.

'Up here,' Tada yelled again. 'I can't get down.'

At the sound of his voice she went cold and realized how much she wanted him dead.

Tada was trapped and fighting like a turtle to extricate himself from piping which had lodged him against the floor. Kaelin was his only hope of survival. 'Put one of those cabinets on its side and then put a chair on top,' he commanded.

I should just leave him here to die. She began to walk away, then made a terrible mistake and turned. 'Where's Omori?' she called up to him.

He seized upon her question with animal-like instinct and yelled down to her. 'I know where he is. I can take you to him, but we need to move quickly. He's injured badly.'

Rendered senseless by love, she looked around for something to stand on. Finding a sturdy wooden chair, she balanced it on the cabinet and pulled herself up.

Tada lay helplessly on his back. 'Lift these pipes off my chest and we'll find Omori.'

Kaelin lifted it just enough for Tada to wriggle out. He rolled over on to his stomach and then slowly lifted himself to one knee.

'Where is he?' cried Kaelin.

'You hairy slut. So you want your little Omori. He's probably dead, and you'll be too if you don't shut up.'

Kaelin broke into hysterical sobs and Tada slapped her in the mouth, splitting her lip and breaking her front tooth. She let out a scream. Then, defeated, she slumped down on the floor and remained there sobbing. Night had fallen, and Kaelin was certain she was going to die.

Hiroko heard a scream and broke away from the crew to find its source. She looked up into the Ministry of Construction but saw nothing. Spotting the lone concrete staircase, she scrambled over the debris while the others in the group shouted at her in the dark.

'Hiroko! Hiroko! Where are you going?' A rescue chopper on its way to the Palace drowned out their voices. Jiroo and the Palace guards headed down the street, oblivious to Hiroko's attempted rescue mission.

Once the chopper had passed, Hiroko could make out the sounds of Kaelin's crying. Her phone line was open and absent-mindedly she put it in her bag.

'Hello!' she cried out.

Tada heard Hiroko and waddled over to Kaelin.

'One word, bitch, and you die,' he whispered.

'Up here. Help. There are two of us. We're trapped,' yelled down Tada. 'I'll grab your arm. Jump on the chair.'

'Okay, I'm coming,' said Hiroko, climbing up the chair.

Just as Tada pulled her up, Kaelin yelled out. 'No, don't. Get out of here.'

But it was too late. Tada had already swung Hiroko up on to the floor.

She was confused. 'My name's Hiroko Fujita. What's wrong?' she said in English.

'Fujita? My name is Kaelin. We have spoken before about – ' said Kaelin just before Tada lashed out and hit her across the face with his forearm.

'How dare you hit a woman, you animal!' said Hiroko, dropping her bag and pouncing on Tada. She tried to scratch his eyes as she had been taught in her Columbia University self-defence course.

'Oh, what have we here? A wild little thing,' said Tada, flinging her off easily.

Hiroko fell badly, screaming out as she landed on a broken desk. She recovered and threw a large paperweight at Tada just as he was turning round. The object glanced off his shoulder. Enraged, he rushed for Hiroko.

'I'm going to kill you too, bitch,' he snarled.

'You're going down. I know everything about you. The Daishin scam. Building pay-offs. The Prime Minister. The Transport Minister. Everything.' She was pointing at him. 'You'll pay for what you did to the people of Tokyo, you murderer.'

Tada's eyes turned cold. 'So you're the bitch at the *Asahi* trying to bring me down.'

Kaelin was on her knees now. 'No, it was me. I told her everything!' she said defiantly, trying to protect Hiroko.

Tada nodded slowly and licked his lips. 'Well, nobody's going to write about our little Daishin scam now. And you,' he said turning to Kaelin, 'I suspected you were the mole.' He struck her again. 'I'm going to have fun playing with both of you. Nobody will ever know what happened to you.'

Like a bear, Tada approached Hiroko. She grabbed her bag from the floor and swung it at him. Tada punched her in the face and swiped her bag over the edge. Hiroko fell to the floor, out cold.

Meanwhile, as half a billion CNN viewers listened to the scuffle, glued to their TV sets and radios, the broadcast went dead. The phone fell on to some mangled concrete which jarred the battery and pin card loose. The world's only link to the quake lay in the dark, indistinguishable from the million other pieces of broken rubbish created by the quake.

After Hiroko was knocked unconscious, producers in Atlanta scurried to fill the blank air time. 'Say anything,' they told Alanda Voltaria, 'until we can get some quake experts on the line.'

'This is Alanda Voltaria at CNN headquarters in Atlanta. Our Tokyo correspondent Hiroko Fujita has just been brutally attacked by Japan's Minister of Construction in a bizarre incident. Our CNN quake team is now in Osaka where they'll enter Tokyo by helicopter.' Then she took a risk. 'The first stop by our news team will be the Ministry of Construction. CNN is committed to its journalists in the field, and we feel it's our responsibility to assist Hiroko Fujita and report back to you, our viewers, where she is. Now on the line from Chile we have renowned seismologist Dr Garcia . . .'

As soon as Voltaria signed off, her international producers started shouting. 'And what the fuck was that all about? What did you mean by "assisting Hiroko?"'

'If you're going to claim Hiroko is "CNN property", then you'd better protect her,' yelled Voltaria. 'If you don't go after her, I'll tell the world that CNN would rather chase a story than save a human life. Isn't it about time we stopped reporting news on a detached basis and became part of the news we create?'

Her producers backed down, partly because Hiroko's disappearance was news itself. Calls were already jamming the Atlanta switchboard, applauding CNN's decision to rectify a situation brought about by its own news-hungry tactics.

Meanwhile, back in Tokyo, as fires lit up the shadows of the night, Tada was advancing on Kaelin.

'You're next,' he said. He picked up an iron pipe and raised it over her head.

33

THE RAPE

'You will shoot to kill all suspected looters.'
Mayor Eugene Schmitz to 1000 hastily sworn-in volunteer
patrolmen during the 1906 San Francisco earthquake

Kaelin was trapped on the seventh floor of the Ministry of Construction with Tada, who had gone berserk. Thousands of campfires in the Imperial Palace grounds gave off a shadowy light by which she could make out the Minister's ogre-like image. Hiroko lay on the ground.

Tada snarled at Kaelin as he held the broken pipe above his head.

She tried to scream, but nothing came out of her throat.

A distant rumble could be heard, like far-off thunder. The thunder gave off a continuous roar, becoming louder and louder. *Please not again*, prayed Kaelin. She cringed, and seconds later another aftershock ripped through central Tokyo. The quake measured only 4 on the Richter scale, though its impact was as if it had been far greater. Tokyo's buildings stood precariously with a joist here and a strut there supporting an entire structure. They were as easily uprooted as a child's loose tooth hanging by a tendril and the Ministry of Construction was itself on the verge of collapse.

The shock sent Tada and Kaelin sprawling backwards over the edge of the floor. They plunged 5 metres and landed with Tada underneath.

'Fuck!' shrieked the Construction Minister, who had broken his leg. Kaelin climbed off him, ignored his screams and called out for her friend.

'Hiroko? . . . Hiroko, are you okay?' Kaelin shouted up to the floor above. There was no answer.

The Ministry, still rocking gently from side to side, was clearly in danger of collapse. Kaelin decided to rescue her and tried to clamber up the filing cabinet which had fallen on its side. The chair was broken and it looked as if reaching the next floor was now impossible.

'Stop, Kaelin. Help me . . .' came Tada's voice from the floor.

'Help *you*?' she replied in utter disbelief. 'You were about to kill me, you animal.'

'Kaelin, I didn't mean it.'

Tada could feel her slipping away from him and thought quickly. 'My anger has driven you away,' he said glibly. 'You are in love with somebody else and I understand.' He began to warm to his lie.

What an idiot. Does he think I believe him?

Tada began to take control. 'I know you love Omori. You can be with him. He's still alive and I can take you to him if you rescue me.'

'Of course you will,' said Kaelin, still trying to find a way up to the next floor. The building was now swaying dangerously.

'Are you willing to take that chance? Once you leave me there won't be any hope of finding Omori. Is life really worth living without him?'

She stopped again, confused. The building lurched sideways. Tada pressed his point home. 'Kaelin, this building's going to fall soon. You must rescue me in order to rescue Omori.'

'Do you really know where he is?'

'I swear to you.'

'Where? Where is he?'

Tada continued his manipulation. 'He's alive and I'll take you to him. Only I know where he is. First you must help me.' Tada had no way out of the building on his broken leg without her help.

'I'm not leaving here unless you promise to tell me where Omori is and you help rescue Hiroko.'

'One thing at a time, my darling. First I will take you to Omori. He's not far away. Then we rescue Hiroko.'

The building rocked sideways again and the seventh floor fell half a metre, then stopped.

Kaelin hesitated. 'Okay. Where is he?'

'Help me up and we'll go to him now. He's in the car park.' Kaelin helped the heavy man up and he leaned on her as they walked to the emergency staircase. It was a metre jump to the staircase and Kaelin jumped first.

'Come on,' shouted Kaelin.

Tada was a coward at heart and couldn't bring himself to jump. The longer he waited, the more pain he imagined. Only the sound of the Ministry falling apart made him choose pain over death.

He threw himself over, barely cleared the precipice, landed on his broken leg and screamed in agony, almost passing out. Then, with extreme difficulty, they struggled to the bottom of the emergency staircase. There Kaelin pulled away from Tada, leaving him to balance helplessly on his own.

'Okay, where is he?'

'Nearby. You'll need my help to find him. Help me and I promise I'll take you straight there. Let's go. He might need our help. Hurry!'

Kaelin let Tada put his right arm around her shoulder.

'The car park.'

'But I checked the car.'

'Do as I say.' Tada didn't care about Omori but he did need his car because it contained a phone. He could not let Hiroko get away and blab to the media about his underhand financial dealings. But one well-placed phone call would take care of her.

The front end of the Mercedes had been crushed by a telegraph pole and there was no sign of Omori in the car. Kaelin left Tada by the rear passenger door, calling for her lover, as he clawed at the door handle and deposited himself heavily on the leather seat.

He dialled Moyama's home number. 'Tada here. Is Moyama-san there?'

'No. He's out. This is Mata.'

'I'm stuck at the Ministry. Can you send two of your men over to help me?' He needed gangster muscle to track down Hiroko.

'Yes, Tada-san. We have units on patrol not far from you. Where are you?'

'In the car park in a black Mercedes. How long will it take?'

A rush of air came through the phone. 'I'm not sure. Early morning some time.'

Tada clicked off. He listened for Kaelin, but only heard faint sobs coming from the side of the car. Curious, he leaned over to the right side of the car and peered out of the window. Kaelin had Omori cradled in her arms. His head had been crushed by the telegraph pole and he had fallen by the side of the car.

'It's all right, my love, I'll take care of you.' Kaelin stroked his hair and kissed what was left of the side of his head. 'We'll have a wonderful life together, you'll see.'

Tada sat back in the seat and tried to ease the pain from his broken leg. *So, Kaelin's gone over the edge. But I still have plans for her*, he thought, dozing off. He went to sleep listening to the purr of Kaelin's voice as she comforted Omori's dead body.

An uneasy quiet filled Tokyo on Wednesday morning, the day after the quake. One look at the sunrise was enough to caution the city's survivors that trouble hung over them.

The Tokyo skyline was normally a pallid greyish white, but today pollution spewed from thousands of fires to create a fiery backdrop. In many ways the customary sterile skyline had become a metaphor for the unproductive and clinical lives of the worker and salaryman. But today the sky was a haunting shade of bluish black, spotted with explosions of orange as if it were a stage set for a war film.

The colourful sunrise woke Hiroko. She sat up and brushed herself off. Her hands and arms were blackened from soot and dirt and her clothes were torn to ribbons. *Where are Tada and Kaelin?* she wondered.

She took a fire-hose from the hallway, tied it twice around a pillar and lowered herself down to the sixth floor. Moments later she was back on the ground. There was nothing she could do about Kaelin now. *I must find Alex and my mother.* She set off in a westerly direction and a few minutes later spotted an abandoned bicycle. Without a second thought she picked it up and began pedalling.

Hiroko had been riding no more than five minutes when she heard foreign voices just out of earshot. Two men were arguing as they dug through a mound of rubble in which lay a toppled sign that said: 'Capitol Tokyu Hotel'.

'Stop complaining! I know the safe is behind the reception desk.'

Two Koreans, Kim and Lee, were arguing in their native tongue. Half the population of Korea answered to the names of Kim or Lee. Lee stopped digging to take a swig from a half-empty Suntory whisky bottle. Both men were drunk.

'So where the fuck's the reception desk?' slurred Lee, who was tired of digging.

'I had the clerk put all our cash in the safe. When he opened it I saw all sorts of jewellery and money. Just shut up and keep digging.'

The pair were salesmen from Korea's Pusan Steel Works, in Tokyo to sell their low-cost steel to Japanese construction companies. They travelled Asia together selling Pusan steel during the day and drinking and whoring at night. Stocky, abrasive and uncouth, both men looked like ruffians in their dirty dress clothes. They had been drinking, digging and sleeping for the past twenty-four hours.

On Monday evening, the night before the earthquake, Kim and Lee had been on the prowl in Shinjuku. They had each paid 20,000 yen, nearly $200, to watch an S & M show at Club Bondage, a popular place where members of the audience whipped the bare backsides of young Japanese girls. Kim had jumped up to take the lightweight cane from the dominatrix mama-san who acted as master of ceremonies to see that drunken guests did not get out of hand. Protests were hurled by the Japanese clients when Kim tried to spank the young girl on stage.

'He's Korean!' yelled the hostile crowd.

'Alien!' These were the worst insults in the Japanese language.

'You can't let a Korean hurt a Japanese woman.'

The Japanese disliked the Koreans and viewed them as an inferior species. The Koreans hated the Japanese with equal vehemence, having been subjugated numerous times in five hundred years by Japanese warlords and other warmongers. For this reason the Korean population of Tokyo had its own bars, restaurants and clubs. Shinjuku, however was yakuza territory and Club Bondage a traditional club despite its S & M performance.

The mama-san had to make a decision. 'Sorry, but you must leave.'

Two burly bouncers appeared and Kim and Lee left without a fight. Both were bitter.

'These Japanese think they own the fucking world. Let's find us some tasty hookers and show 'em who's boss.' Kim wanted to get rough and take his aggression out on a Japanese prostitute in what he termed a 'spite fuck'.

But the two Koreans were to have no luck that evening. They paid a 5000-yen cover charge to watch a strip show down the street and forked out another 5000 yen for two drinks. Kim called over the mama-san of the strip joint.

'How much to buy a girl for evening?' he asked in English.

Standard procedure was to negotiate with the mama-san over a 'bar fine' or payment to management for taking a girl home. Another fee would then be negotiated with the woman. But the mama-san did not like the look of the two Koreans and refused to discuss a bar fine.

'I'm sorry, our girls are not for sale. Try the Filipino bar down the street.'

Kim knew the mama-san was lying. All women were for sale in Shinjuku, but Japanese girls were reserved for Japanese men; Koreans had to sleep with foreign women. Kim was ready to tear the bar apart when he noticed three bouncers, dressed in short-sleeved shirts to show off their tattoos, appear in the doorway. Angry and hung-over, Kim and Lee returned to their hotel.

The next morning they jumped into a taxi for a nine o'clock

meeting. Five minutes into the journey the quake hit. The taxi felt as if it was being pushed from behind like a boat on the crest of a wave and the two Koreans felt sick. All control of the steering was lost, but nobody was injured as the taxi came to a rest like a surfer at the end of a long run. Not knowing where else to go, the Koreans walked back to the Capitol Tokyu Hotel. All they had to drink were two presentation bottles of Suntory whisky intended for their Japanese clients. After downing the first bottle they excitedly decided to dig for the hotel safe, an irrational act since neither man had any of how to open it once they had found it.

Hiroko assumed the men were rescue workers, put down her bike and approached them. She greeted them in Japanese and the drunken Koreans turned around, speaking in Korean.

'Ehhh, what have we here? A tasty piece of sushi.'

'She looks a bit sick – maybe we can give her an injection of raw beef,' joked Lee.

'*Sumimasen, Nihongo-o hanashimasu ka?*' said Hiroko, asking the two if they spoke Japanese. Then she switched to English. Both Koreans and Japanese had to learn English as a second language at school. 'Do you have a telephone?' enquired Hiroko. She wanted to call the Asahi newspaper offices in Osaka to see if there was any word of Alex. Hiroko had no idea that 500 million CNN and Asahi viewers were anxious about her whereabouts.

'A telephone?' He repeated her question in English before switching to Korean. 'I'll sure give her something to put her mouth on. Lee, we're going to show this lady what Korean men are made of.' He staggered threateningly towards her.

Hiroko, sensing danger, slowly backed away. 'I'm sorry, I just thought . . .'

Kim lunged forward and grabbed Hiroko by the waist, dragging her down on top of him. Kim began sniffing Hiroko like a dog on heat, forcing his unshaven face between her breasts.

'I like it when they struggle.'

'Get off me!'

Hiroko kicked him between the legs, but this excited Kim all the more and he held her on her back.

'Let's have some fun with her. Hold her hands down.'

Kim fumbled at his fly. Hiroko fought, but was no match for the large men.

Lee pulled Hiroko's skirt above her waist. 'Hey, wait, I don't want sloppy seconds.' Lee took off his tie and began tying Hiroko's hands above her head.

'Help! Help me!' Hiroko screamed.

The streets were virtually deserted but a nearby yakuza patrol was in the area, led by Mata, Moyama's bodyguard and confidant. Having found Tada and ascertained that he was not too seriously injured, Mata had ordered his men to Akasaka Palace where further relief supplies were being ferried in.

The patrol heard Hiroko's cries and ran over to help.

'Get them!'

Mata's men charged the two Koreans.

The first to the scene pulled Kim off Hiroko while another held Lee. Hiroko loosened her hands and pulled her skirt back down. Relieved but embarrassed, she could not look either her attackers or her saviours in the eye.

'Korean scum,' sneered Mata as he spat on them. A rumour had spread that the Koreans were plundering the city – a rumour partly inflamed by the radio report of Koreans looting a body when in fact they had been administering CPR. Koreans always seemed to be witch-hunted during major earthquakes. Immediately after the 1923 disaster, a rumour went around that Koreans had poisoned Tokyo's drinking water. Vigilante groups slaughtered more than two thousand of them in reprisal. And after the Kobe quake rumours abounded that fires in the city had been started by Koreans trying to cash in on buildings insurance.

Mata went into a rage and, without hesitating, pulled out his firearm. 'Apologize, scum!'

But Kim refused to beg for his life and instead lashed out at Mata. 'You cloven-footed dwarf, I bet you aren't man enough to fuck this young – '

Mata shot him through the head. As Kim dropped to the ground, Lee began grovelling.

'Please don't kill me.'

The yakuza leader motioned for his men to stand Lee on his feet.

'And this is for you,' said Mata, dispensing immediate justice by shooting Lee through the groin.

'That will teach you to try and fuck our women. Korea is the nation of whores, not Japan – remember that. You are not Japanese.'

Writhing in pain, Lee collapsed on to the ground.

Mata turned to Hiroko as a squelch came from his walkie-talkie. He turned the receiver on.

'Patrol two, any sign of the girl yet?' The distinctive, loud voice on the handset was heard by all. It was Tada.

Though still in a state of shock, Hiroko froze.

All patrols west of the Imperial Palace had been issued with a description of Hiroko and told without explanation to apprehend her and return her to the Minister. Hiroko's capture was a death sentence.

The handset squawked again. 'Patrol two, come in. Answer me, have you found the girl yet?' asked Tada.

Suddenly Moyama himself was calling in to Mata on the Satphone at the same time. 'Have you found the girl yet?' the underworld leader asked.

'Yes,' replied Mata.

'Don't let Tada know you've found her. Understand?'

'Yes, boss. He's on the handset.'

'I asked if you'd found her yet,' screamed Tada into the walkie-talkie.

'No. Still looking.'

'Well, call me when you have her.'

Mata turned the walkie-talkie off and came up to Hiroko who sat on the ground, her elbows between her legs.

'Thank you,' she said.

'You're welcome.'

'Why did you come to my rescue?'

'That's our code of honour. And anyway, I have a sister.' Mata squatted down next to Hiroko. 'The thought of somebody raping her made me crazy. I'm not sorry I killed that Korean, but I'm sorry about what happened to you. But we've got to get moving. The boss wants you safely back at his home.'

The yakuza patrol headed back to the Imperial Palace, with Hiroko in protective custody.

34

THE RESCUE

Early Wednesday morning, the day after the quake

'We had a curious spectacle of a city patrolled and guarded by Federal troops, state troops, municipal police and amateur safety committees. As a result there was continued friction and many clashes of authority.'
> Brigadier General Henry Noyes, the army officer in partial
> command of army troops during the 1906
> San Francisco earthquake

'General Mishima, this is Admiral Miyazawa here,' radioed the navy boss from his seaside base in Yokosuka, south of Tokyo. 'We've got a problem. Our reconnaissance planes have just picked up the USS *Ranger* twenty-four hours outside Tokyo Bay. If the Americans send in rescue teams before us, the media will make us look like fools.'

Mishima thought for a moment. 'Just a moment. Let me think.' *We kept the Americans out of Kobe and we've got to do the same thing here.* 'I've got an idea. Look, let's play up the rape angle. First they rape our schoolgirls in Okinawa and now they're after our young girls in Tokyo. If they manage to land, which we'll try to prevent, it shouldn't be hard to scare the public.'

'How are we going to do that?'

'That's why I'm a three-star general and in charge of the Tokyo rescue. Leave it to me. Now, what have you got on standby?'

'I've got fifteen Logistical Support Transport vessels in Tokyo Bay now.'

'The amphibious ones?'

'Yes. They're full of food and water and all ready to move ashore. We can take the wounded straight to naval hospitals.'

'Anything else?'

'I've got thirty-five destroyers there or on the way, ten seaplanes and twenty UH 60J choppers. The air force has twenty C-130 transport planes fuelled and ready to go.'

'Excellent. My choppers are stuck in Hokkaido but should be down shortly.' Most of Japan's military were committed to the north to prevent an invasion from Russia or North Korea.

'When can we move?' asked the admiral.

'When we find the governor.'

'And the Prime Minister?'

'Still in a coma. I'll call you when we can move.'

But the rescue operations remained paralysed. Eighteen thousand firemen, fifteen thousand riot police and twenty-two thousand army troops awaited the command of the governor of Tokyo. At that moment the governor was in French Polynesia, in an unofficial capacity, protesting against nuclear testing in the south Pacific. His protest consisted of drinking vast amounts of cold San Miguel beer out of the bottle, frolicking in the warm waters of the ocean and eating grilled lobster. He was now lying in the arms of a bare-breasted island girl, oblivious to the crisis unfolding in Tokyo.

Not one soldier was allowed into the city without the governor's permission. As General Mishima's troops stood on full alert, he continued to monitor the crisis via his UH-1 observation helicopters. A TV had been wired up to the emergency generators and a translator kept the general up-to-date on the quake through CNN. The general knew that there was a back-up plan in the event of the governor's absence, and he was determined to find out what it was.

'Get me the Tokyo Metropolitan Plan for Disaster Prevention,' he shouted to his aide. 'In the meantime, find me the city's top ten officials.'

General Mishima had already been in contact with the Defence Minister, who had put the navy and air force on full alert. All were waiting for the governor's permission. The radio had first reported that the Prime Minister was dead, then that he had been rescued by a woman news reporter. Medics were trying to revive him at this moment. Nobody could find the head of the National Land Agency to convene an emergency meeting of government heads.

The general's aide immediately sent fifty 'observers' into central Tokyo to locate city officials. Mishima hoped he wouldn't get reprimanded for sending in observers, but hopes of contacting the governor were dwindling, as were the chances for finding his colleagues. The observers crossed names off their lists one by one and in the end discovered that there were only two city officials who were not dead or missing.

Aojima, Yoshi	Governor (on holiday)
Takahashim, Asako	(missing)
Iizuki, Teremo	Assistant governor
Tsuchiya, Ryoichi	Treasurer (dead)
Michiko Nagasawa	Assistant treasurer
Tatekawa, Seizo	(missing)
Morita, Juro	(dead)
Fukumoto, Takeo	(missing)
Goto, Keniichi	(missing)
Kawasaki, Tatsuro	(missing)

'Here's the emergency manual, General.'

Mishima grunted and then quickly flipped through the Disaster Plan. He had to commit his troops or else he could forget his honourable retirement. After five minutes he found what he wanted. In the absence of the Tokyo governor, the city was to be governed by a three-man committee consisting of the assistant governor, the police superintendent and the treasurer. Two of these three constituted a quorum on which binding decisions could be made.

'Find me these three men. Now!' ordered Mishima.

The news was not good. The police superintendent was presumed dead and, though the assistant governor had been found, he refused to act without authorization from his boss, fearful that his move would be branded militaristic. General Mishima swore when he heard this. *Fucking Communist bastard*. In the days of Great-Uncle Tojo, the wartime leader, he would have been able to use a little electric shock treatment to change the assistant governor's mind; now he had to act through official channels. The most the assistant governor would agree to was to abstain from voting against sending in the military. And that was only after Mishima had personally intervened and pressed the bureaucrat, as a fellow graduate of Waseda University, to help save the lives of the citizens of Tokyo.

Tokyo's fate now rested on finding the city's assistant treasurer, Mrs Nagasawa, who was legally able to fill in as acting treasurer in the absence of her boss. She was eventually found in the 'Na' sector of Yoyogi Park covered in blankets. She had broken her leg and her face was badly burned. Feeling a bit groggy and high, Mrs Nagasawa was one of the lucky few to have received a morphine injection.

The army scout, Lieutenant Uma, immediately radioed into General Mishima's office. 'Stand by, Eagle, we have the acting city treasurer.'

The young officer and a battery of ten troops surrounded the poor woman. 'Mrs Nagasawa, I'm Lieutenant Uma of the army. The commander-in-chief has asked me to speak with you.'

He heard a muffled reply from the side of the bandages around Mrs Nagasawa's head.

'We need your permission to send in military rescue teams to save Tokyo. Here's an authorization form for you to sign.'

Uma hurriedly shoved a pen into her right hand. Flattered by all the attention but feeling slightly addled, Mrs Nagasawa signed the document. She was the casting vote on the temporary city board which ruled Tokyo. With the assistant governor abstaining, any order from Mrs Nagasawa was now binding. The navy officers, dressed in their summer whites, also had her sign a form, as did a lone air force officer. Everybody had covered their ass.

'Scout to Eagle, we've got permission to move. You're cleared to proceed.' The army, navy and air force officers than bowed to Mrs Nagawasa before marching out of the 'Na' sector as she lapsed into unconsciousness.

Within minutes the amphibious logistical support ships landed on the shores of Tokyo Bay and disgorged thousands of troops. Giant transport helicopters took off from the escort ships and flew immediately to the Imperial and Akasaka Palaces to ferry the injured to outlying hospitals. Dressed in regulation green, wearing helmets and carrying tents, spades and water, the first division of the Eastern Army started their march into Tokyo from their Nerima barracks. They were trained as the vanguard of a Tokyo rescue operation. The twelfth division were also called up, making a total of thirty thousand troops with another twenty-two thousand reinforcements on the way. All military personnel were armed.

The rescue operations began with unbounded enthusiasm which quickly turned to uncertainty and despair. Nobody had ever confronted such mass hysteria. Civilians grabbed the nearest soldier and begged for help in digging out relatives. Officers found it impossible to refuse such requests and, with no firm directive on how to save those trapped in buildings, the first division quickly disintegrated before they had even reached central Tokyo. With no heavy rescue equipment, the troops were forced to dig through rubble with spades.

Meanwhile the police and fire officials gathered in front of Mrs Nagasawa, waiting for her to wake up. Present were the deputy assistant of the Metropolitan Police, the National Police Agency, the Tokyo Fire Department and the National Fire Agency.

A colonel from General Mishima's office chaired the meeting. Under emergency guidelines, the army, police and fire department were supposed to divide up Tokyo, but nobody really knew what to do.

The army colonel bluffed his way through. 'Anyone heard about the Prime Minister?' he asked.

'Still in a coma, according to the doctors. But more importantly, does anybody know where the governor is?' said the fire chief.

'Probably still getting his winkie wet in Polynesia,' joked the colonel.

The joke didn't go down too well with the acting police and fire chief, both of whom reported to the governor. The colonel moved on.

'While we wait for Mrs Nagasawa, can I ask who has been called up from the police?'

'I've called up the 1st Riot Police at the Takebashi headquarters. We haven't been able to reach anyone, but I expect three thousand of the four thousand men will report for duty. One or two hundred have already straggled in. Fifteen hundred of our men are supposed to direct traffic in this situation – maybe we should vote to change that, since there is no traffic. Most of our men are without supplies or equipment, though, and were at home when the quake struck. If this lady can sign our form, then I can bring in reinforcements.'

'Is the WIDE system working?' asked the colonel.

WIDE was the satellite phone system that the National Police Agency had invented for its own use. Much of the problem in fighting a Tokyo emergency was that every government organization had its own communication system and its own earthquake department. The colonel did not mention that the army's own two-way radio system was not working.

'WIDE is working and we've just called up our off-road bike team in Shizuoka. We've got a hundred motorcycles driving up today. All are equipped with WIDE phones.'

'How about the sniffer dogs?'

'We've only got two German shepherds, I'm afraid. Alex and Sasha. They're already looking for survivors.'

'My emergency sheet says you've got fifteen hundred dogs,' said the colonel.

'No, those are drug sniffers. The rescue dogs don't work so well anyway.'

'What? The newspapers said they were effective. The stores were even selling stuffed Alex and Sasha police dogs.'

The acting police chief turned red, thinking about the propaganda they had sent to the newspapers. Readers loved the romantic notion of cuddly dogs saving lives, and the police did not dispel that notion. 'No. They can only work for fifteen minutes before taking a half-hour break. Any noise and they completely shut down.'

'Great – just great! Let's move on. How about police choppers?'

'Five of our fifteen are in the air. Another seventy around Japan have been called up.'

Next the colonel turned to the Tokyo fire chief. 'Is the Red Bird up?' he demanded, referring to the fire department's observation helicopter.

'It's been up all day, but apart from radio contact it's useless. The camera's working, but the receiver at headquarters is broken.'

'What's the internal damage report?'

The fire chief read down his list. 'Out of 485 pumper trucks, only twenty made it out of their stations and only five of the eighty-two aerial ladders are working. None of this really matters, though, because the water pipes are all broken.'

'But I thought you had back-up water tanks.'

'We did, but they were all made out of concrete. They've all burst or cracked.

'Shit. The city's burning and there's nothing we can do. What else?'

'Ten of the two hundred ambulances are operable, but there's nowhere to drive. Of the sixty-seven foam pumpers, three are operable. They're all fighting the chemical fires at the waterfront.'

'And the fireboats?'

'All nine are working the waterfront. Just pray the wind doesn't change. Five of the floodlight trucks can be driven from the fire command across the street to the Imperial Palace to give the survivors light. That leaves us with four robot squirters, four of our six choppers and five of the twenty-three rescue trucks left. Actually, forget the rescue trucks. They can't go anywhere.'

'Personnel?'

'We can't reach anyone. But under our emergency plan, eighteen thousand men should report into our seventy-seven stations along with another sixteen thousand off-duty volunteers. I'd cut that figure in half.' The fire chief was being somewhat optimistic.

Anxious to get on with rescue operations, the head of the National Police Agency interrupted. 'Do we really have to take orders from this woman?' he asked.

'Yes, I'm afraid so. Hang on, I think she's waking up.' The men excitedly got their pens out.

From her morphine-induced haze, Mrs Nagasawa stirred and wondered what all the commotion was about. In her thirty years working in the treasurer's department, she had seldom been an object of attention. Most of the time she had to make and serve tea for her boss. Mrs Nagasawa looked forward to retiring next year and was thankful she had made it through the quake alive.

The police and firemen slipped authorization slips in front of her, allowing reinforcements to enter Tokyo. Mrs Nagasawa let her hand slide across the paper before slipping back into a dream state.

The race to save lives was on.

35

THE CAMP

'A fine ash settled down upon us and to our horror we realized it was the remains of our friends.'

An Auschwitz survivor describing the burning of Nazi victims at nearby Birkenau

Dougie Douglas had been drifting in and out of consciousness for hours. Once, an hour ago, he had looked up at Yuki in a moment of lucidity.

Yuki smiled down at him, gently stroking his hair as she cradled his head. A moment later his world faded to blackness. Weeping, Yuki hugged his motionless body. *I love this man so much. What shall I do if he dies?*

Yuki's main fear was that Dougie would not make it through the night. It was Wednesday. Though the Salomon Brothers' office was only a few minutes' walk from the Imperial Palace, the journey had taken over five hours. Dougie had gone into severe shock halfway there and started shaking furiously. Yuki had laid him down on the pavement and covered him with a blanket scavenged from the wreckage. Dougie lay in a coma-like state as Yuki pleaded for help from passing refugees. With no tears left, she sat over Dougie, bobbing her body up and down in a rhythmic motion.

Somebody had touched her shoulder. A man spoke but she could not understand him. She pointed to Dougie's hand. The man nodded, helped Yuki to her feet and then lifted Dougie over his shoulder. He carried him to the Imperial Palace, waited patiently until Sato opened the gates, and then set Dougie down before seeking his own family. Yuki gave the man a long hug and was sorry to see him go.

'*Au revoir,*' he said. '*Bonne chance.*'

'*Sayonara.*'

And then he was gone. Dougie lay on the ground, surrounded by thousands of other people. Yuki had to step over and around people, and movement in a straight line was impossible. *I need to get him antibiotics or he will die.* Gangrene would certainly set in.

Yuki turned to a family behind her. They were tourists from Osaka who had luckily been on a walk outside the Palace Hotel at the time of the quake. The hotel, under which the Noichi sisters now lay buried, bordered the Imperial Palace and the walkways were unhampered by buildings.

'Would you mind looking after my friend? I must find him some medicine.' They gladly agreed.

Yuki set off with one hope. Somewhere in the extensive media coverage of the Imperial family an article had been written about Akihito's hobbies. The Emperor, like his father Hirohito, loved botany and kept an extensive herbal and medicinal garden near his home. Yuki needed to find the garden to obtain medicine.

Though darkness had fallen, there was just enough light from the raging fires outside the Palace to guide her. The Emperor's home was in the geographical centre of the gardens and she could just make out the Palace in the shadows. The Emperor would have planted his garden facing the sun-filled south side of his home.

Yuki fell over a low-lying hedge. As she lay on the ground the smell of basil and rosemary wafted over the campfires. *I must be close.* Yuki stood up and walked through the Emperor's herb garden. She knew nothing of plants. How was she going to distinguish a medicinal one from a garden salad?

'Young lady, may I help you?'

Yuki looked up at the man who had appeared beside her.

'Only if you know something about medicinal herbs.'

'What do you wish to know?'

'You know about herbs?'

'A little,' smiled the man.

'My friend has lost his hand. I need medicine or he'll die. There must be something here in the Emperor's garden to help him.'

'I'm sure there is. Let's have a look.' The man led Yuki over to some plants and bent down to smell one. He handed her a sprig as if it were a beloved pet.

'Yes, this is what you are looking for.'

He carefully harvested a handful of greenery. 'This is a common form of antibiotic. Boil four of these leaves for ten minutes. Have your friend drink a cup of the tea. Repeat this every four hours,' he instructed.

'Now your friend will be in unbearable pain. There are no plants to prevent pain, but this leaf does bring on sleep.' The stranger picked some small prickly leaves. 'You may mix this with his antibiotic. A sleeping man feels no pain. He'll be fine.'

He then handed her a matchbook. 'Take some dry branches on your way back and build a nice fire. Your friend will live. Now dry your eyes,' the man said softly.

Impulsively Yuki hugged the stranger. This time she was crying tears of joy. 'Thank you,' she said and ran off to save Dougie.

In complete darkness, save for the glow of cooking fires that dotted the Palace grounds, it took Yuki almost an hour to get back to her sector. When she did, Dougie was gone. Immediately she broke into a cold sweat, thinking that he had died while she had been away. She turned to look for the family who had been guarding him, but they too were gone. Yuki began to panic. All she could see were dark shapes huddled on the ground. The shapes went on forever. Everything looked the same. She was lost.

Yuki started zig-zagging through the compound, hoping she would recognize somebody. *What if he dies while I am looking for him? What if I can't find him?*.

For almost thirty minutes she stumbled frantically over people. Finally somebody grabbed her arm. It was the woman with whom she had left Dougie. Yuki had passed within 5 metres of Dougie without spotting him.

Dougie was now delirious and had a high fever. She made a fire and brewed the antibiotic tea. While he slept, Yuki changed his dressing.

When she unravelled the cloth from his arm, Yuki almost vomited. The stump where his wrist had been had turned a fetid, purplish colour. The blood had congealed into oddly formed chunks of black rock. In desperation she dipped the stump into the pot of water that she had boiling on the campfire. Dougie awoke, screaming. Pus was now draining openly from his arm. She ripped off a clean strip of cloth from her skirt, boiled it and dressed his wound.

Then Yuki prayed, first to Buddha and then to Master Wa. If Dougie lived through the night, he would survive. Unlike Dougie, she did not sleep and spent the whole evening stroking his head. It was the longest night of her life, and at the end of it she watched the sun rise in majestic fashion. The billowing black fumes and toxic gases acted as a prism to form an orange backdrop. Then, just after sunrise, Yuki heard the rescue choppers.

She moved Dougie to the medical aid station which had been established in the south-west area of the Palace. Staffed by a handful of volunteer doctors and nurses, the station was swamped with nearly fifty thousand victims urgently in need of attention. It was like a scene from M*A*S*H*, with bodies, blood, doctors and writhing victims everywhere. All operations were carried out without anaesthesia or proper medical instruments: crude amputations were performed and shrapnel and glass removed.

Yuki led Dougie past neatly stacked corpses awaiting burning. It took five hours to get to the front of the line, where he was given a shot of morphine and a proper bandage. A rumour had spread that the choppers would evacuate the wounded to outlying hospitals. As soon as she heard about it, she rushed to get Dougie aboard. Though he had survived the night, his fever had not broken.

The choppers were filling up even as Dougie was being attended to. Yuki was keen to get him on to one of them, but the doctor would not even consider the idea. Amputations such as Dougie's were commonplace.

'You've got to take him,' Yuki begged. 'He almost died last night.'

'But he's alive,' said the doctor.

No amount of pleading seemed to help. The doctor was just finishing the bandaging when he noticed the medallion around Yuki's neck.

'May I see that?'

Yuki handed him the diamond necklace, which he looked at carefully. The doctor also had a pendant, but his was a simple gold one with the letter 'W' hanging down.

'Master Wa gave it to me.'

The doctor looked up in surprise and a flash of recognition came over him. 'You were the one at the Tokyo Dome.'

Yuki nodded.

'I was there too,' he said excitedly.

'*Dozo*,' said Yuki, offering him the necklace. Anything to get Dougie aboard the chopper.

'No, I couldn't take it. Thank you.'

'Please,' she urged.

'No. But let me help your friend. I can authorize his evacuation to Osaka.'

'Oh, thank you,' said Yuki with relief as she began to bundle up Dougie's belongings.

But Dougie, who had now regained consciousness, spoke for himself. 'I'm not going.'

'What?' said Yuki. 'You could die without medical attention!'

'I'm not going.'

The doctor interrupted. 'There's not much time. If you're going, you've got to leave now.'

'I'm staying, Yuki.'

The doctor slipped her some extra bandages and painkillers. 'Take these,' he whispered. 'Good luck.' He turned to help the next victim.

The choppers were being unloaded when Sato arrived. His armed Imperial police were protecting the cordoned area from frenzied looting. Word had spread among the police that bandits, many of them Korean, had been looting Tokyo for food and water. Sato had seen to it that no such activities would take place in the Imperial refuge.

The government was not well prepared for feeding the refugees. This responsibility fell to the Ministry of Agriculture, Forests and Fisheries, who were supposed to organize with the rice suppliers the distribution of bread, rice and dried milk rations. Though the Ministry had squirrelled away 10 million portions of bread rations, it was not enough. There were 900,000 portions of dried milk for babies, but distribution from the various storage facilities was almost impossible.

A young man in his mid-twenties had raced up to steal a container of food. He was quickly apprehended and Sato felt he needed to use the man as an example to prevent further looting and mob rule. The perpetrator was dragged to an open space and Sato addressed onlookers with his bullhorn.

'This man was caught stealing food. He will not do it again, nor will anybody else.' The man was handcuffed and led away.

There was no more stealing, for reasons more to do with Moyama than the Imperial Household Agency. His yakuza spread the word that anybody caught looting would be shot.

Sato returned to his work and saw Moyama up ahead directing the relief efforts. The yakuza chief was a natural leader and even the Imperial police were taking orders from him. He had reorganized them so that ten armed guards stood on top of the 7-metre-high stone parapet. The wall was a natural lookout post overlooking the moat and inner Palace grounds. Moyama used the wall to protect supplies as they were unloaded. Scarce goods such as morphine, syringes and antibiotics were heavily guarded and stacked in boxes against the wall. The next row of supplies was stacked parallel to the wall, a metre distant. The relief supplies formed five concentric half moons.

Moyama had mastered the art of mob rule during World War II. Rule one was to divide large groups into smaller ones. From the helicopter Moyama had seen the sector boundaries set up by Sato. That was perfect. German and Japanese prison camp commanders had been especially effective in controlling large groups of men with a handful of guards. Moyama had at first found it amazing that five hundred armed guards could contain up to fifty thousand prisoners of war. Why did the prisoners not overwhelm the guards? he had thought until he realized how these large numbers were managed. Rule two was to let the groups believe that enough supplies existed for everyone. The Japanese were accustomed to waiting in line for trains, ski lifts and golf tee times, so Moyama figured they would also wait patiently for supplies. Rule three was a show of force. Though the Imperial police had orders to imprison looters, the yakuza orders to shoot on sight were a far greater deterrent.

When Sato reached Moyama he was surprised at the large amount of supplies being unloaded. 'Thank you, Moyama-san.' He was about to ask the yakuza boss where he had obtained such valuable supplies at such short notice, but stopped himself. He bowed. Moyama, dressed in his disaster wear, bowed back.

A group of doctors and nurses stood on call, assisting as hundreds of silver pads and laptop computers were neatly stacked.

'What are those pads?' asked Sato.

One of the doctors explained. 'They are Biomats, and each one is attached to a laptop computer. A mat will be placed under the seriously wounded such as burn victims, multiple amputees and injured elderly people, with a blanket covering them. Their vital signs such as heart rate and respiration are read out on the computer.'

Moyama had important business to talk over and took Sato aside. 'Sato-san, I will keep the supplies from Osaka coming. There's just one matter I needed to discuss. Just a small favour.'

'What's that?'

'You know the Imperial passage to the parliament building?'

Sato looked up at Moyama and said nothing. The surprise in his eyes, however, told the yakuza leader that the tunnel was still there.

'Sato-san, you're very loyal to your Emperor. None of your men has betrayed the secret tunnel. When I was a young supporter of the Emperor during the war, we used the tunnel as our hideout. I just need to use it for storage. I give my word that nothing illegal or harmful will be placed there.'

'Hmm,' said Sato, deep in thought. He was in a difficult position. The notion of *giri*, or obligation, overwhelmed him. Moyama's relief effort had put Sato in deep debt. 'Yes, you may use the Imperial tunnel. I only request that you use the garden entrance in the parliament building for unloading your supplies.'

Sato was careful not to use the Emperor's name in approving of this plan. Plausible deniability was his trademark. *The Emperor does not need to know everything that occurs under him*, reasoned Sato. *This is a small price for saving the lives of Tokyo's victims*. But Sato could match Moyama in *giri*-jousting and, as Moyama's choppers were preparing to return to Osaka, he turned to the yakuza leader.

'Moyama-san, we have many thousands of wounded victims. Could you please fly the most serious to Osaka General Hospital?'

It was Moyama's turn to hesitate. He wanted to assist the wounded but had special plans for the supply helicopters. He had been out-foxed. No excuse would suffice to extricate him from the request, and with a smile he said he would be delighted to help transport the victims. Both men knew that Sato was already loading the choppers with the injured.

Later that day Sato made his rounds of the compound. 'Find me a priest,' he ordered one of his assistants.

A few minutes later a Shinto priest arrived. Sato bowed and said, 'I want you to perform the burial rights for the dead.' He pointed to the stack of corpses. 'They must be burned before the summer heat spreads disease.'

Sato apportioned a secluded corner of the southern Palace grounds across from the Metropolitan Police Headquarters as the funeral site. 'Chop down the pine trees on the southern slope,' he ordered his men. 'I want pyres erected immediately.'

Giant fires were built at the bottom of a sharp slope. This was a stroke of genius. The bodies were too weighty and cumbersome to be thrown on top of a fire, but with this arrangement they could be rolled down the slope into the waiting flames. The Imperial police had sealed off the area. Gawkers and rubberneckers throughout the Imperial gardens stared at the dead and dying. Curiosity had no shame.

For hours the process of rolling the corpses down on to the flames continued. Then, as a small child went tumbling into the inferno, his mother became so overwhelmed with grief that she hurled herself into the fire, unwilling to let her child be consumed alone.

By noon the sweet, sickly smell of burning human flesh filled the air. A gentle rain of light human ash fell upon the million squatters within the Imperial Palace, not unlike the tragedy of the Nazi death camps earlier in the century.

The real horror was about to come.

36

THE BLACK DEATH

'He picked black chunks of skin off his own body as a man would peel an avocado. Only the chunks were larger.'

A Calcutta doctor describing a patient afflicted by bubonic plague

Before the quake, a stowaway had made his way from Calcutta to Yokohama by steamer, jumped ship in Yokohama and boarded a local fishing vessel bound for the Tokyo docks. The stowaway, an Indian wharf rat the size of a small cat, sat about half a metre high on his haunches. His hairy fur was running with dozens of rat fleas infected with a bacterium known as *Yersinia pesticis*, contracted in the offal of the Calcutta slums. These bacteria obstructed the flea's gut so that during his next blood meal he regurgitated them. The disease caused by the bacteria was commonly known as the Black Death.

The Black Death, or bubonic plague, is the world's most infectious disease and one of the most easily preventable. The term 'Black Death' came from the necrosis seen in victims, whose skin turns a greyish-black before they die. The disease was best known for its devastation of Europe during the Middle Ages. Infected rats had been carried in the supplies of Tartar armies who besieged Genoa in 1397, leaving a terrible legacy. The plague began in Italy, travelled north and west to Spain and France and onwards to Germany, Scandinavia and England. In three years half of Europe was wiped out: 25 million people died.

Victims felt first sore, then feverish. Glandular soreness set in, followed by dizziness and vomiting. Their flesh turned black and fell off. Death came in three days. A plague vaccine was discovered in 1897, and, although outbreaks in rat-infested countries such as India still occurred, the disease had become easily treatable through antibiotics.

The Calcutta wharf rat scurried along the bowline and jumped ashore in Tokyo Bay. Hungry, he rooted through garbage until his nose picked up the scent of fresh fish. It was 3 a.m. and the fish auctions had not yet begun. Finding a juicy piece of tuna, he licked it and then gnawed off a small chunk. He then spotted a workable piece of squid and left the tuna, dragging the squid off to a quiet corner. No trace was left of his foray into the tuna but a dribble of contaminated saliva. The bacteria-ridden saliva dried quickly, and by the time the tuna was sold on to a local sushi bar owner there was no visible trace of the rat's deadly nibble.

The sushi bar owner served up the tuna that morning to four dock workers, who ate and then went out drinking in local bars. Drunk, the four made it to the Imperial Palace by noon on the day of the quake, intent on selling Imperial koi to the refugees.

The fishmonger who had been apprehended by Sato early in the evening broke out in cold sweats later that night. When he began vomiting, his friends laughed.

'Can't hold your liquor,' they taunted him.

Shaking, he made it to the medical area. In pain, he squatted behind a pine tree to defecate. A watery, rice-coloured emission squirted from his back-side.

The fishmonger's glands swelled, his eyes became sore and a high fever set in. The next morning he coughed blood. Under pressure, the doctors quickly diagnosed light pneumonia: nothing serious and certainly not worth drugs, given the thousands of mutilated quake victims. The fishmonger cried out for water continuously, his thirst unable to be sated. A while later areas of his skin began to haemorrhage. When black patches appeared on his face and hands his friends immediately brought him back to the same doctor, who recoiled. He had never seen such rapid putrefaction of the human body. The rotting skin stank. The doctor isolated him and secretly prayed that the man would die so his body could be burned.

Later that afternoon one of the toilet volunteers discovered something strange on the hill of the public toilet. As he threw Refreshing Gel down the hillside nearest the infirmary, he noticed speckled white diarrhoea in a latrine. The doctor had told him to watch for strange bodily excretions along the hillside. The volunteer ran back to the infirmary to report his find.

The doctor went immediately to the latrine dressed in a pair of waist-high, rubber fishing waders. He strode down the faeces-covered hillside, and scooped up the slippery white diarrhoea in a plastic bag. Back at the infirmary he put a little of the sample on to a slide and placed it under a microscope. Two sets of microbes appeared: one was cholera and the other he quickly identified as bubonic plague.

The doctor immediately quarantined the entire infirmary, ordered all medical staff to be given antibiotics and then called Sato by walkie-talkie.

'Overlord Two, this is Doc One. Do you read?' The doctor tried not to sound alarmed. Panic itself was contagious, and dozens of Imperial police, Imperial Household staff and organizers had handsets.

'Overlord Two here.'

'Sato-san, I need fifty thousand shots of antibiotics within the next twelve hours.'

'What's the problem?'

'I can't say.' The doctor did not want to give any information over the airwaves.

'It's impossible to get so much medicine so quickly.'

'You must,' said the doctor with urgency, still trying to disguise his panic.

'Be more specific, Doc One. What's the problem?'

'I must tell you in person.'

'No, tell me now or there will be no antibiotics.'

There was a slight pause before the doctor replied.

'It's bubonic plague. None of us will survive if we don't have an immediate airdrop.'

The news sank in. 'What specifically do you need, Doc One?'

'Fifty thousand initial vaccines of Streptomycin, with 2 million to follow.'

'I'll procure the vaccines. Nobody may enter or leave your medical compound.'

'You must also find a way of killing off the rat population.'

'Roger. Overlord out.'

Sato picked up his phone, called Moyama and explained the problem. Fortunately Osaka was the pharmaceutical centre of the world: Takeda, Tanabe, Shionogi, Dai Nippon, Yoshitomi, Fujisawa, Green Cross, Santen and Fuso Pharmaceutical all had their headquarters and factories in the Osaka/Kobe area. Most produced antibiotics and there were ample stores in their warehouses.

Osaka and Kobe yakuza gangs controlled much of the distribution of Japanese drugs in western Japan, so this request was readily obeyed. 'Convert your production lines to the output of additional vaccine,' Moyama ordered the drug companies. He shipped up the initial fifty thousand vaccines and within a week a further 2 million survivors would be vaccinated.

The Calcutta wharf rat that had started the plague died in the liquefaction of the low-lying Nihonbashi/Tsukiji area. Millions of rats drowned underground as the water pressure forced mud into dark fissures, holes and crannies. Like the humans, the rats swarmed to the safety of higher ground. As if by instinct, Tokyo's rat population avoided human contact and moved west into the government district. In need of food and water, they soon lost their fear of humans. Rats were seen in batches of a thousand, even taking turns sipping water from the banks of the Imperial Moat. Sato was alerted to this phenomenon by guards on top of the stone wall.

'Police Chief One, this is Overlord Two. I want ten men by the west gate immediately. Over.'

'Roger, Overlord. We read you. Over.'

'Chief One, bring the jerry packs.'

'Yes, sir. Over and out.'

Ten minutes later Sato was at the west gate. His ten men were fitted with portable jerry packs strapped to their backs like knapsacks, the jerry cans filled with gasoline. Each man held a hand-controlled nozzle in his hand, with a control lever in the shape of a petrol pump. The flamethrowers had been used to speed up the burning of corpses.

'These flamethrowers can throw up to 16 metres,' instructed Sato. 'You must evacuate each area before commencing. Your first goal is to protect the Imperial Moat from rats. Most of the rats have come down from Kasumigaseki. Your second goal is to exterminate them, and this means locating their new nests. Listen very carefully: nobody is to use these flamethrowers in rubble where survivors might still be located.'

Nine of the ten exterminators shook their heads in acknowledgement. The tenth, a man named Furuno, was adjusting his helmet and did not hear Sato's last sentence.

'Okay, let's move.'

Dressed like firefighters, the ten exterminators made a sweep of the outside moat. They roasted the rats, leaving behind their charred oval corpses. Clean-up crews picked up the melted hairballs and threw them into a wheelbarrow. Five men patrolled the moat, while the other five ferreted out creatures hiding in the rubble further west in the government headquarters. The exterminators were guided by sound – the high-pitched squeaking made by rats in large groups.

Furuno had a good time playing with his flamethrower. He called it the 'Tongue'. Furuno was able to propel the Tongue up to 35 metres, not the 16 specified by Sato. His blood up, Furuno hunted down the furry beasts, spying and torching holes they had scurried down. He learned a few tricks. He found that if he injected the nozzle of the Tongue into a hole, a flame would leap out of a hole 10 or 12 metres away. Like most Japanese, Furuno was disgusted but slightly afraid of rats. The more he incinerated, the better.

As Furuno circled eastwards towards the Palace Hotel, he became more adept with the flamethrower. If he spotted a rat 20 metres away, he could flick the throttle to the Tongue and, with amazing accuracy, roast the beast alive. But Furuno tired of single-action target practice and wanted to shoot for quantity. The rats, he felt, were hidden in the wreckage of buildings. Outside the Palace Hotel Furuno fired up the Tongue, working the flame deep into the rubble.

Meanwhile the Noichi sisters lay helplessly awake, buried beneath the fallen masonry.

Furuno methodically worked his way through the hotel. The screeches of the dying rats sounded almost like humans and drove him onward. The flames, burning at temperatures up to 1000 degrees Fahrenheit, closed in on the twins. The whooshing sound of the advancing flames sounded as if a giant gas stove was being lit.

'Help us!'

But Keiko Noichi's voice was drowned by the cries of the terrified rats.

The deadly flame approached.

'No. Please. No. Help!'

The twins' tomb was now illuminated as the Tongue licked the sides of their hidden lair. Mushka the cat had the chance to run and save her own life, but stayed behind with Keiko. Keiko's hair and Mushka's fur began to curl, smoke and singe.

Three metres to go and I will be finished, thought Furuno to himself. Suddenly the Tongue began sputtering and the flame died. Furuno pressed hard against the throttle. The Tongue coughed and sputtered and only a thin trickle of flame dribbled out of the nozzle. *Darn, I'm out of fuel. I'll get a refill, then come back*. The exterminator turned to walk back to the Imperial Palace.

37

WHERE IN THE WORLD?

'Try to appear to be working hard if filmed by a TV crew.'
From a brochure issued by the Chiba municipal
government in 1995 after the media blasted government
rescue attempts during the Kobe earthquake

Though he was a traditionalist, Ken Moyama had had a satellite dish fitted to his roof. The modern black device clashed with his elegantly tiled house, but for Moyama it was a necessity. 'I must watch business news from around the world,' he solemnly told his men.

Each night Moyama turned on his TV and secretly watched old reruns of *I Love Lucy*, broadcast on European satellite. Only Mrs Moyama and Mata knew of his passion, and Mata had been sworn to secrecy. He knew, in any case, that Moyama would banish him from the yakuza if any gang members ever found out. Not that Moyama could understand all Lucille Ball's jokes – it was her acting and expressions that thrilled him.

The first thing that Moyama's men repaired after the quake was the satellite dish. On Tuesday evening he had been watching *I Love Lucy* in the dark, his TV plugged into the emergency generator, when the channel interrupted its telecast to bring viewers an update on the situation in Tokyo. Hiroko's CNN commentary was replayed and Moyama followed her broadcast and subsequent disappearance with special interest.

Mata had now evacuated Hiroko to Moyama's stronghold and, on arriving, introduced her to the yakuza leader. Hiroko had entered the compound with a mixture of fear and curiosity, but was quickly put at ease by Moyama and wondered why he was being so nice.

'Miss Fujita, we're glad you're safe. I understand the world's looking for you, including our dear Minister Tada.'

'My son . . .' said Hiroko.

'And your mother?'

'She lives in Mitaka at my apartment.'

'Yes, I know your mother,' replied Moyama. 'She owns the Gaslight, doesn't she?'

'Yes,' said Hiroko, rather surprised. She had never spoken to anyone about the Gaslight and certainly never mentioned that her mother owned it.

'First let's sort out Tada, and then we'll find Alex and Michi-chan.'

Hiroko noticed the affectionate use of her mother's name. As Moyama considered what to do next he curled his lower lip outside his mouth after he spoke. Nobody but she and Alex had ever been able to do that trick, and here was Moyama performing it absentmindedly.

Moyama dialled Tada's number.

'Uhhhhhh,' grunted the Construction Minister as he answered his phone back in his Kojimachi apartment.

'Tada-san, this is Moyama here.'

Moyama felt the Minister straighten up.

'Yes, Moyama-san?' asked Tada in an obsequious voice.

'Miss Fujita is with me. Please let me make this clear. She's my guest and my friend. If anything happens to her I should be very unhappy.'

Moyama did not need to be explicit. If Hiroko died, then Tada died. Tada knew this.

'But Moyama-san . . .'

'Maybe I didn't make myself clear. She's under my protection and if any harm befalls this beautiful lady, even accidentally, I'll attribute it to you.'

'But . . . she'll destroy us.'

Moyama had hung up before Tada's reply was out of his mouth. Nobody ever countermanded an order of Moyama's.

Meanwhile the hunt for Hiroko Fujita had captured the world's imagination as the media converged on the Ministry of Construction. Craig Huntley was broadcasting live, using the concrete shell of the Ministry as a backdrop. It looked like a cutaway view of a doll's house. To Huntley's irritation, a camera crew from ABC and WTN were on the scene. The world had caught Hiroko fever and, though all the news teams were ostensibly reporting on the quake, their secondary purpose was to find Hiroko. Human interest in her disappearance was immense. News reporters, curious survivors and bounty hunters swarmed to the Ministry building like bees to honey.

'This is Craig Huntley reporting to you live from Tokyo, where the greatest earthquake ever to hit Japan has devastated the nation's capital. The quake,' he went on, 'registering a massive 8.6 on the Richter scale, has killed hundreds of thousands, left millions homeless and destroyed Japan's central government. Over 60 per cent of Japan's major companies have their headquarters here in the capital and all business has ground to a halt.' Huntley then read from a piece of paper handed to him by a researcher. 'The great Kanto earthquake, which destroyed Tokyo in 1923, wiped out 37 per cent of the nation's annual production and caused 6.2 trillion yen of damage. Just forty-eight hours after this quake, Tokyo lies in a state of anarchy. Rescue teams are only just beginning to arrive from around the globe to search for survivors and treat the injured.'

The CNN broadcast was interrupted by excited voices.

'We've found her!' shouted an ABC technician.

Involuntarily, Huntley paused, excited at the thought of Hiroko being saved. 'We've just had word that rescue workers may have found Hiroko Fujita, our CNN correspondent lost on Tuesday evening,' Huntley told viewers. 'Our crew is now making its way over to the rescue site,' he said as the TV cameramen walked over to the commotion.

'We've found her. She's buried under a wall,' said an exhausted worker.

A semi-circle had formed around the body of a young woman dressed in a grey skirt and cream blouse. It was difficult to identify her since her face had been badly lacerated. She was dead.

Huntley studied the woman's face. He looked over and saw ABC already reporting Hiroko's death. Huntley motioned for his crew to film the scene, but he remained silent. Listening to the ABC telecast, he motioned for his own team to hold off.

'We're here at Japan's Ministry of Construction where ABC brings you an exclusive report on the tragic death of Hiroko Fujita, the brave newspaper reporter who first broke the story of the great Tokyo quake to the world. Viewers will recall that Miss Fujita had been assaulted by Japan's Minister of Construction. A frantic search for Miss Fujita began and a collective prayer from around the globe sought her safety. We are sad to report that the search for Miss Fujita is over – a courageous reporter and lovely woman dead at age thirty-four. The world will mourn her passing. This is John Davidson reporting live from Tokyo for ABC News.'

Huntley noticed that ABC made no mention of Hiroko's affiliation with CNN. *Petty journalistic rivalry*, he thought. Something bothered

Huntley, though. He looked at the dead woman's body, which indeed looked just like Hiroko. But something was not right. He studied the body for a moment and then a sense of relief came over him. This woman was wearing black shoes. He distinctly recalled that Hiroko had been wearing sneakers. When Jiroo dropped the camera during his shot of Hiroko in the Japan Meteorological Agency, video footage had picked up an accidental leg shot. Huntley had to make a snap decision. Should he let the world believe Hiroko was dead? He turned to camera.

'Unconfirmed rumours in Tokyo believe that Hiroko Fujita, our CNN correspondent, has died from a cave-in here at the Ministry of Construction. We haven't yet confirmed this report and CNN's search for Miss Fujita continues. We'll bring you an update shortly. Now over to Chanda Kapura at the Imperial Palace. This is Craig Huntley reporting live from Tokyo.'

CNN cut to the Imperial Palace in order to buy Huntley time to work out how to handle the Hiroko Fujita story. Chanda Kapura was slightly rattled at the death and suffering he was witnessing and rambled through his broadcast.

'The eyes of the world are here, upon the Imperial Palace, where the injured, shocked and hungry have flocked by the millions. For some, the most important victim here is Japan's Prime Minister who remains in a coma. We will bring you updates on Mr Mori's condition. Meanwhile, the commander-general of earthquake relief, General Mishima, has sent teams of scouts to find members of the Prime Minister's cabinet and the thirty-three members of the Central Disaster Prevention Council who are required to restore the nation to normality. We understand that General Mishima has also despatched an air force jet to French Polynesia to locate Tokyo's governor.

'I can't express the horror of this disaster. To some, the Imperial Palace has become not a sanctuary but a graveyard as nurses and doctors try to inoculate the survivors against bubonic plague which has already claimed untold lives. And the survivors? They've taken solace in prayer, an interesting contrast to the residents in the 1989 San Francisco earthquake. Having covered that quake, I remember that huge crowds turned to drink and gathered outside the city's liquor stores where owners illegally hiked prices 200 or 300 per cent. The reaction of the Japanese has been different, one of spirituality. Tens of thousands of small shrines have been erected here and offerings made to appease the gods. Tokyo has turned to prayer to find its way out of this nightmare. This is Chanda Kapura, reporting live from Tokyo.'

Meanwhile at the Ministry of Construction the ABC crew were crowing over their victory as Hiroko Fujita's body was covered by a blanket.

'Sorry, buddy, you lose this round,' said ABC reporter John Davidson, coming up to Huntley and patting him on the back. The ABC team sniggered while the CNN crew remained silent.

Davidson was normally quite arrogant enough, but with a victory against CNN he was unbearable and began needling the rival crew.

'What does CNN stand for? "Certainly Not Newsworthy"? Or how about "Catatonic Nasal Newshounds"?'

'How about fucking off?' yelled Huntley.

The CNN M-phone beeped.

'Craig, it's for you.'

Huntley was thankful to get away from the odious ABC reporter.

'Huntley here,' he answered.

'Mr Huntley, this is Ken Moyama speaking.'

Craig put his hand over the mouthpiece and whispered the name, trying to figure out who he was speaking to. He had no idea who Ken Moyama was.

'How can I help you, Mr Moyama?'

'I believe you're searching for Miss Hiroko Fujita?'

'That's right, although ABC just reported they found her body.'

'They're mistaken.'

'You know where she is?'

'I should. She's a guest at my house. My men will escort your helicopter to my home. They should be above you now.' Huntley could barely hear Moyama now as the chopper blades thumped 100 metres or so away.

'Yes, I see them,' shouted Huntley into the phone. 'We're on our way.'

Huntley waved the crew into the Daiei chopper. John Davidson, meanwhile, wondered what CNN was on to and his journalistic antennae were going haywire.

'Load up our equipment fast,' he yelled to his team. 'We're going to follow those bastards.' The CNN team were away within ten minutes, just as the ABC crew had finished packing.

Moyama's helicopter took the lead, with CNN right behind. Nobody noticed the ABC pilot slip in 500 metres above and behind the CNN crew. The race to Hiroko Fujita was on.

Ten minutes later the CNN crew were shown into Moyama's

garden. In the centre stood Hiroko Fujita. The ABC helicopter hovered overhead, looking desperately for a place to land.

Moyama extended his hand. 'I'm Ken Moyama. You must be Mr Huntley.'

'Yes, sir. Thank you for finding Miss Fujita.' He turned to Hiroko, who was staring at a photo of Alex cupped in her left hand.

'It's a pleasure to meet you, Miss Fujita.' He extended his right hand, which Hiroko accepted. He felt her warmth and kept his hand pressed against hers longer than propriety allowed.

'For a moment we thought you were dead.'

'So did I.'

Huntley turned back to Moyama and immediately noticed the striking resemblance to the photo of Alex which Hiroko had flashed across CNN. Huntley registered the fact and moved on.

'Congratulations, Mr Moyama. You're about to become a global hero.'

Moyama beamed. 'Thank you, I umm . . .'

Moyama was at a loss for words, but Huntley solved the problem. 'I have one request. See that helicopter up there? We need to get that noisy aircraft out of the area. Would you be able to help us?'

Moyama turned to his assistant. 'Mata, warn off that helicopter. Now.'

Mata ran over to his men, who aimed wide of the ABC chopper and fired off a round of warning shots. Huntley was shocked at this aberrant behaviour but said nothing.

Aloft in the chopper, John Davidson tried to coax the pilot into landing. 'Take it down, take it down,' he yelled, gesticulating to the pilot. But the Japanese pilot knew he was intruding on Moyama's turf. The shots from Mata were enough for him to veer off to safety.

'Tell that crazy man to shut up or we'll all get killed,' the pilot shouted to an ABC translator. But Davidson was beyond reason.

'Take this fucking thing down now!' he spluttered, unfastening his safety belt and grabbing the pilot.

The pilot pushed the throttle, hit the joystick and sent the chopper forward and up at a forty-five degree angle. Davidson shot to the back of the craft, his head bouncing off the side of a metal camera case. With Davidson out cold, the pilot returned to the Imperial Palace.

'That's better,' said Huntley.

'We'll be ready to go live in four minutes. First, I'd like to ask you a few questions, Hiroko – you know, about what happened to you. Then I'll cut to you, Mr Moyama, and ask how you saved Miss Fujita.'

Moyama suddenly looked nervous. 'I'll be right back,' he said quickly to Huntley, who thought the older man was going off to urinate or even vomit. Instead, Moyama returned a moment later with his family.

'My wife, son and maid,' he said proudly, ready for the cameras to roll. 'Get into this picture,' he ordered his son.

Like most Japanese, Moyama was a trigger-happy, camera-toting tourist when he travelled abroad and viewed the CNN interview as a similar photo opportunity.

'Father, I'm not sure.'

'Everybody smile,' said Moyama. 'This is okay, isn't it, Mr Huntley?'

Craig smiled. 'Just fine, Mr Moyama.' Moyama and his son were both unconsciously rolling their lower lip outwards.

He turned to Hiroko and studied her. Hiroko noticed him staring.

'Is something wrong, Mr Huntley?'

Craig snapped out of his trance.

'Hmm. No, nothing. I was just wondering if you were okay.'

'Yes. No. I mean, well, I miss my son. A lot's happened in the past two days.'

'I know. I've seen your coverage.'

Huntley moved a bit closer. 'Listen, I really do hope you find your son. From his picture he looks like a great kid.'

'You saw his picture?'

'Yes. I also saw you staring into your hand. His father must be proud.'

'His father's no longer alive.'

'Oh, I'm sorry. Did he – '

Huntley's producer interrupted him. 'Cameras are ready, Craig. Give us the sign.'

Huntley turned to camera, nodded and then waited for the producer's cue. 'The best news of this hour out of Tokyo is that the CNN's news team has just located Hiroko Fujita, the CNN star reporter who was mistakenly reported missing by ABC.' He moved over to Hiroko so that the cameraman could pan on to her. 'Hiroko, first let me say how happy we are that you are safe.'

'Thank you,' said Hiroko, bowing her head slightly and still looking at the picture of Alex cupped in her hand.

'More than half a billion people were worried about you. Now that you're safe, can you tell us what happened? The last time we heard from you was when the Minister of Construction hit you. Why would he want to hurt you?'

'I was about to break a story about Minister Tada's kickback scheme and how the collapse of the Daishin Trade Towers was the result of his corruption. Tada recognized me and knocked me out.'

Huntley broke in. 'Your son's in Mitaka, which I am told is far west of Tokyo. It would have taken you days to reach his school.'

'Yes?'

'Forgive me, Miss Fujita. But many of our viewers find it amazing that you would consider walking days to find your son instead of waiting for rescue teams.'

'All I know is that I must find him.' Hiroko's eyes misted over. Unlike most American reporters, who would have mercilessly held her in the camera's eye, Huntley turned to Moyama who had been standing at attention with his family. He had held a tight smile the entire time, unsure if the camera was zooming in on him.

Huntley quickly looked down at the notes handed him by his research assistant. 'We'll come back to Miss Fujita's remarkable story in a moment. Now we would like to introduce the man who saved her, Ken Moyama. Mr Moyama is best known as a philanthropist and the godfather of the Liberal Democratic Party, Japan's once-ruling party. Mr Moyama, how did you discover the whereabouts of Miss Fujita?'

Moyama stared at the camera and froze. He understood the English, but his response would not come out. There was an awkward moment of silence; then Hiroko, thinking quickly, asked Moyama the same question in Japanese. Moyama responded immediately, also in Japanese, and she translated for CNN viewers.

'I remembered World War II and the chaos that reigned afterwards. Thinking we needed order, I helped organize patrols to rescue those trapped in buildings and offer relief. When we heard that CNN were trying to locate Miss Fujita, we alerted our volunteers.' Moyama had said 'troops' in Japanese, but Hiroko changed it in translation. 'My assistant located her and flew her straight here by helicopter.' Moyama made no mention of the attempted rape. He was still smiling into the camera, his arms around his wife and son.

'Thank you, Mr Moyama. I know the – '

'The man to thank in the rescue efforts is our Imperial Highness, the Emperor. He organized the entire relief effort.'

'And Hiroko, what about your son?' asked Huntley. 'What will you do now?'

'I'll start walking home to Mitaka. It's all I can do.'

'Not true,' jumped in Moyama. 'I'm lending Miss Fujita the use of my helicopter to fly to Mitaka to find her son,' said Moyama magnanimously.

Hiroko was surprised. '*Honto ni*?'

'Yes, in fact you can leave now and be at your son's school within half an hour.'

Huntley again showed his empathy by diverting the camera off Hiroko and on to himself. 'And so a small note of goodness and hope amidst the horror and death of a city that has been destroyed. We at CNN will continue to bring you the reality and drama of the quake as events unfold here in Tokyo. From CNN in Tokyo this is Craig Huntley. Now back to the Imperial Palace.' Huntley handed his mike to the technician.

'Well done,' he said to Moyama and his family. Then he quietly approached Hiroko. 'And you too, Hiroko – you saved the day by translating for Moyama.'

'Thanks.'

'Do you mind if I join you in the search for Alex?' he asked impulsively.

Hiroko was surprised. 'But why?'

'It's a great ending to a captivating story.'

'You're welcome to come along,' she said. 'Just clear it with the godfather,' she added, laughing. 'You know *who* he is, don't you?' she asked.

'Well, I guessed he's sort of a fixer.'

Hiroko smiled to think that his Japanese CNN staff had not come clean and said he was head of Japan's yakuza.

'Yes, you could say that,' she mused, and did not add anything further.

Ten minutes later Hiroko, Huntley, Moyama and the CNN crew were airborne for Mitaka.

The twins had now been trapped beneath the Palace Hotel for two days, and it had been thirty-six hours since Keiko had spoken with her sister. Keiko had lost track of time through disorientation and fatigue, thinking it had only been a few hours. She squeezed some toothpaste out of the tube on to the wet cardboard, and slowly chewed her meal. The toothpaste gave her food an unexpected peppermint taste. Luckily water had filtered down from above and been absorbed into the cardboard. Mushka was luckier and feasted on the large supply of rats running around the rubble. She was careful not to bring any rats near Keiko and carefully cleaned herself before returning.

'Kiko?'

There was no reply.

'Kiko!' she screamed. 'If you can hear me, tap once.'

A faint scratch was heard. Kiko was unable to talk but rubbed her left slipper against a piece of concrete.

'Kiko, listen carefully. Conserve your energy. When I ask you questions, one sound means yes and two means no. Do you have enough to drink?'

Kiko again rubbed her slipper once, in an effort not to worry Keiko.

'Are you okay?'

She again rubbed her slipper once on the concrete.

'You must eat something. I'll call for you again in an hour. I love you, Kiko.'

Kiko rubbed her left foot once more before both twins went back to their sleep cycle.

38

THE QUEST

Wednesday afternoon

'To survive, I scavenged leftovers from NHK reporters. The state news service had 12 full time choppers ferrying food to its reporters during the Kobe Quake.'

A UK journalist covering the disaster

'What does that say?' As they walked, Craig Huntley pointed to a cardboard sign with Japanese characters written in large black ink. Hiroko translated. 'Kyomi, I am at the school park. Meet me there. Love, Hitoshi.'

They passed the remains of a house, with only the tiles visible above the crushed wooden structure.

'And that one?'

'Here lies my wife Kimiko and daughter Tomoko. I had a wonderful life with them and will be starting over in Osaka. Please leave this area in peace. Signed K. Takamatsu.'

'And what are those?'

Under the sign were a bunch of flowers, two oranges, an egg, an open can of orange HI-C and a stuffed animal.

'Offerings to his family in their afterlife,' shouted Hiroko. The sound of low-flying choppers made it hard to hear. As they flew overhead Hiroko made out the letters 'NHK' on the underside. The state news service and was using helicopters for food runs for its news teams.

They were now passing through an undamaged part of Mitaka. 'Look at those guys. They sure are efficient in this country,' said Huntley. He was referring to a moving van labelled 'Mitaka Removals' which was parked near a house. Neatly dressed removal men were carrying valuables from the house to the van.

Hiroko got suspicious. 'They can't really drive anywhere except that warehouse 500 metres down the road. I bet they're stripping the area.' She began to move towards the men but Moyama diverted her attention.

'The school's just ahead. We've got to find Alex,' he said exuberantly, looking nervously over his shoulder at his removal men. When Hiroko wasn't looking, he signalled for them to leave.

Hiroko walked briskly, turned left down a street and then went right. In front of them stood the concrete rubble of the Mitaka Primary School. The playing field was filled with survivors and there were tents everywhere. The CNN camera crew were busy filming footage for later broadcasts.

Hiroko rushed up to a woman boiling water over a fire. 'The children? Where are all the children?'

'Over there.'

The woman pointed to a row of tiny black plastic rubbish bags. There were three dozen bodies laid out neatly with name tags on them.

'No!' screamed Hiroko, running over to the bags. She worked her way down the row, looking frantically for Alex. The bodies were in order and she quickly scanned the name tags.

'Fuji, Hitoshi.' Hiroko closed her eyes and turned away, unable to read the next tag. 'Please, please not Fujita.' Slowly, and with considerable difficulty, she forced herself to open her eyes and look down. There, written on the tag, was the name: 'Fujiyama, Satoshi.'

'Oh God, please, please, please let him be alive!' Hiroko collapsed into Craig's arms and broke down into sobs, not sure whether to be relieved.

Craig just held her tight, gently stroking her back and making soothing sounds. 'We'll find him, Hiroko. Don't worry – we'll find him, I promise.'

The CNN crew filmed the tiny body bags and then moved on to a squatter camp that had been set up in the school playing field.

Moyama's men were busy interrogating survivors about what had happened at the school. Moyama himself was showing them a picture of Alex. 'Have you seen this boy?' the burly yakuza leader asked.

The survivors, already shocked by the quake, were intimidated and shook their heads.

'Call this number if you find him,' said Moyama, handing out his card. When Hiroko was out of earshot he secretly offered money for Alex's safe return. 'A big reward to anyone who can find him.'

A small group of victims sat expectantly around a radio, listening to a local radio station run down a list of names. The station was running off emergency generators and providing a service to the community. Locals could call up and tell the station where they would meet relatives. Hiroko moved closer to the group so she too could listen. Craig put his arm around her shoulder for comfort.

'Fujihara, Akihibo . . . Fujihara, Densei . . . Fujise, Toyama . . . Fujita, Alex . . .'

'No!' Hiroko became hysterical and shook a man standing nearby.

'What is this list of names? Tell me!' she pleaded with the startled man.

'It's a list of survivors in Mitaka,' said the man, pulling away from Hiroko and looking at her as if she were mad.

'Yes! Yes! Yes! Thank God.' She grabbed Craig's M-phone. 'What number do we call for the radio station?' she demanded of a woman in the group who was writing down names. The woman told her. Hiroko was so nervous that she dropped the phone. She picked it up and dialled the radio station. The lines were jammed. She hit auto redial, but the lines were engaged.

'Oh, please, please pick it up.'

Finally, after almost ten minutes, the phone rang. 'Radio Mitaka, please hold.'

Hiroko paced the grass, holding the phone and biting her nails. 'Please pick it up. Please.'

Three minutes later a man answered the line. 'What name, please?' Phones were ringing and people shouting in the background.

'Fujita, Alex.'

'Survivor or dead?'

'Survivor.' She could hear the man turning pages.

'Fujita . . . yes. Fujita, Alex. He's alive and uninjured, according to this list.' Hiroko covered her mouth and started crying. It took a moment before she could speak. 'Where is he?'

'Just a moment. Let's see . . . try the Mitaka Primary School shelter.' The man hung up and moved on to the next call.

'We're at the Mitaka Primary School shelter,' shouted Hiroko. 'Where can he be?'

Moyama, meanwhile, had been systematically combing the field, forcing everyone to look at Alex's picture.

'Yes, the children who made it out of the school alive are over there,' said one of the teachers, pointing to a group of children playing.

Moyama strode over to the children. 'Alex, where are you?' He surveyed the group. No one raised their hand. 'Where is Alex Fujita?' he said a little louder.

He saw a small hand go up.

'Is your name Alex?'

'Yes. Why?'

'Your mother's here.'

Alex looked up. 'Really? Where is she?'

Moyama smiled and came over to him. 'Climb on my back and I'll take you to her.'

The little boy jumped on Moyama's back and they jogged over to where Hiroko was standing with her back to them.

'Look who I've found.'

Hiroko whirled around, and Alex dropped off the yakuza leader's back and into his mother's arms. The CNN crew were already rolling the cameras.

'Mommy, mommy!'

'Alex!' Hiroko shouted, hugging him and twirling him around in her arms. 'Oh, precious,' she said smothering him with kisses. 'Are you okay? Is there anything I can get you?'

'How about a teriyaki burger from McDonald's?' asked Alex, much to the amusement of the group.

Moyama broke off from Hiroko and Alex and made a quick call to Osaka. 'I want ten teriyaki burgers flown up from McDonald's. They're for my grandson, so don't complain.' Later the next day Alex was munching away contentedly on his burger.

As the CNN cameras swept the poignant scene Huntley started to speak, but he was interrupted by the loud clacking of mah-jhong tiles. To relieve the stress, amidst the chaos four women were avidly grabbing, thrusting and swearing over a mah-jhong table retrieved from the school, where the game was played every Wednesday night. To add to the confusion they had their radio blaring. 'This is American Forces Radio, bringing you the best rock music in Japan.'

'Hey, could you please turn your music down and hold up your game for a minute?' he politely asked them in English.

The ladies ignored him and kept playing their game.

Exasperated, Huntley began shouting into the microphone over the noise of the tiles and the joyous cries of the reunion.

Alex, now tired, fell asleep in his mother's arms. Hiroko turned to Moyama and thanked him, then suddenly remembered Michiko: 'Oh, my God – Mother!'

'Don't worry. We'll walk over to her building – it's not far. Here, I'll take Alex,' offered Moyama affectionately.

Hiroko politely refused, unwilling to give up her son after so long a search. But as the party began walking Hiroko found she was suddenly tired with all the emotion and handed her child to Moyama.

They arrived at the Mitaka apartment building only to find it flattened.

'Mother – no!'

A sound was coming out of the rubble, and as they moved closer the voice became clearer: 'Quick. Dive under the table! Quick. Dive under the table!'

'Our alarm. Mother's dead. She must have been buried alive,' said Hiroko in a sad, distant voice.

With all the commotion, Alex woke up. 'What's going on?' he asked.

'Darling. I'm sorry, Alex. It's grandma. She's dead.'

'Dead? What are you talking about? We left her playing mah-jhong at the school. She's probably still playing.'

Hiroko looked at Moyama with relief and they both laughed. The yakuza boss had a twinkle in his eye.

Huntley turned to camera, ready to broadcast. 'This is Craig Huntley reporting live from Tokyo, where a fairytale ending has just given hope to millions of survivors . . .'

Moyama flew the Fujita family back to his compound and Craig broke off from the crew to spend the night there with them. Later that evening Hiroko and Craig celebrated with sake, and by the fifth cup both were tipsy. Hiroko put her head in Craig's lap and he played with her hair.

'I'm so happy,' she murmured.

Alex was fast asleep on the floor and Michiko was nowhere to be found.

'Where's your mother?'

'Probably with Moyama, catching up on old times.'

'Doesn't his wife mind?'

'No, at one time she was wife number two and accepted by Mrs Moyama.'

'He's your father, isn't he?'

'Uh, Craig?'

'What?'

'Shut up and kiss me before I sober up.'

Though Michiko never showed up that evening, the risk of her sudden appearance made their lovemaking all the more exciting.

The next morning Hiroko and Craig fell out of bed with hammer-head hangovers. Craig lit a fire outside the cottage, then Hiroko boiled water and added Magic Rice retrieved from some relief package. The rice tasted like paste and the two ate breakfast in silence.

'I'm certainly not going to marry you for your cooking.'

Hiroko laughed and leaned over to kiss him just as Michiko appeared. Craig quickly pulled away.

'Hello, Mother,' greeted Hiroko mischievously.

'Hello, little daughter. Alex still asleep?'

'Yes. Why don't we wake him up?'

Mother and daughter went into the cottage together and Michiko whispered in Hiroko's ear, 'You put your skirt on inside out.'

Hiroko blushed and quickly ran behind a screen to reverse the situation. 'And I suppose you slept soundly through the night, Mother?'

'At least one man in Tokyo still appreciates my body.'

'Shhh. Mother! Alex is awake.'

'Good morning, darling,' cooed both women as Alex jumped out of bed.

Hiroko went to join Craig outside. 'About last night . . .'

'Wonderful, wasn't it?'

'It was. But do you think we slept together because of the situation? You know what I mean – the quake . . . finding Alex . . . the sake.'

'I can only speak for myself. I'm head over heels in love with you. But you don't sound so sure.'

'No, it's just my hangover. Things will be fine,' she said as she kissed Craig on the lips. 'I just need time.'

'There's no such thing as 'time', Hiroko – only feelings. Any woman will leave anything she's doing for a man she loves. Anything. She could be married to the richest man in the world, meet an enchanting pauper and be gone the next day. Time is nothing where love is concerned.'

'And how about for a man?'

'I've never thought about it – but yes, I suppose a man would give up everything for a woman he loved.'

Craig kissed Hiroko on the lips and left to jump aboard the CNN chopper that had just landed.

39

THE HEIST

Tokyo's Narita airport on Wednesday night, thirty-six hours
after the quake

'There was gold everywhere!'
An awestruck investigator after the raid on political
fixer, longtime MP, former cabinet minister and godfather
Shin Kanemaru in 1992. Investigators also found billions
of yen in illicit stocks and bonds used to finance
Japanese politics

'How many fucking hours?' Tony Berman shouted when he
was told how long it took to fly from Las Vegas to Tokyo.
'You can fly to the fucking moon in fifteen hours.' To calm
his nerves the mafia lawyer drank heavily on the flight. Vodka always
calmed him, as it did most alcoholics, and Berman spent most of the
night asleep.

Narita airport outside Tokyo was officially closed, but Moyama's
men lit one runway with lamps and flashlights and signalled the
plane by flare to distinguish the runway from the thousands of fires
that burned in the distance. The Hercules transport plane thumped
heavily down on the tarmac, crammed full of tents, sleeping bags,
blankets, morphine, amphetamines, penicillin, antibiotics, vitamins,
syringes, Beretta nine millimetre pistols, AK-47 assault rifles and
ammunition.

Japanese drug dealers made most of their money from peddling
uppers to overworked taxi-cab drivers and dock workers. Amphetamines had been given to soldiers during World War II to stave off
hunger and generate euphoria in battle. Moyama had kept the
post-war soldiers addicted to 'soft' drugs. Though the current
sentence for drug dealing was severe – seven years to life – this
did not deter the yakuza. Through Moyama, Berman's hope was to
flood the Japanese market with cheap uppers and keep medical victims
hooked to morphine long after the quake's effects had subsided.

The landing jolted Berman, who awoke in a vile mood. Jet lag, lack of sleep, turbulence and the uncertainty of the journey had worn him down. He had bags under his eyes and a migraine-intensity hangover.

As he and his five side-kicks landed, one of the boxes broke open. Out fell fifty packs of strawberry frosted Pop Tarts in shiny silver wrappers.

'Who the fuck are those for, boss?' asked Vinnie Antolo, Berman's number two man. Every sentence uttered by Berman or his men seemed to contain a swearword.

'Don't fucking ask. And don't fucking swear.' He eyed his men. 'Listen to me, you guys. No messing around here. This man Moyama is a god in Japan. No slant-eye or gook jokes. I'm warning you.' Unfortunately for Berman, Moyama did not hold the mafia lawyer in the same regard, viewing him as a crude hoodlum whom he could exploit.

Berman had ordered his men to bring suits and dress shirts. He himself was dressed in a brown polyester suit with a silk shirt and a wide, bright red tie. On his feet he wore expensive designer shoes. His men were similarly clothed.

The plane taxied to a group of helicopters. Fifty of Moyama's yakuza stood by to move the supplies from the plane to the choppers.

Berman opened the side door of the Hercules and spotted Moyama and his lieutenant down below. The yakuza wheeled the mobile staircase to the side of the plane and to Berman's amazement Mata bounded up the steps and handed out business cards printed in English. Berman focused on one of them: It read: 'Mata Akio, General Manager Fuji Waste Products'. He stuffed the other cards in his shirt pocket without looking at them. Moyama's men were dressed in disaster wear: khaki outfits and army-style boots. This new fashion trend had swept Japan after the Kobe quake, and all Japanese households had disaster outfits in their wardrobe.

Berman staggered down the steps and remembered not to hug Moyama as he did his consiglieri in the States. He started to bow, but Moyama came up to him and gave him a bear hug.

'I didn't think you did that sort of thing,' said Berman.

'Special circumstances call for special behaviour. Good to see you, Berman-san.'

'Good to see you too, Moyama-san.'

'Did you bring my special request?' he asked. Berman took a pack of strawberry frosted Pop Tarts out of his pocket.

'Both of them.' He handed Moyama the Pop Tarts and also slipped him a bag of Semtex, the high explosive favoured by terrorists. 'We brought an explosives expert to use this.' Berman wondered what Moyama needed the Semtex for and hoped the yakuza boss would remember to reciprocate – he looked forward to hosting a private party for young Japanese boys.

Moyama signalled his men to begin loading the choppers, then ripped open the pack of Pop Tarts and started wolfing them down. Moyama loved strawberry frosted Pop Tarts. He had discovered them in a local Seven-Eleven during a visit to the States and was instantly hooked. Moyama's kitchen staff were under orders always to have ample supplies of his two favourite foods: sea slug and Pop Tarts. They could never locate the Pop Tarts, however, and left it to Moyama to sort out his own supply lines. His son had brought some back from Los Angeles but they were not frosted. It was the only time the younger Moyama had ever seen his father angry. 'Throw them away!' Moyama had ordered, almost hitting him.

'We must go now,' said Moyama. Berman noticed that all five military choppers on the runway were painted over with the Red Cross insignia. He wondered where the hell Moyama had obtained Chinooks. Moyama, Berman, Mata and one of Berman's lieutenants jumped into a smaller UH1-J helicopter.

'Home,' Moyama ordered the pilot.

Once airborne, Berman looked out in amazement at Tokyo. It was two in the morning and the city was lit up like a Christmas tree. Fires burned out of control throughout the city. Vinnie leaned over and whispered in Berman's ear. 'We shouda brought marshmallows.'

Berman elbowed Vinnie, then looked out the window at the fires. He suppressed the urge to laugh.

It was 3 a.m. by the time the chopper dropped the four men off at Moyama's home. Mata, the yakuza lieutenant, showed Berman and Vinnie to a cottage. The two Italian-Americans jumped into bed without undressing and fell fast asleep.

Once Berman had left them, Moyama took Mata aside to check on another project. 'Are the acetylene torches, welding rods and blasting caps here?'

'Yes, sir.'

'Okay. I want our advance team ready to leave in five minutes.'

Four men specially picked by Moyama boarded the small helicopter with him and Mata. Each wore an asbestos suit and a welding helmet with a lantern on top, making them look like spacemen. Among them was Berman's explosives expert. The chopper took off, flying east near

Ginza and the Imperial Palace. When they approached the financial
district, it began to descend. The area was devastated: the remains of
buildings seemed to have subsided into the earth, which had turned
into a grey sludge.

Moyama pointed to the Bank of Japan. 'Land on that building.'

The Bank of Japan was a granite structure built to convey a
sense of majesty and permanence to the nation. This sturdy building
had partially sunk into the mud and tilted slightly to one side.
Across the street Moyama could see the remains of Mitsukoshi's
headquarters.

'Okay, you know the plan. Go!'

The four spacemen, well drilled in their task, jumped out. Moyama
carried some rolled-up blueprints in his hand; his phone was hidden
deep in the pockets of his disaster wear. The spacemen pushed their
equipment on a small luggage trolley and none of them spoke as they
went about their work. Some diligent official had locked up most
of the Bank of Japan's doors before evacuating; they broke open
an entrance. Moyama produced a powerful flashlight from another
of his pockets. *The war was never this exciting*, he thought.

The spacemen turned their lanterns on. After five minutes of
wending their way down corridors, stepping over dead bodies and
breaking down doors, the team came upon a wrought iron gate.
Asking no questions, the four professionals lit their torches and
made a circular incision around the lock. The door lock popped
out and the group moved on. After two more similar doors, they
stopped. Moyama checked his blueprints.

'This is it.'

The four spacemen lit up their torches again and worked for
half an hour. Then they produced a drill and embedded Semtex
in four different locations. After setting the blasting caps, the small
team retired up the passage and hid behind a wall to await the
explosion.

A roar filled the air, and when it had subsided Moyama hurried back
into the ante-chamber. The mangled vault door lay on its side.

'Shine the lanterns in here,' Moyama ordered.

The nation's gold repository lit up in a brilliant glow. Thousands of
gold bars lay stacked on wooden pallets. Tears welled up in Moyama's
eyes. It was the most beautiful sight on earth – a billion dollars' worth
of gold.

Collecting himself, Moyama instructed the spacemen to hook up
the portable generators and lights. He dug into his khaki pants
to find the phone and tried to call up his second team, but it

was impossible. Moyama had forgotten how far underground they were.

'Mata, you and I'll go back up top . . . The second team will be here in a moment,' he told the spacemen. 'Just wait here.'

Moyama and Mata walked back up through the passages. When they emerged into the darkness, Moyama flipped open his phone and dialled.

'Okay, team two, move into position.'

Two helicopters appeared out of the darkness and a squad of fifty yakuza scrambled down a rope ladder.

'Mata, you make sure the gold gets aboard those helicopters. It'll take two trips. The men can then be paid and sent on to the next mission in Ginza,' he shouted.

Mata nodded, smiling. He was armed with an AK-47, while the fifty lackeys assigned to loading the gold were unarmed. Nobody would ever mess with Moyama, but he was taking no chances. Just like the war. Trust nobody.

Next Moyama called his third team. This group were his enforcers, just in case they ran into problems. Another chopper appeared and thirty army troops scaled down a ladder. Mata looked at his boss in fear.

'Don't worry – they're just my men dressed in army uniforms. Now get going.'

The yakuza troops surrounded the Bank of Japan building, guarding it against curious refugees, looters, police and real members of the army. Before the quake, Tokyo residents had been curious and nosed into everyone's affairs. But the new law had become 'fend for oneself' and survival was now all that mattered. Refugees were interested only in food and water.

Everything secure, Moyama flew off, daydreaming about the billion dollars' worth of gold that was now his.

40

THE RIOT

The Mitsukoshi food warehouse, Thursday afternoon, two days after the quake

'The penalty for speculating in the rice markets is death.'
Edict issued by an Osaka Tribune on 28 September 1663, after merchant profiteering in rice had led to severe shortages, price increases and riots

'Most countries have race riots. Japan has rice riots.'
A sociologist tracing thousands of years of violence due to food shortages

A crowd of two dozen people, many of them women, had gathered in a circle with yen banknotes in their hands. Not prepared to queue six hours for free food and drink, they began bidding.

'Ten thousand yen.'

'Eleven thousand.'

'Eleven five.'

The man standing on the plastic container reprimanded the last bidder.

'Only lots of a thousand. It makes things go quicker. Do I hear twelve thousand?'

'Twelve thousand.'

Then there was silence.

'Any other bids? No? Sold for twelve thousand yen.' Nearly $120 for a canned drink.

The auctioneer handed the winner a can of Pocari Sweat and pocketed the notes. He then held up a bag of rice.

'I'll start the bidding at ten thousand . . .'

A lively black market had sprung up in food and drink, and overnight Japan had become a cash-and-barter society. Most families paid for supplies in yen notes, one of the few commodities readily available in Tokyo. It was reminiscent of Tokyo after the great Kanto earthquake of 1923 and in the late 1940s. Men hid yen notes in silk money bags tucked under their bellies, while women nestled their jewels in tiny sachets down their bras. Though families had slowly come to trust banks during the years of Japan's economic miracle, it was a guarded sort of trust. As Japan gradually changed in fifty years from a ravaged post-war society to the greatest industrial power on earth, another change also took place: control of wealth passed from the male breadwinner to the housewife. Housewives kept wads of money tucked in their *tansu* – a wooden dresser that doubles as a staircase, under the floorboards and in unused decorative vases. Japan could get away with such old-fashioned notions since robbery was unheard of and deposit interest rates were derisory. Most of the black marketeers were therefore women.

After a long wait in the food queue, some refugees were prepared to sell off their food. A great many people were still lined up at Watanabe's relief shelter.

A peasant woman, known as a 'prawn-back' on account of the distinctive arch in her spine, approached the shelter. She had patiently waited six hours just for a drink.

'Please may I have some water?' asked the prawn-back.

Thousands of refugees stood behind her. Alerted by radio broadcasts that the Mitsukoshi warehouse was doling out free food and drink, the numbers had grown. Although weary, the crowd emitted a low drone, like a restless swarm of bees.

'We're out of water for the moment, but I can offer you fruit juice or soda.'

The stooped woman was hard of hearing and put her hand to her ear. 'Eh?'

The young girl behind the counter repeated her words loudly.

'I said we're out of water – '

'Out of water?' cried a man behind her.

His cry rippled through the queue like a wave. The fear-laden phrase travelled to the end of the kilometre-long line in less than ten seconds.

'Out of water!'

'But I see drinks up there.'

'They're lying.'

'They're keeping the water for themselves.'

Those at the back began pressing forward. Very slowly fear turned to anger. Men, women and children scrambled to push to the front before supplies ran out. The straight line now resembled a giant pulsating amoeba, constantly changing shape.

The man who had begun the run on the drink stand elbowed his way past the old woman.

'I see plenty of drinks here. You can't hide them. Let me have a drink.'

He jumped behind the stand, followed by others. The old woman fell to her knees and was unable to get up.

Watanabe heard the commotion. He and his daughter had crossed Tokyo Bay by powerboat, docked at the Sumida River and walked back to the food warehouse. He had Naomi on his back. Official-looking squads, ten men strong, were patrolling the financial district. They were Moyama's men, dressed in khaki disaster wear and armed. Watanabe and his daughter walked by the 'patrols' unhindered. Near the warehouse, Watanabe saw the chaos and instinct told him trouble was afoot. He quietly took Naomi down the side entrance to the depot.

'Wait here, Naomi-chan, I'll be right back.'

The young girl behind the counter was now in danger. The more able-bodied had jumped over it and were madly opening drinks, chugging down liquid as it dribbled down their chin and clothes. Those behind, scared that supplies were about to run out, but spying the remaining drinks, pushed forward. Those at the rear simply thrust forward through a combination of fear, anger and desperation. The old woman at the front of the line was now on her stomach, pleading for help as people climbed over her. Her breathing became more laboured.

Kozo Taishowa, meanwhile, had come to the young relief worker's rescue and pulled the old woman to safety. He then turned his attention to the crowd.

'Stop!' he shouted into his bullhorn. 'Stop, or I'll be forced to use this stun gun.'

He turned the weapon on but the rioters continued to root through boxes for drinks. Those at the back felt cheated.

The man who had incited the riot turned to Kozo. 'Look, he wants to keep the drinks for himself.'

This made perfect sense to the irrational mob, who surged forward. 'Get him!' somebody yelled.

A swarm of bodies covered Kozo. Though he was a feeble old man, the mob was indiscriminate. The man took Kozo's stun gun and turned the high voltage rod on him. A shock wave tore through Kozo's body, knocking him out. The mob had drawn its first blood. Hungry for more, they turned on the rescue workers. The angry crowd tore, punched and scratched at them. Watanabe ran to save his volunteers but checked himself. He rushed back into the concrete depot, grabbed Naomi and ran out through a side entrance.

Two hundred metres down the main street he spotted the patrol. 'Help!' he yelled to them.

The patrol turned to Watanabe and marched quickly up to him. 'A mob is killing our rescue workers – please help us.'

The yakuza patrol, eager for action, clicked off the safety catches on their assault rifles. Watanabe showed them the side entrance.

'Single fire position,' the patrol leader ordered. A few disappointed moans could be heard from wannabe Rambo types. The soldiers wanted a chance to spray a crowd with automatic fire. Now they were being forced to take aim at their victims.

The patrol marched quickly through the food warehouse and up the concrete ramp. The mob began to move in on the warehouse. Dozens of bodies lay trampled or beaten near the loading dock. The mob was busy overpowering the remaining rescue workers who were blocking the loading bay entrance. The patrol lost no time in taking careful aim at mob leaders. Only one shot need have been fired, but the gangster-led police were in no mood for compromise: they wanted blood. Five leaders in the crowd fell, and the sound of the rifles sobered the mob.

'Stop shooting,' yelled Watanabe.

But the soldiers did not listen. Blind anger turned to abject fear. Panic seized the crowd, who changed direction. Men, women and children began running away from the warehouse. The old, weary and infirm were crushed underfoot. Having survived the earthquake, they died by suffocation.

'Cease firing.'

Nevertheless, the foot soldiers pursued the mob. Their shooting had stopped, but they knocked laggards over the head with their rifle butts. Watanabe followed the patrol. Bodies were strewn everywhere.

'Kozo, Kozo, where are you?'

He spotted his friend under an overturned table. With his daughter firmly held in one hand, Watanabe rushed to Kozo's side. The old man had turned a greyish blue colour. Watanabe checked his pulse and felt only a weak beat.

'Medic!'

The emergency medical team were already attending to survivors of the riot. A medical student appeared, took out a stethoscope and examined Kozo. The old man was still unconscious.

'He's alive, but barely. His body looks as if it has suffered a severe electrical shock and his heart may have been weakened. We'll get you a blanket. There's nothing else we can do,' he said, turning to treat the next victim.

Watanabe began to fall apart. Watching Kozo slip away brought home the reality of his family's death. Watanabe held the old man's hand and began to weep.

But then his eight year-old daughter hugged him. 'Daddy, don't worry. I'm with you. Let's sit by your friend. Remember when grandma died. You said it was okay because she had lived a long and good life.'

Naomi's words sent warmth through Watanabe. She had only been five when his own mother died and she had remembered his words all those years. He hugged her.

Kozo stirred and opened his eyes slightly. Watanabe was still holding his hand. Kozo felt the warmth, looked up and saw the man and the small child. He smiled weakly.

'Your daughter . . .' Kozo instinctively knew that Naomi was all that Watanabe had left. 'Reach into my jacket.'

Watanabe pulled out the tattered papers he had retrieved from the safe. It seemed like years ago.

'I have no family. These papers are now yours. I've already signed them over to you.'

'But you'll recover – let's stop this talk.'

'Take these papers. Please.'

'Okay, anything to get you to rest,' said Watanabe as he put the documents in his pocket.

'I'm sorry about your family. Start a new life. You're a good man.'

'Taishowa-san, please rest . . . 'Naomi,' he said, turning to his daughter, 'please run over and get me a drink for Taishowa-san.'

Watanabe turned back to Kozo, whose hand had now gone limp. There was still a smile on the old man's face.

41

THE CRASH

Thursday afternoon on the Salomon trading desk in
New York

**'We were genuinely a full service casino – a customer didn't
even need money to gamble in our house.'**
Michael Lewis describing Salomon Brothers
in his bestseller *Liar's Poker*

'How many zipperheads we up to?'

'Twenty thousand and rising.'

Ralph Gazinsky had been promoted to head of Asian trading at Salomon Brothers and was shouting across the trading desk, betting on how many Japanese had been killed in the earthquake.

'What spread you makin'?' asked Gazinsky.

'Twenty bid, thirty offer,' replied Freddie.

'I'm in for a thousand bucks at thirty.'

He had just bet Freddie that more than thirty thousand Japanese had been wiped out in the earthquake. Gazinsky figured that with his new promotion he could afford to blow a grand.

Freddie was running a book on the Tokyo death toll; it was called the 'FDI' or Freddie Death Index. Word had spread quickly, and Salomon's trading lines were jammed. Freddie was doing more business in the FDI than he was for Salomon. Salomon clients placed bets with Freddie in his personal capacity, many for $50, $100 or $1000. If they believed less than twenty thousand Japanese had died, then they sold a contract at 20. If they felt more than thirty thousand had died, they bought a contract at 30. The 50 per cent spread was theoretically Freddie's profit.

Betting was more hectic than Freddie had anticipated. He had over $50,000 riding on the body count. As in most international crises, the information on which to base an informed decision was scarce, or, as Freddie so aptly put it, 'nobody knew jack squat about shit'.

He was right. Minutes after the quake, initial estimates placed the death toll at a 'few hundred'; by the end of Tuesday it was two thousand, a day later ten thousand, and now the estimates had risen to twenty thousand. The smart money was buying Freddie's contracts and he was worried. While world news reports issued Tokyo death estimates of around twenty thousand, traders all over Wall Street were calling up Freddie to buy FDI contracts at thirty thousand. Something was wrong. Freddie had to move his 'sell' price up to forty by the end of trading. Instinct now told him that more people had died in Japan than anyone had imagined.

He decided to protect himself against disaster and insure his 'book'. Freddie quietly dialled the London number of Ladbroke's, the gaming company, with whom he had a special account. Salomon Brothers frowned on traders gambling during working hours when they were supposed to gamble for Salomon Brothers, not themselves.

'Ladbroke's, may we help you?' answered a sensuous voice. Ladbroke's knew that pleasant voices, beautiful women and alcohol eased the inevitable pain of losing.

'Yes, this is Frederick Bruton from Salomon Brothers in New York. Is Mr Barber-Pike in?'

Freddie only used his full first name when dealing with Brits. Frederick not Freddie, Jonathan not Johnny, Albert not Al and Stephen not Steve.

'One moment, putting you through.'

Francis Barber-Pike picked up the phone. 'Frederick, so nice to hear from you. What can we do for *you*?'

He lingered on the 'you', conveying the impression of a discreet, personalized service. Freddie was designated a good credit risk by Ladbroke's and able to bet up to half a million dollars on his own account.

'I need to lay off some bets. I want to bet a hundred thousand dollars on how many people died in the Tokyo quake.'

Freddie heard a clicking and scratching on the line that was not overseas interference. Ladbroke's taped its calls. Despite the time-honoured phrase 'My word is my bond', securities and gambling houses trusted nobody and taped all their calls. The Ladbroke's representative asked Frederick to hold for a moment.

A bet of this size did not raise any eyebrows in his world. Ladbroke's owned Aspinall's, the exclusive casino in Mayfair where Arab sheiks, Taiwanese billionaires and African dictators frequently won and lost millions. Punters called Barber-Pike, Ladbroke's customer liaison, when the itch to have a flutter was too strong to resist a phone wager. Bets of up to £500,000 were not uncommon. Ladbroke's was famous for its diversity of betting. Just as Lloyd's was known to insure the noses of wine tasters, the voices of singers and the legs of dancers, so Ladbroke's accepted a variety of bets: how many trees fell in Hyde Park during a storm, the sex of an unborn royal child or the number of people killed in a bomb disaster. Freddie's bet was not out of the ordinary. Sick, but not out of the ordinary.

Barber-Pike came back in less than a minute. 'Our spread is twenty-five, thirty-five for a hundred thousand.'

Freddie was excited but out of propriety hesitated. *Pack a lunch, you fucking double barrel hairy-assed tuna fish, I'm taking you to school.* He calmed himself before speaking. 'Okay, I'm a buyer of a hundred at thirty-five,' said Freddie casually. 'I'll wire the funds immediately.'

'Thank you, sir.'

Freddie hung up and shouted a stifled cry for joy. He had bet $100,000 that more than thirty five thousand people had died in the quake.

Ralph Gazinsky overheard Freddie's conversation. As the new head of Asian trading, he was interested in any influence that Tokyo's body count might have on the stock and bond markets. The Salomon executive committee had forbidden Ralph to buy any Japanese securities for the Salomon house account, but no mention had been made about 'shorting' or selling securities. Ralph had a simple theory. The more zipperheads killed in Tokyo, the further the Japanese stock and bond markets would fall.

'Freddie, my gut tells me you're long on corpses,' probed Ralph. 'Long' meant he was a buyer. 'Where's the FDI now?'

'It's moved up to thirty bid, forty offer, way ahead of the official body count. I'm playing the hunch that more people bought it than the public expects.'

Ralph was interested. 'The smart money agrees with you. Keep me posted, buddy.'

Though trading in the Japanese securities markets was closed in Japan, eager, aggressive and greedy traders were shuffling Japanese paper around in the hope of making a killing. The financial vultures first swooped down on the hapless yen. Foreign exchange traders hammered the Japanese currency and sold it from 100 to the dollar to 200 in less than two days. It was one of the worst collapses ever seen in a major currency. Ever since the almighty yen had taken over as the world's strongest currency in 1987, foreign exchange traders had been helpless against its rise. Now they exacted their revenge. With feigned patriotism, Wall Street traders purchased dollars, Frankfurt traders purchased marks and London traders bought up pounds in selling the yen. Other traders were also busy shorting Japanese shares in a nation that resembled an economic roadkill.

The Big One wiped out almost a trillion dollars' worth of stock exchange wealth – first through the collapse of share prices traded on the black market, and then through the physical destruction of share certificates.

But the financial slaughter produced two ghoulish winners. Osaka Polymer and the Nippon Dry Ice Company were both located in Osaka and safe from the quake. Osaka Polymer was a plastics manufacturer whose product line included body bags, while Nippon Dry Ice produced the liquid carbon dioxide used in the preservation of corpses. Osaka Polymer rose from 1250 yen to 6500 yen a share in six weeks while Nippon Dry Ice only tripled, rising from 650 to 2000 yen a share. Demand for mountain bikes also soared, which sent the Japan Mountain Bike Company from 200 to 1000 yen a share.

As Salomon's trader, Ralph Gazinsky joined the selling frenzy. But he noticed something strange in the sell-off, prompted by an internal call.

'Hi, Ralphie, this is Mike Lawrence in equities. A client of mine is looking for a large block of Toyota. What can you offer in size?' He was asking how many shares Ralph would sell at one time, preferably in a large block.

Mike Lawrence was a New York-based salesman selling Asian stocks to American pension funds and institutions. His clients were based in the Mid-West.

Ralph was surprised. American institutions were notoriously conservative in their purchase of foreign shares, especially during a crisis. Something was up and Ralph's sensors were on full alert.

'Who's the client, Mike?' he probed casually. 'Is there more behind it?'

Traders had to be careful, even in their own firm. The traders ran a separate profit and loss account to the Salomon salesmen. Salesmen tried to protect clients, while traders 'tried to rip clients a new asshole'.

The client's identity would tell Ralph a lot of things. Was it someone of integrity? Ralph did not want to sell the client a big block of Toyota shares only to discover that that market was cleaned out of stock and Salomon was unable to buy the Toyota shares back elsewhere. Unscrupulous clients sometimes called three traders at once to buy stock. This practice, called double dealing, was unethical.

Mike Lawrence got annoyed. 'Look, the client wants anonymity and hasn't told me about any other orders. It's not a big deal. Give me a price for five million shares or I'll trade away.' Mike was a successful salesmen and one of the few who could bully a trader.

'Okay, offer him five million shares at 1250.'

'Thanks. I'll be straight back to confirm.'

From across the room, Ralph could see Mike on the phone. *I need to know who the client is*, he thought urgently. A five million share buy order was highly suspicious in a falling market. Something big was going on. Ralph called Mike's sales assistant to grill her for information, but his eyes never left Mike who was still on the phone.

Shelly Andrews was an Ivy Leaguer whom Ralph had dated a few summers ago, and one of the few ex-girlfriends with whom he was still on speaking terms.

'Hi, Shel, this is Ralphie. Shhhh. Don't mention my name. Listen, who's Mike talking to now?'

'Detroit, why?'

When discussing a client, brokers usually spoke in terms of geographical location such as Houston, Singapore or London. A client name was seldom used. Each brokerage house had different nicknames for clients. At Salomon, traders called the major Detroit-based institutions by nickname: 350 for General Motors, after their classic 350 Chevrolet, Mustang for Ford, and Captain Kirk for Chrysler's largest shareholder, Kirk Kerkorian.

Ralph decided to lie. 'I didn't know if you wanted the trade booked to Captain Kirk or to 350.'

'I think it's Captain Kirk, but I'll ask Mike and call you back.'

'No, no, Shelly – do me a favour and don't mention I called. I owe you one. Thanks.'

Mike called Ralph a moment later. 'Okay, my client will take the five million Toyota at 1250. He's interested in more large blocks but promised he won't buy in the market until you've covered.'

Ralph filled out the internal trading ticket selling 5 million Toyota shares to the sales desk. He knew Mike also had to fill a form out and watched across the room as he handed the slip to Shelly. The salesman's ticket contained all the important information. Shelly put the ticket in the out tray for the settlement team, who would send the client details on payment.

Mike got up and headed towards the men's room. It was a good moment for Ralph to walk over to the sales area.

Why would Chrysler be buying shares in Toyota? Most American car manufacturers had Japanese partners, but these ties had proved ineffective in selling into Japan. Chrysler had purchased 15 per cent of Mitsubishi Motors in 1971 at a price of 100,000 yen a share. After share splits, Chrysler's stake had increased to 140 million shares in 1988. Mitsubishi Motors had been ineffective in selling Chrysler vehicles to Japanese consumers and Chrysler president Lee Iacocca had ordered his investment team to dispose of the holding. It had taken five long years as Chrysler sold the shares on the Tokyo Stock Exchange, but by 1994 Chrysler was out of Mitsubishi, pocketing hundreds of millions of dollars in profit.

Ralph reasoned that the buyer of Toyota shares could only be the Chrysler pension fund or the cash-laden Chrysler Corporation. The board of the Chrysler pension fund trustees were a bunch of old ladies and would never allow investment into Japan during a crash. The buyer must be Chrysler Corporation itself.

Ralph walked past Shelly's desk and peeked in the out tray. Under 'client' Mike had written 'CC' in his chicken scratch handwriting. Ralph had been right – the buyer was Chrysler Corporation.

'And what are you looking at?' asked Shelly suspiciously.

'Nothing, babe. Look, I just don't want to take a bath on this trade. Let me know if there's more coming down.'

'Why, Ralph, that would be breaking client/broker privilege,' she said playfully. 'What's my bonus?'

Ralph smiled. He owed Shelly a poke. It had been about eight months.

'You name the time.'

Back at his desk, Ralph thought the Chrysler purchase through. He knew that Chrysler was sitting on a cash pile. He knew that Kirk Kerkorian, the largest shareholder, wanted to improve its pay-out to shareholders. He also knew that Chrysler had been unsuccessful in selling its cars and vans to Japanese consumers. Trade barriers and labyrinthine webs of middlemen pushed the retail price of a $25,000 luxury car up to $48,000 in Tokyo.

Then it dawned on Ralph that Chrysler was plotting to take out Toyota! The Toyota share price had taken a beating, falling from a post-quake level of 5000 yen a share to less than 1250 yen. Meanwhile the yen had lost half its value against the dollar.

Anyone like Kerkorian with the balls to attempt a takeover bid of Chrysler itself, as Kerkorian had in 1995, was aggressive enough to have a go at Toyota while the Japanese were on their knees. It was a cruel move, but shrewd. Ralph punched a few numbers into his calculator. Toyota had 3.5 billion shares. *Wow*, he thought, *Toyota's* *worth only $21 billion.* Fifty per cent of Toyota could be bought in a falling market for around $10 billion, a bargain to high-flying asset-strippers. Ralph checked his *Japan Company Handbook* which listed the assets of Toyota. The car manufacturer had over $8 billion of cash in the bank, much of it in currencies other than yen. A week ago Toyota had been worth nearly $80 billion.

Ralph could make a killing with this knowledge. But Salomon's executive committee had forbidden him to buy any shares for the house account. *The dickbag compliance officer's not about to waive those rules,* he thought.

But this was Ralph's big chance to make a fortune. He bought shares in Toyota anyway.

42

THE RATS

Noon in Tokyo, Thursday, two days after the quake

'In China the appearance of rats is an officially designated earthquake precursor: in May 1974 it saved the lives of a family in Yunnan province. A housewife had seen rats running about her house since May 5. On the night of May 10 they were so noisy she actually got up to hit them. Then she suddenly recalled a visit to an exhibition on earthquakes and evacuated the house. The following morning an earthquake registering 7.1 on the Richter scale occurred and the house collapsed.'

From Andrew Robinson's *Earthshock*

'Boss, boss, wake up.' Vinnie was shaking Berman.

The mobster opened an eye. He had popped a blue bomb – a Halcyon tablet – before flopping asleep in Moyama's cottage eight hours earlier. Berman threw his feet over the side of the bed and shook his head. *Good, no hangover*, he thought. He sniffed his left armpit and realized he needed a shower.

'Yo, Vin, what the fuck time is it?'

Vinnie looked at his watch. 'Seven doity, boss.'

'Not in the States, you fucking bonehead. What time is it in fucking Tokyo?'

'Dunno, Tony, mus' be 'bout noon. The boys say sumtin' fucking big went down this mornin', you betta check.'

Berman showered, threw on his suit and wished he had brought a pair of jeans. Then he ate the toast that Moyama's maid had left. Moyama knew Americans did not like Japanese breakfasts – the idea of eating rice, fish and pickled ginger was revolting to them.

Berman rounded up his five men. 'Okay, what's the scoop?'

Berman's Semtex explosives expert had laid the charge in the Bank of Japan vault and filled in Berman on the heist. 'Fuck, boss, they musta taken a hundred million dollars of gold outta that place.'

Berman was excited. 'Where'd they fucking take it? Where'd they take it?' *Fuck, if I supplied the explosives and the detonation expert it's only fair I get a cut of the gold.*

'I dunno. They all spoke in fucking gook. All I know is we loaded the gold, took off and landed across the street from a big park with millions of fucking people. We set down in the garden of some mansion or some fucking palace. All the zipperheads began unloading the gold into a small hut,' said the explosives expert.

'You knucklehead. You were near the Imperial Palace. Can you find the place again?'

'I'll try, boss, but things are all jumbled. All I remember is a lot of broken coloured glass in the church we passed over. You know, like the glass at St Mary's where we grew up in Brooklyn.'

'Whaaat? A fucking church in Tokyo?'

Moyama was seen approaching the guest house, and the Italian Americans fell silent.

'*Ohayo*, Berman-san. *Genki*?' greeted Moyama.

'Very well, thank you. Did you get any sleep? I hear your men have been busy?'

The yakuza leader was a master of non-verbal communication. He saw the excitement in Berman's eyes, the greed. Obviously his man had been telling him about the Bank of Japan job. Americans were so predictable. Still, Moyama did not underestimate how dangerous Berman was, even off his own territory.

'No sleep. This is time to help people and make money.' The subtle indictment in Moyama's words criticized Berman for sleeping. The inference was that samurai did not sleep.

'Moyama-san, we would like to survey Tokyo. Two of my men can fly helicopters.'

'Your assistance is welcome. I'll leave one helicopter at your disposal. My pilot and crew will take you anywhere,' said Moyama, waving off Berman's objection.

'But . . .' Berman wanted his own men to ferry the chopper.

'Please no need to thank me, I am at your service.' Moyama bowed and walked away, leaving Berman's gang in the hands of the yakuza.

Ten minutes later the helicopter took off. The crew all put on headsets with built-in microphones designed to speak above the roar of the choppers. Moyama's pilot was at the controls.

'Keep a look out. Stained glass ruins . . .'

The chopper took off and headed west. They passed over the Ministry of Transport, the Ministry of Construction and the Parliament building. The smell of burnt human flesh and tons of human excrement wafted over Kasumigaseki.

'Boss, what's that smell?' asked Vinnie, almost gagging.

'Who the fuck knows? These zipperheads eat funny things.'

Berman turned to his explosives expert as they flew near the Imperial Palace. 'You recognize anything here?'

'That's the park I saw. But I don't see no big mansion.'

'Is that your church?' Berman shouted into the microphone, pointing down at the Parliament building. The afternoon sun sparkled off the jagged edges of what stained glass remained on the rooftop.

'Ya, boss, dat's it! Da fuckin' choich.'

Berman motioned to the pilot to take the chopper down. Five minutes later his gang were on the ground. The six men made a dash to a gardener's hut about 30 metres away.

The Japanese pilot and his assistant secured the chopper and ran after Berman, shouting in Japanese. '*Abunai! Abunai!*' they yelled, telling them to stop.

The Americans didn't understand and, more importantly, didn't care.

'What the fuck's wrong with these pinheads?' asked Berman as the Japanese ran towards him. Berman knocked the pilot down, knowing that his four men were armed. The co-pilot then jumped Berman. Instinctively, Vinnie pulled his gun and shot the man through the head. The Japanese pilot froze and began speaking fast into his headset.

Berman quickly pulled out his pistol, lifted the pilot's earphones and pushed the weapon against his temple. 'Shut the fuck up.'

The pilot stopped talking.

Berman turned to one of his men. 'Archie, can you fly one of these babies?'

'In my sleep, boss.'

Berman nodded, then turned to the pilot and spoke slowly. '*Sayonara*, baby.' He pressed the trigger and shot the pilot through the head.

'We'd better hurry – that little nipper was telling somebody what we were up to.'

'Hey, boss, Moyama's gonna be upset when he finds out you whacked his pilot.'

'Fuck Moyama. We're gonna be rich. Let's go.' They descended in search of gold.

The funnel had a number of old wooden doors leading to storage rooms, and it was the same tunnel through which Hiroko had walked. The secret rooms that had once housed the Imperial treasures during

World War II now lay empty. Berman scrutinized the locks. None looked recently opened and they moved on. After five minutes the gang came upon an oak door. There were no cobwebs in the corner of the door and the floor had been scraped, as if by heavy traffic. Berman took out his Beretta, switched it to single fire and blew the lock off. He kicked the door, but it didn't move. He motioned to Vinnie to give it a try. Vinnie threw his shoulder into the door and it budged. Three men pushed and the door flew open.

Stacks of grey bricks lay piled high. 'Fuck,' cursed Berman, disappointed.

'Let's get the fuck out, boss. Ain't nothing here. This place gives me the creeps,' said Vinnie.

The men started to leave but Berman hadn't moved. He was looking at the bricks. Something didn't sit right. He walked over and picked up one of the bricks. It was heavy and sticky. He took out a knife and cut into it. The grey paint peeled off to reveal shiny gold.

'That bastard Moyama is smarter than he looks.'

Berman started giving instructions. 'Get this into the chopper. Find some wheelbarrows. We're all gonna be rich. We need to get this load back to our plane at the airport. I'll wait here till you come back.'

'You sure ya wanna wait here, boss? It's kind a spooky,' asked Vinnie.

'Get going, you lunkhead,' said Berman with a smile, kicking Vinnie playfully in the backside. 'I'll be fine.'

After his gang left, Berman put his Beretta down and began cheerfully counting the gold bars. He began singing the theme song to *Fiddler on the Roof*. 'If I were a rich man . . .'

It seemed like hours later when voices down the tunnel woke Berman. Still jet-lagged, he had dozed off on the floor of the storage room.

'Hey, Vinnie, what took you so fuckin' long?' Berman got up and stretched his legs.

Suddenly Moyama appeared in the doorway with several of his men. The yakuza leader was dressed in khaki with rope, a knife, a flashlight and a Satlink phone attached to a utility belt. His belly hung over the belt, making him look like a telephone repair man, but his face was stern.

'Berman, you killed two of my men.'

This was not put as a question but as fact. Moyama did not even bother using the honorific term 'Mister' in front of Berman's name. A Japanese speaker would have realized that this insult meant trouble.

'A misunderstanding. . .', began the American, not yet appreciating the seriousness of his position. 'They – '

Moyama broke him off in mid-sentence. 'And you intended stealing our gold.'

'No, we were just protecting it. We heard that – '

'Silence!' shouted Moyama. Even his own men cowered.

Berman slowly looked around for his Beretta. No luck. He had left it in the dark somewhere.

The leader motioned for his men to bring a prisoner forward. It was Vinnie, who was sobbing.

'Look what they did to me, boss!' wailed Vinnie, holding both his hands up. They were covered in a bloody cloth, and as Moyama pulled it off Vinnie screamed in pain. The mobster's fingertips were missing. Yakuza tradition decreed that wayward gangsters chop off the tip of their little fingers as penance for misdeeds, but never an entire row of fingertips. Moyama had extracted extra revenge on Berman's gang for their greed.

Berman was paralysed with fear but did not show it.

'Don't worry,' said Moyama. 'We're not going to kill you. We're not even going to harm you.'

Berman relaxed. 'Where are my other men?' he asked.

'They didn't make it,' said Moyama.

Then, as if at some unseen signal, Moyama's men took hold of Berman. 'This way.' They led him down the main tunnel.

The group of men came to an open wooden doorway hidden deep in the side of the tunnel and entered the chamber. Moyama took out a pair of handcuffs and handed them to Berman. An iron ring hung from the wall. 'Fasten those to your right wrist, and then fix the handcuffs to the ring,' the leader ordered.

Berman got aggressive. 'Listen, you fat gook. What the fuck do you think you're doing? Do you know the Di Angeles family? Do you know who I am? You fucking slope, I'll – '

Moyama took out his gun and fired a shot through Berman's left foot. 'Now!' he shouted.

Berman quickly snapped the cuffs around his wrist and slipped them through the iron ring.

Moyama then came forward with a hacksaw. 'If you wish to escape, you may use this to cut through your wrist.'

Berman awkwardly grabbed the hacksaw with his left hand. There was no escape from this dungeon except by sawing through his wrist. 'No, c'mon, you're joking.' There was no pain in his left foot, but he could feel his shoe filling up with blood.

'My men are going to seal up this chamber.'

Berman could hear the wheelbarrows dumping loads of bricks outside the doorway.

The yakuza leader took a canteen of water and laid it on the floor near Berman's feet. 'If you cut through, here's some water.' Moyama laughed evilly.

Berman began to whimper. 'No, please. Anything you want you can have. Money. Land. Girls.'

Moyama laughed again. 'I own plenty of land, I am no longer interested in young girls and I have a billion dollars in gold. What can you give me?'

He waited for a moment, actually intrigued to hear what Berman might offer, but the Italian-American had no response. Instead he spat in Moyama's face.

The yakuza leader calmly wiped his face with his sleeve and turned to one of the bricklayers. 'Lay a reinforced double wall.'

Moyama left with his gang, pushing Vinnie in front of them.

'No!' wailed Berman as the bricklayers began cementing in the chamber. Berman looked at the men with new hope. 'Listen, I'll give each of you a thousand bucks.'

None of the workers looked up.

'Ten thousand! Yes? Yes?' yelled Berman, shaking his head up and down with a big smile on his face.

One of the men looked up, then went back to work.

'A hundred thousand!' he shouted in desperation. 'Don't you fucking buttonheads understand fucking English?'

The wall was getting higher and Berman tried to switch to Japanese, but without success. The workmen ignored him. Berman started to scream. His screams turned to raves. By the time the builders had finished, Berman was half-mad at the thought of being trapped in the dark.

Meanwhile the yakuza had climbed out into the sunshine outside the Parliament building. Mata was holding Vinnie, who was now in serious pain.

'Ya gotta give me sumtin',' yelled out Vinnie.

'Don't worry, my men will give you a painkiller,' replied Moyama in English. He then switched to Japanese.

'Mata, give him some morphine. Make sure he never wakes up.'

Vinnie looked up with tears in his eyes. The pain was unbearable.

'*Domo arigato gozaimasu*,' he said, thanking Moyama in his own language. Then Vinnie bowed.

Moyama looked at the compliant mobster and was suddenly filled with pity. He was also impressed that the crude Italian-American had learned Japanese customs so quickly.

'Mata, forget what I just said. Give him a dose to take away the pain. After that he's yours. Teach him Japanese. He'll make a good servant.' With that, Moyama jumped into the helicopter and headed back to his hillside retreat.

Meanwhile, deep underground the rat migration sought out the cool, dark confines of the Imperial tunnel. Their first instinct was to find water and, dehydrated by their journey and the fires of Tokyo, they licked the cool sides of the tunnel to slake their thirst. As they moved by the thousands into the tunnel, the smell of fresh water from Moyama's canteen was like a beacon to the thirsty rodents.

Scientists have recorded rats gnawing through solid concrete walls in the frenzied pursuit of water, and the newly laid brick wall leading to Berman's dungeon came away easily in their teeth. Rats are born with sixteen chisel-like teeth covered in heavy enamel. These are ideal for gnawing any material and are in a continual state of growth. Between the razor-sharp incisors and cheek lie a set of molars. While digging, the rats place their inner cheek between the two sets of teeth so as not to swallow dirt and debris.

The rats took turns excavating through the newly laid brickwork. Berman heard them long before he saw them. Soon they had carved a small hole through the bricks. As they poured through, Berman lost control of his bladder. He lifted the hacksaw to his wrist and made a light incision which drew blood, but could not find the courage to begin cutting deeper into his flesh.

Finding the canteen, the rats ripped away the plastic top and spilled the water on to the ground. Creatures continued to pour through the ever-expanding hole. Soon the dungeon was filled with their squeaks and squeals. Unable to quench their thirst, they turned to Berman. Attracted by the congealing blood, the rats began sniffing at his feet. He began kicking wildly but after a few minutes stopped from exhaustion.

The rats moved in on the blood draining from his left foot. Berman began hacking away at the tenacious creatures, which were climbing up his legs and clinging to his clothes. At first Berman fended them off successfully, but numbers were on their side. He tried cutting away at his wrist, but the open wound only attracted them. For several more minutes Berman tried to free himself, but the pain and effort were too much. All he could do was shake his head violently to keep them gnawing at his eyes, ears and nose. His screams had turned his throat raw so that blood trickled from his mouth too. Sound was no longer possible.

By now the rats had chewed through his clothes. They swarmed over him, ripping chunks of juicy flesh from his body in their search for liquid. Their numbers growing by the minute, the rats moved on in search of water. Half an hour later nothing was left of Berman but a skeleton.

43

THE USS RANGER

The Pacific Ocean off Tokyo Bay, Thursday

'We rule the world . . .'

A crew member of the USS *Ranger*

As the USS *Ranger* raced north to Tokyo Bay, Captain McFlynn leaned out over the flight deck and watched his aircraft carrier churn through millions of dead fish.

'Pull up some of those fish. I want a lab sample,' ordered the captain.

Meanwhile the *Ranger*'s chief of operations noticed a strange array of military vessels on his radar screen. 'Captain, I think you'd better come up to the bridge,' he radioed down.

Captain McFlynn was on the bridge in two minutes. 'What's up?'

'Look, sir.'

He pointed to the Global Positioning System. Fifty green lights were blinking madly on the screen, each light indicating a military vessel. Invented by the US Defense Department in 1975, the system worked off twenty-four satellites revolving 18,000 kilometres above the earth. Each monitor took in four or more of the repeating signals, so that by measuring the speed of radio waves the GPS could calculate to within a few centimetres the location of a ship, car, tank or pedestrian. The GPS system became a favourite of yuppies in the 1990s, who installed it in their Porsches, Ferraris and BMWs.

Rigid and motionless, a fully uniformed Marine guard with sidearm stood watch over the *Ranger*'s Global Positioning System at all times. This was not a standard GPS system but one that could track any military vessel in the world.

'Close up.'

'Yes, sir.

The operations officer pointed the computer's turbo mouse at one of the green vessels on the screen, and clicked twice. The fifty ships in Tokyo Bay zoomed in size on the metre-wide screen, showing Tokyo Bay as a jumbled mess. Each ship appeared as an outline, with its size and identification registered underneath.

'Hostile or friendly?'

'Friendly, sir.'

The fifty anchored ships were in fact rescue vessels from the Japanese navy.

'Establish radio contact.'

'Yes, sir.'

'This is the USS *Ranger* contacting the SS *Muromachi*. Come in, please,' radioed the officer.

'USS *Ranger*, we read you. Over,' replied the lead Japanese vessel.

'We're on our way to provide rescue assistance. Wish to anchor in Tokyo Bay, over.'

'Hssss. Very difficult, *Ranger*. *Chotte matte kudasai*. Just a moment, please.'

'What the fuck do they mean, very difficult?' yelled Captain McFlynn. 'It's either yes or no. This is a disaster area. What's the problem?'

The Japanese captain radioed to the head of the navy, Admiral Miyazawa: 'Sir, the USS *Ranger* is about to enter Tokyo Bay to begin rescue operations. What shall we do?' he asked.

The American communications officer intercepted the Japanese radio conversation, but could not understand it.

'Tape it,' ordered Captain McFlynn, 'and call up Ito, on the double.'

Admiral Miyazawa was tired of all the criticism of the Japanese military, who had been lambasted in the media as weak and ineffective. Why should the Americans get all the glory? He wanted to make a stand against the US navy. Fifty of his own ships were already committed to the rescue operations.

John Ito, chief surgeon of the USS *Ranger* and a second-generation Japanese-American, ran up to the bridge.

'Sir.'

'Tell me what these guys are saying.'

The communications officer put the conversation on speaker phone. The sound of Japanese filled the bridge as Admiral Miyazawa spoke to his captain.

'. . . Make something up to keep them from coming ashore. Anything. They mustn't know we have no authority over them.' Ito gave Captain McFlynn a simultaneous translation.

The Japanese naval captain was not about to act without a direct order from the admiral, and did not sign off. 'I'm awaiting your instructions, sir.'

'Okay, captain. Tell them that the constitution of Japan does not allow foreign powers to land on Japanese soil without permission from the government. First I must contact General Mishima, who controls all rescue operations. Then I must contact the Defence Minister, the Foreign Minister, the head of the National Land Agency, the governor of Tokyo, and then the Prime Minister. After we have obtained the permissions of all these officials, the Americans can land. Even we can't figure out our own bureaucracy, so for them it will be impossible.' The admiral laughed, obviously pleased with the tortuous and impossible task he had set the Americans.

The Japanese captain immediately contacted the *Ranger* and repeated the admiral's order. 'Regret, *Ranger*, that you cannot enter Tokyo Bay until formal government permission is granted. This is the SS *Muromachi*, over and out.'

Captain McFlynn smiled. As a Vietnam veteran with 195 combat missions under his belt and a Distinguished Flying Cross pinned to his chest, he was not easily beaten. He turned to his colleagues on the bridge.

'Gentlemen, under the revised 1960 US Japan Security Pact, a commander of the US military may, with permission from his commander-in-chief, rescue American civilians whose lives are threatened. Such a rescue is subject to the laws and customs of Japan and must be supervised through an official of the state,' said McFlynn. 'Point one. Our commander-in-chief has approved our rescue mission. Point two. American lives are in danger. Point three. We need a state official to grant us permission to land. I have an idea. Get me the radio frequency and call signal of the Imperial Palace.'

Captain McFlynn played hard but he played by the rules, and he would never have landed without formal permission. The communications officer pirated the radio frequency used by the Japanese army to contact the Imperial family.

'USS *Ranger* control to Overlord. Come in, please.'

Sato's walkie-talkie crackled. He had been giving Emperor Akihito an update on the relief work and the two were sitting in the Emperor's study.

'We read you, *Ranger*,' Sato responded on behalf of the Emperor. It would not do to have his Imperial Highness engaging in radio communication.

'This is Commander McFlynn of the USS *Ranger*. We seek permission to come ashore with medical and emergency assistance. Communication through other official channels is impossible. Over.'

'*Ranger*, we request you seek permission from the government.'

'Negative, Overlord. We understand the Prime Minister's in a coma, the Foreign Minister can't be found and the governor of Tokyo's on holiday.'

'What type of assistance are you offering and what will be your means of landing?'

'We are authorized by the President of the United States of America to provide you with any care necessary to save lives. This will include field hospitals, mess halls, tents and latrines. Our helicopters can be with you in ten minutes to unload supplies and evacuate your injured. Over.'

'A moment, *Ranger*.'

Sato pressed the handset and spoke to the Emperor. 'We do need American help but we can't act on behalf of the government.'

The Emperor hesitated a moment. 'Why not?' he asked.

Sato couldn't believe what he was hearing.

'Imagine what the headlines would read: "Emperor approves first landing of American troops since 1945. Japanese independence threatened."'

'My dear Sato, this is a time of crisis. One must think only of what is necessary to save lives. I will accept the consequences. Please tell the captain of the *Ranger* that the Japanese people thank him for his kind offer.'

Sato knew that the Emperor was right, but was worried that proper consensus had not been reached in governmental circles. Usually a decision of this nature took politicians weeks to debate. The Emperor had made a decision with unprecedented speed.

'Do you promise me you'll evacuate to Kyoto if this proposal is accepted?'

'Sato, you're always pushing. Yes, I'll join my family in Kyoto.'

Sato smiled, then turned on the handset to talk.

'Overlord to *Ranger*. Our country gratefully accepts your offer . . .' Then Sato added an amendment of his own. '. . . On the basis that while on Japanese soil or in Japanese airspace your efforts are coordinated through the Imperial Household Agency initially, and then through proper government channels once they have been established. Is this acceptable?'

'Affirmative, Overlord. Please relay your GPS position for unloading and evacuation.'

'Our GPS position is 21 degrees south, 15 degrees east.'

'Roger, Overlord. We're on the way. Over and out.'

One addition to the *Ranger*'s civilian arsenal was a complement of ten V-22 Osprey helicopters. The choppers were special tilt-rotor jets specifically designed for disaster relief. Boeing and Bell had delivered 1200 Ospreys to the US military in 1990, at a cost of $16 million each. On each forward wing lay a propeller which tilted upwards to transform the plane into a manoeuvrable helicopter. The Osprey folded up neatly into a compressed bundle aboard the USS *Ranger*. Maximum speed was 480 kilometres per hour. What made it unique was its large cargo space in which to lay stretchers and load supplies.

Captain McFlynn turned the rescue operation over to the 'Air Boss', who controlled the airspace around the *Ranger*. The primary flight deck resembled an air control tower. The air team was colour-coded: yellow- and blue-shirted troops were taxi handlers, purple shirts fuel handlers, red shirts were armaments, while green-shirted troops were mechanics. All were now moving busily about the *Ranger* in full sight of the flight deck.

'Air Boss to Raptor One.'

'Raptor One.'

'You're cleared for immediate take-off.' The captain took his aide aside. 'Call the lab. I want to know if anything came up on those fish samples.'

'They've already called back, captain. The lab doesn't want to touch the fish.'

'Why not?'

'High levels of radiation.'

Captain McFlynn let out a low whistle. 'Those sons of bitches. Seal up the fish and tell the boys in the lab everything they've seen or heard is classified. As of now.'

'Yes, sir.'

Captain McFlynn watched as the Raptor whirred to life, its giant blades turning over. Four minutes later it was airborne, with nine Ospreys closely on its tail. A moment later McFlynn was on a secure line to Washington.

The Captain of the SS *Muromachi* immediately radioed to Admiral Miyazawa, who gnashed his teeth at having been unable to stop the American rescue operation. He was not about to let a bunch of hairy, unclean barbarians upstage his own forces. The admiral immediately called General Mishima to put their own plan into action.

44

YANKEE GO HOME

Thursday afternoon

'I wouldn't call us racist. All non-Japanese are strange to us. We just have a curious fascination, maybe even fear, of black people.'

Four thousand US Marines, Navy Seals and sailors came ashore. Support from the USS *Ranger* was massive as the ten Osprey rescue choppers airlifted electric generators, lights, field kitchens and field hospitals, water purification units and field latrines to the Imperial Palace. A thousand seriously injured victims were ferried to the *Ranger* while sailors prepared for another five thousand survivors on and below deck.

Among the first to disembark was Lance Corporal Denzel Carver from Tarrytown, New York. Strong, proud and athletic, Carver marched effortlessly with his 76-kilogram field pack. General Mishima's men had no problem choosing Carver as the perfect candidate for their plan since he was big and, as the general aptly noted, 'blacker than calligraphy ink'. The fact that he was extremely tall was a bonus.

Carver had not been ashore more than an hour when a beautiful young Japanese woman ran up to him screaming.

'My sister. She's trapped. Please help me,' she cried in perfect English.

Carver threw off his field pack, grabbed his spade and ran after the girl.

'There she is,' cried the girl, pointing to a teenager stuck under a wooden beam.

Carver lifted the beam with ease as the girl cleared herself.

'Are you okay?' asked the Marine.

The trapped girl was remarkably agile, given her narrow escape, and ran off before Carver had time to check her condition.

'Oh, thank you for rescuing my sister,' said the woman, running up to Carver and hugging him. 'Please just hold me for a minute. This earthquake's been so traumatic.' Carver wasn't sure what happened next, but just as he put his arms around the woman she began screaming again.

'Help! Rape! Help me!' she screamed in Japanese as one of Mishima's men sneaked up behind Carver and hit him hard. With Carver out cold, the woman lifted her skirt and lay on her back while Mishima's men unzipped Carver's pants and laid him on top of her.

'Make sure you get a picture of the smiling black ass,' said one of the army men to the photographer. The woman pretended to struggle, showing her pained face to the camera as she pounded on Carver's back with her fists.

'Okay, we've got all the pictures.'

'Did you plant the other photos in his field pack?'

'No problem. A bunch of black men gang-banging a Japanese girl who's tied up.'

'Perfect.'

'Take this ape to the navy brig. The ship's waiting.' It took six men to lift all 113 kilos of Denzel Carver into the back of the jeep, unload him into the SS *Muromachi* and throw him into a cell.

That evening the Japanese military sent out a press release saying that it had laid charges of rape, sodomy and attempted murder against Lance Corporal Denzel Carver of the US Marine Corps. Accompanying the press release were photos of his rape of a young civilian woman. By Friday afternoon demonstrators had called for the withdrawal of all US troops from Japan, and there were reports of civilians running in fear from Marines and sailors. Later that day the US Secretary of Defense recalled all American military personnel from Tokyo.

Denzel Carver woke up in a navy brig with a headache, wondering what had happened. Six months later his captors released Carver for 'lack of evidence' and he was turned over to the Marines. Because of media scrutiny the Marine Corps were forced to give Carver a dishonourable discharge. Not even the $200,000 which mysteriously found its way into Carver's bank account from Fuji Bank New York could repair his life. One day the former lance corporal took a drive into the Adirondack Mountains, parked his car and blew his brains out with his service revolver. Only ten people attended the funeral, including what Carver's few relatives termed 'one of them funny-lookin' Oriental types'. Each year until he himself died, General Mishima returned to Tarrytown, New York to pray and put flowers on the grave of Denzel Carver.

45

THE ROLL OF DEAD

Friday morning

'Amidst the death and chaos of the quake's aftermath, an undertaker squatted outside his funeral parlour, completely absorbed in polishing coffin handles.'

Susy Ponson, a 1906 San Francisco survivor

A group of forty survivors in 'O' block huddled around a lone radio. Survivors in 'ka' block were gathering to do the same. It was six in the morning and the sun was just coming up over the East Gardens of the Imperial Palace.

'Oku, Samu, of Odawara . . . Oku, Satoshi, of Nerima . . . Oku, Seniichi, address unknown . . . Oku, Soma, of Nikko . . .'

Somebody screamed further down 'O' block.

The radio announcer continued reading with a nasal drone: 'Oku, Sumitoshi, of Ojima . . . Omori, Hayashi, of Hiroo . . . Omori, Hayato, of Shinjuku . . . Omori, Iishi, address unknown . . . Omori, Yoshi, of Ikebukuro . . . Omori, Zeniichi, of Mitaka . . .'

Another wail was heard. Heads turned to see who the unlucky relative was.

The announcer kept reading: 'Oyama, Mitsu, address unknown . . . Oyama, Naomi of Kitasenju . . . Oyama, Natashi, of Ebisu . . . Oyama, Motogoro, of Yokohama . . .'

Yet a third cry went up in 'O' block.

'May I speak Mr Di Angeles, please?'

'Who's calling?'

'Moyama from Tokyo.'

'Hang on, pal.' Moyama endured the seconds of silence before a gruff voice came on.

'Di Angeles here.'

'Mr Di Angeles, Ken Moyama from Tokyo.'

Di Angeles knew of Moyama and his Asian power. The mafia

leader also knew that his son-in-law, Tony Berman, had flown off to cut a deal with the yakuza chief without family permission.

'Yes, Mr Moyama, so nice to hear from you.'

Di Angeles was usually guarded on the phone and even more so now since learning of wiretaps placed by the New York Attorney General's office.

'Mr Di Angeles, my English no good. My son speak to you, please.' Relieved, Moyama handed the phone over to his son.

'Mr Di Angeles, I have bad news.'

'Yes?'

'I'm sorry to say your son-in-law has died.' The younger Moyama waited for a reply but, hearing none, continued. 'He and his men entered a building which collapsed on them. We take full responsibility for not watching them more closely.'

The old man did not respond at first. This was the best news he had heard in a long time and saved him the trouble of whacking Berman himself. Nobody smacked his daughter. Nobody.

'My daughter will be devastated.' Actually she hated her husband, and had only stayed married because of the shame of divorce within the close-knit Italian Catholic community.

'When can we bring home the bodies?'

'I'm afraid that the Tokyo authorities require us to burn all bodies because of an outbreak of plague. I'm sorry.'

That was even better news for the mafia don, and saved him a lot of expense. Di Angeles wanted to get off the phone. The New York authorities would be all over this. He asked for Moyama's number so that he could call from a safe phone later.

'Mr Di Angeles, one more thing.'

'We have some things that belong to you.' The younger Moyama was referring to payment for the supplies that Berman had air-lifted over.

'Yeah, thanks,' said Di Angeles hurriedly. 'I'd better call my daughter now. She's gonna be all broke up over this. We'll speak in a few weeks after our funeral service. Goodbye.'

Moyama's son hung up and turned to his father, who had a look of adolescent excitement on his face.

'How did it go? Do you think he believed us?'

'Dad, I don't know. These guys aren't stupid. My guess is that even if they think you killed Berman, they'd be too unsure of your power to take revenge. I suggest we pay them gold for the supplies and then try to buy all our drugs from the Di Angeles pipeline in America.'

'Why from America? We make all our amphetamines in Osaka.'

'Dad, it costs us a quarter the price to ship uppers from the States. Our production costs are too high. We need to begin producing offshore like all the electronics companies and car manufacturers are doing.'

'I'll leave all our relations with the US mafia in your hands. Just keep me informed.'

'Sure, Dad.'

Young Ken Moyama had big expansion plans.

46

THE RACE

Friday, three days after the quake

Fifteen minutes.

The time it took the National Guard to mobilize after the 1994 Los Angeles earthquake.

Four days.

The time it took the Ground Self Defence Forces to respond to the 1995 great Hanshin earthquake.

'Next.'

Mrs Nagasawa was still flying high on morphine and enjoying her newly found status as the initiator of rescue operations. Tokyo's assistant city treasurer and saviour was seated comfortably on a pile of blankets in Yoyogi Park. Somehow word had got out that foreign rescue operations had to be authorized by her, and a long line of foreign representatives had formed in the park. Somebody had even put up a wooden sign at the main entrance, 'Mrs Nagasawa this way'.

A Frenchman, next in line, approached her. He handed her a form permitting the French navy and air force to land and begin distributing supplies.

Pen in hand and ready to sign the authorization, Mrs Nagasawa decided to try out her memories of schoolgirl French. She wanted to ask him how long he had planned on staying, but her French was a bit rusty.

'How long is your penis?' she mistakenly asked him, accompanied by a drug-induced smile.

The blushing officer looked at her with bewilderment and she repeated the question. The proud Frenchman finally answered.

'Seven inches, *madame*.'

'Oh, how nice,' Mrs Nagasawa said to her aide. 'He says he's staying seven days.' As she signed his form and handed it back to the Frenchman she had one more go at her high school French. *Let's see, it's been forty-five years. How do I say, 'My people will show you around'? Oh yes, I think I remember . . .*

'Please show it to me,' said Mrs Nagasawa with a sweet smile.

The Frenchman hurried away shaking his head.

'Next.'

A representative from the People's Republic of China stepped up with his form, which Mrs Nagasawa willingly signed.

'How nice, a Chinese man,' she babbled. 'You know, I just love Peking duck.'

Nobody noticed the surprise on the man's face, not evoked by Mrs Nagasawa's comment but the fact that she had permitted the Chinese military to enter Japan. The government would never have allowed the Communist People's Liberation Army set foot on Japanese soil. The Chinese hated the Japanese, whom they considered bloodthirsty tyrants – the memory of their rape and pillage activities in World War II was still fresh in their minds, in particular the Rape of Nanking. In turn the Japanese distrusted the Chinese, whom they considered an ill-mannered, barbaric people attempting to get economic and military control of Asia.

The Chinese liaison hurried off to tell his government the good news, and within two hours twenty thousand Chinese troops were en route to Tokyo by sea.

Mrs Nagasawa's morphine was wearing off and the burns on her face began to sear through the pink flesh, but the doctors in Yoyogi Park had run out of the precious painkiller. Now in intense pain, she called out to her assistant that she would only sign authorization forms for another five minutes. As a result, a fight broke out in the queue. The Italian emissary took advantage of the confusion and pushed in front of the Spanish and German representatives. His blood up, the Spaniard pushed the Italian to the ground. The Italian jumped up and lunged at the Spaniard. As the police broke up the fight, the German calmly took both their places and got his form signed.

Mrs Nagasawa signed as many authorization forms as possible before collapsing in pain. Her assistant went off to look for some more morphine.

Meanwhile, international rescue teams began to clog Osaka's international airport. Flights laden with emergency supplies from ninety-five countries tried to land there, creating chaos. The Japanese had no central authority to coordinate the rescue aid, so that food, water, blankets and clothes were piled high in an unused hangar. Once that hangar was filled, the supplies piled up on the unused runway. The rat population soared as the rodents feasted on the food. On the fifth day of the crisis, in the absence of a national government the Osaka municipal authority refused all international aid. This created an outcry: 'Cold-hearted Osaka leaders refuse aid for Tokyo citizens,' read the headlines.

Mrs Nagasawa was also asked to coordinate relief supplies in Tokyo, but this was difficult: survivors refused much of the aid. Later that day, when doctors found Mrs Nagasawa some more morphine, she tackled the problem of aid distribution.

'You're telling me that we have two tonnes of clothing and the survivors won't accept any of the donations?' asked Mrs Nagasawa with incredulity.

'Yes, ma'am.'

'What's the problem?'

'It's used,' replied the aid worker.

'So what?'

'Nobody will wear used clothes. They'll only accept new clothes. We had the same problem after the Kobe quake. We need you to appeal to foreign nations to stop sending used clothes.'

'I'll send a form letter saying that we now have enough donations. In the meantime burn the used clothes. Now what's the problem with the goods shipped up by the Catholic church of Osaka?' asked Mrs Nagasawa.

'Most of the donations came from Filipina maids who make up the Catholic community. They couldn't offer much, so gave whatever money they had to buy goods. The problem is that they could only afford basic kitchenware and utensils. Nobody will eat off them.'

'Hmmmm . . . I may have a solution.'

'Yes, ma'am.'

'Send a letter of thanks to the Catholic church saying the goods have been gratefully accepted by the survivors and put to good use. Then find somewhere to dump the supplies so that nobody finds them.'

'Okay.'

'Has the army located the governor yet?'

'Yes, they found him on a small island in Polynesia and he'll be back tomorrow.'

'Good, I can't wait for this to be over,' said Mrs Nagasawa. 'What's next?'

'Next on the list is how to handle a clever fraud being perpetrated by the Kobe yakuza.'

'What have they done this time?' asked Mrs Nagasawa, curious and slightly amused at the money-making antics of Japan's underworld.

'They've posed as a relief organization and played upon the emotions of the listening public. For two days they've solicited contributions over the radio in the Kobe/Osaka area, running ads like "Please help the orphans of Tokyo, remember your own dead and your own grief from Kobe," with the sound of children crying for their parents in the background. "Send your donation to account 331–05567 at Sumitomo Bank head office in Kobe. These orphans need food." The account has brought in over 150 million yen in donations in two days. If we expose the fraud it means our legitimate cash donations will dry up.'

Mrs Nagasawa had another idea, and called the yakuza leader directly.

'Moyama here.'

'Mr Moyama, this is Mrs Nagasawa,' she said, introducing herself and then explaining the Kobe relief fraud.

'How outrageous. What hoodlums!' exclaimed Moyama. 'I'll clear the matter up immediately.'

'Thank you, Moyama-san.'

'You're welcome,' said the yakuza leader. The next day suitcases full of money arrived by helicopter, stuffed full of banknotes totalling 75 million yen. Moyama had kindly donated half of the illicit gains to the relief effort.

'Last on our list is the barge full of goods sent by the Osaka municipal authorities.'

'What goods?'

'All the foreign donations that were flown to Osaka. They stored them in a hangar, then finally just took a bulldozer and dumped the whole lot on a giant rubbish barge. They told the captain to send the barge to Tokyo for offloading.'

'Have the media picked up on this yet?'

'Yes. NHK has a full-time chopper following the barge.'

'So we can't turn it down.'

'No, ma'am.'

'That's a tough one. Put me through to Admiral Miyazawa.' A few moments later the admiral came on the radio.

'Mrs Nagasawa, thank you so much again for approving our rescue operation so quickly. How can I help you?'

She explained the problem with the Osaka relief barge. 'Can you assist me?' asked Mrs Nagasawa.

'Leave it to us,' said the admiral. 'We owe you a few favours.'

The next day NHK reported that navy medics had boarded the Osaka barge and found plague-infested rats aboard. For medical reasons all personnel had been offloaded and the ship scuttled.

The Imperial Palace, late Friday afternoon

The Prime Minister sat up in bed surrounded by aides, cabinet ministers and assorted government heads. An intravenous drip hung out of his arm, both legs were encased in plaster casts and his entire right side lay exposed under a seamless white hospital gown. The doctors hoped to save both his legs and, to prevent stress, had recommended that the meeting should last no more than half an hour.

The Prime Minister wanted to begin a cabinet meeting while two dozen other bureaucrats and their assistants idly sat smoking in an adjacent tent, but then changed his mind. 'There's no point in having a cabinet meeting without first deciding what we need to vote on.' The Prime Minister was unable to act without prior approval from his cabinet. He nodded to the Parliamentary Vice Minister of the National Land Agency who, under emergency procedure, became Chief Secretary of the Headquarters for Disaster Countermeasures. General Mishima was commander-in-chief of the rescue, which meant he was the operating head of whatever plans were made. All this had been quickly confirmed by the Prime Minister's legal adviser, who stood nearby.

A moment later forty men filtered into the tent, dressed in disaster wear. Many had their heads wrapped in bandages or their limbs encased in plaster. As they walked in, the Prime Minister looked at his white toes protruding from the cast. *At least they can walk. I pray to all the gods that I shall be able to walk again.*

The newly appointed Chief Secretary opened the meeting, much to the annoyance of General Mishima and the Minister of Defence, who felt they should be in charge. The Prime Minister tried to wiggle his toes.

'The main priority now is how to feed the survivors,' said the Chief Secretary. 'I'd like the Minister for Agriculture, Forests and Fisheries to brief us.'

'Sssss. Mmmmmm. This is very difficult. As you know, we have stored 9 million rescue portions of biscuits and milk throughout the capital. Unfortunately the storage facilities have been destroyed. Despite this, we have a back-up plan with rice manufacturers in Osaka to distribute rice this weekend.'

A cough was heard from the head of the National Fire Agency. 'Don't you think we had better concentrate on putting out all the fires first?'

'Speaking of fires, why don't I see more firemen at work?' asked Construction Minister Tada.

'Maybe if we had water we could fight the flames, Tada-san,' retaliated the fire chief. 'All our water pipes are broken, and if I recall that falls under your territory.' Tada rose menacingly towards the fire chief, but the Prime Minister politely told him to sit down.

'What's he doing at this meeting anyway? The Fire Agency falls under the Ministry of Home Affairs,' spat out Tada.

'Look, we've got our priorities all wrong. We've got to focus on finding survivors,' said General Mishima.

'What? And just let the chemical fires burn in Tokyo Bay?' said the fire chief.

The Chief Secretary tried to take control of the meeting again. 'We each have our own tasks. Let's just focus on those.'

'Then why can't the fire department contain the Tokyo Bay disaster?' someone asked.

This really upset the fire chief. 'I'm sick of taking all the blame. We're trying hard, but technically it's not even our responsibility. All toxic waste falls under the Ministry of Health.' That was a surprise to the Deputy Minister of Health, who stubbed his Mild Seven out on the ground and began to protest, but the fire chief was on a roll. 'You all remember the last oil fire we had. It took fifty trucks to contain the blaze. What do you expect me to do when we can't even get our mobile trucks on the road?' He glared at the Deputy Minister of Transport.

'Gentlemen, let's take this one step at a time. How do we stand on rescue equipment?' asked the Chief Secretary, turning to General Mishima.

'Bad news. We were allocated hardly any money for rescue equipment in our annual budget. All I got were a bunch of useless radios,' said the general.

'That's a start. Is everybody linked up to the emergency radio system?'

'No,' replied the general. 'Each branch of government has their own communication network. The police can't even talk to the fire department. I suppose we could use satellite phones. We've recovered a number of them in Parliament.'

The Chief Secretary instructed an aide to hand out phones to everyone and began jotting down their numbers.

'And rescue equipment?'

'The military doesn't really have much heavy-duty construction machinery. The Ministry of Construction is supposed to lend us everything. We could use some bulldozers, front-end loaders and demolition balls.'

Everyone turned to Tada, who was chain smoking. 'We've got *some* equipment, but in a situation like this we have a loose arrangement with construction companies to borrow their equipment.'

'Maybe if you people built the bridges to a decent standard and inspected a few buildings, this might not have happened,' said someone from the back of the tent.

'Who said that?' growled Tada, rising once again.

Nobody answered.

Again the Chief Secretary intervened. 'General, as commander-in-chief why don't you fill us in on the rescue efforts?'

'We've finally evacuated the Emperor to his villa in Kyoto.' There was a small round of applause. 'We've now committed well over fifty thousand troops to the rescue. My biggest problem is authority. I'm not allowed to give orders to anyone outside the army – and even then I need the governor's permission.'

'You've certainly used your talent and authority to destroy our US relations with the stunt you pulled with that Marine,' said the Minister of Foreign Affairs.

'What are you implying?' said General Mishima defensively.

'Nothing – except that I'll be trying to salvage American relations with the Secretaries of State and Defense for the next year. The people are screaming at us to throw out the Americans. I tell you, if they're forced to vacate their bases we're vulnerable to attack, and it won't do wonders for the local economies.'

'It's not my fault that that Marine raped one of our women.'

'Can we please concentrate on the present? General Mishima, please continue.'

'As I see it, we need to save lives, put out the fires, distribute food and clean up this mess.'

'What about gas and electricity? Should we be shutting everything down or putting everything back on line?'

The general shrugged his shoulders.

From the back of the tent came a sound as a short, balding man with big black glasses spoke up. 'I'm from Tokyo Gas. As you know, we're the biggest gas company in the world.'

'Spare us the fucking sales pitch,' yelled Tada.

This flustered the Tokyo Gas man, who began to stammer. '. . .

Ummmm. We ... ah ... serve ... ah ... 8 million households. Each house has an "intelligent" gas meter, so most gas is shut off automatically.'

'Good. What about your gas mains?' asked the Chief Secretary.

'Well, mains and pipes are a problem.'

'What do you mean, problem?'

'We have 50,000 kilometres of pipeline – enough to circle the earth. Most of it's PVC, but the mains are connected by G-type cast iron.'

'So?'

'Well, the quake was over 50 on the spectrum intensity scale – twice the danger point.'

'Look, we don't care about spectrum intensity. What happened to the pipes?'

'Ummm ... well ... ahhh ... there's no way to tell for certain. The microwave network system we developed was wiped out. But my guess is that the PVC pipes stretched and the cast iron mains were destroyed. Also, many of our 'egg' tanks rolled off their platforms.'

'General, can you please send an army detail to sort out the leaking gas?'

The general nodded as the Prime Minister's legal adviser spoke up. 'Please excuse me, but we can't do that. All orders must go through the cabinet. I'd just like to remind the Prime Minister that under Cabinet Law number 63, no orders are binding without cabinet approval.'

This really got the general worked up. 'As I see it, none of us has authority except as a group. The governor's in charge of the police and fire department and signs off on all rescue missions. I'm commander-in-chief of the rescue but can't give orders. You,' he said, pointing to the head of the National Land Agency, 'are the Chief Secretary of this group and can't give orders either. The Prime Minister runs the cabinet, which has emergency powers but only under special conditions. My vote is we change things now and pick one man who can run this operation.'

The Prime Minister nodded as he tried to wiggle his toes. At that moment the meeting was interrupted by the doctor.

'Everybody out. The Prime Minister needs his sleep.'

'But what about the rescue operation?'

'Who's in charge?'

'I'm in charge,' said the general.

'No, you're not. That's unconstitutional,' shouted a voice.

'Shut up, everybody!' yelled Tada. 'I've got an idea. We all agree we've got to act quickly, so each group will take care of their own area of responsibility and then get approval from the cabinet afterwards.'

The Prime Minister thought he saw movement in his big left toe and nodded in excitement.

Everybody liked the idea and left the smoke-filled tent smiling, each in charge of his own little empire.

47

CATATONIA

The Urbannet Building and Imperial Palace, Friday, three days after the quake

'HOTEL STANDS UNDAMAGED AS A MONUMENT OF YOUR GENIUS. CONGRATULATIONS.'
Cable from Baron Okura to Frank Lloyd Wright whose
Imperial Hotel withstood the 1923 Tokyo quake

Dougie and Yuki had cut across the Imperial Palace in order to reach the Urbannet Building. The former Salomon headquarters lay in a mangled heap of twisted wire and concrete. Both of them stood there for several moments before Dougie broke the silence.

'I can't believe we made it out of there alive.'

'It was a miracle.'

Dougie looked at her. 'You really believe that, don't you?'

'What?'

'In miracles. Couldn't it just have been luck?'

'No. Master Wa said that the earthquake would come to purge evil from Japan. And it came. I survived because of my faith and because of the purity of my heart.'

'And me? Why did I survive?'

'Because your heart is pure too. You just don't realize it.'

Dougie thought she was being sarcastic, but decided it was best not to ask. Supernatural events often required supernatural beliefs.

They fell silent again.

There was no movement near the building but there was quite a bit of activity nearby. A number of businessmen were walking down the middle of the street, briefcases in hand. Dougie was puzzled.

'Yuki, what are they doing?'

'Going to work.'

'What? The city's been destroyed.'

'That doesn't matter.'

'Come on, Yuki – that's not loyalty; that's blind stupidity.'

One man was standing in front of the wreckage of the Urbannet Building as if he were waiting for an elevator. There was nobody to tell him what to do and he had nowhere else to go.

Dougie shook his head and he and Yuki returned to the Palace. Anxious to hear of survivors from Salomon Brothers, Dougie got on the line to the receptionist at the Salomon office in Osaka.

'Hello, this is Dougie Douglas from the Tokyo office.' He heard a squeal on the other end of the line as the receptionist heard his voice.

'Mr Douglas, you survive. I'm so happy.'

'Thanks. Yuki also survived.'

'That's wonderful. Douglas-san, it's difficult to get news about Tokyo. Tell me, how bad is it?'

'Worse than you can imagine. Worse than Kobe. Do you have any relatives in Tokyo?'

'My mother and father live in Sendai, just outside. I still haven't heard from them.'

'I'm sure they're okay. Maybe it wasn't so bad outside Tokyo. Listen, do you know how many people survived from our Tokyo office?'

'No. You're the first to phone in.'

Ran Miyaki, the office manager, snatched the phone from the receptionist, who left the desk weeping. The treatment of women in Japanese offices was abysmal, and most male office managers felt their role should be restricted to serving tea, answering phones and holding open elevators. A receptionist had no business talking to a top Salomon trader.

'Ahhh, Dougie-san, you arrive.' He meant to say 'alive'. 'We're happy but I think you even happier,' said Miyaki.

'Miyaki-san, they tell me I'm the first to check in. Surely somebody else survived?'

'Dougie-san, I'm sorry. You are first call. I think you are only survivors. But you are very lucky man, Dougie-san. You very rich man now. Rumour in Salomon says you make firm over $300 million. Your bonus maybe $30 million. Big chairman from New York call me every day. I call him now to tell him you alive. He be happy, even though Salomon only make $270 million with you alive.'

Dougie wasn't really listening – he realized that all his colleagues at Salomon had been killed. Over three hundred workers. Dead.

'Dougie-san, you still there?'

'Yeah, sure, Miyaki-san.'

Dougie drifted off again. He was about to hang up when Miyaki asked, 'Where can we reach you, Dougie-san? What is phone number?'

He gave him the number. 'I've got to go now, Miyaki-san. Could you call me if you hear from Sugimoto or any other survivors?'

'Yes. Yes. Oh, Dougie-san, you very lucky man . . .'

Miyaki prattled on, but Dougie had already hung up. He didn't feel lucky. A wave of guilt washed over him as he chided himself for not trying to find Sugimoto on his way out of the building. He had been selfish. Suddenly he felt dizzy and overcome by thirst.

After a few minutes the phone rang. Dougie picked it up listlessly.

'Yo, Dug*eeee*! I'm glad you made it, bud*eeee*,' shouted Ralph Gazinsky down the phone from Salomon's New York office. Miyaki had called him to say that Dougie was alive.

'Thanks, Ralph.'

'Hey, dude, word at Solli is that you are one rich mother-fucker now. What say you put some money into the FDI?'

'What's the FDI?'

'The Freddie Death Index. Bet how many buttonheads bought it in the quake. It's sixty thousand bid, eighty thousand offer and rising.'

Dougie wanted to throw up. *How many buttonheads bought it in the quake?* He stood there thinking of Sugimoto lying crushed inside the wreckage of the Urbannet Building.

'Yo, earth to Dougie. You still there?'

'I'm here.' The back of Dougie's throat was parched. He needed a drink.

'You're gonna make some heavy-duty shekels, buddy. I mean, you're right there in the action. You'll clean up – you know, opportunity-in-a-crisis. If you can do a body count on the dead Nips, you'll make a killing.'

Silence.

'Yo, Dougie, what's wrong?'

'One of those buttonheads was my best friend.'

He hung up on Ralph without waiting for a reply, staring into the distance and trying to overcome nausea and dizziness. He had been staring for fifteen minutes when Yuki returned.

'Dougie, what's the matter?'

He didn't respond.

'Dougie?'

She was worried. Yuki put her arm around the man she loved and whispered in his ear. 'Dougie, speak to me. Please.'

'Mmmm.'

She stepped away and looked into his eyes. He wore a vacant expression and his eyes were focused somewhere in the distance. She panicked. What could have happened to him? Gently she unclipped the phone from his belt and pressed the redial button.

'Salomon Brothers *de gozaimasu.*'

'*Moshi, moshi.* This is Yuki. I need to – '

'Yuki!' interrupted the secretary. 'Dougie told me you were alive! I am so happy.'

'Was Dougie just on the phone to you?'

'Yes, why?'

'How did he sound?'

'Fine. He then spoke to Miyaki-san.'

'Can you please put me through to Miyaki?'

'Sure.'

The line went quiet for a moment.

'Yuki-san! This is Miyaki. We are so glad you are alive. Dougie told me – '

'What did you say to him, Miyaki-san?'

'What?'

'What did you say to him? He can't even speak now. He just stares into space. What did you say?'

'Maybe he's happy. I told him Salomon was going to pay him $30 million and that he was a rich man.'

'What!'

'Yes, he is very, very rich. Maybe that made him so happy that – '

'Miyaki-san, what else did you tell him?'

Miyaki thought hard. 'I told him that you two were the only survivors from the Tokyo office.'

The Satphone beeped, indicating that there was a call holding. Yuki hung up on Miyaki, took the call and pressed the green button. It was Ralph Gazinsky from Salomon New York again, who began speaking before Yuki could talk.

'Hey, Dougie, why'd ya hang up? Look, I'm sorry that one of the gooks who died was your friend. I only thought we could make bucks. Dougie? Are you there?'

Yuki switched the phone off, walked back to Dougie and looked at him. He hadn't moved. She had seen the same behaviour in other survivors who had suffered a traumatic experience or the loss of a loved one. She hugged him, but there was no response.

'I'll be right back,' she whispered in his ear, kissing him

gently on the cheek. Then she went off in search of a doctor.

Earlier the doctor had warned her that amputee victims often lapsed into depression, which could be triggered by anything. She was to call him if Dougie went into depression, since it required special care to prevent psychological damage. Yuki's volunteer work at the infirmary gave her an inside track to speaking with the overworked doctors, but none was able to leave the care of emergency patients. Mental trauma was not a priority.

For two days Dougie sat in a state of semi-catatonia. He did not speak, eat or sleep. If a doctor had examined Dougie's body he would have discovered that his metabolism had slowed, much like that of a bear during hibernation.

Yuki washed his face gently and tried to open his mouth for him to drink, but it was no use. She persuaded a doctor to insert an intra-venous hook-up into his arm, and then she just sat and watched the drip.

48

THE PLAN

Salomon's New York headquarters, Monday, six days after the quake

'Besides life itself only three things matter. Your family, friends and bank account balance.'

> The president of a large Japanese conglomerate in and interview with the author

'So that lucky son of a bitch made it.'

John Williamson took the distinctive orange band off his $30 Cohiba cigar. Williamson was head of Salomon's compensation committee and responsible for paying Dougie his bonus. He lit the Havana and a wisp of blue-grey smoke rose in the board room.

'Stop bitching that Douglas is alive. Just pay him out,' said Derek Hunt, Salomon's chief executive.

Many securities houses deviously tried to fire traders before their big pay-outs became due, but Salomon had never resorted to this tactic. As head of compensation Williamson wanted to save Salomon the $30 million, but was meeting resistance from Hunt. As chief executive, he knew that Williamson's strategy of screwing employees out of bonuses would lose him the support of the trading and sales team.

Hunt had once been head of Salomon's profitable Tokyo office and had been selected by the board to take charge of the firm. Clients had been calling him ever since the quake, asking how to buy undervalued Japanese companies.

'We need a trader like Douglas in Tokyo. Our American clients want to kick Japan Inc. in the teeth by buying up Japanese shares. Pay him out. And find him . . . so we can start trading in the black market.'

But Williamson was not through having a go at saving $30 million. He puffed contemplatively on his Cohiba, then twirled the cigar between his fingers, studying it.

'Look, Derek, I've got a proposal. We won't fire Douglas and we'll pay him out provided he continues to work for the firm until bonuses come due. If he leaves voluntarily before bonus time, then we're under no legal obligation to pay him.'

Hunt laughed. 'Okay, that's fair.' *What idiot wouldn't wait six months for $30 million?*

Williamson smiled as he blew a ring of smoke skyward. He had a plan.

Yuki had gone to find Dougie a replacement IV drip. He was sitting bolt upright as he had been throughout the weekend, still in a state of catalepsy brought about as a result of post-traumatic stress. As she walked over to the infirmary, the phone rang.

'*Moshi, moshi.*'

'Hello, this is John Williamson from Salomon Brothers in New York. May I speak with Dougie Douglas, please.'

'This is Yuki Naguchi. How can I help you?'

'Well, I really need to speak with Dougie,' the Salomon executive persisted.

'You can speak with me. I work with Salomon Brothers and I'm his fiancée.'

This registered with Williamson. 'Ah . . . we just wanted to know how he was,' he said, adding rather too quickly, 'and when he was returning to work.'

Williamson was taping the phone call and hoped to record Dougie saying he would not be returning to Salomon Brothers, thereby saving the firm the $30 million. If Dougie had been in any condition to speak, that is precisely what he would have told Williamson. Now Williamson hoped that Yuki would fall into the trap instead.

'He's had an accident and lost an arm.' Yuki waited for a reaction or a sign of sympathy, but there was none. 'The doctor says he shouldn't move for a few months.' This wasn't exactly true, but Yuki wanted to test Williamson. She knew that Salomon taped all its phone calls, and added something for the record. 'You don't have a problem with that, Mr Williamson, do you?'

'No.'

Williamson had spoken softly, hoping that the tape would not pick up his voice. Maybe he could alter it later.

'Please give him our best.' Williamson hung up. 'Shit,' he said softly to himself.

Yuki immediately dialled Salomon's Osaka office and was put through to Ran Miyaki's office.

'*Moshi, moshi.*'

'Hello, Miyaki-san, this is Yuki from Tokyo.'

'Ahh, Yuki-san. Are you okay?'

Yuki noted a touch of sincerity in his voice. 'Yes, thank you. Miyaki-san, can you think of any reason why Salomon Brothers might not want Dougie to return to work? You told us yourself that they owe him $30 million. There's no way they can weasel out of this, is there?'

Miyaki was in a difficult position. He was the new ferret for Salomon, unofficially reporting directly to New York on affairs in Japan. Yet he hated to see Dougie lose out on a bonus that was due to him. 'Ummm, Yuki-san, this is a very difficult subject to discuss. Perhaps I might suggest that Dougie stay with Salomon until the year end.'

Yuki understood.

'You mean he doesn't get paid out if he quits.'

Miyaki said nothing but let out a 'mmmmmm'.

'Thank you, Miyaki-san. Both of us appreciate this.'

'There's another thing, Naguchi-san.'

'What's that?'

'Don't trust Williamson. If he can avoid paying Dougie, he'll find a way.'

'Even after a tragedy like this?'

'We're talking about $30 million.'

'Sounds like Dougie's got to sort this out with New York.'

'That's not a problem, is it?'

'I'm not sure. Thanks, Miyaki-san.'

'No problem. Good luck.'

Yuki resumed her search for a doctor to give Dougie another IV drip. While she was gone, somebody walked up behind him.

'Haro.'

The voice behind him was struggling to say 'hello' in English, and Dougie blinked as his mind wrestled with the voice.

'Haro.'

Dougie could not speak, but closed his eyes and thought about where he had heard that voice before.

'Hey, fuckwad, what's the matter?'

Dougie struggled, unable to utter any words himself.

'I figured I'd find you here.'

This time the voice was straight ahead of him. Dougie opened his eyes and saw Sugimoto, his best friend, standing in front of him.

Dougie blinked. Sugimoto knelt in front of him and took his hand. Tears welled up in Dougie's eyes.

'What's the matter? Cat eat your tongue?'

Dougie squeezed Sugimoto's hand and stammered a response. 'Cat got your tongue,' he corrected his friend. With that, Dougie shook his head once as a man warding off sleep, stood up and stretched.

'What's that for?' Sugimoto asked, holding the IV bag.

'I don't know, buddy.' Dougie gently pulled the IV needle out of his arm and hugged Sugimoto. 'But I'm glad you're alive.'

Yuki returned to find the pair chatting away, raced up to Dougie and embraced him. 'You're okay!'

'Of course I am, but Sugimoto is the one you should be hugging. He's alive.'

Yuki bowed to Sugimoto. 'You saved him,' she whispered in Japanese into his ear.

'Eh?' Sugimoto gave Yuki a quizzical look. The quake had been a strange time for all of them, and he passed her comment off as yet another inexplicable event.

'Let's eat,' said Dougie, and from that moment Yuki knew things were going to be all right.

As Dougie wolfed down three days' worth of rations, Yuki explained that he had lapsed into catatonia. She then told him what had happened during her phone conversations with Salomon Brothers. 'All you need to do is tell them you'll work till the year end. Then the money's all yours. There's no way they can screw you out of the $30 million.'

'I can't.'

'Can't what?'

'I can't go back to work. Not after the quake and what happened. Three hundred people have just been wiped out and they expect me to go back to work? Forget it.'

Yuki and Sugimoto dropped the subject.

49

THE SAVE

The Palace Hotel, fourteen days after the quake

'This shows the inferiority of American construction methods.
And you want us to allow in American contractors?'
> A Ministry of Construction official after the
> San Francisco earthquake killed fifty people

'We might have to re-examine our building methods.'
> A Ministry of Construction official after the Kobe
> quake had killed over five thousand people, more than
> one hundred times the number of deaths in San Francisco.
> The quakes were almost identical in magnitude

'Kiko?'

There had been no response from her sister for the last two sleep cycles. A stench was coming from her sister's direction, and the sound of flies could be heard buzzing in the rubble.

Keiko sniffed an open tube of toothpaste and then left the tube near her nose to keep away the odour. How many hours had she been trapped? As she drifted back into another sleep cycle, Keiko dreamed she heard loudspeakers announcing the free distribution of food. Warm miso soup. Rice.

'Rice and soup,' blared a bullhorn far off in the distance.

'Please come in,' advertised a clean-cut young man near the Happy Science field tent set up outside the East Gardens of the Imperial Palace, 100 metres from the Palace Hotel where Keiko lay buried.

'Fresh obento and cold drinks,' blared a competing rescue service. This field tent was hosted by the yakuza, and a thin, tattooed man with sunglasses was brazenly soliciting business. Both Wa's religious followers and Moyama's yakuza had flown in fresh food from Osaka to hand out to survivors. A line of three hundred people stood in front of each tent.

'Eat our food and drink our water with a clean conscience,'

broadcast the Happy Science bullhorn. This not-so-subtle attack on the yakuza's morality had the desired effect, and a few people jumped from the yakuza line to Master Wa's line.

The tattooed gangster was not to be outdone. 'Eat our food without fear of contamination,' he countered. The yakuza leader had cleverly planted the idea that the Happy Science food was tainted. The public had been wary of fanatical religious groups ever since the Aum Shinrikyo gas attacks, and the fear of mass poisonings, gas attacks and bombings was ever-present. Two dozen people scurried away from the Happy Science line.

Both sides stepped up their attack. The yakuza organizers called in two hundred heavies to stand in their own food queue to give the appearance of successful numbers. This did not please the religious organizers, who increased their verbal warfare against the thugs.

'Don't support pornography and corruption,' they shouted at those in the rival ranks. The beleaguered and bewildered refugees, caught in the battle, just looked on.

Meanwhile, some well-manicured gangsters had infiltrated the Happy Science field tent, posing as hungry survivors. After being served food, they ate their meal and then swallowed a vomit-inducing drug. Gang members were soon heaving their guts inside and outside the Happy Science food tent.

'Poison!'

'Dirty food!'

'Impure!'

The threat of contamination put off hungry families, while the overpowering smell of vomit in the sweltering sun forced even the Happy Science volunteers out of the food tent.

The conservative religious volunteers were not accustomed to such under-handed behaviour but quickly went on the counter-attack. Within two hours five hundred Happy Science supporters converged on the yakuza food tent, besieging hapless survivors.

'They're evil.'

'Don't eat their poison.'

'Blood money.'

'They're serving rat meat,' and indeed a rat was seen conveniently scurrying from the yakuza tent in full view of all those in line. A Happy Science organizer took full advantage of the rat's flight. 'Aha, one got away before they could serve it,' he said over the loudspeaker. Afraid of bubonic plague, the crowd ran from the tent.

Yakuza heavies moved in on Wa's followers and began beating them up. Fists flew and only the police could break up the fight. They disbanded both groups and banished their relief tents to opposite sides of the Imperial Palace.

Across the street Keiko tried to gasp.

'Help.'

She had made a mental note to cry for help every hour, but, losing track of time, she had only managed a cry every ten to twelve hours.

'Help.'

Tired from her two cries, Keiko squeezed some of the remaining toothpaste from the tube and swallowed it. Her cardboard food supply had run out, and her body had almost completely shut down. She intuitively knew that Kiko was dead. Keiko tried to stay conscious, aware that if she fell asleep this time she might not wake up. But sleep was just so tempting. *Just a short nap, then I can start shouting for help again.* She closed her eyes and fell asleep.

Up above, a Swiss rescue team was busy at work with their dogs. At first, Ministry of Agriculture officials at Osaka's international airport refused to let the dogs into the country without the proper quarantine period, but they relented when the Swiss threatened to go to the media and trumpet Japan's ineptitude in the crisis. As a compromise, the Swiss doctors agreed they would not practise medicine when Ministry of Health officials in Osaka pointed out that they were unlicensed in Japan. 'We Japanese have different medical requirements,' they told the Swiss, who shook their heads, crossed their fingers behind their backs and swore they wouldn't save any lives if it involved medical attention.

Above the rubble, the Bernese mountain dog barked once, then twice. The Swiss team immediately ran over to the huge dog, who was trained to bark once when he sniffed a dead body and twice if he sniffed a live one. The dog barked again, pawing at the concrete.

'Quick, get the Jack Russell,' ordered Pierre, the team leader. 'We've got a hot one. Let's move.'

The Swiss team were systematic. After a larger mountain dog sniffed out a body, the smaller dogs were brought in for a 'surgical strike', working their way into the concrete to pinpoint the exact location of the survivor. The Bernese mountain dog moved on, barking once every fifteen seconds or so. Pierre attached a heat-sensing device and mini-cam to the terrier, whose name was Jack. He began squirming his way through the rubble as the team tore off layers of concrete.

'Hello . . . hello,' called Pierre.

Keiko was in a sleep/death cycle and did not respond.

As Jack crawled through the wreckage, the mini-cam played back an image to Pierre on a hand-held TV screen. Nothing so far. Then Jack began barking 3 metres below the rescue workers.

'We've got the victim in view,' shouted Pierre. 'Straight down.'

Jack was trained to sidle up to the body to allow the sensors to pick up heat. A small red light lit up, indicating that Keiko was still alive. Jack whimpered slightly and nuzzled the surviving twin, trying to wake her, but there was no response.

Pierre and his companions frantically cleared rubble with their hands, desperate to save this survivor. Though the Swiss team had saved hundreds of people over the past two weeks, their frenzied rescue attempts were a means of purging their failure in Kobe several years earlier. The government had held up their entry into Japan for some days, and when they finally reached Kobe most of those who might have been survivors were dead. 'All we dug up were corpses,' Pierre had been quoted as saying in a newspaper interview. 'Japanese families were adamant that we recovered their dead bodies, which prevented us from tracking down possible survivors.'

Fifteen minutes later, Pierre pointed a flashlight down a black hole on to Keiko's body. He could not tell if she was dead. A putrid smell hit Pierre's nose.

'Give me a mask.' He put it on, then climbed down to Keiko's body and checked her pulse. 'I've got a live one. Alert the medical team. We need a chopper. Crank up the saw!' shouted Pierre. Up top, his team fired up a chainsaw with a blade specially tempered to tear through iron and concrete.

Pierre covered Keiko's face with a small hand towel just before the team handed down the saw. He took off the clear plastic protective cover, put on his goggles and guided the saw between Keiko's crushed legs, cutting a pillar in half. Concrete particles and dust flew back on to her. Pierre turned off the saw, handed it back up and tied a rope around one of the pillars.

'Pull.'

The pillar came up. He then put another rope under her arms and threw it up.

'Up she comes. We've got to hurry.'

Pierre guided her limp and emaciated body up to the surface, where a chopper was standing by. Keiko's legs had been pulverized into a flattened mass of splintered bone, blood and flesh. Fortunately the weight of the pillar had acted as a tourniquet. They quickly loaded Keiko into the helicopter. The prop wash from the chopper drowned out any sound.

The Jack Russell began to growl. Pierre looked down into the dark hole and saw Mushka's green eyes. He crawled down to pick up the cat, whose scorched hair was matted to her body. With Jack still growling, Pierre put Mushka on the stretcher with Keiko, leaving Kiko's decomposed body covered in flies.

Across the street at the medical tents the laptop computers beeped continuously, warning that a patient's vital signs were flagging. Dougie put all his energy into helping the medical staff, having not contacted Salomon Brothers about his whereabouts or bonus. Unsure of his future, he simply lived in the present and avoided his old firm. Nearby an alarm went off, and he shouted for Yuki since no doctors were around. The normally self-confident Douglas hesitated.

'What should we do?'

'Get that green bottle and bag,' yelled Yuki.

A middle-aged man lay on the silver mat and it was clear he wasn't breathing. Dougie grabbed the green bottle, missed with his right hand and without hesitating switched hands.

Thousands of green bottles the size of the water bottles used by bike racers littered the infirmary. They were known as O-Max bottles and were used to produce oxygen. Bulky oxygen cylinders were heavy and unwieldy. These do-it-yourself oxygen kits only weighed just over a kilo and produced four litres of oxygen every four minutes.

Dougie quickly poured water into the plastic bottle, then added the organic chemicals which forced the oxygen out of the water up into the mask. He put the mask over the man's face. The man's breathing slowly returned to normal, as did Dougie's, and a doctor came running over to relieve them.

'Good work. You saved his life.'

'Thanks.'

Dougie and Yuki returned to their camp where Sugimoto was making tea when the head of Salomon's Osaka office called. Risking his job, Miyaki warned Dougie that Williamson, Salomon's head of compensation, did not intend paying his bonus if he didn't return to work. For the first time in over a week, the three discussed the future.

'What are you going to do?' asked Yuki.

'Work in a soup kitchen – I don't know. But Salomon isn't the answer. One year we make half a billion and the next year we lose it. What's the point? It's a life of four-minute trading miracles. Going back there's absurd.' The fast lane as his sole purpose for living held little attraction for Dougie now.

'Why don't we do what we've always talked about? Let's start our own firm,' said Sugimoto.

'Here? In Japan. Land of the corporate samurai? Come on – get real.'

Yuki got excited and spoke up. 'Look, it was a crazy idea before the quake. We both thought you were dreaming. Nobody started up their own financial firm in Japan. But now there is no Japan. Why not? You're a trader. That's your profession. What's happened to your confidence?'

'Dougie-san, for two years we've discussed this idea. Now's the time,' said Sugimoto.

'Brilliant idea, Einstein-san. Now just what exactly will we do for money?' asked Dougie.

All three of them smiled at once.

Dougie grabbed the phone and dialled Salomon Brothers' New York office. As he waited for the satellite connection, he cupped his hand over the mouthpiece. 'If they're greedy, they'll jump at my proposal.'

'Hello, Salomon Brothers.'

'John Williamson, please.'

'Going through.' The phone rang.

'John Williamson's office.'

'Is he in? This is Dougie Douglas in Tokyo.'

'He's in a meeting, but I'll tell him you're on the line,' said the secretary, who was under firm instructions to track down Williamson the moment Douglas called.

Williamson raced out of his meeting and frantically indicated to his secretary to transfer the call to his private meeting room. He tried to act calm, but was still panting when he picked up the phone.

'John Williamson.'

'Hi, Mr Williamson, this is Dougie Douglas from the Tokyo office,' he said, wanting to sound like a permanent fixture at Salomon Brothers.

'Oh, hi, Dougie. Listen, all of us are thrilled you made it. And by the way, please call me John.'

'Well, John, this has been some experience.'

'Dougie, anything we can do to help out . . .,' said Williamson, sounding grossly insincere.

'The reason I was calling was about my bonus.'

The line went silent for a moment. 'How can I help you?'

By paying the fucking $30 million into my bank account, you asshole. 'I have a proposal for you,' said Douglas instead.

'Yes. Go ahead.'

'I understand that I have approximately $30 million coming due this December, and a condition of my receiving this bonus is that I'm still employed by the firm.'

Williamson did not comment, not wanting to commit himself on a tape-recorded conversation. 'Please go on.'

'I'd be prepared to cut a deal with Salomon,' said Douglas.

'What kind of deal?'

'I'll accept $20 million if you pay me out immediately and waive my restraint of trade clause which prevents me from transacting business with Salomon's clients once I leave the firm.'

There was a pause. 'I've got some bad news for you, Dougie,' said Williamson. 'Your trade was unauthorized, and you'll be lucky if Salomon doesn't press charges against you. You're a gambler, and the only thing that separates you from Nick Leeson bringing down Baring Brothers was that your trade made us money.'

But Williamson's threat did not evoke the response he had intended. Instead Dougie laughed. After surviving the Big One, he had little regard for the petty threats of a button-down bureaucrat in New York.

'Do you have any idea of what's happened here? A quake just wiped out our entire office and killed three hundred people. And you're talking about an unauthorized trade. Get real. You're one to talk about authorization. I bet the board hasn't authorized the threat you just made. In fact, I'll bet the board's told you to pay me out.'

Yuki and Sugimoto were silently clapping in the background.

'Here's my final proposal, John, and it's non-negotiable. Salomon pays me $20 million immediately or I carry out my job till the year end. Then you can cough up $30 million. I'll wait to hear from you.' Dougie hung up.

Williamson had to make five calls to authorize the payment to Douglas, but only one counted: Derek Hunt. And Hunt was ebullient. 'Well done, that's a great deal you've cut,' congratulated Hunt when Williamson told him of the proposal. 'Of course you've got my permission. Pay the man.'

Williamson called Dougie back straight away, worried that he might change his mind and stay till the year end. 'Hi, Dougie, John again. The executive committee has approved the immediate payment of $20 million. There's a short agreement we want you to sign saying that this is in full and final settlement of all amounts we owe you. Can you get to a fax machine?'

'Just a second.' Dougie put his hand over the phone. 'They agreed!' he said exuberantly. 'But we need a fax machine.'

'The infirmary,' said Yuki.

'Will it work?'

'All the Biomats are linked to laptop computers with fax modems. If we can hook the laptop up to your phone, we can transmit.'

'John, we've got a fax machine, but first two things. Make the agreement short, and if it says I have no come-back on Salomon I want to ensure Salomon has no come-back on me. Secondly, the payment can be made directly into the New York account into which you transfer my monthly payments. The details are on record. I'll call you in half an hour to begin transmission.' Douglas hung up.

'Yeee-haaa!' He danced a jig, hugging Yuki and Sugimoto. 'Quick, let's find a fax. This had better work.'

They dashed down the rows of victims until they found a patient who was sufficiently recovered to be disconnected from the computer. They contacted Williamson and told him to send the fax via Dougie's phone. A moment later the agreement printed out.

'We Salomon Inc. agree to pay the sum of $20 million immediately into the nominated bank account of Dougie Douglas. In return, Dougie Douglas and Salomon Brothers agree that such payment is in full and final settlement of all amounts owing to Dougie Douglas, that Dougie Douglas may seek immediate employment in competition with Salomon Brothers and both parties waive all rights to any future litigation in relation to this matter.'

The letter of agreement was signed by Williamson on behalf of the board of directors. Douglas signed it and sent it back. He turned to Yuki and hugged her, them slapped Sugimoto a high five.

Douglas, Sugimoto & Co. could now open for business.

50

JUSTICE

One month after the quake

'We would advocate the death penalty for men who abuse women. Unfortunately we can only suggest women leave abusive situations.'

A bitter, unnamed source at a shelter for abused women
in New York City

Tada locked himself in his study, opened his safe, took out his share certificates and flicked through them. Nippon Steel, Fuji Photo Film, Tokyo Gas, Kumagai Construction, Hitachi and Sony – all the names that had made Japan a world powerhouse. When he came to Daishin Construction he scowled and threw the certificates on the floor.

'That potato-head,' he said in disgust.

The Minister was referring to Kobayashi, the Daishin chairman who had built and owned the Daishin Trade Towers. Those buildings now lay in ruins and the share certificates were worthless. Tada was also angry at not having been able to kill Hiroko. *If only Moyama hadn't come to her rescue.* Now she was alive and still a dangerous threat. She had clearly amassed more than enough evidence to expose the corruption of the Daishin scandal. *Fuck. Not only is the bitch going to make my life difficult, I'm not even going to make money out of Daishin.*

Tada had theoretically been wiped out by the crash. His Daishin shares were valueless and he still owed Sumitomo Bank 2 billion yen for their purchase. In planning his next fraud, Tada was taking no chances that the bank's records had been destroyed.

He took out a piece of paper and carefully made a list, marking down the number boldly stamped in red on the upper left corner of his share certificates. He then listed the number of shares he owned and the total number of shares that each firm had issued.

Company	Certificate No.	Number of shares owned
Nippon Steel	2300000143	200,000 shares out of 6.8 billion in issue
Fuji Photo	9723000	100,000 out of 514 million
Tokyo Gas	3789999	50,000 out of 2.8 billion
Kumagai	8 88018934	25,000 out of 700 million
Hitachi	333978000	38,000 out of 3.3 billion
Sony	4470013	7000 out of 374 million

Now came the scam. Tada giggled with evil delight at the thought of how much money he was going to make. He slowly wrote out an affidavit by hand, swearing that he owned millions more shares than he actually did:

I, Tada Takajire, of 114 Kojimachi Mansions, Chiyoda-ku, Tokyo, do hereby swear the following:

I am the owner of the below-mentioned share certificates, these certificates having been destroyed in the Great Tokyo Earthquake:

Nippon Steel	2300000143–2310000142
Fuji Photo	9723000–982500
Tokyo Gas	3789999–3989999
Kumagai	8 88018934–8 89018934
Hitachi	333978000–335979999
Sony	4470013–4480013

I ask the honourable court to grant me reissuance of these shares. As prescribed under law, I have advertised these share certificate numbers in the forthcoming edition of the government gazette and shall do so over the next six months. In light of the tragedy that has befallen Tokyo, I ask that the court waive the 'six month' waiting period and make it an order of court [*meirei*] for these shares to be reissued immediately.

Signed and sworn,

Tada Takajire this seventh day of August

Under Japanese law, if an investor lost a share certificate he was required to appear before a commercial court and advertise his loss for six months in a government gazette before the share was reissued. The stockbroker through whom an individual bought the shares kept track of details such as when and how many shares were bought, the certificate numbers and so on. Now, with brokers' records wiped out in the liquefaction of the financial district and confusion reigning over the Tokyo financial markets, Tada had hit upon a marvellous scam. He was simply claiming millions of shares that he did not own, to be issued in his name.

Tada coughed in excitement and dislodged a piece of phlegm, which he spat into the wastebasket near his desk. He greedily worked out how many extra shares the commercial court would issue him, and then worried that he was being too greedy putting in for 10 million shares of Nippon Steel. *No*, he reasoned, *ten million shares is fair. I lost everything in Daishin and I might have to pay back Sumitomo Bank the two billion yen I borrowed. After all I've done for Japan, this is very fair.*

'Oi!' he shouted as he put his original shares in the safe. 'Oi, messenger,' he bellowed.

'Yes, Tada-san, can I help you?'

The retired man bowed. He was in his sixties and worked part-time as a messenger at the Ministry of Construction since he was unable to live off his pension. Tada often kept him on call for twelve hours at a time.

The Minister did not return the bow and spoke in a condescending tone. 'Boy, I want you to hand-deliver these to the Tokyo commercial court by scooter. You understand?'

'Yes.'

'Sign this.'

Tada shoved the affidavit in front of the poor man, who did as he was told – too scared even to ask what he had just signed. With the affidavit witnessed, Tada sealed it in an envelope.

'And don't lose these or I'll fire you.'

The messenger depended on this job to feed his family, and was now shaking. 'Yes, sir.'

Tokyo's commercial courts had been temporarily moved into field tents outside the Supreme Court Building across from the Imperial Palace. Hundreds of thousands of small investors had lost their share certificates in the quake, but few of them realized that they could claim them back via the court system. Most Japanese believed that anyone having too much contact with the law was likely to be on the wrong side of it. Japan had one-fifteenth the number of lawyers per person of the USA. Even if small investors *had* discovered the possibility of claiming from the courts, the prospect was daunting. Tokyo's residents had other problems.

Tada, taking no chances, was already busy plotting a back-up scam. He picked up his phone and dialled an Osaka number. Tokyo was ruined, but business was booming elsewhere throughout the nation.

'*Moshi, moshi*, Hanshin Print Works, Tendai speaking.'

Tendai was managing director of the Hanshin Print Works and Banknote Company, which printed all the documents for the Ministry of Construction thanks to a pay-off to Tada. The firm also printed all Tada's personal stationery for free.

'Tendai, this is Tada. I have a job for you.'

'Yes, Tada-san?'

'You don't print high-security paper such as banknotes, do you?'

'No, we haven't printed banknotes since the Pacific War,' said the printer, referring to World War II, 'but we like the name since it gives our clients a feeling of security and confidentiality.'

'Yeah, yeah, but can you print share certificates?'

'Oh yes, almost any modern printer can. The problem is the special paper and obtaining the positives from the printer who did the job before,' said Tendai.

'Impossible. The other printer was Tokyo-based and he was wiped out. Can your artists replicate a share certificate and reprint it?'

'Hmmm. Well . . . hmmm. Yes, well, I suppose it could be done. Our designers could match the design and I could locate the special paper. We need the company's permission, of course.'

'Don't worry about that,' barked Tada. 'You take your orders from me. If anyone ever found out that you bribed me to win the government tender then your firm would be ruined,' said Tada, not pondering what implications such a revelation would have on his own career. 'I'll have the certificates flown down with the serial numbers that need to be run. Call me when you get them.'

'Yes, Tada-san,' said Tendai. The line had already been disconnected.

The Minister opened the safe again and took out his Nippon Steel shares. *The perfect share to forge*, he thought. With nearly 7 billion shares in issue nobody was going to know if 10 or 20 million flooded the market. This was the one share certain to rocket once prices turned up, since the entire city needed to be rebuilt from steel. He felt the high-security paper's granular surface and held it up to the light. *I hope that bastard can duplicate the watermark*.

He put the shares in an envelope without a note. His first rule was never to write anything down. He could phone the serial numbers through to Tendai later. Enough business for one day. *Where is that whore Kaelin?* he wondered. *I need some fun*. He addressed and sealed the envelope and then went off to find her.

In the Tokyo Commercial Court one month later, masses of

chain-smoking plaintiffs and defendants sat on plastic milk crates or on the ground, or else milled about outside. Tada was on hand to hear the judge rule on his 'lost' share certificates. He was in the front row where an attendant had miraculously produced a wooden chair. Most furniture had been burned as firewood.

The court system was still housed in a series of field tents. In the adjoining tent, heavily armed police stood over defendants charged with murder, rape and looting. Both courts were overloaded. The jury system had fallen away after World War II for both civil and criminal cases. Defendants were allowed to ask for a jury, but if they did so they were considered guilty. Since then, prosecutors had delivered a stunning 99 per cent conviction rate in the criminal courts.

'I've reviewed the claim of Minister Tada in regard to the reissuance of shares in his personal investment portfolio,' said the judge from behind a small wooden table. 'I hereby grant Minister Tada restitution of his lost share certificates, waive the six-month requirement to advertise in the government gazette and make it an order of court that the said companies reissue him his rightful share certificates,' he said, banging down his gavel.

'Next case,' cried the court clerk.

An imperceptible smile crept across Tada's face. He stood, bowed to the judge and walked back to his own tent. He was seriously rich.

The next morning, at a coffee shop in Nishi Azabu, Kaelin tried to hide most of her bruises from Hiroko, but the extra make-up couldn't conceal her black eye and puffed lip.

'You must leave him,' Hiroko pleaded in a loud voice, shouting over the noise of jackhammers and heavy machinery outside.

The reconstruction of Tokyo had begun, but it would take many years before the city was fully redeveloped. After the 1923 earthquake it had taken seven dusty and disruptive years for the programme of reconstruction to be completed. Back then over thirty thousand tin shacks had been erected, most resembling third-world squatter camps. A quarter of a million people had been relocated at that time so that the streets of Tokyo could be widened and new parkland created.

Similar tin and cardboard shacks had sprung up this time around Tokyo, but reconstruction was now in the hands of the private sector which had moved quickly to rebuild the city. A Minister of Reconstruction had been appointed by the temporary cabinet, much to the anger of Tada, whose actions as Minister of Construction preceding and during the quake were under investigation.

Hiroko and Kaelin sat on two wooden stools on the ground floor

of the two-storey coffee house. It had no roof, and the sunshine and
dust poured through the open ceiling. Coals were burning in the
floor of the shop on which three or four kettles bubbled away.
Kaelin and Hiroko had become close friends since the earthquake,
but to Hiroko's frustration Kaelin continued to live with Tada and
was now being beaten daily.

'I said you must leave him.'

'I will.'

There was no question that at that very moment Kaelin believed
she would and could leave Tada. But the minute she came back into
Tada's sphere of influence his methodical destruction of her ego would
lead her to believe that her beatings were deserved. With nothing to
offer anyone and with the belief that she was fundamentally a 'bad
woman', leaving Tada would then be unthinkable.

'No. Kaelin, I know you – you won't leave until he kills you. You
know, you can come and live with our family.'

Hiroko, her mother and Alex were living in a CNN field tent in
Nishi Azabu, near the Turner International headquarters.

'Really? You'd do that for me?'

'Of course. You can move in now. Come on, let's pick a time.'

'You're sure?'

'Yes. We'd love to have you.'

'Well . . . I'd have to tell Tada-san.'

'Kay-chan, we've been through this. You don't need his permission.
You're a grown woman. He'll never allow you to leave, and you certainly
don't want him to know where you're going. Just leave now. Come with
me,' said Hiroko, getting riled at the thought of Tada's influence.

'You're right. Let me pack my clothes and I'll come over later
tonight.'

'Promise?'

'I promise,' swore Kaelin, taking Hiroko's hand in hers as the
two women giggled conspiratorially. There was no question that
she thought this time would be different. 'This will be fun.' Kaelin
stood up. 'I'll see you tonight. By the way, when is your story going
to run on CNN?'

'They say today.'

'I'm proud of you.'

'You should be proud of yourself. Without the videotape, I
wouldn't have had any proof and my editors would never have
run the story.'

'See you tonight.'

'Bye-bye.'

Hiroko watched Kaelin leave, wondering how a woman could stay with a man who hit her. She shuddered, paid the bill and walked out into the street.

The sound of jackhammers was deafening and dust was everywhere. A large Komatsu tractor with a jackhammer on one end and a loading bucket on the other was breaking up the remains of the elevated highway that had run over the main street. What surprised Hiroko were the Caterpillar front-end loaders filling up a large dump truck with twisted steel and concrete. This was the first sign of American-made construction equipment in Japan. Blue plastic sheeting had been put up over the façades of buildings and shielded the entire street front. The plastic covers were meant to keep the dust of rebuilding from pouring on to the street. In reality the reconstruction of private offices and apartments had barely begun since the top priority was to clear the streets of rubble, and the plastic sheeting neatly hid the devastation.

Life had not returned to normal in Tokyo, but residents pretended it had. The streets were packed with pedestrians, all wearing white surgical masks. Hiroko kept to the left to avoid the steady stream of commuters on mountain bikes.

She walked up the street towards the CNN headquarters. CNN had recently offered her a post as their Tokyo correspondent and Hiroko, frustrated at being blocked by her editor at the *Asahi* newspaper from running her story on corruption, happily accepted. Her brief was to keep CNN viewers abreast of Japan's reconstruction and the forthcoming elections and to file interesting feature stories. The 'A' team had regrouped at CNN, with Jiroo joining her from *Asahi Shimbun*.

Today was a big day for the 'A' Team. CNN was running the exposé on the Daishin scandal and the rampant corruption that pervaded Tokyo. Hiroko checked her watch: almost time for her telecast.

The remains of the ten-storey building were one of the few sites to have been cleared. The basement had been filled in with rubble and covered with hard soil; canvas field tents, generators, green field latrines and large plastic water tanks filled all the available space. Hiroko wondered what had happened to all the other tenants of the building: ground floor and basement shopkeepers, small shipping and travel agents, an employment agency, consulting engineers and various trading company employees.

An old man who had run a yakitori restaurant in the basement braved the dust and set up a plastic tent from which he sold food. He cooked off a gas stove and a steam vent ran up through his tent. Inside were six wooden chairs for customers. But only a few other tenants had returned.

Hiroko walked over to the tent where CNN's Tokyo headquarters was temporarily situated. Her own 'house' was 30 metres away on the opposite side of the plot. School had been cancelled indefinitely and Alex spent his days exploring the ruins, poking around for treasure. Yesterday he had found a box of pachinko balls, tiny ball bearings, which he and Craig Huntley were now playing with on the ground. Michiko's Gaslight bar had burned down but, with the help of her surviving bar girls, she had retrieved wood from Ginza and built a makeshift bar. Business was booming as men sought out the camaraderie of other men and the companionship of Michiko's women.

Hiroko walked into the tent. 'How are the two men in my life?' she asked, bending down to kiss Alex. He was intent on his pachinko balls and hardly noticed his mother. Hiroko kissed Craig on the cheek and received a warmer response as he stood up and hugged her.

'How do you feel?'

'About what?'

'Very funny.' Craig knew that Hiroko was anxious over her corruption story. Although living under the protection of Moyama, the thought that Tada might have her murdered was ever-present. If it hadn't been for Craig she might never have pursued the story. Since the day they had found Alex, the pair had been inseparable. Hiroko was deeply in love, something she had never thought possible since the death of her husband. Craig was strong, compassionate, funny and romantic. Moreover, he was confident enough in himself to treat Hiroko as a professional equal.

'Let's sneak away,' he said quietly. 'Just the two of us.'

Hiroko giggled. 'Not now, you dirty old man. We've got work to do,' she whispered. She walked over to Jiroo and asked him, 'How long till the story runs?'

'Still five minutes to go. Tada's going to kill you.'

'Don't worry about him. My godfather will protect me.'

Craig interjected. 'Speaking of Moyama, I've been doing some snooping. Did you realize that your godfather is head of – '

'Shhhhh,' said Hiroko, playfully cutting him off. 'Our show is almost on.'

The three of them watched the TV screen. Tokyo Electric Power had run electricity to the corner of every city block, which residents and businesses were allowed to tap from their own power cables. A booming business in electric cabling and installation had sprung up. But power was still rationed, and CNN had two emergency generators chugging away outside the tent.

World Business News was just wrapping up for viewers in Asia and Europe, and the familiar top-of-the-hour jingle was heard.

'This is *World Headline News* with Alanda Voltaria.'

'Turn it up, Jiroo.' The generators, jackhammers, trucks and demolition workers outside made it hard to hear.

'Our top story today. CNN has uncovered evidence of massive corruption in Japan. We go now to Hiroko Fujita in Tokyo.'

A pre-recorded tape of Hiroko came up on the screen. 'CNN has gathered evidence of government and corporate bribery and corruption which we believe cost tens of thousands of lives in the recent earthquake. An extract from a videotape shows the Prime Minister and Transport Minister and the current Construction Minister discussing share manipulation and kickbacks. The tape is in Japanese but has been dubbed into English,' explained Hiroko.

Prime Minister Mori appeared first, discussing how the Liberal Democratic Party would use the proceeds from the Daishin Construction stock manipulation to bribe its members to keep him in office. Tada was next on the screen. He had been cautious, since it had been his idea to videotape the gathering. A voice asked whether all the building inspectors had been paid off, at which point Tada deferred to Kobayashi, Daishin's chairman. In an astounding bit of self-incrimination, Kobayashi launched into detail about kickbacks received from the Daishin Trade Towers project. As he wound up, he thanked Tada as the mastermind behind the entire project. The last clip was of Tada bowing from his chair, acknowledging the praise of his colleagues.

Hiroko's picture then came back on-screen. 'The corruption and greed of the Japanese government swept away five thousand lives on the day the Daishin Trade Towers collapsed. We tried to interview the pro tem Minister of Justice, who refused to comment on whether those responsible would be tried for murder. How many others died as a result of the quest for money and power is not known, but one thing is certain. The Japanese people are tired. They want change. The upcoming elections in November of this year will change the way Japan is run. Meanwhile, Minister Tada continues in office as the nation's Construction Minister and viewers have to ask why . . . This is Hiroko Fujita reporting from CNN in Tokyo.'

Applause broke out in the tent.

'Wow!' exclaimed Jiroo. 'I can't believe they ran the story uncut.'

'Thanks to your help.'

'I see you made a few editing changes, though,' replied Jiroo.

'What are you talking about?'

'You cut the Moyama footage.'

'I don't remember Moyama ever being there,' replied Hiroko coyly.

Tada had just finished watching the CNN exposé and was livid. *Only Kaelin could have leaked the video to CNN. The bitch dies.*
'Oi, driver.'

'Sir?' He appeared a moment later, shaking.

'We're going to my home.'

Tada Toyota Century was parked only 30 metres away but the driver still assisted him – the Minister now walked with the aid of a stick, since his broken leg had still not mended properly.

The blood pounded in Tada's ears. He thought the tape had been destroyed in the quake, and in his fury crushed his fist into the headrest in front of him. The headrest didn't move, so he ripped it from the seat. The driver tensed up, fearing he was next. He glanced in the rear view mirror to see Tada seething, both fists now raised near his chest. Spittle was dripping from his mouth. Then suddenly the Minister relaxed and put his arms down at his side. He knew what he was going to do to Kaelin. He sat back as the driver pulled away from the Ministry of Construction.

All the government buildings had been pulled down and the rubble carted away, and replaced with giant circus-like tents. No vehicles were allowed in central Tokyo except for the official cars of ministers and high-ranking officials, construction equipment and rescue vehicles.

The road was surprisingly clear. Large bulldozers, cranes with demolition balls, dump trucks and lorries drove in the left lane, leaving the right lane open for official cars. As the Toyota Century passed the moving construction fleet, Tada scowled at the foreign equipment: Massey Ferguson bulldozers from Canada, Bell dump trucks from South Africa, and the Caterpillar name on every third vehicle. *Damn Americans*, thought Tada, *fucking crude, greedy barbarians always pressing for trade equality*. Japanese contractors always bought Japanese equipment. But now that the government had handed some of the reconstruction contracts to foreign firms over the last month, Tada was worried that all that might change.

Komatsu was the largest construction equipment manufacturer in the world after Caterpillar. If the Japanese saw how efficient and inexpensive the foreign makes were, they might actually begin buying overseas. Tada scowled again and spat into his brass spittoon.

Kaelin had just finished packing her clothes when she heard the screech of Tada's car downstairs.

'Wait here,' the Minister ordered the driver. He lit a cigarette and walked into the building.

Kaelin's escape was blocked. The emergency concrete staircase was the only way up to or down from the apartment, since the elevators were still not in service. As she heard Tada wheezing up the stairs, she thought about the roof then rushed into the kitchen, picked up a paring knife and hid it in her shoe. At the top of the stairs Tada paused to catch his breath, wheezed, then spat on the floor. He puffed furiously at his cigarette. The apartment still had no front door since the quake had caused the ceiling to drop 7 centimetres. Tada walked right in.

'Kay-chaaaann.' He tried to shout in an adoring tone but his voice emitted a gravelly rasp. Tada was too used to giving orders to recall how to be loving.

Kaelin emerged. *He's in a good mood. Maybe he didn't see the story on CNN. This is a good time to tell him I'm moving out.*

'Hi. You're home early.' Kaelin spotted his stick and quivered slightly. Tada used the cane to beat her.

'Why, didn't you expect me?' he asked suspiciously.

'No, no, not at all. I'm glad you are home. We need to talk.'

'Yes, we do. Sit down, Kaelin.'

His voice sounded abnormally controlled, which worried her. She walked over to the leather armchair but stood behind it, protected.

'You gave her the videotape, didn't you?'

Kaelin felt faint. 'What videotape?'

Her reflex response was a giveaway. She knew that he knew, and he knew she knew.

Though Tada seemed in control of his inner rage, he flicked his cigarette stub at her and lit another. He then began circling Kaelin. He put his hand on a side table and picked up a crystal swan he had given her for her birthday. Kaelin ducked her head, thinking the swan was about to take flight, but she was wrong. Tada calmly dropped it on the floor, smashing it to pieces. He continued stalking her. Next came the Meiji screen she had bought herself months before when she had sought some gesture of independence from Tada. He stubbed out his long cigarette on its delicate gold leaf surface.

Kaelin backed up the stairs into the bedroom, thinking she could climb out on to the balcony for safety.

But the doors were locked.

'Where are you going, Kay-chan?'

He flicked another cigarette stub at her.

Kaelin was in no doubt that she was about to die. Her only possible means of escape was by seducing Tada, so she approached him and placed her hands on his chest.

It was then that he struck, unleashing a barrage of verbal abuse at her. 'You whore,' he screamed, bringing his stick down hard upon the bed.

'No! Please, Tada-san, I can explain. Please don't hurt me again.' Kaelin cringed like a dog frightened of another beating. 'Please don't hit me. Please.'

But Tada had other plans. He pushed against the bed and his force dislodged a corner of the mattress. A photo of Omori fluttered to the ground. There was no hope of a seduction now.

'Oh, hiding your lover's picture, are we? You bitch. You need fucking, and I'll fuck you like Omori never did.'

He pinned her to the mattress and straddled her neck with his massive weight. Kaelin struggled but could not move.

'I'm going to fuck you and then kill you, you whore.'

He raised his hand and struck her hard across the face. Almost immediately the skin turned blue and a welt began to form. Tada had forced her legs apart and was busy unzipping his fly.

Kaelin quickly pulled her legs up to Tada's back and took the paring knife out of her shoe.

Tada began to laugh. 'You'd better enjoy this, bitch. It's the last fuck you're ever going to have.'

Knowing that this was her only chance, Kaelin plunged the knife into Tada's back. He looked at her with confusion as the blade penetrated his ribs, then his heart. Blood spurted through his back like a fountain, retreated, then gushed again, retreated, gushed and then stopped. Tada fell backwards.

Kaelin stood up and looked at the body in horror. She threw down the knife, wiped her hands and changed her clothes. She had to leave quickly before someone discovered the murder – nobody would ever believe her story. On her way down the stairs Kaelin picked up the black bag that Tada had kept so well guarded. She was sure it must be more evidence of his illegal activities which he wanted to keep from Hiroko.

A few seconds later she was in the back seat of the Century. 'Nishi Azabu, please.'

Her voice might have been calm, but the driver could not help noticing her quivering, bloodstained hands. Kaelin opened the bag. Inside was the last thing she had expected.

Demolition work prevented her from continuing past Akasaka. She jumped out of the car and hailed a motorcycle taxi which took her to CNN headquarters. When she arrived her hands were shaking uncontrollably, and Hiroko held her for five minutes before she could speak. The horrible welt on her face was swelling, and Hiroko could only imagine the beating that she had received.

'Kaelin, tell me what happened.'

'He knew I gave you the tape . . . he was going to kill me.' She looked up at Hiroko. 'I had to do it.'

'Do what?'

'I stabbed him. He's dead.'

She began shaking again and broke out into sobs. Hiroko rocked her back and forth in her arms, thinking of a way to save her friend.

'Will I go to jail?'

'No, you're not going to jail.' Hiroko washed Kaelin's face with some of her precious reserves of water. 'Now your hands,' she said in a maternal tone. Hiroko closed the tent flap. 'Turn around and lift up your blouse,' she instructed.

Kaelin gingerly took off her clothes. Hiroko looked at Kaelin's back and gasped. Tada had beaten Kaelin with his stick, breaking the blood vessels close to the skin. A giant black welt ran across her back and upper left shoulder. Hiroko also noticed older bruises too.

Kaelin buried her face in her hands. 'I couldn't take the beatings any more. I'm sorry – I'll turn myself in to the police.'

'Kay-chan, it's okay. Put your clothes back on. We'll get some ointment for your bruises.'

Hiroko picked up her phone and dialled Moyama. Only a few insiders had his private number.

'*Moyama desu.*' The yakuza leader answered himself, his tone slightly rough.

'*Moshi, moshi, Moyama-san. Fujita desu.*'

Moyama's tone instantly changed. 'Hello there, Hiroko-chan. How are you keeping?' he said affectionately. 'I saw your story on the Daishin scandal.' He was proud of her for having run the story and never once worried about being implicated in the corruption scandal. Cutting the footage of Moyama had never been discussed. It didn't need to be.

'Moyama-san, we have a slight problem. I think Tada-san may have had an accident.' Hiroko explained where his body was, but avoided giving him any more details.

'Ah, Hiroko-chan, Moyama will sort out everything. Leave it to me.'

Two hours later his two lieutenants, Mata and Vinnie, were in Tada's apartment and stripping it of valuables.

'Clear the building,' shouted yakuza gang members dressed as housing officials.

'This building's unsafe. It's about to fall.'

'Clear out.'

The ten surviving tenants of the building rushed out into the summer air, clinging to what belongings they could carry. A crane and wrecking ball stood by. Once the tenants were out, the demolition crew knocked down the building. Vinnie handed each of the tenants a satchel, apologizing on behalf of the government that the building had had to be knocked down.

'They don't look like housing officials to me,' said one housewife suspiciously to her husband. The man opened the satchel and gaped at the 10,000 yen notes. There was over 10 million yen – nearly $100,000 – stuffed in the bag.

'Shut up, woman,' he ordered his wife. With 10 million yen they could nearly retire.

In less than an hour Kojimachi Mansions was levelled. Somewhere deep in the rubble lay the 100-kilo corpse of Takamire Tada.

'Okay, start clearing.'

Mata instructed the front-end loaders to shovel the rubble into waiting dump trucks. By next morning it was as if Kojimachi Mansions had never existed. Tada's disappearance became a minor footnote in Tokyo's epic tragedy – one death in a million.

51

THE SCREW-UP

You are fired. Anyone who still wishes to work at Salomon please let us know and maybe we'll be in touch. But don't hold your breath.

> An October 1987 memo flashed over internal
> computers to five hundred workers at Salomon's
> money market and municipal bond teams

Prices rose steadily for a month on the Tokyo Stock Exchange black market as investors, speculators and traders rushed to buy undervalued shares. This was not a good sign for Salomon Brothers, who were still carrying Dougie's short position and hoped the market would fall. Derek Hunt, the Salomon chief, was monitoring the firm's position and didn't like what he saw.

'Please have John Williamson, Ralph Gazinsky and our head of global trading see me immediately.'

Williamson was the first to arrive in the Salomon chief's office. 'What's up, Derek?'

'Let's wait till the others get here.'

Now Williamson knew there was a real problem. Four minutes later all three men were gathered.

'I've just been on the phone to our Osaka office. The Osaka Stock Exchange is set to open tomorrow. The good news is that we can liquidate our futures position. Can anyone guess the bad news?'

Ralph Gazinsky sighed. 'Yah, I've seen the rally. It's eaten into our profits on the short position. The market's incredibly strong.'

'Where do you figure the market will open tomorrow?'

'About 1500. I'm guessing.' Gazinsky whipped out a calculator. 'We took the position at 2000, prices fell to 750 and have since doubled. Let's see. We'll still make 70 million on the position.'

'Seventy million. That's before the $20 million payment we made to Douglas,' said Salomon's CEO, glaring at Williamson. 'That wasn't a great move.'

Williamson piped up to defend himself. 'Hey, we're still in the chips. We're still up 40 million.'

'What about the exchange rate?' asked Hunt. 'Did you guys think of that?'

There was silence. The room suddenly become very hot and instinctively everyone loosened their ties. The profit that everyone expected was derived from the Osaka Futures Exchange and payable in yen, not dollars. The yen had crashed and lost half its value against the dollar over the past two months. The $50 million profit was now halved to $25 million. The world's highest-paid money men had screwed up.

As Gazinsky and the head trader left the room, Hunt signalled for Williamson to stay behind.

'John, I want Gazinsky out of here.'

'Why?'

'It was his job to monitor the position more closely. Somebody's head has to roll.'

'Come on, he inherited the position.'

'He's out, John, and that's final. Unless, of course, you want to take his place.'

'Very funny. His desk'll be cleared inside fifteen minutes,' replied Williamson.

The Salomon chief checked his watch. 'Okay, I'll time you. Oh, there's one other thing. A guy called Freddie ran a book on the Tokyo death count. I want him outta here too.'

'Done,' said Williamson, who ran off. Ten minutes later the security guards dumped all Ralph Gazinsky's personal belongings into a black trash bag and escorted him to the street. As the guards returned to claim their second victim, everyone in the trading room picked up a phone and began talking with their heads down. Instinct told Freddie he was next, so he ducked into the men's room as the guards searched for him. The next moment the trading room came alive as traders, their assistants and clerks took bets on how long it would take to track down Freddie.

'Fifty bucks says he's gone inside a minute.'

'Done,' shouted five takers at once.

'A "C" note says he lasts five.'

'Give me odds.'

'No fucking way. Even money.'

'Okay, I'm in for a hundred.'

'He's in the men's room,' shouted the trader who'd bet on Freddie's discovery within a minute.

'Not fair! That's cheating,' shouted five voices at the same time.

Chased by the two guards, Freddie bounded out of the men's room and jumped on to the trading desk.

'Come and get me,' challenged Freddie. 'A grand says they can't get me out the door in under four minutes,' he shouted to the trading room, his hands held defiantly above his head. As the guards jumped on to the 30-metre-long desk, Freddie tried to escape but slipped. The guards pinned him down and hauled him away.

Everyone looked at their watch and pandemonium broke out again.

'Pay up.'

'No way – you cheated.'

'He was caught in three and a half minutes.'

'Nope. Bet was to the street and they've still got to get down the elevator.'

'Fuck you. I'm never betting with you again.'

'Wanna bet?'

52

THINNING THE RICE CROP

'At first you feel there is nothing to live for. Life is dark. Then one day, in my case two years later, you wake up and the sun is shining. Though never quite as brightly as before.'

A father describing the loss of his son

Watanabe drove across Tokyo Bay once a week to make offerings of oranges, chocolate and green tea at his family's shrine. His wife had liked oranges and his son had loved chocolate, and he wanted them well fed in their afterlife.

Though it was a bright September day, Watanabe was despondent. He and his daughter Naomi were on their way to Chiba to celebrate Matsuo's birthday. His son would have been four today.

'Daddy, is Matsuo having a birthday party with Mommy now?'

Watanabe choked back the tears. 'Yes, darling.'

The two of them sat down on a little bench he had built on the site of their former home, now a memorial. A tiny image of a boy had been placed next to a wooden windmill built by Watanabe to keep his son happy in his afterlife. He opened the basket and took out a small chocolate birthday cake. Naomi carefully pushed the four candles into the cake and Watanabe lit them. He tried to sing 'Happy Birthday', but his voice cracked. Naomi carried on. Watanabe took a present out of the basket and laid it near Matsuo's memorial.

'Can I open the present for him, Daddy?'

'Yes. He'd like that,' replied her father softly.

Naomi undid the wrapping paper and opened the box. Inside were a pair of tiny sneakers and a miniature baseball bat. Watanabe had hoped to teach his son how to hit a baseball.

'Oh, he'll like these.' She put the sneakers down near the memorial and took her present out. It was in an envelope.

'You can open it, Daddy.'

Watanabe opened the envelope and took out a picture. Naomi had drawn their home with four stick people inside.

'That's you and me.' She pointed to the upright figures. 'And that's Mommy and Matsuo.' Both were drawn as if they were sleeping.

'I'm sure Matsuo will like your gift,' he said, putting the drawing back into the envelope and placing it under the sneakers. He then put Naomi on his lap and hugged her. They watched the candles on the cake burn down, each too forlorn to eat. As they sat there, Fujimoto appeared. Watanabe hid his grief and thanked the shopkeeper for his earlier donations, unaware that Fujimoto had mercilessly sent his wife to her grave.

'So what are you going to do with your life?' Watanabe asked.

'Well, times are tough here. It's impossible to buy supplies and my shop is about to close. I'll have to find a job,' Fujimoto complained.

'Why not join me?'

What a joke, thought Fujimoto. A middle-ranking department store executive offering me a job. But he kept his scorn well hidden.

'No, thanks. I've imposed enough on you as a relative.'

'I've come into some land and a large inheritance,' confided Watanabe. 'I'm going to start my own hypermarket.'

The shopkeeper raised his eyebrows. 'Ummmm . . . well, how much did you come into exactly?'

'Some properties in Ginza and maybe a billion yen in cash and platinum.'

Fujimoto's mind was racing to find a way take advantage of Watanabe's naivety. He had already written off the million yen that were owing. It was time to move in for the kill.

'Well, you know, I do have this store and I've invested a lot of time and money in it,' began the crafty shopkeeper, forgetting his earlier complaints. 'The shop's a goldmine, and financially I couldn't afford to leave it.'

Since his wife's death, Watanabe had been lonely. He loved his daughter, but needed to be with people of his own age. Starved of friendship, he felt like a plant without water. 'Look, I need help with this new operation I'm setting up. There aren't a whole lot of people left out there whom I know or trust. I trust *you*. How much is your store worth? I'll buy you out and then you can join me.'

Fujimoto did a quick calculation. His land was worth 50 million yen. But his building was worthless and had to be rebuilt. The shelves, too, were empty of stock – he had sold all his canned goods, toilet paper, tissue and medicine at inflated black market prices to desperate neighbours.

'Well, let's see. The land's on a busy corner, you know. Hmmm . . . 100 million yen plus the building – another 25 million . . . and the stock, say, well, roughly 10 million . . . and of course the goodwill that I have built up in the area. Let's say a round 200 million yen.'

Watanabe was overjoyed. 'Okay, I'll offer you 200 million yen and you can join me.'

'It's a deal.'

He had finally found a friend and trusted associate.

A few days later the Mitsukoshi department store decided to charge Watanabe for additional supplies given away at its Nihonbashi warehouse after September. It was the accountant who had initially protested at Watanabe's relief efforts who was now spearheading the drive to recover the firm's Tokyo losses. Privately the directors of the store were incensed at Watanabe having given away its goods, but it kept quiet for fear of adverse publicity.

Watanabe decided to buy the warehouse supplies from Mitsukoshi so he could continue giving free food and drink to the needy, and to sell the rest of the goods at cost from his own store.

'I'll pay you for the goods,' he told his boss.

'Pay for the supplies?' the Mitsukoshi director scoffed. 'You couldn't possibly afford them! You're way down the corporate ladder.' He burst out laughing.

Watanabe persisted. 'If I can pay for the goods in the warehouse, will you sell them to me?'

The director was still laughing. 'Sure, sure. I'll even sell them to you at cost.' Then he got serious. 'Listen to me. You are a Mitsukoshi man and my instructions are to shut down the free distribution centre now. Our company will barely survive this quake and here you are giving away food. Shut it down. Now.'

Watanabe decided he would just have to leave Mitsukoshi, and the next day he and Fujimoto lifted the bars of platinum from Kozo Taishowa's safe into a wheelbarrow.

'That should keep Mitsukoshi happy,' said Watanabe as he put an old blanket over the bars and then threw some rotten potatoes over the blanket. Looting was rife in Tokyo, and he was taking no chances. 'Take this to my boss,' he instructed Fujimoto. 'He'll be in a green canvas tent on the old Mitsukoshi site.'

'No problem.'

Fujimoto was already scheming out a way of skimming some of the platinum for himself. It was known as 'thinning the rice crop'. As he wheeled the platinum from Ginza to Nihonbashi he was inconspicuous amidst the chaos of reconstruction. Covering a distance of 3 kilometres in a straight line down Chuo dori, he dodged bulldozers, cranes, dump trucks, front-end loaders, steam shovels and clean-up teams. The dust was thick and Fujimoto wore a surgical mask. Despite the short distance the journey took four gruelling hours, and by the time he got there he was covered in dirt and soaked with sweat. Just as the Mitsukoshi tent came into sight, he stopped. *Watanabe owes me for this harsh journey*, he decided, and moved aside the rotten potatoes. He then uncovered a corner of the blanket, looked furtively over his shoulder and, when he was sure that nobody was looking, quickly hid three bars of platinum under a pile of rubble. He built a concrete cairn over his booty, noted a crumpled telegraph pole next to his rock pile and then moved on to the Mitsukoshi tent.

'Oi, where's the boss?' Fujimoto demanded of a young office woman through his surgical mask. She was dressed in khaki disaster wear and Timberland boots which Mitsukoshi had flown in from the USA.

She bowed. 'Over there.'

Fujimoto wheeled the valuable cargo over to the man. 'Are you Watanabe's ex-boss?' Fujimoto was pre-empting his relative's official resignation. Watanabe had wanted to say goodbye to his firm in the proper manner.

'Ex-boss?' answered the man. 'Who are you?'

'I'm Fujimoto, Watanabe's new partner. He asked me to give you this as payment for the warehouse goods.' He tugged at the blanket and the potatoes went flying on to the ground.

'Ehhh! Where did old Watanabe get so much money?'

'Don't you worry about that. You agreed to sell him the contents of the warehouse, isn't that right?'

'Yes.'

'Well, find somebody to count this platinum. Meanwhile I'm going to stand guard over our goods in the warehouse to make sure nothing goes missing.' Now that he was in business with Watanabe, he had an interest in preventing theft. He would take care of any thieving that needed to be done. 'Oh, and another thing. This payment includes delivery of the goods to our Ginza site.'

'That's impossible,' objected the manager. 'No trucks can get through the demolition works on Chuo dori.'

'That's your problem.' Fujimoto was unscrupulous when it came to negotiating. 'Can you imagine what the newspapers would say if they discovered that the renowned Mitsukoshi department store was selling food and supplies for profit instead of giving it away?'

'Okay, okay,' spluttered the director.

'Delivery in two days. May I have the keys to the warehouse now?' His palm was outstretched and the Mitsukoshi man handed over the keys.

Fujimoto walked over to the warehouse and, when he was sure nobody was looking, searched for his platinum. He looked for his pile of concrete but it was nowhere to be seen. *I could have sworn I buried the bars here*, he muttered to himself. Suddenly the revved-up drone of a front-end loader could be heard behind him.

'Move yourself!' shouted the tattooed driver.

As Fujimoto jumped out of the way the bucket scooped up a load of concrete, raced backwards, turned round and deposited the load in a dump truck.

Fujimoto stared at the truck, then at the crumpled telegraph pole next to him. 'My treasure . . .'

All the loose concrete, including his platinum, was now in the back of the dump truck. Frantically Fujimoto raced over to the truck and looked for the lever to dump the load. He pressed all sorts of buttons. Meanwhile the driver, a rough-and-ready character, was smoking a cigarette, relaxing in the cab until the load was ready to haul away. Suddenly he heard the hydraulic gear of his truck slowly rising.

'Ehhh. What the fuck?' he exclaimed, spinning around to see Fujimoto trying to offload the concrete.

The driver leaped out and grabbed Fujimoto by the neck and ripped him off the vehicle. The load had just begun to slide off the back when the driver lowered the back end to its stationary position. He then turned his anger at Fujimoto.

'You stupid thick peasant, I'm going to kill you.' He jumped off the truck and made for Fujimoto who lay on the ground. 'I get paid by the load and that would've cost me two hours' time.'

'Wait, wait,' said the cowering shopkeeper. 'I'll pay you to dump that load.'

'Whaaat?'

The driver backed down for a moment – not out of interest but because he thought Fujimoto must be mad.

'Yes, yes. I'll pay you a hundred thousand yen to dump the load. In return I get half an hour to sift through the concrete.' Fujimoto was warming to his story. 'You see, my wife lost her purse in the rubble and her wedding ring was inside it. It means a lot to her,' he said.

'A hundred thousand, you say. Hmmm. I'd have to split it with my mate.'

Fujimoto instantly upped his offer. 'Make it a hundred thousand each.'

The driver smiled, showing a row of silver-capped teeth. 'Half an hour.'

He lifted the lever, jumped into the cab and drove forward. The entire load of concrete went crashing to the ground.

Fujimoto began to search the rubble, not worried that he did not have 200,000 yen in cash on him.

The truck driver and the machine operator sat down for a smoke, laughing at this crazy man. The concrete was heavy and hard to move, much of it twisted in amongst jumbled iron rods.

After half an hour the two drivers shouted to Fujimoto, 'Okay, time's up. Time to pay us.'

'No, no – just a few more minutes.'

'Nope. We want our money now. Show us your money and you can dig for as long as you like.' The two strode up the pile of concrete. 'Money. Now.'

Fujimoto started to clamber down the pile, but fell. The two men were on him in a flash and, after turning out his empty pockets, kicked the shopkeeper viciously.

'You lying sack of beetle dung. We're going to beat you senseless.'

When they had finished they threw him to one side and, since it was growing dark, left for their tents down the road, leaving Fujimoto for dead.

53

THE SAINT

Central Tokyo, two months after the quake

'Life went on in the shattered city . . . People ate, slept, laughed, complained, cried, hoped and dreamed, and sometimes, forgetting the hurried business of the hour, rose to small, sublime moments of generosity and love.'
from William Bronson's *The Earth Shook, The Sky Burned*

'Good morning, Kroll Associates.'
'Wayne Herman, please.' Dougie was calling from Tokyo and hoped his old Columbia room-mate was in New York. Wayne worked for a global detective agency.
'Putting you through . . .'
'Wayne Herman here.'
'Hi, Wayne, it's Dougie Douglas.'
'Dougie, how are you? My wife and I heard you were transferred to Tokyo before the earthquake. Are you okay? Are you still with Salomon Brothers? What's it like out there?'
'You sound just like a detective. Actually I'm fine now,' he replied, explaining how he had survived the quake but lost an arm. The two chatted for a while and then Dougie explained why he had called.
'I need to compile a secret report on televangelism in America. We'd like to expand in America, using Pat Robertson's Christian Coalition as an example.' Many Kroll employees were ex-spooks with well-placed intelligence contacts around the world, and this type of research was their speciality. Kroll was known for digging up dirt in hostile takeover bids but was most famous for having tracked down Saddam Hussein's overseas investments during the Gulf War. The West had promptly frozen all Iraqi assets.
'Will $30,000 cover it?' Dougie asked at the end. 'I need it in a month.'
'No problem. I'll have a master copy couriered to Osaka via our Hong Kong office.'

'Thanks, Wayne. See you.'

'Bye, Dougie.'

A month later Dougie handed Master Wa the dossier on Pat Robertson. The right-wing, Bible-thumping broadcasting tycoon was best known from his television shows and his 1988 presidential bid. Master Wa was slightly envious at the slick, fund-raising support that Robertson had orchestrated via the medium of television.

As Wa skimmed through the hundred-page report, his 170-IQ brain was hard at work, racing like a finely tuned Ferrari engine. The disaster had created a unique opportunity to convert the wayward public to his Buddhist sect, scaring them as old-fashioned Puritan ministers had once frightened congregations into believing in a vengeful Old Testament God. Japan's evil ways had upset the harmony of the world, resulting in the earthquake – 120 million Japanese souls were now up for grabs and he had to find a way of reaching them. Instead of just publishing best-selling books to reach the people, Wa wanted to use TV to speak to the world. American televangelists such as Tammy and Jim Bakker and Oral Roberts had successfully tapped American viewers, failing only out of greed. To create the world's fifth major religion, Wa needed a TV station and access to the startling growth of America's conservative religious groups.

'What are your thoughts, Dougie-san?'

'Based on Robertson's success, TV is an obvious means of expansion, but for real grass-roots support in America we need an alliance with his number two man, Ralph Reed.'

Wa flipped to the concise biography of Reed. 'Ralph Reed Junior. Born 1961, Portsmouth, Virginia. PhD in American History, University of Georgia. Campaigned for Jack Kemp and Jesse Helms. Conservative. Gave up drinking and smoking in 1983. Anti-porn, pro-life. Head of Christian Coalition's 2 million supporters. Control over Republican swing vote in thirty states.' A more detailed and highly personal biography followed.

'What's this man Ralph Reed like?' asked Wa.

'He's nicknamed the "Saint", which is the image he likes to project. Though his forces are still small – only a couple of million supporters – his influence is very strong in churches across America. More importantly, he can dictate legislation by threatening to withdraw support from Republican candidates. He took over Pat Robertson's presidential mailing lists from the 1988 election when the Christian Coalition began milking the lists. I view him as a possible presidential candidate.'

'Tell me more about the Christian Coalition.'

'Like you, they're anti-porn and anti-gay. Fundamentally they are to America what you are to Japan – except they're Christian and you're Buddhist. While Robertson made his name in TV, Reed has formed activist church groups across America to spread the Christian Coalition word. Some people think that after the President he's the most powerful man in Washington. Every third Tuesday of the month he presides over an Internet, fax and phone update with over a thousand downlink sites across America. In many areas, the Christian Coalition control Congress.'

'Any backlash against them?'

'Plenty. They're accused by some Republicans and most Democrats of putting government back into the lives of the people and in dictating how the public must live their lives. They're also being portrayed as the thought police.'

'That doesn't bother me. How about allies?'

'They're fervently pro-life and don't believe in the free distribution of contraceptives. Though they're Protestant, the Pope likes their stance, so theoretically Reed can plug into the world's Catholics.'

'Distribution?'

'He's the hand-picked spiritual heir to Pat Robertson's TV empire. The Christian Coalition are able to hand out up to 40 million leaflets through their church network, their mailing list has over 10 million names and their fax and Internet lists are also growing.'

Master Wa thought for a moment. 'Can you introduce me?'

'Sure.'

Dougie made a note to call Washington, and was confident of getting in to see Reed. The man was keen to spread his morality across the religious spectrum and already had formed a tie with powerful Jewish groups. Dougie was certain he would want an alliance with Japan's most powerful leader.

The pair moved on to discuss wresting control of a TV station.

'I'd like to give you a little business,' said Wa, 'as a kind of thank you for the donation you made to our group. I'd like your firm to help me acquire a TV station. More specifically, I'm giving Douglas, Sugimoto & Co. a mandate to take over the Yomiuri group.'

Dougie was stunned at the aggressiveness of Wa's plan. The Yomiuri group was the largest media conglomerate in Japan and its morning newspaper alone sold nearly 10 million copies a day. Like most Japanese *keiretsu*, or business combines, Yomiuri was controlled through its real estate company, a listed firm called Yomiuri Land.

'Please buy me 10 million shares of Yomiuri,' instructed Master Wa. 'I'll make the funds available to you immediately.'

Ten million shares was just over 11 per cent of the media giant. Dougie did a rough calculation in his head. Yomiuri had fallen from 900 yen to under 200 yen a share in the recent collapse, making Wa's purchase worth $10 million. That sounded cheap for 11 per cent of Yomiuri.

For the next two hours the two men formed a battle plan to take control of the group. Dougie would spearhead the operation but use Happy Science staff where necessary. Wa had a Yomiuri shareholder register which listed the names, addresses and number of shares held by each owner.

'We need to send a team to call on each shareholder at home and offer cash for his shares,' explained Wa. 'We should buy discreetly and steer clear of shareholders close to the group. If anybody asks, you can say that you have a buy order from a major American institution.'

'No problem. Sugimoto will purchase as many shares as possible on the open market. I can also commit some of my funds – say a further $5 million – to increasing the stake.'

Douglas knew a bargain when he saw it.

The Yomiuri group comprised the *Yomiuri Shimbun*, the largest-circulation daily newspaper in the world, and twenty-three other companies engaged in property, entertainment and media. Most publishers drooled at the thought of owning the Yomiuri newspaper, but Wa was interested in its TV licence and distribution to 125 million viewers. Yomiuri controlled not only Nippon Television but also the Tokyo Dome where he held his annual birthday party for fifty thousand guests on 7 July.

The pickings were rich, and so Buddha made his move to take over Yomiuri and the world's lost souls. Having infiltrated the US economy, the Japanese were now preparing for a spiritual invasion of America.

Dougie left Master Wa, put on his surgical mask, hopped on to his Suzuki dirt bike and made for the Tokyo Stock Exchange to put the takeover plan into action. Driving with one arm was tricky and somewhat dangerous as he veered around construction equipment and piles of concrete. The bike was specially built for a disabled rider, with the brake and throttle on one hand control. On his way back, as he passed an abandoned building Dougie noticed a street urchin, blackened and dressed in rags, drinking from a pool of stagnant water. The waif's hair was long and matted and he slowed down to watch as she lapped up the dirty water. The girl noticed him and took off like a frightened doe from a watering hole.

'Wait! I just want to help,' he called in English.

She ran off into the building. Dougie threw down his bike and chased after her.

'It's dangerous. I just want to help you,' he said in awkward Japanese when he caught up with her.

The little girl stood in a corner shaking, but his words had a calming effect on her.

Dougie noticed that her ribcage was protruding from beneath her tattered pink dress. 'What's your name?' he asked.

She was still scared, but curious that a foreigner could speak Japanese.

'I'm Dougie. What's your name?' he repeated.

In school she had been taught that Japanese was too difficult for foreigners to speak, and as a consequence all Japanese had to learn English. She lifted her head. 'Sachiko.'

'That's a pretty name,' stammered Dougie, who was trying to remember *kirei*, the word for 'beautiful' that Sugimoto had taught him.

Sachiko could see he was having problems and did not correct him. 'Thank you.'

'Mother? Father?' he ventured in Japanese.

Sachiko shrugged her shoulders, looked down again and began crying. Instinctively Dougie picked up the young girl and hugged her. He didn't know what to say.

'Do you want a ride on my Suzuki?' he motioned with hand gestures.

Sachiko's eyes lit up, and she forgot about her family and hunger pains as she jumped on the back of the bike. Dougie headed to the Imperial Palace grounds where he and Yuki shared a tent. Dinner was cooking over the fire when they arrived. The little girl eyed the rice and grilled fish as Dougie unfurled the tent flap and found his wife-to-be inside.

'Yuki, I'm home,' he said as he kissed her. 'Can we do dinner for three? I've brought a guest.'

'No problem. Who is it?'

'Another woman.'

'Very funny. Let's meet her.'

Dougie and Yuki walked outside the tent and looked in amazement as the bedraggled waif devoured the grilled fish off the stick.

'Where's her family and her home?' asked Yuki.

'You can ask her later, but I suspect we're her new parents.'

Yuki put her arm around Dougie's waist as they both watched Sachiko eat her first proper meal in two months.

54

THE SUCCESSION

Ken Moyama's compound, two months after the quake

'The ideology of emperor worship was energetically propagated, the need to counter Western techniques with an Eastern morality was emphasized, and the morality of loyalty and filial piety was disseminated throughout the land.'

> Quote from *The Japanese Social Structure*, explaining
> Japan's feeling of irrational superiority spawned
> in the 1800s, by Tadashi Fukutake

'That's not fair. Why should you keep half?'

'I'm your father. Don't they teach you filial piety at UCLA?'

Moyama raised his voice slightly and pretended to be angry, though he was secretly delighted at his son's business acumen. Ken Moyama junior had begun a cyberporn service at UCLA and launched the service on the Internet. The elder Moyama agreed to provide a juicy hundred-thousand-picture photo library of nubile young Japanese, Chinese, Thai, Indian and Korean women to the on-line service. Wa's anti-porn crusade was beginning to cut into pornography profits in Japan and the yakuza leader was excited at diversifying into his son's cyberporn business, which he had called Asian Babes On Screen.

The elder Moyama pressed his son hard for a deal. 'There's a big demand for Asian women in America – you need my photos. Plus you're my blood and everything you do is a result of me, so there's no more argument. Fifty per cent, agreed?' He watched his son carefully, wondering how he would react.

'Okay, 50 per cent is fine . . . provided you're paid your half after all expenses, including giving me a cut of 10 per cent of gross profit.' Living near Hollywood had taught him always to take a cut on gross, never on net profit.

The yakuza chief was proud, but didn't let on. 'Okay, it's a deal.

But you shouldn't cheat your father in his old age. And I forbid you to sell that dirty American porn.'

'We're a porn service. What do you mean by "dirty"?'

'You know . . . that funny stuff.' The old man was embarrassed to discuss such matters in front of his son.

'No, tell me.'

'Animals, young girls, young boys . . .,' blurted out the old man.

'But Dad, that stuff sells.' Sometimes his father was too conservative.

'No. That's final.'

The young man knew he would lose this battle. 'Okay, but let's compromise on the "young girl" stuff. Let's say no photos of any girls under the age of twelve.'

'Of course – what did you think I meant? Twelve is normal.' That was where much of the yakuza porn magazine profits were derived. 'Just none of the funny stuff . . . Now tell me what else these computers can do.'

The young Moyama explained how he hoped to create an on-line gambling circuit, taking a share of profits away from organized crime, American Indians and gaming tycoons.

'How?' asked the yakuza boss.

'Our clients can play blackjack, poker and slots over the computer. They authorize their bank to credit a chunk of cash to our account, allowing them to play up to that limit. All they need is a computer at home.'

'I like that.'

'I've got the marketing all figured out. We'll announce a big winner – somebody we know – and pay him five grand to play along as if he had won a million dollars playing the computer. Then we program the computer to pay below the odds. I've already figured out a computer program to beat gaming officials who monitor pay-outs. Once they get too nosy, and force our pay-outs up, we'll direct the computer to pay out select friends in the US and abroad.'

The elder Moyama nodded in agreement, but realized the world had changed. He steered the conversation to a topic with which he was comfortable: money. 'I see our investments in the States are doing well.'

'Look, Dad, I can't keep $275 million in US money market funds. You need to invest this money in the stock market. And wait a second . . . these statements are handwritten by you and say you are only earning $12 million in interest a year on your $275 million. Something's wrong here.'

The yakuza leader looked sheepish.

'No, don't tell me . . . are you putting your cash in the bank vault again?' The young man asked this in a tone of voice that suggested his father had not been taking his medicine.

'You know these Americans. Always asking questions, filling out forms. They treat me like a drug dealer. I like knowing my money is mine and nobody else can touch it. Plus if the bank goes under, they can't touch my cash.'

'You *are* a drug dealer. But they only care about American and Latin drug dealers, so don't worry. How much cash do you have in storage?'

Moyama hesitated. 'Hmmm. I'm not sure. It's in different currencies. Maybe $100 million.' He looked sheepish again.

The economics major shook his head in disbelief. 'When I get back to UCLA you're turning *all* your fund management activity over to me. You need to sign a letter authorizing me to handle the balance of your funds on your behalf,' ordered his son.

'But . . .'

The younger Moyama already knew what was on his father's mind. 'The money's still yours and never leaves your account. I can't touch it. It just means that I have authority to invest the funds where I see fit. Only you can withdraw the money.'

Ken Moyama relaxed. 'Okay, I'll sign.' The yakuza boss felt like a schoolchild and turned the conversation to a different subject. 'Now I want to know about the elections. What can you tell me?'

With Japan's government wiped out, nationwide elections had been called in November. For the first time in Japan's history the Prime Minister would be chosen by electoral ballot and not by Parliament. All 512 members of the House of Representatives and 252 members of the House of Councillors were to be re-elected. Though article 45 of the Constitution stipulated that half of all members of the House be elected every three years, this clause had been amended to allow for a general election. An Overseer of Elections had been appointed and, much to Moyama's disappointment, could not be bought. But Moyama had a back-up plan, and this was where his son came in.

Japan's first money-free elections were going to be conducted through an electronic polling station. This was a fancy phrase for voters calling in their ballots over the telephone. The process was quite simple, and the younger Moyama explained it to his father.

'Three tenders have been awarded. The first tender went to Hitachi for a mainframe to handle the 80 million phone calls. The second tender went to Automated Wagering in Montana to oversee the process. They handle many of the world's lottery systems. The third tender went to Electronic Data Systems, who have the software to handle the election.'

All this talk of computers befuddled the yakuza leader. 'But how do we get access to this system?' The idea of voting by phone was frustrating. It wasn't like the old days when he could just buy the Prime Minister.

'Please, just listen,' said his son, trying to calm him down. He wanted to overcome the old man's mental block. 'Every person in Japan has an identity number. That number will be their personal identification number or PIN. They pick up the phone and call the computer toll-free. A voice will instruct the voter, 'Please enter your PIN number now.' Each voter may only call once. Their voting region will already be known to the computer, which will tell the caller, 'Please record your vote for Prime Minister. Press one for Ozawa, two for Miyaki, three for Ouchi, etc.' Then the computer goes on to members of Parliament, first prefectural then local candidates. If a person has moved to a new address, they can press 0 to get an election operator.'

Moyama's face lit up. 'You mean there's a person who punches in votes?' Alert to every possibility of fraud, Moyama began bombarding his son with questions: 'What about Tokyo residents whose phones haven't been connected? . . . What about all the ID numbers of the dead? . . . Where is the Hitachi mainframe located? . . . Can we tamper with it? . . . Can we buy off Automated Wagering or Electronic Data Systems? . . . Can we pay off the election operators? . . . How much discretion do they have? . . . Who monitors the election?'

His son fielded the questions one by one, explaining that anyone without a phone, which meant most of Tokyo, could vote in person. Their hands would be marked with UV paint so that they could only vote once.

Moyama was keen to gerrymander the election. 'Why can't I stuff the ballot boxes?'

'With what?' asked his son.

'We'll cast votes for the dead people. A million extra votes won't carry the election nationwide, so I need you to fiddle with the Hitachi mainframe. It would be dangerous to let the country choose a Prime Minister.'

'If you can pull strings to get me assigned to the election software monitoring committee, I may be able to do something.'

'The what?'

'The United Nations usually sends in observers to third world countries to monitor election fraud – usually where African dictators are involved. We're too advanced for that, and all monitoring now has to be done by computer experts. Get me on the monitoring committee and I can help you.'

The yakuza leader was burned out by this discussion. He finished every computer conversation feeling frustrated, confused and apathetic.

'Okay, okay, okay. I'll get you on to the committee. Let's change the subject.'

The world really was changing quickly. Moyama needed a back-up plan in case election rigging did not work. He would resort to the old-fashioned way of doing business: instead of buying votes, he would wait and buy the elected official. Computers might have ruined the election process but humans would always be humans. Almost anyone could be bought . . .

55

THE DECISION

Tokyo, September, two months after the quake

Sex is the way to win over any man

Japanese proverb

C raig and Hiroko lay squashed together in a double aluminum-framed bed with canvas backing. The American military beds were unpopular with the Japanese, who preferred sleeping on the floor, and so Hiroko had picked this one up easily. Alex was asleep in his own bed.

'I don't understand the problem. You've told me a zillion times that you love the States,' said Craig, puzzled.

'I do. There isn't a day that I don't think about the east coast, but can't we discuss this later?'

'Sweetheart, if not now, when?'

'What if our love was the result of a momentary lapse? I slept with you because I was excited, exhausted, frustrated and relieved over finding Alex and my mother.'

'Don't forget drunk,' added Craig.

'Come on, I'm being serious. I just don't want our relationship to be founded on a single moment when I was emotionally vulnerable.'

Cradled in Craig's arms, Hiroko absent-mindedly played with the hairs on his chest. They both lay silent for a moment. 'Why don't you just stay here with me?' she said. 'I'm going to be running CNN here, and I'm sure you could also work in Tokyo.'

Such a statement would have instantly destroyed a relationship with a Japanese man, who would never move for a woman. What Hiroko was putting to Craig was done with a certain amount of effrontery. She was asking him to put her career and country ahead of his. But she needed to test him. Craig Huntley was a legend in TV broadcasting, and here she was casually asking him to throw away his career.

'Okay. Let me get this straight. You want me to stay here and either work for you or start my career all over again.'

Hiroko looked up and smiled. 'Something like that.' She gave him a lingering kiss. Her breasts touched his chest, her nipples erect. They both glanced over to make sure Alex was asleep before she rolled on top of him.

'Never make a decision with an erection. It's the first rule of manhood.'

Hiroko sensually stuck her tongue into his ear, knowing that this drove him crazy.

'You like being in control, don't you?' he said, raking her back with his nails. They were the last words either of them spoke that evening.

The next day Craig packed his bags for Atlanta. Nothing was mentioned about where he was going to live, though each of them knew that in less than four hours they would be separated.

Craig left Tokyo, as Hiroko knew he would. A month later CNN asked her to fly to Atlanta for the required two-week training seminar before she became Tokyo bureau chief. Craig was there to pick her up at the airport.

As they lay in bed together that night in Atlanta, she started crying.

'What's wrong, Hiroko?'

'I can't do this. I can't just pop over and then walk out of your life again.'

She looked up at him with tear-filled eyes. 'This is the first and last time I do this,' she said.

Craig looked down at her and shrugged. 'I bet it isn't.'

'What's that supposed to mean?'

'I just quit my job for you.'

Hiroko was taken aback. 'What!'

'I can't live without you. And since you won't move here . . .'

'Oh, Craig!' she said, leaping into his arms. 'I promise it will work out. You'll see.'

'I certainly hope so, because we're getting married.'

'What! You want to marry? Me?'

'Didn't I just ask you?'

Hiroko slapped him playfully. 'What took you so long?'

The next day they were married in a civil ceremony with two witnesses. They flew back to Tokyo where Craig joined the ABC/SKY news team, covering Japan and north-east Asia.

56

THE SURVIVOR

'German insurance companies had to pay nearly $100 million worth of policies after the 1906 San Francisco earthquake. Four of them promptly stopped trading in North America to avoid paying out anything.'

From *Earthquake: The Destruction of
San Francisco* by Gordon Thomas

The claims representative from Osaka Life Insurance sat next to Keiko Noichi in the US Navy field hospital. She had survived the Palace Hotel collapse, though her legs had been amputated. Her twin sister was dead but Mushka lay curled up on the hospital sheets. Keiko had an IV drip in her arm.

'I'm sorry about your sister.'

'Thank you.'

'Luckily, you survived.'

'Maybe I'm lucky, but I see no point in living without my sister and without my legs.'

'How about your home in Ueno?'

'Burned.'

'Your shop in the Palace Hotel?

'Destroyed.'

Keiko's only hope of rebuilding her life was her sister's life insurance policy, of which she was the sole beneficiary. She was not eager to capitalize on Kiko's death, but reality was sometimes harsh. Keiko had no other means of existence.

'How much was Kiko insured for?'

'Fifty million yen.'

'When can I receive the money?'

The representative looked down and did not reply.

'You *are* going to pay me, aren't you?'

'Still no reply.

Keiko buried her head in her hands.

'Sssssss. I'm very sorry, but I thought you knew. The government exempts life insurance companies from paying out for deaths that result from earthquakes.'

'Whaaaat?'

'I'm sorry. But please let me explain. Imagine the panic on the Japanese financial markets if the life companies had to liquidate their stock and bond holdings. There's 20 trillion yen in life policies sitting with the nation's major insurance firms. The government forced us to insert a clause that prevented pay-outs in the event of deaths resulting from major earthquakes.'

'My sister's dead and you're not going to pay out her insurance?'

'Yes.'

There was silence.

'None of the victims' families is going to be paid. But the Red Cross is donating 100,000 yen to families whose head of household has died.'

'What about my house?'

The insurance representative kept his head bent.

'No! It can't be true,' she cried.

'I'm sorry.'

'But my house . . .'

'The government forbids insurance companies to pay out more than 15 per cent of insurance claims related to earthquakes.'

'Are you saying I'll only receive 15 per cent of what I'm insured for?'

He nodded.

'But I can't rebuild my home on that. What would have happened if I had had a mortgage?'

'You'd have had to pay it back after a grace period on interest payments.' Then the insurance man looked up sheepishly and asked Keiko a question. 'May I ask how your house was destroyed?'

'By fire, of course, just like everyone else's.'

'And you had fire insurance?'

'Of course. Why?'

'Sssssss. Mmmm. I didn't realize. This is very bad news. Fire insurance does not cover any fire damage caused by an earthquake.'

Keiko closed her eyes and waved the salesman off. She was crippled and penniless, with nowhere to go.

57

THE ELECTION

Tokyo, November, four months after the quake

'Black money and gangland funds poured into politicians' hands when the Liberal Democratic Party was formed in 1955. The yakuza have had a secret influence as national politics ever since.'

A secretary to a member of Parliament in an interview with the author

Moyama and his son were measuring the impact of their election fraud. The yakuza chief was grilling his son, who had taken a semester off from UCLA to gerrymander the elections.

'Dead bodies?'

'We could only forge three hundred thousand names. This had negligible impact at the national level but helped us score heavily in Tokyo and prefectural races.'

'Phone operators?'

'We had three hundred election operators on the payroll and they raised a quarter of a million extra national votes for us and over fifty thousand locally.'

'Computer tampering?'

'Getting me on the monitoring committee helped, but the international advisory team from Seattle were very clever. My guess is that I fiddled the outcome of the national elections by 2 per cent. What worries me is that some of the other advisers were doing the same thing for our opponents.'

'How are you calling the final results?' The gangster was not only trying to throw the elections but wanted to bet on the outcome.

'No way, Dad, it's too hard to call.'

'Come on. Just guess.'

'No way, Dad. You'll just bet on what I say, and if I'm wrong you'll be angry with me.'

'I promise not to be mad at you, and I swear I won't bet on the election.'

His son gave in. 'Okay. For national elections, my computer program says that the Komeito Party will win the prime ministership, followed by the Socialist Party and LDP. Your independent nominee Hayashi Yamaguchi will only carry 5 per cent of the vote, despite our efforts. Where did you dig this guy up, Dad? He looks like a yakuza hit man.'

'That's enough! Yamaguchi is an honourable man and worked his way up through the street stalls. Let's move on.'

The Komeito Party was the political wing of the Soka Gakkai religious group, whose platform of a one-year debt moratorium for Tokyo businesses and homeowners was popular. Their victory in the elections was an annoyance to Master Wa, whose followers campaigned against both them and Moyama's candidates. Posters bearing pictures of candidates from both sides were pictured as burning in hell.

'So Komeito won the sympathy vote. Next.'

'The Tokyo governorship was won by Miss Keiko Noichi, that woman who campaigned in the wheelchair with her cat. Her platform of waiving principal payments on home mortgages was a big hit. We scored some Tokyo city councillors.'

'Couldn't you rig the governorship for our man?'

'No way, Dad. A cripple with a cat isn't only cute, it's unbeatable. Some say she should have run for Prime Minister.'

'The upper house?'

'Of the two hundred reconstituted seats we'll win twenty, with allies winning another twenty. The other parties were evenly divided with about fifty seats each.'

'The lower house?'

'The lower house now has only five hundred seats, and again our independent candidates will take 10 per cent of those with allies in other parties taking another 5 per cent. Komeito scored big here and are likely to have a majority.'

'Shit. I've had enough of these religious groups. What you're telling me is that our election rigging was a failure.'

'Yeah. Sorry.'

'It's a valuable lesson.'

'What lesson's that, Dad?'

'We should have waited for the results to be announced and then bought off the politicians – just like in the old days. We'll wait till the Prime Minister chooses his cabinet and then make our move.'

His son smiled.

'What's so funny?' asked the old man.

'I just thought of a new slogan.'

'What's that?'

'If you can't beat 'em, buy 'em.'

Moyama laughed. His son's ideas were like recycled gifts – the packaging changed, but the underlying item remained the same.

'Dad, there's one last thing we need to discuss.'

'What's that?'

'Your money.'

Moyama had allowed Ken to manage his American portfolio, but retained control over the Japanese investments himself.

'With the Komeito Party in power, I'm worried.'

'What's the problem?'

'The earthquake may wipe out the Japanese banking system. You won't see anything yet, but I'm certain that this waiving of debt will lead to a banking crisis. That's exactly what caused the bank panic of 1927 and led us into World War II.'

Ken gave his father a brief financial history from the perspective of the great Kanto earthquake. The quake had hit Tokyo at noon on 1 September 1923 and killed over 140,000 people. The following day the Yamamoto government had declared a moratorium on bank loans, allowing homeowners and businesses time to work their way out of debt. The country, already in depression, slipped further into financial darkness. While the rest of the world enjoyed the roaring twenties, Japan suffered through despair. Then in March 1927 the full effect of the quake rocked Japan's banking industry. Japan's banks were unable to collect money they had lent out, forcing the government to close the Watanabe Bank. The worst financial panic in Japanese history ensued, in which many of the country's leading banks, including the Bank of Taiwan, had gone under. This depression and eventual reconstruction led to Japan's late imperial ambition in China and South-east Asia, and subsequently to World War II.

'Dad, my recommendation is that you take all your money out of Japan and buy US dollars.'

His son had a knack of instilling panic within the most hardened of financiers. Moyama wanted to run to the nearest bank and withdraw all his money but instead spoke calmly, not giving his son the satisfaction of knowing he had just tweaked a giant nerve ending.

'Your ideas may have some merit.'

Within twenty-four hours all Moyama's liquid Japanese assets were converted to US dollars.

58

THE CORDON

Tokyo, one year after the quake

'Banks reopened with ostentatious piles of cash by their teller windows. Much of the money was printed on only one side, for there had not been time to print both sides.'

From Edward Seidensticker's *Tokyo Rising*,
on the Bank Run of 1927

Moyama bowed his head to receive the award as Emperor Akihito stepped forward to put the medallion around his neck. The Grand Cordon of the Order of the Sacred Treasure was the highest award that could be bestowed upon any Japanese citizen.

'Exactly one year ago, Japan suffered its greatest tragedy since World War II. The earthquake tore our city apart and perversely also brought our people together. We've all suffered as one.' The Emperor looked around the room. 'Every disaster produces heroes. As I looked over the Palace grounds the evening after the earthquake, I was stunned by the sheer numbers of people who had taken refuge there. This was their sanctuary, and it was my responsibility to feed them. The man who came to our assistance helped save a great many lives.' The Emperor was now looking at Moyama. 'The Japanese people owe their gratitude to you, Moyama Keniichi, for your selfless aid and compassion. It is on behalf of the Japanese people that I bestow on you the Grand Cordon of the Order of the Sacred Treasure.'

Moyama bowed deeply.

To the surprise of the observers, the Emperor bowed even lower than Moyama. On very few occasions could the public recall the Japanese Emperor bowing lower than a subject.

'Keniichi Moyama, your unflagging service to our nation during a time of crisis saved the lives of many thousands of people. We thank you. And as a special token of Imperial gratitude, we present you with this gift.'

Sato, the head of the Imperial Household Agency, stood on the platform and unveiled a giant fish tank containing brilliant orange and white koi.

Two hundred media and private guests clapped. The ceremony was being transmitted live to the Japanese public. Mrs Moyama got up on the stage and began taking pictures with a disposable Fuji camera. Nobody stopped her.

'May these Imperial koi give you years of pleasure,' said Emperor Akihito, bowing again.

Moyama beamed.

He had waited his entire life for a moment like this. From his beginnings as a young thug, he had amassed a fortune and gained the unspoken respect and fear of the entire nation. 'Unspoken' was the operative word. For years the media and public had treated him like a crippled distant relative who had to be hidden from sight. The only thing he wanted before he died was credibility and acceptance. Now that he had been awarded the highest honour in Japan, Moyama was a happy man.

Master Wa's driver switched on his indicator and turned left through the green light. It was lunchtime and the intersection was busy, so the driver waited patiently for the pedestrians to cross. But just as he hit the gas pedal, a young boy raced in front of him and bounced off the front of the Lexus, his skull hitting the pavement.

It was Wa who jumped out of the car, checked the boy's pulse and, finding no heartbeat, administered CPR and mouth-to-mouth resuscitation. People gathered around and all traffic came to a halt. Soon the crowd was ten deep and growing. Those towards the back of the crowd were pushed up against the front entrance of the Sakura Bank, which faced the street. To those who had not witnessed the tragedy, it looked as if a mob had formed outside the bank.

One man had just finished withdrawing money from the automatic machine at the corner and was counting his notes. 'Bad luck,' he said, shaking his head over the accident.

This comment was overheard by a woman, who thought he was referring to the bank. Glancing at his stack of notes, she immediately assumed that he had withdrawn his savings. There was no way she was going to be left till last, so she fought her way towards the bank entrance.

'Let me in! I demand my money!'

The crush of people prevented the woman from reaching the doors, but everyone heard her cries. Five members of the crowd who were

nearer to the bank also had accounts with Sakura and, afraid that
their savings were in danger, forced their way inside. The rumour
of Sakura's demise spread quickly through the crowd and people
pushed their way to the entrance. Such was the confusion and panic
that there was no possibility of a queue forming. The bank guards
rushed to the interior doors to assist customers, but their gesture
was misconstrued by the crowd who thought the place was about
to be locked up.

'They're locking the doors!'

'No, please! I have my life savings in there.'

'Sakura's gone bust.'

'There's a run on Sakura Bank. Quick, get inside.' Everyone else
had the same thought.

'There's no way we'll get our money out of there. Let's go to the
branch down the street,' whispered one man to his wife.

The bank manager was so frightened that he finally did instruct
the guards to lock the main doors, which only compounded the crisis.
A passing film crew in their news van took footage for the six o'clock
news. The Sakura Bank assured customers over nationwide TV that
the bank was in no financial trouble, but this statement only seemed
to aggravate matters.

Master Wa had successfully revived the boy, who was now being
rushed by ambulance to the hospital. Nobody took any notice.

By five the next morning a line had formed outside almost every
bank in Japan. The Sakura Bank run had started a financial panic
which the Bank of Japan had unsuccessfully tried to quell. Unfortunately, Tokyo's banks had trillions of yen in unpaid loans from clients
whose houses and businesses had been destroyed in the earthquake.
Though the government had proclaimed a three-year moratorium on
principal repayment, it did ask borrowers to begin repaying interest
one year after the quake. Tokyo's residents were so cash-strapped
that they were unable to meet even these light payments, forcing the
banks to write off the loans. The run on the banks highlighted the
precarious nature of the nation's banking structure.

The financial crisis was only resolved when an elderly director of
the Bank of Japan recalled what had been done during the 1927
crisis. Banks had reopened with cash stacked high alongside the
tellers' positions. When his fellow directors asked where they would
get the money, the elderly man replied, 'We do what the Bank of
Japan did in 1927. We print it.'

The nation's high-security printers worked non-stop during the
three-day banking holiday. Unlike in 1927, when, because of time

pressure, many of the notes were only printed on one side, these notes were perfect. On the morning the banks were due to open, government delivery trucks were seen dropping off bales of money to the country's main banks. Banks cleverly planted in the queues a number of their employees who, masquerading as depositors, ostentatiously flashed their cash. These ruses calmed the jittery public, and shortly the crisis was over.

59

THE SUCCESSOR

Tokyo, four years later

'Japanese politicians, gangsters and corporate kingpins streamed through Kodama's mansion after his death in January of 1984.'

> Quote from a Sumiyoshi gang leader who paid his respects to Kodama. Yoshio Kodama, Japan's premier racketeer, had ruled Japanese politics and underworld for nearly thirty years

A young man in a black suit swept the path clean. Another raked the white pebbles with a short wooden rake, making a series of clean, concentric circles.

A black limousine drove past the white-walled Cadillacs and Lincoln Continentals and pulled up near the tomb. The crowd parted, expecting their leader. The driver ran round and opened the door, and a short, burly man climbed out. He was strikingly handsome, with grey hair and a scar that down his left cheek. Two bodyguards ran ahead of him. As he walked up to the black marble tomb, the sea of heads began bowing down the line like a Mexican wave. He stopped in front of a wall of flowers. This man was clearly important, but he wasn't their leader.

The gathering was divided by gang, sub-gang and personal rank. The lowly soldiers were nearest the limos, while the gang chiefs stood with their bodyguards closest to the tomb.

'Kazuo Tamakawa,' whispered one of the gangsters to another. It was the leader of Osaka's Tamakawa-kai crime family come to pay tribute. Like the rest of the crowd he was dressed in black, but his $2000 suit separated him from the others – all were bedecked in gold jewellery, many in suits too tight to hide their muscular frames, others wearing baggy suits bought off the rack.

Another limousine pulled up and a murmur went through the crowd. Yes, this was their leader. An American chauffeur jumped out of the limo and ran to open the back door. It was Vinnie, the mafia soldier who had had the tips of his fingers lopped off four years earlier. The Sicilian-American had been kept on by the Moyama family to demonstrate their power and social cachet. Few other Japanese leaders had American bodyguard/servants.

Out of the limo stepped the broadly built Ken Moyama. His short, confident walk to the tomb initiated another Mexican wave. The thousand or so yakuza leaders, lieutenants, soldiers and goons who had gathered on this day were tense. The death of his father two years ago had created a power vacuum within Japan's gangland leadership. His son was now at his tomb, paying homage on the anniversary of his father's death. The twenty-four-year-old Ken Moyama was now their hereditary leader while Hatchi Tamakawa, his rival, was making a play to split the Osaka/Kobe gangs from a central leadership. Japan's yakuza were now divided: those in Tokyo for Moyama and those in western Japan for Tamakawa. All eyes were on the young yakuza chief to see whether he paid homage to the elder Tamakawa.

As Moyama approached the tomb, Tamakawa made a courtly forty-degree bow – low enough to be respectful but not low enough to ingratiate himself. Everyone knew the difference. Now it was Moyama's turn, and everyone strained to see whether they were going to war.

Moyama began his bow and stopped when he was at right-angles to the ground. A collective sigh of relief was heard from the crowd. Moyama had opted for peace.

'Your father was a great man,' said Tamakawa politely. *But we will have to wait to see what you are made of*, he thought.

'Thank you for coming. Both he and I are pleased you are here,' said Moyama, signalling that his father still watched over things from his grave. *Underestimate me and it will be your downfall*, thought the young heir to Japan's underworld.

With a billion-dollar fortune, the younger yakuza leader could wage war against Tamakawa for decades. But the young Moyama had another powerful weapon: an alliance with the American mafia which had prospered over the last four years. Moyama had accounted for 20 per cent of the Di Angeles family profits last year, and they would protect him against Tamakawa. Both yakuza leaders knew this, and last night had decided on a compromise. Tamakawa would reign as Japan's yakuza leader as a quasi-regent until Moyama 'came of age'. Moyama would rule eastern Japan on a daily basis, while Tamakawa ruled western Japan.

Then Ken Moyama turned to a beautiful woman dressed in black,

holding her twelve-year-old son by the hand. Moyama smiled and
bowed. The crowd hadn't noticed the woman before, and wondered
who she was and why she was allowed to stand in the place of
honour.

Then Moyama walked up to his father's tomb and bowed as low
as he could manage, paying his deepest respect. Tamakawa could
only envy the respect shown to the dead leader. *Some day they will
all bow to me*, Tamakawa vowed.

Moyama looked up at the tomb. It was the tomb of an emperor, cut
into half the hillside, and had cost 300 million yen – nearly $3 million.
But it was nothing compared to what the old man had bequeathed
him. Even from the grave Moyama was still the provider.

The son spoke in a monotone. 'Father, we've missed you over these
two years. Times have been tough, but I'm happy to report that we
have resolved our differences and that your memory lives on.'

The entire gathering bent down as Moyama bowed. As they rose,
a man rushed forward and handed Moyama a red lacquer saucer
filled with warm sake. Tamakawa lined up behind Moyama, with
the other chiefs in turn behind him. Moyama raised the saucer in
both hands and shouted, 'Rest well, father. We will return on New
Year's Day.' Red saucers filled with sake were passed down the line
from the chiefs to the 'directors', executives, captains, lieutenants,
soldiers, 'children' and apprentices. The yakuza had more ranks than
a Japanese corporation.

A minute later and Moyama was gone. The gangsters walked over
to a giant marquee full of food and drink. Now they could relax.

Moyama escorted the woman and her child back to their car.
'Goodbye, sister,' he said affectionately, before picking up his
nephew and hugging him. Moyama hoped one day to bring Alex
into the family business. 'I'll see you soon, little buddy.'

'Can we play in your game arcade again, Uncle Ken?'

Ken Moyama winced. He'd have to teach this twelve-year-old the
meaning of secrecy. Now he was going to get an earful from his
half-sister.

'Ken, you told me you took him to the zoo! Remember your
promise. Alex and I have nothing to do with the family business, and
that includes taking him to any game arcades, pachinko parlours or
soap lands you own.'

'Aw, come on, it won't do him any harm.'

Hiroko gave him a stare, and Ken reluctantly agreed to keep the
boy away from his operations in future.

'Shake hands with your uncle,' said Moyama.

As Alex took his hand, the gangster slipped a gold coin into his palm and winked at his nephew.

'Goodbye, Hiroko. See you at your mother's ceremony in two months.' Hiroko's mother had died of emphysema two years earlier. 'Say hello to your husband for me and give your little one a hug.'

Vinnie opened the door for Hiroko and then ran back to Moyama's car. Moyama climbed in, happy to be hidden by the black glass. Until last night he had wondered whether he had the courage and strength to fight Tamakawa for the leadership of the yakuza. It was a great honour, but also a great strain. He had considered going back to the States to sit on his great fortune and leave the in-fighting to Tamakawa. But from their graves his grandfather and father called out and drove him on – the coming years were going to be important for the credibility of Japan's yakuza. Already the years had increased the Moyama family wealth and power through the reconstruction of Tokyo – now it was Moyama's turn to channel that wealth into legitimate enterprise, shedding the ruffian-like image of Japan's yakuza. Moyama had a mission. Alone, he pondered the future.

Back under the marquee, the sounds of *kampai*, or 'cheers', were heard late into the night.

60

THE WITNESS

'The pig, snake and cock are the three poisons at the centre of
the Wheel of Life. They represent ignorance, hatred and greed
with the three eating and vomiting one another for "eternity",
until awareness provides them a way out.'

From John Snelling's *The Buddhist Handbook*

Nomo Watanabe got off the subway at Ginza crossing and
walked across the street to work. A giant three-storey sign
ran the length of his hypermarket, beckoning customers:
'Watanabe's: The Lowest Prices on Earth'. This had been his first
store and it took up almost the entire block. His hypermarket was
nothing more than a well-presented concrete and tin corrugated
warehouse sitting in the middle of Ginza. 'Cash only', read the
signs. Crowds came to gape at the goods stacked up to the ceiling:
clothes, bedding, kitchenware, appliances, toys. Shoppers could buy
anything from a futon to a car.

Watanabe had cut out six or seven middlemen involved in the
complicated Japanese distribution system and bought directly from
manufacturers. This might have been a common business practice
in America and Europe, but in Japan the concept did not exist. His
first year had been difficult as the established, upmarket department
stores tried to run him out of business. 'Don't extend him any credit,'
they pleaded with manufacturing companies. But Watanabe didn't
need credit – his customers paid cash, which Watanabe in turn paid
the manufacturers. They loved him. Soon Watanabe's branches were
sprouting up all over Japan. He franchised the name and allowed
entrepreneurial families a chance to get rich. Now there were over
forty Watanabe's hypermarkets throughout Japan.

The biggest winner after Watanabe was Fujimoto, whom he trusted
implicitly, fulfilling his obligation, or *giri*, to the former shopkeeper
for trying to save his family after the quake. Fujimoto was now

president of the hypermarket chain. Watanabe had never paid much attention to the accounts, even less so when he promoted himself to chairman of the chain. Fujimoto had been cleverly skimming cash nationwide from the hypermarket chain, building himself a fortune in excess of 5 billion yen, nearly $50 million.

On this particular day Watanabe was late for a meeting and hurried into the store. The security guard bowed as his chief ran past. Fujimoto rushed up to Watanabe and practically dragged him to a group of waiting Chinese VIPs who were interested in adopting Watanabe's techniques on the mainland. An automated forklift beeped as it drove slowly past the delegation, automatically restocking a load of Apple Mac computers which had been sold out. Watanabe's was filled with American and European consumer goods previously blocked from sale in Japan.

'Ahhh,' nodded the Chinese, pointing as the robotic forklift moved past. The hypermarket was clean and efficient. The floor sparkled.

'This is the latest in inventory control,' explained Watanabe. 'Once the scanner reads a sale, the ticket item is deleted from inventory and replaced when stocks run low.'

One of the group was smoking furiously, notebook in hand. The Chinese were like the Japanese of the 1950s – touring factories to pirate ideas to take back home. The Chinese note-taker was clearly excited and stubbed out his cigarette on the floor. Another spat in a corner. Promptly a woman appeared with a mop and broom to clean up the mess. The ill-mannered note-taker took a ginseng sweet from his pocket, unwrapped it and threw the paper on the floor where the woman was cleaning. She picked it up.

Watanabe continued the tour, moving to a large display of refrigerators. A middle-aged woman turned and noticed the group.

'You're Nomo Watanabe, aren't you?'

Watanabe nodded. He had just begun to engage the woman in conversation when Fujimoto stepped between them. He wanted to clinch the China deal without any interruptions and attempted to send the woman on her way, but she continued to talk.

'You may not remember our family. The Hatanakas of Chiba. We lived down the street from you.'

'Why, yes.'

He moved away from his delegation and closer to the woman, to Fujimoto's consternation.

'How are you? And your family?'

'My husband was killed . . . ,' she began, but her voice trailed off. Most people had lost relatives in the quake.

Watanabe could sense her pain. 'I also lost my wife,' he offered in sympathy.

Fujimoto was now irritated. 'The delegation is waiting.'

Watanabe ignored him. Talking to this woman brought back bitter-sweet memories. 'I hope that the rest of your family . . .'

'No, no, they're fine thank you. My daughter is with me now.' Mrs Hatanaka called over her ten-year-old daughter, who was opening and closing all the refrigerator doors: 'Naomi!'

The girl quickly ran over, and her mother put her arm round Naomi's shoulder. 'You remember Mr Watanabe.'

Naomi looked up at him in confusion and stared for a few moments.

Mrs Hatanaka was embarrassed. 'Naomi, what do you say when you are introduced to someone?' she scolded.

'I'm very pleased to meet you.'

Watanabe patted her on the head. 'Well, you certainly have grown into a young lady.'

The Chinese were growing impatient at this intrusion. Fujimoto tugged at Watanabe's jacket, indicating they had business to attend to.

Suddenly the young Hatanaka girl looked up at Fujimoto and a look of shock registered on her face. She began screaming hysterically. Her mother tried to calm her down but she continued to shout: 'That's him! That's him!' She lunged at Fujimoto, who pushed the girl away. He didn't know what was going on and didn't appreciate being mauled by a ten-year-old. The girl's mother was holding Naomi back as her screaming continued.

Fujimoto motioned to a security guard. 'Get them out of here.'

The guard moved towards the woman and her daughter.

'Naomi, stop it!' shouted her mother.

'That's him, that's him.' She was pointing at Fujimoto. 'He started the fire!'

Fujimoto suddenly went cold as a reptile. 'Take them away now,' he shouted at the guard.

Watanabe stepped in. 'Wait.' He turned to the little girl, who was now sobbing uncontrollably. He took her hands. 'What fire did he start?'

The repressed memory of four years ago had suddenly come back to Naomi and she looked up at Watanabe with an expression of horror. 'He burned down your house.'

Everyone turned to Fujimoto. 'She's just a child,' he protested. 'Crazy. Why would I burn down your house?' Fujimoto motioned again to the security guard but the man hesitated, waiting for Watanabe to give instructions.

'It was you,' she shouted, pointing at him again. 'It was the day of the quake. I remember everything now. I was on the street playing.'

Watanabe motioned for the guard to stay put, and was now focused on Fujimoto.

'You're not going to believe this little girl, are you? I wasn't even near your house that day.'

'You were,' screamed Naomi. She turned to her mother. 'That man had a newspaper in his hand.'

She looked at Watanabe. 'I heard screams coming from your house and went to look. Before I could go inside he lit the newspaper, started a fire and walked away. I went to put the fire out but an explosion knocked me out.'

'She's lying!'

'It's true!' said Mrs Hatanaka, turning to Watanabe. 'I found her unconscious a few hours later. Your house was burned to the ground. But Naomi remembered nothing till now.'

A look of anguish spread over Watanabe's face as the full horror of his wife's immolation hit him. He could hear her screams as she tried to escape the approaching flames. It was as if someone had punched him in the solar plexus. He turned to Fujimoto who suddenly bolted and snaked his way to the entrance. For a moment nobody moved. The security guards didn't know what to do – Fujimoto was their immediate boss. Watanabe was the first to recover, and gave them a signal to apprehend Fujimoto before he reached the front door.

The Chinese delegation spared their hosts any further embarrassment and quietly left as Fujimoto was brought back kicking and screaming. Pale, stunned and confused, Watanabe looked at Fujimoto as a store full of customers and workers looked on.

'Why?'

Watanabe could never have prepared himself for what happened next. With a look of jealousy and hatred that chilled him to the bone, Fujimoto spat on him and then growled, 'It was *you* I wanted to kill that day. I only wish I could've heard your screams, like I heard those of your precious wife as I lit the fire.'

Fujimoto wanted to inflict as much pain as possible on Watanabe. 'Can you imagine the flames burning her body as she cried for help?'

Watanabe rushed to grab Fujimoto's throat and the guards had to pull him away. The police had just arrived.

'She wasn't alone when I killed her,' spat out Fujimoto, enjoying the first sense of total power over Watanabe. 'I heard a man's voice,' he lied.

Watanabe gripped his own chest and fell to his knees. The guards had hold of Fujimoto, who was no longer struggling but defiant.

'I hope you rot in hell,' Fujimoto shouted at Watanabe as the police led him away.

Watanabe was curled up on his knees in a sitting foetal position. Mrs Hatanaka began shooing away the shoppers.

'Give him some air. Please leave him alone,' she said pointedly to those still curiously gaping. She pointed to a guard. 'And you. Please help me lift him up.'

With their assistance, Watanabe got slowly to his feet.

'Come, we had better get Mr Watanabe home,' said Mrs Hatanaka to her daughter. She put her arm around him and guided him outside. The three got into the back seat of a taxi.

'Don't cry, Mr Watanabe,' said little Naomi Hatanaka. She pulled at the arm of Watanabe's suit jacket. 'Watanabe-san, that man was lying. There was no other person in the house except your wife.'

Watanabe looked down at Naomi. He put his left arm around the little girl but clenched his right fist. Fujimoto would pay for this. One year later a judge sentenced Fujimoto to life in prison.

61

THE ESCAPE

'Suicide rates more than quadruple after earthquakes.'
From a research study conducted to determine why an
abnormal number of people take their lives after large quakes

'I want to thank you for being such a good friend.'

Kaelin was lazing in the bath, feeling wonderfully relaxed as she spoke to Hiroko on the portable phone. The bubble bath hid the welts on her legs, but Kaelin could still feel the space where her front tooth was missing.

'Have you seen the psychiatrist I suggested?'

Hiroko had pressed Kaelin into seeking help. The latest in her string of abusive boyfriends was a heavy drinker and freeloader. Hiroko was worried for Kaelin's safety and had given her the name of a psychiatrist who specialized in abused women.

'Have you seen him yet?' repeated Hiroko.

'Hmmm . . .' said Kaelin dreamily.

She cast her mind back three years. She had thought that the night she had killed Tada and walked off with his black bag marked the end of her worries. She had opened the bag in the car and discovered more than 2 billion yen in bearer shares. She was rich! Keeping the shares was the only dishonest thing Kaelin ever remembered doing. Whenever she needed some spare cash she sold off a few shares. The realization that she was rich did not have much effect on her life other than to attract a steady stream of indolent boyfriends. She kept hoping that one of them would turn out to be another Omori, the only one who hadn't hit her. *But I would have done something even for him eventually to hit me, I suppose*, she thought. Kaelin eased back into reality and realized she was on the phone.

'No, I haven't seen him yet. But I won't need to – things are going to be fine.'

'I hope so, Kay-chan. You take care.'

'Goodbye, Hiroko. Thank you again for everything. I'm lucky to have you as a friend. Remember not to feel badly about this.' Kaelin hung up.

At the other end Hiroko held on to the phone for a moment, confused, then shook her head and put the phone down. She felt pleased that Kaelin was finally getting her life together.

Kaelin lay back in the bath as the sleeping pills worked through her body. *How many did I take? Twenty? Thirty?* She breathed deeply, felt no pain and wondered what the end would be like. She read that drowning was supposed to be a pleasant experience and like asphyxiation, where the victim experienced orgasm in the throes of death. But Kaelin wasn't a thrill-seeker – she just wanted to be set free.

As her eyelids closed for the last time she got her wish, slipping beneath the bath water to freedom.

62

THE TAKEOVER

Los Angeles

'If the Coalition grows large enough then everyone running for President . . . will have to come to us.'
Ralph Reed to a group of New Hampshire activists in 1995

Dougie gave the driver instructions over the internal phone. 'Dodger Stadium, please.'

The driver had already been briefed and, since a secret service agent was sitting in front, the destination of Dougie's two passengers was no surprise. As the two police motorcycles escorted the limo to the stadium through heavy LA traffic, Dougie turned his attention to the 'Saint'.

'Congratulations on your nomination.'

'Thanks, Doug.' The 'Saint' turned to Master Wa.

'Like you, I promised never to run for office, but this was too tempting.'

The 'Saint', Ralph Reed, had just been nominated as the Republican presidential candidate. The two had forged an interesting alliance. Master Wa had contributed $10 million to Reed's presidential campaign (washed through ten thousand donors pledging $1000 each), while Reed had given Wa access to America through a series of joint speaking engagements, introductions to the media and sympathy from the Christian Coalition.

Dougie looked at the two religious leaders and thought of the collective power that these two men held. Dougie himself was now very influential – he was now a centimillionaire, thanks to his investment in Wa's TV and media interests, and he managed all Wa's investments. But his companions epitomized the meaning of the word 'power'.

The 'Saint' controlled the American Right and the US Congress, while the ever-serene Wa controlled both the Japanese Right and a quarter of Parliament. It looked as if Happy Science would indeed become the world's fifth major religion, while Reed was about to have a shot at controlling the most powerful nation on earth. Most importantly, both men held sway over the spiritual lives and attitudes of hundreds of millions of followers.

As they approached Dodger Stadium, Wa could hear shouting and saw what he took to be supporters lining the street. He lowered his window and waved. To his horror, it was an angry crowd and some of its members gave him the finger.

'Go home, you fucking gook!' somebody shouted.

'Remember Pearl Harbor!' shouted another demonstrator.

A tomato came sailing through the window and splattered all over Ralph Reed's shirt.

'Close the window!' yelled the secret service agent.

Wa pressed the button and the window hummed closed.

Reed looked down at his shirt. 'Shit.' He leaned over and pulled out a new one from under the seat.

Wa was confused, then looked at the signs. 'Down with the Nazis' and 'Vote Ralph Reed for Prison Warden', they said. A few of the signs were more pointed: 'Hang Ralph Reed', demanded one, while 'Fuck the Japs', read another. Wa winced.

Ralph Reed always kept a change of clothes with him, and as he was changing his shirt he prepared Wa for America's violent minority. 'Wa-san, you are now a public figure in America. You've got a large following but a vicious few who hate you. Ignore them. They're trying to rattle you. Also remember this is California, our weakest state. We'll have much more of a welcome down south.'

The entrance to Dodger Stadium lay just ahead. The limo was instructed to ride straight on to the infield. As they approached the main gates, the shouting increased. Police officers held back the angry crowd, but they were clearly outnumbered. A dozen demonstrators broke through and ran up to the car.

'Tip it over!'

They began to rock the limo, but the police intervened and tried to handcuff the men. This angered the mob, who made a run at the police lines and pushed through them to the limo. Rocks pelted the bullet-proof glass.

'Don't open the windows or doors,' ordered the secret service agent. 'We're completely safe.'

'Put a rag in the gas tank and light it,' yelled one of the mob.

Dougie had one hand on the door and was ready to throw Wa and Reed out of the back of the limo, but the secret service agent yelled out again: 'Don't panic! The gas tank's secure.'

Dougie released his grip on the door.

The three men certainly didn't feel safe. The car was rocking up and down and the police were outnumbered. A carpet of human beings had laid themselves out on the road, preventing the driver from moving forward. All he could do was sound the horn, which accomplished little except make the mob rock the limo faster.

Suddenly the rocking stopped. The men trapped in it looked outside to see absolute mayhem as the riot police grappled with demonstrators. For another fifteen minutes the mêlée continued until the crowd was brought under control. Nervous laughter broke out inside the car. Without the assistance of supporters, the car would have been overturned.

Unimpeded now, the limo made its way into the stadium where a large banner waved behind the scoreboard. It read 'Welcome to America'. Several minutes later cheers erupted as Ralph Reed and Master Wa took the field.

63

THE SECRET

'The Japanese were nine months away from the bomb in 1945.
Emperor Hirohito personally authorized the procurement of
uranium. Why is it improbable to suspect they have the
capability half a century later? Our research indicates Japan
is now nuclear.'

From an internal CIA document leaked
to Congressional Japan-bashers

'Can you meet me tomorrow at eight?' the eighty-four-year-old
professor asked excitedly. 'I've got all the proof I need.'
  Though Tokai was still professor emeritus of seismology
at Tokyo University, he had long since resigned as one of the Six
Wise Men. He insisted that earthquakes could not be predicted and
that the Great Lie was an invention of the government to keep
society stable.

'Are you sure the quake was a result of nuclear testing?' asked
Hiroko carelessly.

The phone went dead. Tokai was paranoid about wiretaps and,
certain his phone was being bugged, wasn't taking any chances. He
had been working for four years on his own investigation into the
origins of the 'Big One'.

The shockwave graphs that he had torn away from the Japan
Meteorological Agency on the day of the quake suggested that an
underwater nuclear explosion had triggered the earthquake. Nobody
in the new government had offered any assistance to his investigation.
In disgust, Tokai interviewed nuclear physicists and determined that
the test had been conducted in an underwater trough deep in a fault
line off the Japanese coast. Local fish samples had produced a high
trace content of radioactivity, while a dramatic increase in cancer
had been noted in Tokyo hospitals.

The new Prime Minister's cabinet met to discuss Tokai's snooping.
No minutes were taken, and no assistants were allowed to be present.
The cabinet was a bit testy since elections were being held again in

two months' time. The entire cabinet consisted of elected members of Parliament who held office for four years. If they lost the forthcoming elections in their constituency, they were out of power.

'He's getting close to the truth,' said the Minister of Defence, referring to Tokai.

'Have all the papers been destroyed?' asked the Prime Minister.

'Yes, sir, all except for Tokai's. But I'm more worried about that nosey journalist Hiroko Fujita. Can't we stop her from reporting on this?'

The Prime Minister was surprisingly aggressive. 'Nobody's to touch the girl or hamper her in any way. She's old Ken Moyama's daughter and, even though he's dead, Moyama's son will protect her . . . Why don't we just tell the public the truth?' said the Prime Minister. 'After all, we were all put into Parliament on a 'clean hands' platform. Doesn't the public have a right to know?'

The other cabinet ministers looked at him as if he were mad.

'Tell them the truth?' The Minister of Defence was incredulous. 'Tell them that we consider China to be an economic and military risk and that the previous government detonated an underwater nuclear bomb? Testing, I will remind you, that we are still carrying on.' The Minister laughed and then continued: 'Think about it. The Chinese would go to war if they knew the truth, and the public would throw us out of office tomorrow. Let me make this clear. Everybody in this room is privy to the state secret that Japan has the bomb. Anybody violating that secrecy will be branded a traitor and sentenced under our new treason laws. Our Minister of Justice will back me up.'

The Justice Minister nodded silently in agreement.

The Minister of Finance spoke next. 'We've built a free society. The economy is booming and small businesses are flourishing. Why ruin it by telling the people the truth?'

The Prime Minister sighed. 'You're right. I'd prefer us not to test at all, but if necessary I'm told we can still detonate south of Okinawa without attracting undue notice. Is this true?' he asked the Defence Minister.

'Scientists assure us that the fault is fully sealed against leaks. The blast will register on a few of the world's seismographs, but can be detonated to coincide with the French underwater testing. It will prove impossible for anyone to pinpoint the blast or to suspect us of testing.'

'The last Defence Minister also claimed that the testing was fully sealed. Then the captain of that American aircraft carrier went and took samples of the dead fish. The only reason the Americans don't leak this story is because they've opened up our local markets and strong armed us into keeping American bases on the coast. Anyway, tell us, are the residents of Okinawa in danger?'

'No. The blast's too far offshore,' replied the Defence Minister. 'Who cares, anyway? Nobody lives in that part of the world except hookers and US servicemen.' The cabinet members chuckled. 'So I take it I have cabinet permission to continue testing under Okinawa?' asked the Minister.

Everyone in the room nodded, a sign which the Defence Minister took as tacit approval. Japanese body language was sometimes handy in creating plausible deniability in government circles. The cabinet members knew that no minutes were being taken and that none of them had actually said 'yes' or raised their hand in an official vote.

'Meeting adjourned.'

The cabinet members bowed in the direction of the Prime Minister and left the room.

As the meeting broke up, the Minister of Defence left by a private exit where three men stood waiting. The Minister simply nodded and the men left.

The next morning Hiroko walked up through the leafy campus of Tokyo University. It was a beautiful autumn day and the leaves were just turning colour. Tokyo's privileged few in their penthouses had a clear view of Mount Fuji.

When Hiroko walked into Professor Tokai's ground-floor reception room she knew immediately that something was wrong. She looked from the ante-room into his office and saw two bundles of flowers in clear plastic on his desk. They were funeral flowers. The office looked a mess, with storage boxes being filled.

Dr Tokai's secretary of forty years wasn't there. Instead a temporary secretary was busy filling boxes. Tokai's secretary had not missed a day of work in the past and certainly would not have allowed somebody else to pack up her belongings.

'You work with Dr Tokai?' asked Hiroko.

The girl looked up at her suspiciously. 'Only on certain research projects,' she replied, than added, 'Who are you?'

'I'm Hiroko Huntley. Is the professor in? I have an eight o'clock appointment.'

'I'm sorry. Haven't you heard?' said the secretary, lowering her head.

'Heard what?'

'Dr Tokai died last night in his sleep.'

Hiroko was incredulous. 'But I spoke to him just yesterday.'

The secretary was more taken aback than grief-stricken. 'I'm sorry.'

Something was very, very wrong. Hiroko was about to ask where Tokai's secretary was, but thought better of it. Instead she pretended she thought nothing was out of the ordinary.

'What a terrible tragedy! Such a nice man, but I suppose he was getting on in years. How old was he? Sixty-five?'

She had set the trap: anyone close to Tokai would know he was over eighty.

'Yes, what a tragedy,' the secretary remarked, letting Tokai's age go unchallenged.

'How did his wife take it?' continued Hiroko, wanting to confirm her suspicions.

'She's very upset.'

Hiroko went cold. Dr Tokai's wife had died over twenty years earlier.'

'I'll give my condolences to the family.' Hiroko bowed and walked out of the door.

Once outdoors, Hiroko walked along the building and peered in through Tokai's ground-floor window. The secretary had locked the door and was busily taking files out of his personal filing cabinet and throwing them in boxes. A few minutes later two well-groomed, official-looking removal men arrived, knocked on the door and spoke to the secretary. They took Tokai's boxes to an unmarked truck and when they were finished, sped away. Hiroko took down the licence plate number.

Then she walked round to the front of the building again to Tokai's office in order to question the secretary. The door was open but the phoney secretary was gone. The entire office had been cleaned out.

A month later an earthquake registering 8.5 on the Richter scale struck Taipei, south-west of Okinawa.

Hiriko flew high above the city in a CNN chopper, reporting live. 'Here in smouldering Taipei the death toll is still rising. Survivors are trying to salvage their lives, asking, "Why us, why me?" Although we can't bring back their loved ones, we can finally give the Taiwanese an answer to their tragedy. Highly placed sources in the Japanese government finally admit that they have repeatedly conducted underwater nuclear tests over the last four years. According to scientists, this testing may be responsible not only for the Taipei quake but also for the killer quake which struck Tokyo over four years ago. The Japanese government has sent a chill through the world by admitting that it now has the Bomb. With general elections less than a month away, it's widely expected that the ruling Japanese government will be overthrown and cabinet members charged for violating Japan's constitution, which expressly forbids the manufacture of nuclear armaments. It is also reported that some families of Taipei's victims are considering manslaughter charges against Japanese cabinet officials. The inquiry into the death of Dr Tokai, who himself was investigating Japan's use of nuclear weapons, has now been reopened as a murder investigation. This is Hiroko Huntley from CNN reporting live over the ruins of Taipei . . .'

REALITY CHECK

M ost of the characters in this novel are based on historical and current personalities, while events stemming from the earthquake are meant to be plausible.

1. The Omen   China does have a high proportion of the world's low-quality manganese reserves, some of which is still mined by hand near Wuzhou. Manganese is critical to the production and bonding of steel. Some Japanese steel producers have been guilty of using cheap manganese, which has put a number of Japan's buildings and other structures at risk.

2. The 'A' Team   I must thank Dr Robert Geller of Tokyo University's Department of Earth and Planetary Physics for information on this chapter and scepticism regarding earthquake prediction.

Buildings have a natural frequency of vibration and can be rocked back and forth as described. The issue of chemical coagulant fraud poses a danger in Japan where firms fail to meet hardening standards. The most famous fraud resulted in the collapse of the Shinkan Tunnel in 1990, which subsequent investigative reporting by the *Yomiuri* helped uncover.

The *Time* magazine cover story on earthquake prediction (a subject subsequently abandoned by researchers in the USA) appeared coincidentally on 1 September 1975, on the fifty-second anniversary of the great Kanto earthquake.

3. The Salaryman   Nomo (meaning 'hero' in Japanese) Watanabe is a fictional character. *The House of Mitsui* was written for the firm in 1937 at a time when world domination by the zaibatsu (Japanese family conglomorates) was considered a noble goal. The book may be found in second-hand bookshops in Kanda.

4. The Party   This is a fictional chapter.

5. The Spaceship   Master Wa is loosely based on the personality of Ryuho Okawa, founder of the Kofuku no Kagaku (translated as 'Happy Science'), Japan's largest religious group. Okawa's beliefs – the migration of a billion people from Orion, the Ninth Dimension and the beauty of Venusians – are factual in that he does believe in them. They are derived from his written works, in particular his manuscript *The Path to El Cantare*. Okawa is passionate in his hatred for his religious rival the Soka Gakkai, the publishing group Kodansha, and organized crime. Okawa has been written about in the *Los Angeles Times* and *Far Eastern Economic Review*, but remains a hitherto unrecognized phenomenon.

Okawa throws a birthday party for fifty thousand people on 7 July each year in the Tokyo Dome, though this chapter was dramatized.

6. The Catfish   The EQ Utility Bucket described in this chapter is available in the United States.

7. The Scam   This chapter is entirely fictional, as are all the scenes in which *Asahi Shimbun* reporters and editors appear.

Professor Geller's opening quote, stating that 'No earthquake has been predicted for the history of mankind', is based on his own criteria, I quote from a letter he wrote me after editing parts of this manuscript: 'An earthquake prediction must give the time, place and size of an earthquake large enough to cause significant damage within narrow enough limits for public authorities to take specific steps to mitigate the damage; must be based on objective scientific criteria, and must have a high degree of confidence. No successful prediction has *ever* been issued in the history of mankind, although false claims have occasionally been made, as in the case of China in 1976.'

The *Asahi* is one of Japan's most daring and ethical news organizations, and I apologize if any of my dramatized characters such as Sam Tanaka or Nakamura are slightly evil. Hiroko Fujita's heroism makes up for her colleagues.

The Quakemaster was my invention.

The Daishin stock scam is based on political fund-raisers which use the Tokyo Stock Exchange. This 'ramping' is commonplace and a fixture of Japanese finance. For those interested in further reading, my book *The House of Nomura* gives an insight into ramping.

Nomura Securities sued me for libel in the UK High Court in 1990 because of this book, but after two years of litigation withdrew their charges.

8. The Gaijin   Dougie Douglas is a fictional character based on an amalgam of dozens of such traders whom I have known in Tokyo, London and New York. All the conversations by Dougie, the Salomon executives and traders accurately represent the way these people think and talk in their daily life.

Earthquakes do have a financial impact on society. Nick Leeson's billion-dollar gamble with Baring's capital was a bet that Japanese share prices would rise. This was thwarted by the Kobe earthquake, which sent Japanese stocks into a six-month nose-dive and destroyed Baring's. Dougie's bet happens, by accident, to be right.

The Urbannet Building is popularly known as the Tower of Bubble; Salomon resided on the top floor, with the Nomura offices beneath.

The AV Bar exists – you just have to find it.

9. The Provider   Ken Moyama and his son, also Ken, were based on the master yakuza fixer Yoshio Kodama, who funded much of the Liberal Democratic Party from 1955 until his death in 1984. According to US army intelligence reports, Kodama's interests were worth more than $175 million in 1945. That's in 1945 dollars! The son is my invention.

10. The Prophet   The biographical information on Okawa was provided by his public relations team in the form of his manuscript *The Path to El Cantare*.

11. The Net   The Japan Meteorological Agency is located in Takebashi in central Tokyo, next door to the Tokyo fire headquarters. All emergency calls come into this station and ambulances and fire engines are then sent out. Hiroko's comment about the JMA building being the last place she would like to be in an earthquake reflected my sentiments after leaving its ill-lit, box-strewn corridors. The description of the 'command centre' in the JMA is based on an interview that I conducted there.

The sample warning is taken verbatim from their brochure.

On 26 May 1983 the JMA issued a tsunami warning to residents of the northwest coast of Japan. Residents were told to head for high ground after an earthquake measuring 7.7 on the Richter scale struck the Sea of Japan. The warning was issued six minutes after the tsunami and 104 lives were lost.

Technical information in this novel is based on the JMA brochure *Earthquake and Tsunami Monitoring and Countermeasures*.

A very special thanks to Peter Hadfield and his book *The Sixty Seconds That Will Shake the World*.

12. The Animal   Though Construction Minister Tada is a fictional character, bureaucratic and political stock scams, in concert with the yakuza, have formed the backbone of Japanese political fund-raising for fifty years. While I was living in Tokyo and working for a British stockbroker, our firm would belatedly receive faxed 'political' stock recommendations, well after a stock had run 300 or 400 per cent. Raids on politicians' homes in the 1990s (in particular Shin Kanemaru's) show that my fictionalization is perhaps understated.

The electronic bug hidden in his pen is real and manufactured in Osaka.

13. The Twins   These characters are entirely fictional, though Keiko's survival was based on accounts from survivors in the Armenian and Kobe earthquakes and Choi Myong Suk's survival of the 1995 Seoul department store collapse. Choi survived on cardboard and rainwater.

14. The Train   The Sobu line from Shinjuku to Akihabara does have a green bridge after the Ochanomizu station, from which Hiroko and Jiroo climb down. The train conductor gave me a funny look as I examined the underbelly of the carriage to see if it had a ladder attached. This was the week of the Tokyo gas attacks.

The 'Yuridasu' system for braking high-speed trains was developed by Dr Yutaka Nakamura of the Railway Research Institute and is only in use on the Tokkaido Shinkansen, but will be extended to other lines in future.

15. The Army   The Self Defence Agency was very helpful in outlining rescue procedure to me. They were adamant that I should not use the phrase 'army' in the book when referring to the Ground Self-Defence Force, 'navy' for the Maritime Self-Defence Force or 'air force' for the Air Self-Defence Force. Sorry, but that's what they are.

The three-star general who heads the 1st Army out of Nerima is commander-in-chief of all Tokyo rescue operations.

The quote from the Defence Minister ('because nobody asked me to') when he failed to send troops into Kobe the day of the quake seems part of the bumbling which I characterize here. Each governmental organization seems to have an earthquake department, but nobody can act without somebody else's authorization.

16. The Ginza Crossing This part of Tokyo lies on reclaimed land and the liquefaction in the chapter, though in the realm of the possible, is my invention. Quakes do have primary and secondary waves as described here.

17. The Hand The amputation of Dougie's hand may sound dramatic, but research into the 1923 Tokyo quake and 1995 Kobe quake uncovered a high number of emergency amputations performed by those who wished to survive oncoming flames or an impending gas explosion.

18. The Six Wise Men These mostly comprise Tokyo University Professors emeritus. The government's assumption that these old men can be collected in anticipation of a big quake to issue a general warning is ludicrous. Quakes cannot be predicted, as Robert Geller of Tokyo University so frequently mentions – to the annoyance of the Japanese government.

19. The Fire There are 7 million wooden buildings in Tokyo, but otherwise this chapter is completely dramatized.

20. The Tongue Moyama's house is based on the Hattori family's compound in Shirokane on a hill overlooking Tokyo. Tessie the maid is based on our Filipina maid who ran up £2000-a-month phone bills from London to Manila.

Ken Moyama saves his family by observing the thrashing of koi, a phenomenon which Dr Robert Geller feels is groundless. I must quote him in a letter to me! 'It's certainly true that such phenomena are reported from time to time but these claims are as groundless as reports of UFOs.'

21. The Campaign The Marayama Securities sales campaign to ramp the shares of Daishin Construction is a normal stockbroking practice and would be very close to my description here. Retail brokers are under enormous pressure to churn and burn clients.

Those who have read my book *The House of Nomura* may

assume that Marayama is based solely on Nomura. This is not the case, since stock campaigns are too prevalent to be restricted to one firm.

22. Top Gun   The USS *Ranger* was the Top Gun of the Pacific Fleet. Captain McFlynn (in real life Captain McGinn) was its real captain, as Mike Berensky was its Air Boss. The *Ranger* does have civilian rescue equipment, but the addition of the Osprey (actually purchased by the US government) was fictional.

23. The Great Lie   This chapter is based on a feeling that the Japanese government, at all levels, has kept Tokyo sane by not admitting the danger facing its residents.
   The 134 Special Evacuation Areas of Tokyo do exist.

24. Little Buddha   The success of Master Wa's spiritual following is the result of superb marketing, much of it the result of desk-top publishing as explained in this dramatized chapter.

25. The Wave   The thought process of the traders is unfortunately based on reality, and readers may turn to Michael Lewis' humorous bestseller *Liar's Poker* to learn more about this mind-set of traders at Salomon Brothers. The basket of stocks liquidated by Ralphie would have been done in the fashion described, though it is improbable that a bond trader would ever be allowed to touch an equity trade.

26. The Credit   Craig Huntley is the fictional grandson of Chet Huntley of NBC. The Satlink phone system as described throughout this is slightly ahead of commercial application. CNN and other major media networks do use an M satellite phone in the field, at a cost of about $10 a minute. Some day these phones will be available to everyone and used through out the world. All the CNN characters are entirely fictional, though the equipment they used in this novel was described to me by a prominent CNN correspondent.

27. Overlord   The Imperial Palace is the first place to which the survivors of the Big One will run, hobble or be carried.

28. The Tunnel   The existence of a tunnel between the Imperial Palace and the Parliament building is a matter I will neither confirm nor deny.
   All the government buildings described do exist.

29. The Scatterlings   A sad effect of the 1923 quake was the huge number of orphaned children which it produced.

30. The Looting   Few Japanese or Western reporters wrote about the plundering in Kobe after the quake. In my interview with staff in the mayor's office in Kobe, I was surprised to hear how much undisclosed looting had taken place. Their story of neatly dressed yakuza posing as removal men was amusing. The yakuza wished to be portrayed as humane by handing out food, but in fact sent in trucks to loot residential areas.

31. The Ring   The description of oil and chemical storage tanks is factual, though the chapter is dramatized.

32. The Pipe   This is a fictional chapter.

33. The Rape   Koreans are blamed for a number of problems in Japan, and vice versa. Animosity between the countries runs so deep that for years Korea banned the import of Japanese cars. The worst insult that a Korean can hurl at a Japanese is to call him a 'cloven-footed dwarf'.

34. The Rescue   The army cannot be sent into Tokyo without the governor's permission, with a three-man committee (treasurer, police superintendent and deputy governor) presiding in the event that the governor is not present. The numbers on troop, fire and police deployment were all based on interviews with the Self-Defence Agency, Tokyo Fire Department and National Police Agency. The governor is all-important in a rescue, since the fire and police departments work for him.

A brochure called *Earthquake Preparedness of the Tokyo Fire Department* was helpful.

The National Police Agency have two 'live people sniffer' dogs, one of whom is named Alex. I made up the other name.

Chaos will reign when the Big One hits, with lines of authority crossed in both Tokyo and national government. One critic of a draft of my manuscript asked to see more about the detailed inner workings of a quake rescue plan. Forget it. Every government organization lives in its own little earthquake fantasy world with separate budgets, communications systems, seismograph stations and preparedness plans. There is no central authority.

35. The Camp   This chapter was fictionalized.

36. The Black Death   Disease may be one of the worst problems confronting city officials if a quake occurs in summer. Details of the plague were drawn from medical texts.

37. Where in the World?   This chapter is dramatized.

38. The Quest   A fictionalized chapter, although the 'Shaking Boy' alarm from Omron is on the market. The raiding of people's homes after the quake is based on stories told by the Kobe mayor's office in which yakuza heavies posed as removal men and cleaned out whole areas.
   American Forces Radio brings you the best rock music in Japan, even during an earthquake crisis.

39. The Heist   The introduction of the mafia to Japan is fictional. There is, however, a lot of gold sitting in the Bank of Japan vaults waiting for somebody like Moyama to seize it during a crisis.
   Tony Berman (not his real name) is based on an abusive, alcoholic lawyer who uses the law to further criminal activity for his corporate clients.

40. The Riot   The riot was based on descriptions of rice panics during the 1600s.

41. The Crash   This is a fictional account of the financial conse- quences of a large quake hitting Tokyo. Speaking of fiction, there is a theory in the Western world that when the Big One hits, all the value of Tokyo's trillions of dollars in the stockmarket will vanish as the Tokyo Stock Exchange and its records are wiped out. This is not the case. The TSE is simply a place where buyers meet sellers. All records are kept by stockbrokers and all stock certificates by clients, stockbrokers, the Japanese Securities Agents, or the Japan Securities Deposit Centre in Kayabacho.

42. The Rats   The description of the rats' teeth and their ability to eat through brick and concrete was verified by Herman, the rat who ate through the concrete air vent in our Johannesburg guest house as I sat there writing this book.

43. The USS *Ranger*   As already mentioned, the Self-Defence

Forces may not enter a city or prefecture without that city or prefecture's authorization. This caused the delay in helping the victims of Kobe. With twenty-three ministries and government organizations having earthquake bureaux, the Japanese ideal of consensus is taken to a dangerous extreme. I tried to juxtapose this with America's high-handed moral intrusion – 'I am going to help you whether you like it or not.'

44. Yankee Go Home The rape of a Japanese schoolgirl by American servicemen in Okinawa has raised the question of why the USA is still allowed to operate in Japan.

45. The Roll of Dead   Radio stations were very helpful during the Kobe quake in matching lost families and in reporting both the living and the dead.

46. The Race This chapter is based on meetings with various government officials. See the *Earthquake Disaster Countermeasures in Japan* brochure, issued in 1993 by the National Land Agency and the Prime Minister's office.
   Foreign aid is the biggest nightmare for quake-stricken city officials. Hardly any of the aid is of any specific use, and in the case of Kobe much of it was thrown away. The story of the Filipino goods being tossed away was based on my meeting at the Kobe mayor's office. The Catholic church took up an offering from its Filipino congregation, only to find the residents of Kobe turn away used clothes and useful household items.

47. Catatonia Dougie's condition was based on interviews with doctors who told me about post-traumatic stress. The Freddie Death Index, though fictional, is the type of bet one may take out with London bookies – from guessing the number of windows blown out during a bombing to the sex of an expected royal baby.

48. The Plan   This is a fictional chapter.

49. The Save   The Swiss Relief Agency, one of the world's foremost rescue services, uses dogs which are trained to identify dead and live bodies by means of their bark. The details of the Biomat are based on Scandinavian ingenuity.

50. Justice   The Tada share scam, in which he files in court for

the reissuance of share certificates, is based on current Japanese legislation. The problem still exists. What does an investor do if he loses share certificates? Answer: apply to the commercial court. And if you don't know the number of the certificates and the brokerage house has no record of their purchase? Answer: tough luck unless one is prepared to commit fraud.

51. The Screw-up The dreaded black plastic bag was a feature of Wall Street during the redundancies in the late 1980s.

52. Thinning the Rice Crop Immediately after the 1923 earthquake, retailers such as Mitsukoshi set up emergency stalls in Shinjuku and other districts in Tokyo. These later became the sites for their current department stores.

The emergence of retailing discounters has already begun and their rise is inevitable.

53. The Saint Ralph Reed is the spiritual heir to Pat Robertson and the Christian Coalition. There are no links between Happy Science and the Christian Coalition as detailed.

54. The Succession Cyberporn and on-line gambling are the next horizons for organized crime and hungry profiteers.

55. The Decision This is a fictional chapter.

56. The Survivor This chapter is based on the incredible financial toll that a quake will take, not on insurance firms but on individuals. The major insurance companies of Japan are protected by legislation from paying out exorbitant sums in a crisis.

57. The Election All the equipment necessary for electronic polling stations already exists. What's the hold-up?

A very compelling argument can be made not only that the great Kanto earthquake caused the banking panic of 1927 but that the reconstruction and depression led directly to World War II, or the Pacific War as the Japanese call it.

58. The Cordon This chapter is fictional, though the yakuza drive for credibility is a theme to be watched as their money purchases legitimate businesses around the world.

59. The Successor   This is a fictional chapter.

60. The Promotion   This is a fictional chapter.

61. The Witness   This is a fictional chapter.

62. The Escape   This chapter is fictional, although Kaelin is based on an abused woman who baffles her friends (as many do) by having long-term relationships with abusive men.

63. The Takeover   This is a fictional chapter, although Ralph Reed's powerbase in America is portrayed in the probability that he can use Pat Robertson's base as a platform for a presidential campaign.

64. The Secret   Although Japan's constitution and the nation's psyche outlaws the development of nuclear weapons, the manufacture of such weapons is within Japan's grasp. Recently declassified World War II documents show that the Japanese government had been working hard to build its own bomb towards the end of the war.

   The greatest piece of fiction in the world today is the notion that all conspiracies are fictional.

ACKNOWLEDGEMENTS

I would like to thank the following for their help:

My friend, the Japanologist and well-known financier Stephen Barber.

Dr Robert Geller of the Department of Earth and Planetary Physics at the University of Tokyo for his detailed critique of *Quake*.

Craig Gardiner for his editing of *Quake* at a time when he was writing 10 episodes of the hit soap opera *Suburban Bliss*. Inspiration for *Quake* came during a poker game in 1995 when an editor for the *Daily Telegraph* newspaper phoned me about the effect a Tokyo quake would have on the world financial markets. I had a full house at the time (queens over eights) and Craig Gardiner tried to get me to fold the hand. I kept the *Daily Telegraph* on hold while we finished the hand.

Victoria Waddell for her reading of *Quake* during a time when she was finishing her first novel. The literary world will hear more from her as a novelist and editor.

Also Mr and Mrs Okubo for their hospitality while I was in Japan; Tadashige Oku for his kind help; Tachi Nagasawa at the Japan Uni Agency; Mr Tokuma and Mr Iwasaki at Tokuma Shoten for believing in this project; the crowd at Bloomsbury Publishing; Harriet Cohen; Jonathan Lloyd; Pat Murray; Charles Bothner; Gabriel Russell and James Tregear; Shu Lin for her interpreting skills; Etsusuke Masuda of James Capel on construction related matters; Marcus Brauchli and Maggie Farley; Kozo Nomura for the inspiration of Kozo Taishowa; Yukihisa Oikawa of the Kofuku no Kagaku; Yuko Higuchi of the Kofuku no Kagaku; Brian Waterhouse of James Capel for his financial expertise; Tatsuhiko Kawamura, Nobuo Mashimo and Taka Nakamura of the Tokyo Fire Department; Taro Karasaki of the *Asahi Evening News*; Dr Tameshige Tsukuda of Todai Earthquake Research Institute; Kunihise Kawasaki for arranging interviews; Karen Zaugg of the Kobe mayor's office;

Peter Hadfield; The Japan Meteorological Agency; Mr Kawai of the Self Defence Agency; Mr Yamazaki of the National Disaster Countermeasures Security Division of the National Police Agency; Mr Shimizu of Tokyo Gas. And, of course, special thanks to Anne, my wife.